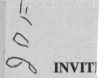 
Whitey stared at Bonner, his flat, dead light-gray eyes showed no expression. "You better wish that bullet you put in Tobey's head was in your own. We damned shore gonna make you wish it before this is done."

"Well, well, you white-headed bastard, you've scared hell outta me." Bonner moved the barrel of his rifle slightly. "You, Manse, get your horses from in front. If you ain't back here by the time I count to ten, I'm gonna start eliminating your saddle pards. You got it?"

"Be right back, mister. Ain't gonna pull nothin'."

In less time than it takes to tell about it, Manse came back tugging the reins of four horses, including the dead man's.

Bonner said, "Load your friend across the saddle an' get outta here 'fore I decide to let the rest o' you go outta here the same way."

Whitey still stared at Bonner. "Wantta get yore face stamped in my brain. I know what parcel o' land you filed on. I'll be out to visit with you."

Bonner smiled coldly. "Didn't take the government clerk long to let you know, did it? Well, I'm here to tell you I ain't of the same stripe as those poor bastards you've already run off, so bring it to me; I will welcome you with open arms."

THE
HOMESTEADER

JACK BALLAS

BERKLEY BOOKS, NEW YORK

THE BERKLEY PUBLISHING GROUP
Published by the Penguin Group
Penguin Group (USA) Inc.
375 Hudson Street, New York, New York 10014, USA
Penguin Group (Canada), 10 Alcorn Avenue, Toronto, Ontario M4V 3B2, Canada
(a division of Pearson Penguin Canada Inc.)
Penguin Books Ltd., 80 Strand, London WC2R 0RL, England
Penguin Group Ireland, 25 St. Stephen's Green, Dublin 2, Ireland (a division of Penguin Books Ltd.)
Penguin Group (Australia), 250 Camberwell Road, Camberwell, Victoria 3124, Australia
(a division of Pearson Australia Group Pty. Ltd.)
Penguin Books India Pvt. Ltd., 11 Community Centre, Panchsheel Park, New Delhi—110 017, India
Penguin Group (NZ), Cnr. Airborne and Rosedale Roads, Albany, Auckland 1310, New Zealand
(a division of Pearson New Zealand Ltd.)
Penguin Books (South Africa) (Pty.) Ltd., 24 Sturdee Avenue, Rosebank, Johannesburg 2196,
South Africa

Penguin Books Ltd., Registered Offices: 80 Strand, London WC2R 0RL, England

This is a work of fiction. Names, characters, places, and incidents either are the product of the author's imagination or are used fictitiously, and any resemblance to actual persons, living or dead, business establishments, events, or locales is entirely coincidental.

THE HOMESTEADER

A Berkley Book / published by arrangement with the author

PRINTING HISTORY
Berkley edition / March 2005

Copyright © 2005 by Jack Ballas.

ISBN: 0-425-20146-5

BERKLEY®
Berkley Books are published by The Berkley Publishing Group,
a division of Penguin Group (USA) Inc.,
375 Hudson Street, New York, New York 10014.
BERKLEY is a registered trademark of Penguin Group (USA) Inc.
The "B" design is a trademark belonging to Penguin Group (USA) Inc.

PRINTED IN THE UNITED STATES OF AMERICA

10 9 8 7 6 5 4 3 2 1

1

TREY BONNER TAPPED the map on the desk between him and the land office agent. "That's the land I want to file on."

Timothy Rogers, the agent, shook his head. "You don't want that land, Mr. Bonner; Matt Tedford runs cows on that land. He won't take it kindly if you try to move in on 'im."

"He or anybody else filed homestead rights on it?"

Rogers shook his head. "That land hasn't been surveyed yet; cain't nobody file on it yet."

"You ever hear of the Preemption Act, passed by the U.S. Congress in 1841? You have; you know it doesn't have to be surveyed." He nodded. "It was passed in response to demands by the Western folks to be allowed to settle on public lands. That's what I'm filin' under; one hundred sixty acres, live on it fourteen months, then I can buy it for one dollar an' twenty-five cents an acre. Where I pointed? I want it to stretch across the mouth o' that box canyon."

Rogers leaned back in his chair, stared at Bonner a moment, and slowly shook his head, a slight smile breaking the corners of his mouth. "Don't need to make no papers out; you ain't gonna live fourteen months, fact is you prob'ly won't live long enough to ride out to that canyon once Mr. Tedford finds out what you done."

Bonner's face muscles hardened, froze. "I reckon soon's I leave your office you gonna make damned sure Tedford knows that land's been filed on."

The thin, cold smile never left Rogers's lips. "You must understand, Mr. Bonner, Tedford's my friend." He nodded. "Yep, soon's you leave here I'm gonna ride out and tell Whitey Yadro what you done. Ain't no need to bother, fact is I don't never bother Mr. Tedford with stuff like this. Yadro will make sure you don't stay out there."

Trey stared at the man a moment. He couldn't believe that a civil servant would so blatantly profess to bend the law in one person's direction, but, he shrugged mentally, this was what he'd ridden halfway across Texas to find out.

He shook his head. Sure, there were many who worked for the government who were so crooked they had to screw their britches on every morning, and that included congressmen, judges, lawyers, and others, but very few would look across their desk and tell a person that the laws made no difference where powerful men were concerned.

"This Yadro you mentioned, he Tedford's foreman?"

Rogers shook his head. "More'n that. He takes care o' most things Mr. Tedford cain't; fact is, he never tells Mr. Tedford 'bout the problems he's got. He just takes care of 'em."

Trey thought about that a moment. Maybe Tedford didn't know about the squatters' homes being burned, or those who had been run off from their holdings. He'd have to study on this. It looked like this assignment would take longer than he figured—and he might need help.

He tapped the map again. "Gonna tell you somethin'. You make damned sure these papers get sent to Austin in the next mail, or I'm gonna do everything I know how to get you kicked outta this office."

Rogers's smile broadened, still cold as winter's wind. "You go ahead, Mr. Bonner, there's them who've threatened me before." He chuckled. "I'm still here—they're gone."

Trey gave a jerky nod. "You do as I say; we'll see about the rest." He nodded and left.

Out on the street, still smoldering from his confrontation with Rogers, he snorted the dry smell of dust from his nostrils and stared at the town, a cluster of gray, weathered clapboard buildings, most of which looked as though they wouldn't last another month before falling in upon themselves.

The livery stable, which also housed the blacksmith shop, stood at the end of the street, separated from the general store by maybe fifty yards. Next to the store a small building with a sign hanging over the door that labeled it as a gun repair shop, then the hotel, a narrow, mean, shotgun building of six rooms, each room built behind the other with a narrow hall down the outside wall allowing single passage from one room to the next. At the side of the hotel the town's only saloon stood, squat, dark inside with a raw board plank that served as the bar. Trey knew what each of the buildings were inside because he'd made it a point to visit each building.

The only place he'd not been stood across the street, the only structure on that side of the trail. It was neat, white-washed, with an attempt to have a few wildflowers in a bed on each side of the door. The sign over the door named it "Linda's Cafe."

His gaze swept the town, then back to the cafe. A saying he'd heard sometime in the past came to him: "Too poor to paint, and too proud to whitewash." Well, whoever Linda was, she wasn't too proud to try to add a bit of sunshine to this squalid jumble of little more than shacks. He thought to meet Linda, see what kind of woman she might be, but he'd already made up his mind to like her. She had to be a spunky lady.

He stepped out onto the dusty, rutted trail, crossed it, and went in the door. He was the only one in the room except for the pretty woman behind the counter. He smiled. "Bet a day's pay you're Linda."

"Reckon your pay's safe. Yep, I'm Linda, Linda McKinsey. Take a seat at either of those two tables, or sit up here to the counter." A smile wrapped around the words she gave him.

•

Trey nodded. "Sit at the counter—we can talk better that way."

"In this town what you want to talk 'bout must be dust, heat, weather, cows, folks? You name it, I'm just glad to have someone to talk to."

Trey edged onto one of the three stools and glanced around the empty room. "Been in business long?"

"Little over a year. My husband took a Comanche arrow on the way west; I got away and took with me the money with which we hoped to start anew over in the New Mexico Territory." She shrugged. "This's as far as I got."

A slight frown puckered her forehead. "Business gets better 'bout noontime; pretty good at breakfast too." The frown disappeared. She smiled. "You came in sort of in between. Know you did it just so's we could visit."

Trey stared at the counter, a questioning frown puckering his brow. "Well, now, if that don't beat all. I never was much good at visitin' less'n I had a cup o' coffee in front o' me."

"Oh my goodness, sometimes I forget that I have this place to serve people." She went to the cast-iron stove, pulled her apron into a pad, picked up the coffeepot, poured two granite cups full, set them between them, then pulled up a tall stool across the counter from him and nodded. "All right, now we can visit. What's your name? What're you doin', just ridin' through?"

Trey shook his head. "Name's Trey Bonner. I'm figurin' to stay awhile. Gonna take up some land down yonder at the base o' those hills some would call mountains."

His words wiped the glow from her face, the sparkle from her eyes. "Mr. Bonner, that's been tried before." She frowned as though thinking what to say, or whether to say it, then she shrugged. "Reckon I should tell you, when I came in here there were five families livin' out yonder at the base o' those mountains; today there ain't any. They been burned out or run off."

Bonner blew on his coffee, then took a careful sip. He looked at her. "Ma'am, I ain't never run from nothin' in my life, an' to burn me out they gotta get within rifle range. This man Tedford the one doin' the runnin' an' burnin'?"

"There's them who say it's him." Her face hardened. "But I'm tellin' you, Mr. Bonner, I just flat don't believe it. He ain't the kind. He, his daughter, an' his wife live out there along with what's left of his crew. I've met the family, an' most o' the hands, the old ones. They seem like right nice folks." She glanced at his cup apparently to see if he needed a refill, then locked eyes with him. "Maggie an' me—Maggie's Tedford's daughter—well, we've gotten to be right close friends, but when we start to talk 'bout the ranch? Well, that's somethin' she don't talk 'bout, almost like she's ashamed of what's happenin'."

Trey frowned, sipped his coffee, and shook his head. "Wonder who's doin' the burnin' an' runnin' people off then?"

Linda shook her head. "I got my ideas, Mr. Bonner, but I ain't gonna say." Her eyes widened, and her lips tightened to a straight line. "I got everything I own put into this cafe. Don't want to lose it; cain't afford to."

In Trey's opinion she looked scared. He figured it best to change the subject, then next time he came to town he might talk to her at greater length. He drank the last swallow of his coffee, now cooled enough such that it didn't burn his mouth. He held up his cup for a refill. "Since I'm gonna be in these parts awhile why don't you call me Trey? The only Mr. Bonner I know is my pa, an' yeah"—he nodded—"my grandpa."

She smiled. "All right, but you call me Linda and, uh, Trey, I'd be obliged if you'd forget what we talked about. Maggie an' now you are the only ones I've had a chance to talk to. Most people come in here, eat, and leave. Reckon I let my tongue wag more'n I should have."

Bonner shook his head. "Don't you worry your head any 'bout that, little girl." He smiled. "I've heard people say if I didn't greet them with a wish for a good day that I wouldn't have anything to talk about."

He tossed a quarter to the counter and stood. "See you next time I get to town." He grinned. "Fact is, I'll try to make it 'tween the mornin' an' noon meals so we'll have a chance to talk more. I figure that along with Maggie, you now have two friends."

A rosy glow flushed Linda's cheeks. Her face sober, she stared him in the eye. "That's a nice thing to know, Trey; me bein' a widow, people been sorta standoffish. I'll look forward to seein' you."

On leaving the cafe, Bonner walked to the livery; the wagon yard sat in back of it and he needed a wagon. There were things he needed if he would get his cabin started, and he intended to do that as soon as he got to the mouth of the box canyon.

The liveryman greeted him with a smile and a handshake. "What can I do fer ye, young'un? Know you don't need no horse. Seen ya ride in with a packhorse in tow."

"Thought I'd like to look at your buckboards; gonna need one to haul my gear out to where I figure to build my cabin."

A quiet, questioning look slid across the old-timer's face. "Yeah? An' where you gonna set up to build?"

The reaction of the old man when Trey announced he wanted to build caused him to draw rein on any more information. "Don't know how to tell you, old-timer. All I know is it's 'bout twenty miles from here." Then he decided to muddy the waters a little. "That young fella down at the land office was right helpful, steered me away from the land I thought I might want. Said somebody had already spoken for it, so he located me on land I hadn't seen yet, but he said it was right nice for buildin' a place on."

"You already seen Mr. Rogers?"

At Bonner's nod, the old man visibly relaxed. His shoulders came off the rigid, high way he'd been holding them, a smile came back to his face. "Well, now. Yes suh, I might have what you need. C'mon, let's git on out there to the wagon yard. Make you a good price on one if you find what you need."

While walking the short distance to the yard, Trey puzzled over the old man's change in attitude when he said that Rogers had practically picked out his land for him. Could Tedford have the entire town in his pocket? He shrugged mentally. Only time would tell—if he lived long enough to find out, and he figured to have something to say about that.

As soon as they got to the wagon yard, Bonner swept the wagons parked there with an appraising glance. With that glance he knew the one he wanted. He stayed away from it until he'd looked at most of them. Then approaching it, he frowned. "Now that wagon there looks like it's been used mighty hard, but maybe I can afford it if the wheels been kept greased, the axles ain't cracked, an' the bed's good and solid."

The old man cocked his head to the side, one eye squinted almost closed. "Now gosh ding it, knowed you wasn't no pilgrim right off the bat, but didn't figger you'd try to cheat an old man. You know that there wagon's the best o' the lot."

Trey chuckled, then nodded. "Yep, you're right on both counts; I ain't no pilgim, an' that wagon is the best o' the lot, an' no, I don't figure to try to cheat you long's you're fair with me."

They haggled a few minutes, then when the liveryman seemed to decide they'd played the game long enough, he looked Trey in the eyes, gave a jerky nod and said, "Gonna give you my rock-bottom price. Take it or leave it. Ain't gonna talk 'bout it no more."

"Okay, old-timer; let's hear it."

"Seventy-five dollars. That's it. No lower."

Bonner grinned. "You just sold a wagon. You got the trace chains, leather, all the gear to go with it?"

"Figgered all that stuff went with it. Yep, I got it."

Trey paid the old man, bought a mule to pull the wagon, and with that session of negotiating ended, he hitched up and headed for the back of the general store.

Inside, he met and introduced himself to the proprietor, Tom Parsons. "You settling around here somewhere, young'un?"

Trey's jaws knotted, then he said through tight lips. "Yep, I'm settlin' here. Figure to stay, an' I'll blow anybody who says different to hell and gone." He pinned the storekeeper with a look harder than granite. "You know anybody big enough to run me off—or burn me out?"

Parsons held his arms out, palms toward Bonner. "Hey, young man, I didn't mean anything by my question; but I did mean to let you know there've been those who met bad luck by squatting on land others have taken for granted was theirs by right of bein' there first."

Trey shook his head, slowly, then let a sheepish grin wipe out the anger. "Sorry, Mr. Parsons, reckon I been gettin' nothin' but warnin's from everybody 'round here; sort o' like don't no one want me to stay. Not one soul has given a word o' welcome—no show of friendship anywhere."

Parsons frowned, stared into Trey's eyes, then nodded. "Mr. Bonner, their failing to welcome you might've been the best show of friendship they could've offered." He pulled his pipe from his vest pocket, packed it, then held a match for Trey to light his—seeing Parsons packing his pipe, Bonner had done the same.

Getting their pipes lighted, Bonner stared into the glowing bowl of his own pipe, then pinned Tom Parsons with a questioning look. "How you figure bein' unfriendly is doin' me a favor?"

Parsons shook his head. "Mr. Bonner, I've said enough. I'm not a fightin' man, and it wouldn't be healthy for me to say more." He slipped Trey an embarrassed smile. "You see, young'un, I want to stay in business."

"Will it cause you trouble to sell me the things I need? The next closest place to this town is Marfa; danged near in the Big Bend, take me a while to drive over there an' come back."

"If I let them stop me from sellin' to legitimate customers, I might as well close my doors now, tuck my tail 'tween my legs, an' get gone." He nodded. "I said I wasn't a fightin' man; I didn't say I was a runnin' man. Go ahead an' select the things you need, then I'll help you load them."

An hour later, Bonner placed the last thing on top of his stack of supplies, frowned, thought a moment, then went to where he'd seen ammunition. He brought two cases of rifle and handgun shells, and one case of shotgun shells to the pile. "Add it up. I'll pay you, then I better get goin'. It's 'bout twenty, maybe twenty-five miles to my place; don't wantta spend more'n one night on the trail."

While Parsons boxed and bagged his supplies, Bonner went out the back to pull his wagon up to the loading dock. As soon as he cleared the back door, his look took in four men showing more than normal curiosity in his buckboard. They apparently hadn't seen him come out the back door.

The white-haired man, slim, built like a throwing knife, looked across the wagon bed to the two men on the other side. "Unhitch that mule, then we gonna flip this wagon over onto its back."

"Hell, Whitey," a beefy, short man on the other side of the wagon said, "let's jest build a fire in the bed an' watch that mule take off with that there fire burnin' 'hind 'im."

Whitey apparently thought about that suggestion a moment, then nodded. "Good idea, Manse. You men gather some o' this hay scattered 'round here, throw it in the bed, set it afire, take the brake off, an' watch 'er run."

Bonner slipped back into the store, picked up his rifle, checked to make sure it had a full load in it and went back out the door in time to see two of the men throw an armful of hay into the bed.

He jacked a shell into the chamber, and only quiet enough to be heard by the five said, "Stand away from that buckboard. Keep your hands clear o' your guns an' come around to this side o' the wagon where I can look at all o' you. Go around the tailgate; don't want my mule gettin' hurt."

Whitey stared at him a long moment, then bit off words that sounded as though they came from a gristmill. "Who the hell are you?"

"Don't make any difference who I am 'cept I'm the man who owns that rig there, an' if a-one o' you even touches it I'm gonna blow you in two." He moved the rifle barrel from one to the other. "Now, slow-like, come to this side so's I can see you."

The two circled toward the tailgate, then the one lagging behind made a move for his side gun. Bonner moved the rifle barrel only a fraction of an inch and squeezed the trigger. He wouldn't have to worry about that one anymore. He'd seen the black hole punched into the man's head just inside his hairline.

"Don't!" The hands of the remaining men froze in their

sweep toward handguns. "Your feeble brains just saw I ain't gonna take nothin' offa none o' you. Now, you, still behind the tailgate come on out here where I can see all o' you. Gonna count three an' you better be standin' rigid right there beside your partners. One . . ."

Before Trey got the word two out of his mouth, the man stood beside his cohorts.

In the few seconds that had passed, Whitey stood there staring at Bonner. His flat, dead, light-gray eyes showed no expression. "You better wish that bullet you put in Tobey's head had been in your own. We damned shore gonna make you wish it 'fore this is done with."

"Well, well, well, now, you white-headed bastard, you've just scared hell outta me." Bonner moved the barrel of his rifle slightly. "You, the one Whitey called Manse a few seconds ago, I'm gonna send you to the hitch rack in front to get your horses. If you ain't back here by the time I count ten, I'm gonna start eliminatin' your saddle pards. You got it? No round about way. Go an' get back or your bunkhouse's gonna be mighty lonely tonight."

"Be right back, mister. Ain't gonna pull nothin'."

Whitey twisted his neck to look at Manse. "Git there an' git back. Don't try nothin' funny; this gent's done showed us he ain't messin' around."

Trey waved the barrel toward the trail. "Git."

In less time than it takes to tell about it, Manse came back around the corner of the store tugging on the reins of four horses—three for those men still alive, and the dead man's.

"Load your friend across his saddle an' get outta here 'fore I decide to let the rest o' you go outta here the same way."

Yadro, his white, lank hair falling across his forehead, still stared at Bonner. "Wantta git yore face stamped in my brain. I know what parcel o' land you filed on. I'll be out to visit with you."

"Didn't take Rogers long to let you know, did it? Well, I'm here to tell you I ain't of the same stripe as those poor bastards you've already run off, so bring it to me; I'll welcome you with open arms."

Without more bluster, Yadro flicked his hand toward their horses. They toed the stirrup and rode off.

As soon as they rounded the corner of the saloon, Tom Parsons stepped through the back door. He held a Winchester in his hands. It was fully cocked. He let the hammer down carefully, then shot Trey a half-scared grin. "Didn't want 'em to see me in case you opened the ball, then I thought I might get at least one of them."

"Thought you said you wasn't a fightin' man."

"Did. And I was scared, but, Trey, I never felt this good in a long time." He glanced at Trey's wagon. "C'mon, let's get your wagon loaded."

2

LINDA PULLED THE curtains aside only a sliver, enough to watch the slim, high-shouldered man ride out of town, his saddle horse and packhorse tied to the wagon's tailgate, his rifle resting across his knees. She frowned. Why would she now feel hope for this town she'd chosen to make her home? Along with her feeling that maybe things would get better, fear ran a chill up her spine, fear for the slim stranger.

Before seeing Trey take his wagon out of town, maybe thirty to forty-five minutes before, she'd heard the sharp crack of a rifle shot, then soon after, the man called Yadro, along with two of his saddle pardners, had ridden out sitting in their saddles. One of the three who had come into town with the white-haired man lay facedown across his. Linda knew Trey Bonner must be responsible for the man his friends rode out with, and that man was obviously dead.

She had no personal reason to fear for Trey, but another shiver ran up her spine. Yadro had been in her cafe only about six times in the year she'd been in business. He'd always been a gentleman toward her and never caused trouble with any of her patrons, but when she was near him she felt dirty, felt like she'd feel if a rattler had slithered through her front door. He personified evil.

Her thoughts again centered on Bonner, and she tried to think what it was that gave her the feeling that things would get better. Was it the way he wore his revolver? Was it the set of his chin? Or was it the quiet confidence that seemed to envelope him?

She shrugged. Why should she think of him in any way? After all, she'd only met him long enough for him to drink two cups of coffee. She sniffed, smelled the spicy aroma coming from the kitchen and turned her steps in that direction. Her stew smelled like it might be about done.

Bonner glanced back at the town before a land swell cut it from view. Creases furrowed his brow. The ones he met, except for Yadro, his bunch, and Rogers, appeared to be solid citizens, but all seemed afraid. He chuckled to himself. Parsons had been afraid, but was ready to back him if trouble erupted. He liked the slightly graying, middle-aged man.

His mind turned to the trail. He swept every ridgeline, land swell, and swale with searching looks, then his mind centered on Linda McKinsey. For some reason she'd trusted him enough to open up and speak her mind. She didn't want the topic of their conversation to get out of the cafe, but she'd had enough gumption to say what she thought. She was quite a woman.

Unconsciously he reached to his shirt pocket, fingered the smooth, round metal object there, and pulled it from his pocket. He stared at the silver circle with the star in the middle, then the imprint came under his gaze: "Texas Ranger." He slipped it back in his pocket. Every time he looked at that small piece of metal a surge of pride swelled his chest, forcing blood to his head.

Colonel John Salmon Ford, was called RIP by most who knew him, because he uttered the words "Rest in Peace" so often during his illustrous career in the service of the Republic of Texas, and then the State of Texas, both as a soldier and as a Texas Ranger. Bonner shook his head. If it hadn't been for him, he figured he'd have wandered onto the wrong side of the law. He was too good with a gun and had never backed away from a fight.

Trey nodded. Those two things had been fast taking him down the wrong fork in the trail until RIP got ahold of him when he was only nineteen years old. He'd been a ranger ever since.

Bonner jerked his attention back to the present, searched the area again, then studied what he'd learned. The only thing that glared at him was that he needed help. This assignment, despite what they said about one riot, one ranger, would take more than one man to ferret out the facts.

He'd been sent to find out who burned out or ran off settlers. He'd never expected to run into trouble during his long ride out here, but someone figured it differently. Twice on his ride from Austin he'd been fired on from ambush. It couldn't have been anyone from this area because no one out here knew of his coming, or that he was a Texas Ranger.

Mentally, he shook his head. In recent years he'd made enemies—men he'd sent to prison and relatives of men he'd been forced to shoot. He frowned. Maybe those shots were an attempt at revenge.

By midafternoon Trey looked for a place to camp, one he could defend. The past hour he'd felt the familiar tightening of the leaders at the back of his neck. Someone shadowed him and was close enough to see him. That was too close. It had to be Yadro. The white-haired man, in Bonner's judgment, was not one to lose a friend and let it ride. Also, he'd had time to get back to Tedford's ranch, bury the man Trey had shot, and get on the trail to try to even things with the ranger. Bonner pulled his side-gun holster around to his side so he could get his six-shooter in action if they got that close. He put his twelve-gauge Greener on the seat beside him and checked to make certain he had a cartridge in the magazine of his Winchester .44 carbine. Hell, let 'em come.

A couple of hours later, after passing up three places in which he thought he might keep anyone from slipping up on him, he settled on one: a huge pile of boulders with enough room in the middle to spread his blankets and have a fire for his supper. Another stack of boulders, although smaller, lay about twenty-five yards to the south of the one he selected. There he would wait for them; he could also hide the wagon, mule, and horses behind that pile.

Bonner spread his blankets, pushed brush under them, put his hat at the head against a large rock, built a small fire, took out a strip of jerky, and moved to the smaller arrangement of rocks. He carried his rifle, pistol, and shotgun with him. He settled down to wait.

He chewed on the jerky until past sundown. The flicker of his fire in the other pile of rocks had long since ceased to flare and reflect on the rocks above it. He waited.

For the hundredth time in his estimation, he glanced to his back to make sure he'd picked a spot such that he couldn't be approached from the rear. That side of him was covered. He lay flat, his rifle pointed toward the jumble of boulders he figured would be the place they'd attack.

His muscles tightened, ached, felt like they'd tear in two. Occasionaly he moved enough to relax them. Time passed— eight, nine, ten o'clock by Bonner's reckoning—then when he thought he couldn't lie still another moment he heard what he figured was cloth scraping on a rock and what sounded like a body's muffled slide across desert sand. He centered his rifle toward the slight noise. With no moon or dim starlight, he could trust only his ears. Then all hell broke loose.

A lucifer flared, then a pile of brush his attackers had piled up burst into flame, flared to a bright light, then died followed by the sharp staccato burst of rapid rifle fire. Bonner had nothing to shoot at except flashes from gunbarrels.

He fired and jacked shells into the chamber of his rifle as fast as he could pull the trigger. One shot—only one— slammed back the slap of a slug hitting flesh. A high-pitched scream followed, a moan, then quiet.

Bonner lay still. They'd been busy attacking the camp around the glowing embers of the small fire he'd built. He doubted they'd seen from where his shots came. He dared not move a muscle. Then from inside the circle of the other boulders someone grunted, but the words came clearly to his ears. "Let's get outta here. He done tricked us."

"Gotta take Jim with us, Whitey. Sounded like he done bought the farm, but we gotta take 'im."

"Ain't takin' 'im nowhere. Let's get the hell outta here."

"He might not be hurt as bad as it sounded. I'm gonna check 'im, load 'im on 'is horse, an' take 'im with us."

"All right, all right, get it done."

Bonner's finger tightened on the trigger, then relaxed. He still had nothing to shoot at except sounds, and there were two of them able to fight. He didn't like those odds. There would be another day.

After some stirring around and grunts as though lifting something heavy, Yadro led the way from the rocks. After a few moments the sounds of their horses' hoofbeats faded in the distance.

Trey waited another few minutes, maybe fifteen, then moved back to where he'd placed his blanket and hat. He thought a moment, grunted, and gathered enough brush to have a small fire. He wanted a cup of coffee and thought it unlikely his attackers would be back.

While drinking his coffee, he thought of the day's happenings. Everything added up to Tedford having gathered around him a few salty gunslingers with their charge being to keep anyone from settling on land the cattleman figured as his. He even had the land agent under his thumb.

Bonner again went over the things that happened and Linda's words that she couldn't believe Tedford was that kind of man. She might be right, but from what he'd seen thus far, it would take a lot to change his mind. He drank the rest of his coffee, picked up his bullet-riddled blanket and hat, went to the wagon, and spread his blankets and ground sheet there. He soon slept.

He awoke before daylight and headed for the box canyon he'd filed preemption rights on. He'd selected a place that would force action from those who burned and ran off any who wanted to settle there. He'd scouted the area for a couple of weeks before deciding on the one he'd filed on.

Back close to the end of the canyon, a steady spring flowed from between rock cracks, the runoff of which made a stream that flowed down the center of the canyon and exited close to where he figured to build his cabin. Thinking about it caused him to smile. If he got the troubles settled, RIP Ford might lose himself a ranger. Trey thought to settle down before some gunhand settled him down—permanently. While thinking, he'd constantly searched the country around him. A slug from a rifle would end his troubles right sudden—and now he had the ambusher *and* Yadro's bunch to worry about.

The mouth of the canyon yawned ahead of him only a mile or so away. Bonner glanced at the sun, figured it to be about three-thirty, and nodded to himself. He'd made better time than he'd thought. The mule pulling his wagon had done a good job. A few minutes later he pulled the wagon to a stop behind a rock shoulder that folded out toward the middle of the canyon's entrance, unhitched the mule, and tethered him.

He'd have to build a corral first. Even if he turned the stock loose, they'd wander back into the canyon and he didn't want to have to search for them on foot. He tethered the horses and set about unloading the wagon.

An hour later, sweat running in rivulets down his face, his shirt soaked, dried, salt rimmed, and then soaked again, he sighed, walked to a small boulder and sat, his legs dangling off the edge. He studied the lush grass from the stream outward. The grass thinned to tufted, wiry clumps before it grew to the edge of the rock upon which he sat. While looking on this piece of land he'd spiked out as his, a peace settled within him. He nodded; yep, Old RIP might've lost himself a ranger, but he'd take care of this assignment first.

He ran his gaze back over the area, picked a land swell above the stream, a hump of land he figured would be above high water should a flash flood push the stream out of its banks, and decided that he'd build his home there.

It never entered his mind to have anything less than a

comfortable place to live, not a shanty, but a home with good thick walls of stone carefully fitted to keep out the heat of summer and cold of winter.

He sat there a few moments longer, stretched the kinks from his tired muscles, stood, and went about setting up a permanent camp, one he could defend as well as one he could work from during the building of his home. The spot he selected spread between the wagon to the inside of the rock shoulder.

That night, finished with supper, he poured his old granite cup full of the strong black coffee, walked to the fold of rock that stood about fifty feet from the canyon floor to its top. He sat, faced inward toward the great slash in the earth, and relaxed. Nothing could get at his back, and he reckoned he could stand off anything that came at him from in front.

Trey dawdled over his coffee a long time, wondering what was wrong with him. He thought it might be tiredness, then shook his head; he wasn't that tired. He pondered the reason another fifteen or twenty minutes, then he faced up to it. He was lonely for the first time since his saddle partner got killed in a shoot-out down in Nuevo Laredo.

He missed having someone with whom to share his thoughts. He wondered why now, what made *now* any different than the many other nights he'd spent by his fire, sipping coffee in the quiet of the evening?

He twisted to look out at his homesite. That was the reason. If a man had a home without someone to share it with, it would only be a house, an empty structure, a place devoid of laughter, tears, comfort, and tenderness. Without those things a man would be cheated of doing the things a man was put on earth for. He'd not have anyone to fight for, to work for, to create a safe, loving haven for.

He shook his head. What was the matter with him? That badge in his pocket made all the people in Texas the ones he wanted to keep a safe place for. He smiled to himself. Who the hell do you think you're kidding, Trey Bonner? You want a *home*, a woman, maybe children. He chuckled. Bonner, you ain't even got one stone laid, and here you are, suddenly got it filled with a wife and kids. He tossed the grounds from his cup, picked up his supper gear, and went to the stream to wash them.

With camp cleaned for the next day, he crawled in his blankets, wadded his hat such that it made a sort of pillow, breathed the hot smell of desert earth, and went to sleep.

The next morning he set about cutting willow trees and dragging them from the stream bank to up close to the escarpment, which he figured to use as one side of the corral.

By midmorning, Trey had two sides of the corral built to his satisfaction and had pulled his rope from another bunch of saplings when the pad of soft, dust-muffled hoofbeats sounded. He dropped his lariat, glanced out at the rolling desert, then walked to the wagon and picked up his Winchester.

The rider on the black-and-white paint horse held the paint to a steady walk until about a hundred yards from where Trey stood. He recognized now that the rider was a woman, a very beautiful woman. She rode as though she owned the universe.

From where he stood he saw that she wore a side gun and had a rifle in her saddle scabbard. He didn't put his gun aside as he was wont to in the presence of a lady. "Ride on in, ma'am. You got time I'll boil us some coffee."

"I didn't come to visit, Mr. Bonner. I came to see what kind of man you might be."

"You know my name, ma'am; who might you be?"

"Margarite Tedford here, and Mr. Rogers sent word out to the ranch that you were here and the name you go by."

"Well, Miss Tedford, you don't seem to want to make this a friendly visit, but my ma told me to always be a gentleman, so I'll ask you to step down and rest your saddle. Maybe you'll tell me why you're reluctant to be friendly."

The square set of her shoulders slumped a bit, she opened her mouth as though to say something then closed it until her lips showed a straight line. Her shoulders slumped more. She stared at him a moment, then she slipped from the sidesaddle she had so majestically sat. "Mr. Bonner, I don't want to be unfriendly. I came out here to warn you. They're not going to let you stay. You should know that. They'll run you off—or burn you out, or kill you—maybe all three, so why don't you pack up and leave before you get yourself killed?"

Trey stared at her a moment. She truly didn't seem to be belligerent. She really seemed to have come to warn him. "Miss Tedford, I too don't want to be unfriendly, but I'm here to tell you—I don't run, an' I'm damned hard to kill. You can go back home, tell your father, and tell that sickly lookin' gunhawk your pa's done hired to bring it on; they ain't enough of 'em to take care of me." He pushed anger from his head and pinned her with a stare he hoped told her he meant business. "You go home an' tell 'em that, ma'am. I'll be here when they try to ambush me the next time. Last night didn't work, not nearly."

She stared at him a moment. "I thought you might be the one when I rode out here." She pulled in a great sigh and let it out. "You shot the one Yadro brought in across his saddle. He's dead. And you shot the one, Jim, they brought in last night, a bullet in his stomach. He'll probably die." She shook her head. "They won't let you live."

Bonner's face stiffened such that he had to push the words from between his teeth. "Like I said, ma'am, it ain't gonna be easy. There's a few already tried it. I'm still here."

She looked around his camp, then moved her eyes back to him. "Mr. Bonner, if you don't mind, I believe I will have that cup of coffee you offered."

Trey's face softened, he looked from her to his belongings. "Wish I had a chair, or somethin' for you to sit on. I'll fix the coffee."

"I've sat on the ground more times than I ever sat on a chair, sir. I'll sit while you get the water, then *I'll* put the grounds in. I never saw a cowboy make coffee 'less it was thick enough to plow."

"What makes you think I'm a cowboy?"

She chuckled. "You sure aren't a sodbuster. Your boots, bandana, hat, jeans." She shook her head. "Nope, you don't look to be a man who would be comfortable doing anything but cowboyin'." Her eyes shifted to his gunbelt. "But the way you wear that six-shooter says you might be somethin' else."

A film of caution settled over Bonner. She was fishing

for information. "Well, ma'am, I ain't a gunslinger if that's what you're implyin'." He nodded. "An' yeah, reckon I've done enough cowboyin' so's I could lay a claim to bein' one." He picked up a bucket and headed for the stream for water. "Be back in a minute."

He felt her eyes study his back while he headed down the slope. Margarite wasn't what he had expected according to the way Linda had described her. He'd expected someone nicknamed "Maggie" to be sort of a tomboy. The girl he'd met only a few minutes ago fit the pattern of a lady, although a rather haughty one. He wasn't ready to judge her yet, but somehow, he couldn't associate her with condoning the actions of Yadro and his cohorts.

He walked to the stream's edge and dipped the bucket in the cold stream. As for Miss Tedford, he'd have to wait and get to know her better; for now, he'd hold back any trust he might be inclined to offer, despite Linda's opinion.

Over coffee, they talked of his plans, the location of where he planned to build his home, when he expected to bring a herd in; each of them careful to keep the conversation away from how he'd manage to keep his skin from getting punctured by a rifle bullet. When finally she stood to leave, she locked eyes with him. "Mr. Bonner, I'll ask you not to judge my father, mother, *or me* by the things that have happened around here, or by what Yadro has attempted. We're not the kind you may think." Without waiting for a reply she swung to the saddle, and riding sidesaddle as easily as a man would ride astraddle, she headed for home.

In the three hours it took Maggie to get home, she studied what she'd learned of the man she knew was going to face a stiff fight. She realized that he'd talked freely when the conversation was on his plans for cattle, where he'd build, etc., but he'd never spoken about where he came from, what the things were he worked at when not cowboying, and she wondered about those things. She wondered if he was to be the man who would free her father from the demons that had him in their hold.

When she rode her horse into the stable, she noticed that every lantern in the bunkhouse had to be lighted, then she saw the doctor's buggy parked in front. He must be caring for Jim Seely, the man she now knew had been shot by Trey Bonner.

She wanted to determine for sure the purpose of the doctor's visit, but turned her steps toward the main house instead. She thought her mother would know.

When she walked into the family room, her mother sat next to a window apparently to catch any vagrant breeze blowing through it. She had a lamp at her back and a book in her lap. She looked up. "I was beginning to worry about you. Where've you been?"

"Tell you in a minute. What's going on down at the bunkhouse?"

Her mother shrugged. "I suppose Seely is doing more poorly than they thought when Yadro brought him in last night. They sent for the doctor."

Maggie frowned, shivered, and looked her mother in the eye. "Mom, it's a terrible thing to say, but if he doesn't make it, I'll feel no sorrow or pity whatever. Good riddance."

Her mother stared at her hands folded in her lap, slowly shook her head, then raised her look back to Maggie's. She nodded. "Yes, it *is horrible* that we've hardened such that we can feel that way about another human being." Her gentle features hardened. "But, my daughter, I'm afraid I've allowed myself to adapt to this country just as you have. I feel the same way." She pinned her daughter with a no-nonsense look. "Now tell me where you've been. It's dangerous for a young woman to ride alone at night in this country."

Maggie braced herself for a reprimand. "Mom, I went to see our new neighbor. Wanted to see what kind of man he is; wanted, hoped he wasn't of the same stripe as Yadro and his bunch." She chuckled. "Don't reckon I can refer to what Yadro has left as a bunch since Mr. Bonner thinned 'em down a mite."

"Well, what kind o' man is he? From what you just said, he's just another hardcase."

Maggie shook her head. "Nope, I don't think I'd call 'im a

hardcase." She shrugged, then nodded. "Oh, you can bet he's hard as granite. I sensed he'd not be a man to push around, but he seemed fair, a man who believed in live and let live—as long as you'd let 'im."

"Then he's the one who shot up Yadro's men?"

"Yes. He didn't hedge on admitting to it, almost as though he hoped I'd carry a message to Whitey to try 'im again."

"Sounds like you think he's put us in the same basket with our uninvited guest."

Maggie shook her head. "I don't think so. I'd say he's tryin' to make up his mind about us. I hope so, because from what I've seen of 'im, I like 'im."

Bonner poured himself another cup of coffee, walked to the base of the escarpment, and sat. Miss Tedford had stayed much longer than he'd thought she would. In addition to having coffee with him, she'd stayed for lunch—in fact helped him fix it.

Her queenly, haughty demeanor she'd shown him on her arrival had thawed to the point he thought he might like her—if he worked at it, but he had no intention of doing that.

He finished his coffee, cleaned his campsite, and sat by the dying embers of his fire. It would soon be dark, too late to continue the job he'd started. He'd finish the corral soon after first light during the morning hours.

He stared down the now-dark confines of the canyon and decided it was time to turn in. He rolled to his knees—that's what saved him.

The sharp report of a rifle ripped the silent twilight. Almost simultaneously, a bullet whined past his head and spattered into the fold of rock behind him. He grabbed his rifle, rolled beyond the small flicker of his fire, and in the creeping shadows of darkness searched the surrounding cliffs. He waited for another shot. None came.

He lay where he'd fallen, sweating, wondered when another shot would come, wondered if a bullet tearing through his flesh would hurt as bad as it had several times before, and all the while wondered if Yadro had come back to make sure tonight was different than the night before. Finally, he shook his head. He didn't think the white-haired gunman would try again this soon; Bonner thought he'd try to find a more sure way to get him.

That thought took him back to the shots fired at him on his ride to the Big Bend country. He decided to finish the corral in the morning, then try to find tracks that might lead him to whoever carried a grudge against him. His jaws knotted; hell, as long as he'd carried a badge there were probably many out there who would like to see him dead.

He lay there for another thirty minutes by his best guess, then moved his blankets about a hundred yards from his campsite and went to sleep.

The next morning he finished the corral, then walked from his campsite into the canyon, searched, and found no indication the rifleman had fired from it, then he climbed to the rim-rock and searched, still on foot.

He'd been looking for about two hours when the morning sun caught a reflection of something shiny. He walked to it and found a spent .44 shell. That didn't help. Probably 90 percent of people out here carried a .44 in their saddle scabbard.

He spent another couple of hours looking for horse tracks, then well back from where he'd found the rifle casing, he found where the person had tethered his horse. The horse's hoofprints showed no distinguishing marks.

Trey studied them, frowned, then considered getting his horse and trying to track the ambusher. He shook his head; there had been a brisk wind across the tops of the hills the night before that would have wiped out any chance of tracking the shooter. He headed back to camp.

There, he measured and with a stick drew in the powdery dirt the outlines of where he'd begin laying rocks for the walls of his home. From that point, it was nothing but sweat and muscle-tiring work.

The first layer of rock went well. He'd search for the right boulder, drag it to the site, chip off the rough edges, dig it into the earth, and fit it to the stone next to it.

He finished the first layer, then rigged a tripod and block

and tackle to lift the heavy boulders in place for each succeeding layer.

Four days later, he had two and a half layers in place. He took a breather, studied the work he'd accomplished, and felt a surge of pride swell his chest. This was the first time in his memory that he'd done anything for himself. He'd helped others build their homes, but never anything for himself.

He looked to see where the sun sat in the heavens. It stood at about four-thirty. A trip to town would get him there well after dark. That was the way he wanted it. He thought if there were those lurking close by to do him harm, or to wreck his camp, they'd be less likely to know he'd left for the night. He stashed his provisions and equipment in a jumble of rocks, hobbled his livestock deep in the canyon, saddled his horse, and left. He hoped Linda's Cafe showed a light when he got to town. He'd be hungry, and he wanted to see the lady again.

True to his reckoning he got to town about eight-thirty, late for ranchers or townfolk to eat supper, but a light showed at the back of the cafe. He sat his saddle, studied the light, wanting company, but not wanting to intrude on Linda's rest time. His wanting and needing company won.

He rode his horse to the back of the cafe, tied it to the hitching post, and knocked gently on the back door. Linda's soft voice answered. "Yes. Who's there? I'm closed for the night."

"Ma'am, it's Trey Bonner here. Just thought we could talk some more. I'll come back in the mornin'."

"No, Trey. Stay right where you are. I'll unlatch the door."

The scrape of wood on wood sounded when she removed the bar. The door swung open. "Come on in. I'd like you to meet Maggie Tedford; she's stayin' with me tonight."

Trey swung his head to look where Linda motioned. "We've already met, ma'am. Had a right nice visit."

"Hello, Mr. Bonner. I never expected to see you again this soon."

Trey smiled. "Same here, Miss Tedford. I been thinkin' 'bout ridin' over to your place to meet your folks, but didn't know what kinda greetin' I'd get."

"You come. I'll see to it you get greeted right."

Linda studied the two of them and for some reason felt resentment that she had to share the tall man during this visit. She quashed her feelings. "I believe the stew's still warm, Trey. Have you eaten?"

"No, ma'am. Don't want to bother you though. Just havin' the company of two pretty ladies'll be right nice."

"Nonsense. I'll never let a hungry man go back out my door with the same feelin's. Sit. I'll dish you up a bowl." Although she was reluctant to leave Maggie and Trey, she went to the kitchen for his food.

The stew still simmered on the yet warm wood-burning stove. She hurriedly ladled a bowl full, sliced a big helping of cornbread, and went back to the room. "Sit and eat, hungry man." She placed his food on a small table she pulled over in front of him, stood back, and looked at them both. "Tell you what, why don't we get rid of the mister an' misses an' use our first names?"

Trey nodded. "Reckon I'd like that. Make me feel like I got two friends in this town."

Margarite grinned. "It's a deal if Trey'll promise to call me Maggie." She locked gazes with him. "You call me Margarite an' I'll figure you don't want to be very friendly."

Linda, studying them, wished Trey would call her friend Margarite, then thought how catty a turn her thinking had taken. She forced a smile, then nodded. "Good, that's settled. Now, Trey, tell me what brought you to town?"

He told them about the lone rifleman who'd fired at him four nights before, that he'd not been able to find anything that would give him an idea who it might have been, and told them only that he'd found a .44 cartridge casing. "At first, Maggie, I thought it might've been your hired hand Yadro," he said with a smile, "but on second thought, I figured he didn't want to lose any more men."

Linda looked at Maggie, watched her stiffen, and with a cold, sort of frozen smile, spear Trey with a look. "Tell you what, Mr. Bonner, Whitey Yadro is not one of our hired hands." Abruptly her attitude changed. "Oh, Trey, I don't know what is goin' on out at our ranch. Maybe next time we talk together we can figure it out."

"Next time we talk." That phrase determined Linda even more to talk with Trey as often as did Maggie. She didn't know why it made a difference—but it did. The tall man was a nice, decent man. Plus, she couldn't remember seeing a more handsome man. He was easy to be around. Well, maybe not all *that* easy, and it was too early for her to think about that.

The ride back to his canyon filled Bonner with thoughts not at all related to finding and stopping the killing of squatters. He'd enjoyed the visit. When riding to town, he'd almost tasted the bite of good bourbon; yet when he'd sat with probably the two prettiest ladies in the Big Bend country, he'd forgotten all about going to the saloon. Damn, Bonner, you gonna get civilized right fast if you don't watch it mighty close. He cast a smug grin into the darkness soon to become daylight. Now he had another long day ahead of him. Well, what the hell, it was worth it.

Whitey Yadro looked at Jim Seely lying on the bunk, his face white as new-fallen snow, his bloody red longjohns showing only a darker red, almost black where his life had come close to spilling from him. "Jim, we gonna get that damned squatter off 'n this here ranch; then we gonna git rid o' this here Ted-ford an' his whole family. I ain't gonna run that there damned squatter off. Gonna kill 'im; gonna kill 'im hard, like maybe gut-shoot 'im an' stand there an' watch 'im die slow-like. You jest git well, pahdnuh, we gonna take care o' him."

3

SEELY, HIS EYES closed to slits, stared vacantly, nodded slowly, then his head lolled to the side. Yadro pinned his partner's eyes with a searching look, then moved to his chest and saw signs of shallow breathing. He nodded. Yeah, there was no way Bonner was going to live.

He turned his head to look at the doctor. "He gonna live, Doc?"

The old man shook his head. "Don't know. Maybe if he's kept still, gets his bandages changed mornin' and night, an' gets fed some chicken broth every time you can get it down 'im; he might pull through—if infection don't set in."

"He'll git the care you talkin' 'bout, Doc. Gonna take care o' him personal."

The doctor stowed his equipment in his black bag, nodded, and left.

Yadro looked at Manse Allard, the only man he had left still on his feet. "Manse, we gonna take care o' Jim first, get 'im back on 'is feet, then we gonna take care o' that damned nester; gonna make sure he dies reeeal slow-like."

He looked toward his bunk, then back to Allard. "You go

ahead, turn in. I'll sit with Jim awhile, then I want you to watch over 'im."

Manse walked to his bunk, pulled his boots off, and flopped onto his bed.

Trey worked sunup to sundown, dragging rock, shaping it, fitting it in place, and each time he had a layer completed, he measured the height against his own. He wanted it at least two feet higher than his head.

Finally, the walls completed, he studied the floor. He was damned if he'd walk around on a dirt floor; he'd done that when as a small boy his folks came to Texas from Tennessee. He studied the idea of buying a wagonload of lumber, then decided he'd make the floor of smoothed stone also; his money had to be spent on cattle, furniture, and food.

That question settled, he flexed his shoulders, tried to get the tired kinks from them, built a fire, and cooked supper. He'd shot a jackrabbit that afternoon, and although poor, stringy eating, that rabbit would have to do for supper.

He pulled a leg from the dripping carcass, poured a cup of coffee, and sat back to relax, making certain no part of him showed where he could take a shot from the rimrock.

He stripped the last bite from the leg and sat chewing, then swallowed, took a sip of coffee, and saw a flicker of movement only slightly outside the firelight. He pulled his Colt and, never taking his eyes off the place he'd seen something move, waited.

After several minutes, maybe ten, he shook his head. He must be jumping at shadows. Then he heard a whine, one as though from an animal, or a hurt human. He pulled the hammer back on his .44 and pointed it toward the sound. "You friendly, come on to the fire; you ain't, I'm gonna start shootin' right soon."

Another whine, then, front paws stuck out in front and dragging his belly along the ground, a wolf, or maybe a dog, inched its way into the firelight.

Trey studied the animal a moment. The wolf or dog he

looked at was the scruffiest, dirtiest speciman of whichever it turned out to be that he'd ever seen. Cockleburs clung to every place there was hair on which to cling, and alkali dust covered the animal and burrs.

His eyes raked from tip of tail to the wolflike head and saw no wound. He pulled another hind leg from the rabbit and tossed it gently toward the animal.

His visitor sniffed at the meat, eyed Bonner, then snapped at the scrap of food, chomped, crushed the bones, chewed rapidly, swallowed and again stared at Bonner.

Trey pulled another piece of meat from the rabbit and held it out to the cocklebur-infested length of fur. He'd decided the animal was a dog, even though it resembled a wolf.

The dog, still dragging itself along its belly, as though not sure he'd met a friend, inched toward Trey.

"C'mon, boy. Ain't gonna hurt ya. Be a good idea though 'cause you're eatin' my supper." Bonner waved the piece of meat in front of him. "C'mon, fella, b'lieve you need a friend as much as I do. C'mon now." The dog dragged himself closer, his nose seeking the smell of that which Trey waved in front of him, then close enough, he moved his huge head within Bonner's reach.

With careful, slow, deliberate movement, Trey eased his hand toward the dog's head, reached its ears, and scratched between them.

Apparently, wanting the meat Bonner held enticingly close to his mouth, the animal wanted human companionship more. He whined again and moved closer to Trey, holding his head tight against the hand that caressed him. With his other hand, Bonner held the piece of rabbit to the dog's mouth. Before taking the meat, the huge animal licked Trey's hand. Bonner had found a friend, or the friend had found him. Without finishing his supper, he carefully pulled cockleburs from the matted hair and tossed them into the fire.

After a long while, time spent cleaning the dog's coat as much as possible, Trey stood, went to the stream, washed his hands, and came back to the fire. The dog stayed at his heels going and coming. He and the dog finished what was left of the rabbit.

Trey had taken to sleeping within the confines of the walls of his home. Still with no roof, it was home, and a bullet from the rimrock couldn't hit him where he bedded down. The dog slept stretched across the doorway.

Bonner pondered where the animal came from, then decided he had belonged to one of the families who were run off or burned out. He wondered about the dog's name and decided to just call him Dawg. He glanced toward the yawning space where he'd eventually hang a door, looked at the animal stretched out there, and felt safer, turned on his side and went to sleep.

The next morning he decided that he and Dawg would go hunting. They'd both be hungry before the day was done, plus he wanted to take another look at the area from which the ambusher fired at him. He went to the ambush area first.

There were no tracks, not even broken brush to clue him which way the killer had gone. Trey shrugged, and thought he'd have to wait for another attack. If he lived through it he'd find the murdering bastard—maybe Dawg could help.

He walked the high mesa thinking to take an antelope or anything else Mother Nature provided for his evening meal. Dawg still stayed at his heels, close enough that he got underfoot a couple of times. "Hell, Dawg, I ain't gonna leave you. Now stay from under my feet; I gotta find us somethin' to eat." With the words barely out of Trey's mouth, the big animal, ears peaked, swung his head to look across the arid land. Trey followed his gaze. Out about three hundred yards, a big buck grazed.

Careful to not make a sudden move, Bonner raised his Winchester, sighted, and squeezed the trigger. The buck jumped, landed on all four legs, then crumpled. "Let's go, Dawg. Just now got us some supper." For the first time the huge animal tracked out in front of Trey.

When they walked to the deer, Bonner apprached it with care, saw the animal was dead, stared at it a moment, guessed it would weigh a couple of hundred pounds, and decided to dress it before starting to his cabin. It would be a lot lighter.

While skinning the buck and then wrapping the meat in the hide, he used care to not get hair on the meat, but several times while working on the carcass he tossed Dawg a few bites. Only then did he wrap the meat in the hide. Finally he shouldered the bundle and he and his new friend headed for home.

He walked to the edge of the rimrock, looked toward the mouth of the canyon, and frowned. Smoke floated lazily from the chimney he finished only the day before. He'd finished the floor the week before.

He placed the bundle of meat on the ground at his feet and studied the grounds around his home. After only a few moments he decided that an enemy would not have announced his presence by building a fire.

He sighed, picked up the bundle of meat, and stepped down the steep path that would take him to the bottom of the canyon. Dawg stepped out in front of him. "Gonna tell ya how it is, Dawg, I'm doin' all the work so's we'll have somethin' to eat, and you're just traipsin' along for the company. I'll find somethin' to keep you busy."

When within about fifty yards of the walls of his home, he stopped, dropped the bundle to the ground, pointed his rifle toward the unfinished building, and yelled, "Hello the camp."

His words still echoing down the canyon, Maggie stepped around the side wall of his cabin. "Come on in, Trey. I won't hurt you." Her gaze shifted to his shoulder. "Glad to see you took care of gettin' the meat. I brought vegetables and an apple pie. Took the liberty of rummagin' through your provisions an' found your coffee." She smiled. "Bet you could use a cup right now. Weather's chilled a bit since sundown."

"You hit that target dead center, pretty lady, on both counts." While talking, he walked toward her. Damn, she *was mighty pretty,* and not at all the cold, standoffish woman he'd at first thought.

Her eyes shifted to the animal leading Trey. "See you found yourself a friend."

Bonner chuckled. "Nope, didn't find *'im,* he found me, but

I gotta say I'm almighty happy to have 'im; it gets right lonely out here with nobody to talk to."

They walked on to the cabin together, side by side. Then, inside the walls, Trey dropped the bundle of venison to his makeshift table, unwrapped it, proceeded to slice two steaks, stopped, looked at Dawg, then sliced a couple more. He looked at Maggie. "Danged dawg's gonna cause me to hunt more, slow down my work on my home. Reckon I'll make 'im sleep out in the cold this winter."

A throaty chuckle greeted his words. "Trey Bonner, from what I've already seen, that dog's gonna be sleepin' right there beside you." She looked at a stone shelf Bonner had incorporated into the wall, pulled two cups from it and poured them coffee.

Bonner took the cup of steaming liquid Maggie held out to him. While taking the cup from her hand, he looked her straight in the eye. "Yeah, Maggie, reckon he'll be there, but somehow there's gotta be more than a dawg at a man's side."

A rosy surge pushed to her face. She nodded. "Yes, Trey, I think you're right. Think about what you just said; that's true with a woman too."

Bonner took a swallow of the coffee, burned his mouth and tongue, wondered how to change the subject, then made the situation worse. "Yeah, but, Maggie, you got your ma an' pa to keep you company."

Maggie looked him straight in the eye, a slight smile breaking the corners of her lips. "Someday, Trey Bonner, I'm gonna explain the difference to you of the kinds of company a man an' woman needs," she chuckled, "but for right now, I'm tellin' you if you don't get those steaks on the fire, I'll be ridin' home in the black dark again."

Trey couldn't remember when he'd been so happy to have been let off the hook, allowed to shake off a noose, allowed to just plain get out of a box that he'd put himself in.

While he busied himself with the venison, he kept glancing at the beautiful woman setting the table, putting the pie close to the fire to warm, putting the vegetables and potatoes on to boil. Aw hell, a cowboy, a Texas lawdog, a, well hell, a real nothing in the eyes of women, shouldn't be getting so damned far into the future. He'd better take care of the job he'd been sent here to do. Then she made his problem worse.

"Trey, if we run past night dark, will you ride partway home with me?"

To hell with putting his head in a noose. He looked into those blue eyes he somehow wished he could drown in, nodded, and pulled the noose tighter. "Ma'am, I'll ride *all* the way with you, ride back, an' do it all over again if that'd keep you safe from harm."

That throaty, deep-chested chuckle again greeted his words. Geez! When the hell would he learn he didn't know one damn thing about women—or how to talk to them. He glanced at the open space above. "Reckon I'm gonna have to take the wagon to town so's I can haul a load o' lumber out here. Need to finish the roof 'fore we get a good soakin. Gettin' right cold at night too; need somethin' over my head."

Maggie swept the room with a glance. "You've done a beautiful job on your home, Trey. Where'd you learn to do all this?"

He took a swallow of coffee, which now had cooled enough to drink. He smiled. "Ma'am, I never built anythin' for myself before; helped many a friend put up their cabins"—he shrugged—"but never anythin' for me. Reckon I just wanted to do it sort o' special." He almost put his foot in his mouth again. He came close to saying that he wanted it good enough to bring a bride into, but held his tongue in the nick of time.

While eating they talked of the town, whether it would ever amount to anything, when they might get some law in the area, but Trey kept the conversation on things he could talk about comfortably. He *did* say he hoped the town wouldn't grow much more; that he liked small towns.

While Maggie washed the dishes, Bonner saddled their horses, glanced at the sky, and realized that it would once again be long after dark before she got home. He thought it might be pushing toward daylight when he got back to his own home. He wanted to meet her father and mother, wanted to see what kind of people they were, wanted to see if he thought her pa was the kind of man that would bring in the likes of Whitey Yadro.

The dark, comforting night closed in around them, and in doing so made conversation an intrusion on something that seemed to be intimate. Bonner held his tongue. He wanted nothing more than to know there was a woman at his side.

They rode for several hours that seemed like warm minutes to him, topped a rise, and the lights of a large ranch spread before him.

"There she is, Trey. All that Mama an' Papa have worked, sweated, and fought for. There's Box T, headquarters. An' really the only home I remember—or want to remember. C'mon. Want you to meet my folks."

Bonner smiled into the darkness. If he'd planned it, it couldn't have worked out better. "Been wantin' to do that, Maggie. Let's get on down there. We don't an' I'll be settin' up to the breakfast table in your crew's quarters."

Fifteen or twenty minutes later, she showed him the stall in which she kept her horse, and while he unsaddled for her, Maggie went to the ranch house to tell her folks they had company.

Her horse comfortably in his stall and Trey's tied to the hitching rail in front of the wide veranda, he walked to the porch. Maggie met him when he topped the last step. "C'mon in. Mama an' Papa want to meet you." She laughed that deep throaty laugh he liked so much. "I told 'em you were a right nice cowboy. That way they won't shoot you."

"Aw now, ma'am, I been worryin' 'bout that durin' our whole ride." He chuckled. "Really, Maggie, I was hopin' we'd get here early enough so's I could meet 'em." Then, thinking he'd better offer a reason for wanting to make their acquaintance, he said, "A man should always get to know his neighbors."

Her retort, "Of course, Trey," took him back to his cabin when he squirmed so uncomfortably. If there had been enough water here, he knew he was in over his head.

Trey had pictured Maggie's mother as a chubby, huggy, motherly woman; instead, she looked nearly as young as

Maggie, and every bit as beautiful. Her father stood well above six feet, an inch or two taller than Trey, with a mane of white hair, an imposing figure in Bonner's estimation, a man used to command. Hell, put him beside RIP, and Trey would have to wonder who was in charge.

When introduced, Bonner called up all the training and education RIP had insisted he strive for. "Mr., Mrs. Tedford, I'm pleased to meet Margarite's mother and father." He stood back and waited for a response.

Matt Tedford shook Trey's hand and scowled. "Maggie told us you seemed like a cowboy, a nice cowboy; you sound like a city boy, one steeped in the niceties of a proper society. Which one are you, Mr. Bonner?"

Trey stiffened, pinned Maggie's father with a look he hoped to make rock hard. "Sir, I am unaware that being a cowboy requires that I be unschooled, uncouth, and stupid. Perhaps I'd best not bother you tonight, Mr., Mrs. Tedford." He nodded, then stepped toward the door.

Maggie caught his sleeve. "Trey, please. Can we just start over. You're not what I told Mama an' Papa to expect. I described you to them as what I'd met over yonder in the foothills—a really nice young cowboy. You sounded like a city boy just now. Don't think Papa was ready for that."

Bonner stared at her father a moment, then nodded. "Reckon, sir, I'm just what Maggie described. I'm a cowboy, but one with a little education. If that offends you, I'm sorry. Most o' the time I like bein' a rough, illiterate, workin' man— 'cause that's really what I am. That's what I been around Maggie. I figured she liked that kind o' man, an' that's what I am."

"You tryin' to be the kind o' man Maggie likes? Why?"

Again Trey's back stiffened. His neck felt like the hair stood straight out on it. He softened his voice, and almost in a purr, said, "Sir, I like Maggie, want to be her friend, that's all. If you folks don't understand a man wanting to make friends, then reckon I've wasted my time ridin' over here." He picked up his hat, which he'd hung on the rack when he came through the door, placed it on his head, nodded, and stepped toward the door. "Good night, folks, have a nice evening."

The two women stood there, stared at Bonner, then each of them cast angry glances toward Matt Tedford.

On the ride back to his cabin, Bonner tried every way he knew how to justify Tedford's attitude. The only reason he came up with was that the man wanted to make sure his daughter was not getting involved with some drifter, one without a sense of honor. Despite his thinking, he simmered beneath the surface. Hell, why should he care what the man thought of him; besides, Tedford might be the man Trey had been sent out here to nail for the treatment of those who had tried to settle along the foothills.

Still a couple of hundred yards from his cabin, a deep growl came from the darkness. "It's me, Dawg. You keep good care o' our things?"

This time he got a pleased whine from the beast. He'd told Dawg to stay at the house and to not let anyone mess with anything. Dawg had done a good job.

Bonner took care of his horse, glanced at the Big Dipper, and thought he might get three or four hours' sleep before hitching up the wagon and heading for town. He needed that load of lumber for his roof.

He slept in until the sun showed a thin halo above the horizon, rolled out of his blankets, fixed breakfast, hitched up, and headed for town. He motioned Dawg to come with him.

On the ride in, he decided to buy enough lumber such that he could build himself a bed. He'd also see if Tom Parsons stocked ticking. He'd find a woman who sewed for other people and have her stitch a mattress covering together so he could stuff it with fresh, dried-on-the-stem grass, and gain a little more comfort.

He drove the buckboard faster then he normally would. He wanted to get to Linda's Cafe in time for lunch. He figured to eat slow-like, slow enough for her other patrons to finish their dinner and leave. He wanted to talk with her again, see why he might have been treated the way Tedford had treated him.

Linda looked up from the wood-burning range just as Trey came through the door. She smiled, waved toward one of the only two vacant seats at the long table closest to her, and went about dishing up steak and potatoes for the man who'd ordered before Bonner came in.

She poured a cup of coffee, put the steak order in front of the man, and took the coffee to Trey. "We'll talk as soon as most of these people clear out. It's good to see you, Trey."

He nodded, looked toward the pegs on the wall and hung his hat on one of them. Most men coming in off the range wore their hats indoors, but RIP had taught him that it was impolite to keep your hat on if there was a place to hang it.

His thinking switched to the smile Linda had flashed him when he walked in. That had surely been one hell of a lot different than the way Tedford had treated him. He shook his head; he'd been blaming Maggie for the way her father had acted. That was unfair. Neither she nor her mother had been inhospitable.

He again glanced at Linda. Standing over the stove, her face flushed from the heat, he thought she made a mighty pretty sight for a lonely man, a sight that would be even prettier if it had been over his own stove in his own home.

Without waiting for him to order, she brought him a steak, potatoes, and fresh collard greens. She explained that there was a lady in town who had a garden, and if she had an abundance of things, she'd sell those she didn't need to Linda. "Ya'll must've already had a frost over here for her to be harvestin' 'er collards already."

Linda nodded. "Just the other day."

Bonner dawdled over his dinner until the cafe emptied, then Linda poured herself a cup of coffee and sat across the table. "Well, busy man, how's your cabin comin'?"

He nodded, chewed, swallowed, and took a sip of coffee. "Comin' right good, pretty lady, all except the roof—that's why I had to come to town. Figure to put a wood roof with some o' those tin sheets o' metal over the wood; that is if Parsons stocks anything like that."

She nodded. "Bet he does. I never went in his store for anything he didn't have." She swept him with a glance. "See nobody's been shootin' at you." She smiled. "At least there's no sign they hit what they were shootin' at."

He frowned through a grin. "That's no jokin' matter, lady." The frown disappeared, leaving only the smile. "But I gotta tell ya. I got me a dawg. Big fella, looks like a wolf at first glance. He took to me right away."

He told her how he'd come to get the dog, told her about the things he'd been doing, thought to tell her about Maggie's visit, and meeting her folks, but shied away from talking about Maggie at all, and wondered why it should make a difference. He'd never showed either of the ladies anything but friendship. He wondered about that and knew that eventually he'd search his thinking and see if he really wanted more than friendship from either of them.

They talked until midafternoon, then he said he'd better get on over to the general mercantile store and see what Tom Parsons had that he needed. Warmth flooded his face. "Reckon I wore these flat-heeled brogans figurin' I had a lot o' work to do here in town that I couldn't do from horseback." He sighed. "Wish I could."

They talked a while longer, then he left knowing he'd not found out anything more than he already knew. He stepped toward the door and turned back. "You got any scraps, or maybe a whole steak? Dawg oughtta be mighty hungry by now."

Linda smiled. "I'll fix 'im as much as he can eat."

Parsons had the tin roofing, lumber, everything Trey needed, including more provisions along with pipe tobacco. Bonner glanced at the regulator clock hanging on the back wall, then looked toward the door. It was late fall and the sun set early. The clock showed five-thirty, and his glance toward the door showed that the sun had almost set. "Think maybe I'll stay in town tonight an' get an early start in the mornin'." He grinned. "Reckon the real reason is I'm gonna have a couple drinks o' that tarantula juice down at the saloon."

Parsons frowned. "Be careful in that saloon, Trey. There's a crew in town, back from a trail drive. They're tired, wore to a frazzle, an' salty as hell." He glanced at Bonner's shoes. "They gonna take you for a sodbuster dressed like you are. That might cause you some trouble."

Bonner's shoulder muscles tightened and heat flooded his

face. "Parsons, I came in town on business an' figurin' to have a couple o' peaceful drinks. They ain't no tireder or more frazzled than I am. They lookin' for trouble, let 'em bring it to me."

Tom frowned, then smiled. "Damn, boy, don't take much to set you off. All I meant was—be careful."

Trey shook his head. "Hell, Tom, reckon I'm ridin' a hair trigger. I been shot at from ambush, some have tried to burn my wagon, some want to run me off—an' ain't no damn way I'm takin' anythin' from anybody. I been up the trail myself— three times—know how they feel, but what I said stands. They want trouble they can bring it to me." He stepped toward the door. "I'll pick up my stuff in the mornin'. What time you gonna be open for business?"

"Six o'clock. You want it 'fore that, let me know an' I'll make it a point to be here for you."

Bonner shook his head. "No. I'll probably have breakfast over at Linda's place 'fore I leave. I'll be here 'bout seven."

Tom nodded. "Your stuff 'll be ready."

Bonner took his time getting to the saloon, then before pushing his way past the bat-wing doors, he thumbed the thong off his handgun. Stale sweat, the smell of yesterday's beer, whisky, and tobacco smoke assailed his nostrils, and bedlam exploded against his ears as soon as he entered. The tinny piano mixed with all in the room talking at once made more noise than he'd heard since he left Austin.

He walked along the wall toward the end of the bar, careful to avoid bumping into anyone; a little thing like that could bring on gunplay. Bonner, about to take a vacant spot down the bar, saw the puncher at the end leave for a table. Bonner walked to the vacated place and motioned the bartender to bring him a glass and bottle.

He stood there sipping his drink, feeling the raw whisky burn all the way to his stomach. Lousy whisky but better than nothing, and the burn fit his mood.

He'd finished half his first drink when a young puncher, drunk, stood in the middle of the floor behind him and yelled so most should be able to hear him. "Damn, men, look what we got here. We got us a sodbuster."

Bonner had only to turn his head a mite to know the cowboy looked at him. "Don't want any trouble, young'un. Get on back to your drinkin' an' havin' fun." With his left hand he took a swallow of his drink. "I ain't botherin' ya, so don't bother me." He bit the last sentence off as though the words were nails.

The ranny stared at Trey through red-rimmed, blurry eyes. "Yeller, huh? Well, I'm already botherin' ya; gonna bother ya 'til I see what you're made of."

Bonner stood there a moment, measured his man, nodded, and took another swallow of his drink—that was when the young'un gripped the handle of his six-gun.

The ranger, in a draw that would be called lightning in any company, drew his Colt, stepped toward the puncher, swung his six-shooter alongside the cowboy's head, and stepped back. The kid dropped like a patty from a tall cow.

Bonner swung his revolver in an arc to cover all in the room. "Gonna 'splain somethin' to you men. I been up the trail twice as a drover, an' once as trail boss. First time was to Abilene." He nodded toward the young puncher only now shaking his head and trying to push himself up off the floor. "That young'un was still wettin' his diapers the first time I ate all that dust. Now I don't want trouble. I came in here for a drink, nothin' else. Keep that young'un away from me—an' anybody else who's lookin' for a fight."

He holstered his Colt and turned back to the bar, but not so far that he couldn't see those in the crowd.

The cowboy stood, shook his head, grimaced, looked toward Bonner, and stepped toward him. One of the trail crew caught the kid's arm before he could bring on more trouble. "Cut it out, kid. That man wasn't givin' you no mess; fact is, I'd say he's seen the ass end o' more cows than most o' us put together." He tried to twist the young puncher such that he could steer him to a table. The kid shrugged him off and turned back toward Trey.

"Sodbuster, you hit me without no warnin'. Draw that six-gun you're wearin'."

Bonner knew he couldn't reason with the drunken cowhand. He stared at the young'un a moment, flicked his hand to his side, and without most in the room having time to react, had his Colt pointed at the cowboy. "Don't move your hands. Don't even twitch. I'll kill you next time. I've had enough."

The cowboy stared at him a moment, opened his eyes wide, then squinted toward Trey. He stood there, a much more sober man than had called Bonner to draw the first time. "Mister, dumb as I am, you shoulda shot me." He wagged his head slowly from side to side. "You right handy with that there handgun." He reached to his pocket, pulled a sack of Bull Durham and brown corn-shuck papers from it, and fashioned himself a cigarette. He dragged a match across the seat of his jeans, put fire to his smoke, squinted at Bonner, grinned, and said, "Thanks for not killin' me."

Bonner felt the tension go out of the room. Talk again filled his hearing, laughter filled the void of angry expectancy. The kid stepped toward Trey, his hand extended. Bonner took the man's hand with his left one. Damned if he was going to take a chance the kid was putting on an act.

He drank more that night than he had intended when he came in the room. Members of the crew kept wanting to buy him drinks. Finally, he told the cowboys he had to get out of there; he had a hard day's work ahead of him.

His bed that night, made of fresh corn shucks, felt like a featherbed. He slept like a baby.

4

TREY WOKE WITH an aching head and fuzzy thinking. He could still taste the cheap rotgut he'd put down the night before, rotgut that had begun to taste like "good" whisky before the night ended. Despite the night before, he wakened before daylight, washed up, and headed for Linda's Cafe.

As soon as he walked in some of the bunch from the night before greeted him, then the young'un he'd had the trouble with stood, held out his hand, grinned, and looked Trey in the eye. "Mr. Bonner, I'd shorely be beholden if you'd let me help load yore wagon this mornin'." His grin widened. "See you got yore sodbuster shoes on so reckon you ain't gonna be workin' from atop a horse like a normal human bein'."

Bonner nodded, and his smile showing through his hurting head that he appreciated the offer, said, "You gonna be sorry you made that offer. I got a full load. Can use all the help I can get."

The trail boss looked across his shoulder, took a sip of coffee, and flicked his thumb toward the puncher. "Seems like you made a friend, but gotta say, you got a damned strange way o' doin' it. Maybe next time I need a friend I'll just clock 'im 'longside 'is skull with a six-shooter."

He turned back to his plate, took another bite of fried potatoes, then, still chewing, turned back to Trey. "Tell you what, you go on an' eat, then we'll all help load that wagon."

Linda, busy scurrying from table to table pouring coffee and bringing hot biscuits only had time to nod and smile at Bonner.

After ordering, and sitting over his second cup of coffee, he wondered if he'd been approaching people in the right way. Hell, maybe he should start out by knocking a knot on their head. He chuckled to himself.

After promising Linda he'd come back over for a cup of coffee before leaving town, he and the trail crew went to the back of Parsons's store where he'd parked his wagon, and in only thirty, maybe forty-five minutes had all his equipment aboard. He shook hands with them all before they headed for the livery to get their horses and head out.

Parsons, having heard the story about the night before, stared at their retreating backs and shook his head. "You cowboys are a strange breed, fight each other one minute, drink and raise hell together the next." He again shook his head. Bonner laughed.

He and the storekeeper went inside where Trey stripped a heavy money belt from inside his trouser's waist and settled his bill. Tom Parsons stared at him a moment. "You always carry that much money around with you?"

Bonner nodded, then grinned, "Most times, but if I visit your store many more times, I won't have to worry 'bout it."

"It's no jokin' matter, Trey, there're a lot o' hard cases in this country who'd take it; take a lot less than you're carryin' in that belt."

Bonner shrugged. "Didn't have much choice. Figured when I left Austin I wouldn't be returnin' there very soon. Figured to stay wherever I stopped. Well, I've stopped."

"I'd offer to keep it for you, but I don't have any safer place than you do."

"No worry. If someone is successful in takin' it I won't be needin' it anymore anyway." He strapped the money belt back around his waist, told Tom he'd pick up his wagon in a few minutes, then went back to Linda's. The aroma of baking made his mouth water. "That apple pie you have in the oven?"

She raised her eyebrows and smiled. "Sure is. Had to have some way to draw you back over here. It's not quite ready; another ten minutes maybe. You want a slice?"

"Could you spare a half a one? Don't want you to cut yourself short for your customers."

"I can always put another one in the oven. I'll bring it soon's it's ready."

They visited while Trey ate his pie and never got around to talking about Matt Tedford, then before leaving he told Linda he'd probably get back to town in two or three weeks. Her face sobered. She frowned. "You work too hard. You need to come in, attend one of the dances we have about once a month. It'll keep you young."

He smiled. "I'll give that some thought, pretty lady." He tipped his hat and left.

Before pulling away from the back of the store, he placed his Winchester on the seat beside him, took a spare six-gun from a box he kept down at his feet. The box contained another Colt, and a couple hundred rounds of ammunition.

"You fixin' to start a war, Trey?"

"If I figure on one happenin', Tom, I'm always ready." He slapped the reins against the horse's back.

He drove slowly, but still the sheets of tin roofing clanged and rattled, making such noise he couldn't have heard a buffalo stampede. Every quarter of a mile, more or less, he drew rein and listened. All the while he searched the land swells, arroyos, and ridges for any indication he might be watched or followed. Even with the caution, the sharp crack of a rifle shot, accompanied by the slap of a bullet into the side of the wagon, jerked his nerves tight. He hit the ground, rolled under the vehicle, and lay there on his stomach. His breath came in short, ragged gasps; his neck muscles pulled against his head, still pounding from the whisky he'd drunk the night before. Fear flooded him. How could a man fight someone he couldn't see?

He lay there under the wagon, eyes searching every break

in the landscape. No more shots came at him. After a long while; thirty or so minutes that seemed like that many days, he rolled out and stood. Still no shots. And the sound had echoed off the sides of the hills such that he couldn't tell from what direction it had been fired. He stood alongside his horse, still trying to see even the slightest hint of another human. Nothing.

Finally he climbed back into the seat and urged the horse to pull. Whoever the bushwhacker was, he had set a pattern. He'd take one shot and leave—but Bonner couldn't bank on that. When you thought you had a man figured, and he broke the pattern, that's when you die.

He looked to his back trail. Dawg followed at a distance. He pulled the wagon to a stop. "Come on, Dawg. It's time you rode up here with me. Know you must be gettin' tired."

When the big beast came alongside, Trey jumped down, slipped both arms underneath the animal, and lifted him to the top of the pile of supplies. "You an' me, Dawg, we gonna see if we can find that bastard shootin' at me, but can't do it now; need a saddle hoss for that."

While standing on a surface that didn't bump and jolt, he packed his pipe, lighted it, and climbed back aboard. While sitting on the bumping, swaying seat, he pondered who might be after him. He discarded Whitey Yadro and the one man he had left who could sit a saddle. The white-haired gunman was the kind who would want as many around him as possible.

Then he went back over his past, thought of the men he'd brought before the law, men who'd been hanged. He shook his head; there were too many to settle on only one. He drew on his pipe. It needed to be lighted again.

He struck a lucifer on the rough board seat, put the fire to the bowl, and puffed life to the tobacco. He glanced at Dawg. "Yep, you an' me are gonna go huntin' again, only this time we gonna hunt a two-legged animal. Think we can get 'im, Dawg?" The big animal put his head on Trey's thigh, then whined, a friendly, "I love you" kind of sound. Bonner rubbed the animal's ears.

After a few more hours of tight nerves, taut, tired muscles, and aching eyes, Trey pulled rein in back of the shoulder of rock, unhitched the horse, and turned him into the corral.

He glanced at the stark, bare-bones walls of his home, then sank to hands and knees, then his stomach. Might not be anyone there on the rimrock, but he hadn't lived this long by taking chances. His rifle in the crooks of his elbows, he slithered toward the back; there was only one window there.

At the window, he raised his head far enough to see inside—but only rock walls, rose tinted by the setting sun, greeted him. He sank back to his knees and studied the problem. No way he would just go blaring in without some assurance he had the place to himself. Finally, he nodded, picked up a rock about the size of his fist, and tossed it toward the inside corner. Silence. Then Maggie's voice said, "Come on in, Trey. I'm the only one here."

He stood, climbed through the hole that soon would hold a window casing, struck a lucifer, and lighted a lantern. "What you doin' sittin' here in the dark like this?"

"It just seemed so peaceful, no noise, no one to get upset with—only me and the crickets chirpin'."

"What's the occasion, Maggie? Seemed like I wasn't liked very well last time I saw you." He kept his voice level; not warm, not cold.

"Oh, Trey, please don't treat me this way. I don't know what got into Papa. He's been riding a hair trigger every since Yadro an' his men showed up. Mama an' I were embarrassed at the way he treated you. I came to apologize if you'll accept one."

"Maggie, neither you nor your mother owe me an apology. Your father? Well, that's a different story. One of these days I'm gonna find out what's eatin' on 'im."

He glanced at a tow sack sitting on the ground beside the beautiful woman. "Don't tell me you brought your supper again?"

She looked at the bag as though she'd not seen it before, then gasped. "Oh my goodness! I thought to have supper fixed by the time you got here, then I sat here on the ground, in the quiet, and it was so nice, no tension or anything; I reckon I let time go by."

"Sit there. I'll fix us somethin' if you think you could eat what I put on the table—course I don't have much of a table yet, 'cept that one I sort o' nailed together, so there's another problem."

She unfolded her legs from under her and pushed against the ground as though to stand. Bonner held his hand out to help. When she stood, her face was only about six inches from his. Her breath caressed his cheek. His first inclination was to pull her to him and kiss her. Better sense took over. She was the kind of girl who would consider a kiss as meaning something more. He wasn't ready for that. Besides, there was Linda.

He didn't want to make either of them think there was—or could be—a promise of something permanent. But he knew one thing right then. Maggie would have let him kiss her, and he wanted to, but he didn't want to confuse a woman hungry for a stronger, longer-lasting emotion. He stepped back. "I'll start the fire. Then we can see what I might have in my provisions."

Her mouth slightly parted, her breath coming in rough little gasps caught in her throat. Then in a husky, throaty voice, she said, "Trey, I brought everything I thought we'd ever need." There was a hint of promise, yet disappointment in her words, words that carried a meaning far beyond a need for food.

Wanting, yet not wanting this to go further, Trey went to where he had wood stacked by the fireplace and studiously laid the fire.

Damn! In all his thirty-two years he'd never met a woman he thought he would want to spend the rest of his life with— and now there might be two.

They sat in near silence, an almost embarrassed silence, then with the lantern light flickering on her cheek but shadowing her eyes, she stared at him across the short distance that separated them. "Trey, you knew I was ready for your kiss— and maybe more. Why'd you shy away from me like a skittish colt?"

He looked from her to the fire dancing in the fireplace, then back to her. She was so very beautiful, so desirable. She deserved an honest answer. "Maggie, gotta tell you like it is. I knew what might come, wanted to, started to, but I let the way I was raised step in 'tween us.

"I realized there might be more than a kiss, or whatever more might come. I didn't want to ruin it. *And,* I didn't want you to do anything you might regret come daylight in the mornin'. There's gotta be more than just wantin'. Wantin' is good, but you throw in all the rest, an' wantin' comes up on a short rope in the long run."

She sat there a long moment, staring into the fire, then so softly Trey barely heard her, said, "Thanks, Trey. We'll give it a chance like we properly should. I was raised like you were, an' yeah, we'd both maybe been sorry in the mornin'."

Abruptly she chuckled. "You don't let me get to fixin' supper I might be here all night. My folks'll believe we did what we almost did, an' we'll both be in trouble. Nobody's folks ever b'lieve their kids've got sense enough to do right."

They both worked at preparing the meal, then sat to eat. After supper, Trey smoked his pipe while they drank coffee. After several minutes of silence, Maggie glanced at him, then moved her eyes back to the fire. "This is nice, Trey. I wish everything and everywhere was like this, nobody fussin', nobody fightin', makin' demands on others." She sighed. "Maybe someday."

"Yeah, but you should have been with me this afternoon. Another shot came at me from ambush."

"Oh, Trey, who could it be? I know for a fact that Yadro was at the ranch. Tell me about it."

He told her about it, then shrugged. "Don't know who it could be, but you might as well know—I've lived a life that would make a many a man want me dead." He came close to telling her that he was a Texas Ranger, then bit down on his words.

"Someday I hope you'll tell me the things you've done. You seem to be a man who minds his own business."

"I try, Maggie, I surely do." He nodded. "Yeah, someday I'll tell you more about me."

They finished their coffee, cleaned the open room, washed the dishes, and Bonner went out to saddle their horses.

Trey rode to within a couple hundred yards of the ranch house with her, then, her small but strong little hand resting on the pommel, he covered it with his own work-hardened one. "Won't ride on down there with you, little lady. Want this visit to be free of disagreeableness. I'll see you in a few days; gotta get my cabin finished."

They parted, and on the way home Trey pondered the differences and likenesses of the two women he'd only recently met. Then came the thought that Linda had once belonged to another man and that she might not want another man to take his place. "Don't want to take nobody's place; just want to make my own place." He mumbled the words as though there was someone there to hear him.

The next morning he sat drinking coffee, Dawg curled up at his feet sleeping. He glanced at the sleeping animal. "Told you we were gonna go huntin' this mornin', but reckon we gonna wait now 'til he takes another shot at me. Can't do any decent kind o' trackin' in that damned dust up yonder on the rimrock. Figure if we get a rain we might find better sign."

Then his look took in the pile of building supplies he'd bought from Tom Parsons. He sighed, stood, and picked up tools he'd left by the door.

The next week he spent measuring, sawing, and nailing joists for his roof. He spent agonizing moments making absolutely certain every measurement was accurate to the sixteenth of an inch, then he took the same care when he put saw to wood. He chuckled to himself; some of the care he took was such that he'd not make a mistake and mess up a length of good lumber, but another reason was that he'd always been accused of paying too much attention to detail. Hell, if a man's gonna do something, he might as well do it right.

Over a week had passed since Trey had been to town, and each day Linda spent more time searching the trail in front of her cafe checking each rider, hoping it might be the man she looked for and knew so little about. She scoured her mind as to why she wanted to see him again. Why did it make a difference?

Always truthful with herself, she admitted she was lonely. She'd been married, was needful of having her man around, missed having him in bed with her at night. She chuckled, yeah, even missed having him to fuss at when things failed to go according to her wishes. Was it only loneliness, or could there be a deeper feeling? She'd have to study on that.

She took another look out the front window. Maggie stood out there tying her horse to the hitching rack. Linda smiled to herself; of the people she'd like to see Maggie was her second choice. She hadn't seen her friend in several weeks.

There were no people in the cafe during the midafternoon lull. Linda poured two cups of coffee and placed them on the long table closest to the kitchen. She looked up when Maggie walked through the door. "Hi, Mag, was just wantin' company of some kind. Reckon you'll have to do 'til somethin' better comes along."

"Well, for pete's sake, if that isn't a heck of a way to greet a friend."

Linda laughed. "C'mon in. I just poured us a cup o' coffee. What's been going on since I last saw you?"

Maggie told her about visiting with Trey, about how his house was progressing, about him getting shot at again, even told her about the uncomfortable way her father had treated the tall man.

While she talked, Linda stiffened inwardly. Jealousy threatened to cool her pleasure at seeing her friend, her only friend in this sunbaked little town. She swallowed, then swallowed again. She couldn't let feelings she had not admitted to herself stand in the way of friendship. She looked straight on at Maggie. "Know somethin', girl? One day that man, whoever's shootin' at Trey, won't miss, then we're gonna be missin' a friend, one I suspect we both hold with special feelin's."

Maggie's look dropped to her cup. She picked up the cup of steaming liquid, took a sip, and placed it back on the table. Then her look moved to Linda's eyes, sharpened, and, her voice soft, asked, "How special, Linda? Figured we'd have to talk 'bout this sooner or later. Glad you don't beat around the bush." She sighed. "Might as well talk now."

The mouthwatering aroma of fresh bread baking seemed to suddenly fill the room. Linda stood, went to the oven, opened the door, and peered in. The bread had only browned slightly, but she was glad for the chance to gather her thoughts. She went back to the table. She nodded. "Yes, this is something we better make sure won't strain our friendship—or destroy it. Yep, we better talk." She took another swallow of coffee and wished that women smoked so she could take up time filling and lighting a pipe. She could use that time to sort out her thoughts.

Finally, she shrugged. "Tell you how it is, Mag. I'm lonely. I like Trey—very much. Can't say as how I feel any stronger than that 'bout 'im." She looked at the table, then back to her friend. "If I decide 'bout that, I promise I'll let you know." She pulled her mouth aside in a grimace. "But, whatever I decide, I refuse to let it stand between our friendship. I value that as much as anything."

She pinned Maggie with a look as sharp as a sewing needle. "You made up your mind 'bout your own feelin's toward that man?"

Maggie's face turned a shade of red that had nothing to do with what the sun might have done to it. She looked Linda squarely in the eye. She nodded. "I almost let 'im kiss me the last night I took supper out to 'im." She shook her head. "Nope, I said that all wrong. I almost begged 'im to kiss me—an, an anything else he wanted to do." Her eyelids drooped to cover her eyes. "He was raised right; if he hadn't been, don't reckon I'd still be a virgin." She shrugged. "Like you, Linda, I don't know how I feel 'bout 'im, 'cept I want 'im. I never wanted a man before."

As serious as the conversation was, Linda felt laughter rumble deep in her chest. "I gotta tell ya, honey, that man's some sort o' animal. We're lucky he doesn't know it."

Maggie smiled timidly. "His not knowing it only adds to his charm." She took another swallow of coffee, then looked in her friend's eyes. "Make a deal with you; when one or both of us decide 'bout our feelin's let's play it square with each other, put all our cards on the table, and do our darnedest to keep our friendship intact."

Linda held her hand across the table. "Deal."

They shook hands and Linda turned the conversation to another topic. They visited until the supper crowd began to arrive. Maggie stood, and when walking out the door, almost bumped into Yadro. She cast him a hard look and left.

Linda saw that look and became more convinced that Maggie and her family had nothing to do with Trey's troubles.

Bonner slammed the last nail into the cap strip, swept his roof with a searching look, then nodded and mumbled, "Good job, Bonner. Now all you gotta do is case the windows an' we'll be warm an' dry this winter."

A vagrant breeze swept the ground-level dust in swirls. Trey shivered. Winter would soon be upon the country; that breeze across his sweat-laden back had been chilly. He reckoned he'd better once again put off trying to find the man shooting at him. He'd get the windows set first.

A glance to the northwest showed low-hanging, gray clouds. He hoped they weren't a harbinger of one of those weeks so common in this country: a week of slow, cold drizzle, a week during which a man stayed damp, cold, and miserable regardless what job he cut out for himself. He climbed from the roof, satisfied that he'd done a good job.

He looked at the sun and judged he had time to get started on the windows before dark. He figured it to be about four-thirty. His watch might tell him closer to the correct time, but he never wore it unless he was going to dress up for some special occasion.

Thinking of special occasions, he thought of the dance they would be having—let's see, when had the girls said it'd be? Finally he nodded. It would be the coming Saturday night, and this was only Tuesday. If he could get the windows done by then, he thought he'd go—but he'd go alone.

If he asked Linda, she lived right in town, and he wouldn't have to ride for hours to get her home. If he asked Maggie to go with him, he'd not get back to his cabin before midmorning—the dance would last until almost daylight. He sighed, grinned, and thought about the problems a man could bring on himself. He picked up his saw and framing square. Better get to work.

Three days later he sat on the floor in the middle of his home, all finished except for putting in the walls to separate the rooms.

One load-bearing wall cut the one-hundred-by-eighty-foot structure in half. He stared at what he'd accomplished and marveled at how nice it looked, then he shook his head. He had no idea how to divide the rest of the house into rooms.

He pondered that problem until it was time to start the fire for supper. He still had no plan where to divide the rooms, how many to make, or what size they should be. He looked across the room at the big-headed dog. "What you think, Dawg? I'm thinkin' to get Maggie an' Linda out here together an' let them put their reckonin' to the problem. Think that might be a dumb idea?"

Dawg only looked at him like he'd lost his mind.

Bonner stood, went to the fireplace, raked ashes aside until he reached hot coals, put kindling on them, blew it to a flame, and placed firewood in the flames.

He finished supper, cleaned up the pots, and sat drinking coffee. Dawg, curled at his feet, abruptly stood, a low growl deep in his throat. His ears peaked; he looked toward the door.

As soon as the animal stood, Bonner came to his feet and picked up his Winchester. While jacking a shell into the magazine a yell came from a distance. "Hello the house. Mind if I ride on in?"

"Ride in, hands empty an' crossed on the saddle horn. I'll look you over."

A few moments later, the rider showed dimly in the light from the door. Bonner studied the man a moment. Long gray hair streamed to bony shoulders; his beard, even whiter than his hair, hadn't been trimmed in weeks, maybe months, and judging by the layers of dust coating his face and clothing, he hadn't bothered to take advantage of any water he'd come across in that time.

"You missed supper, but I'll throw a hunk o' venison on the fire. I still got coffee in the pot. Climb down an' rest your saddle."

"Done et, made camp, an' then when it got dark I seen light from your cabin an' allowed as how I'd like a body to talk to, but the way you keep holdin' that there rifle on me don't reckon you wantta do much friendly talkin'."

"Climb down. Come on into the light, then I'll decide how friendly our conversation's gonna be."

Inside, Bonner put a few more logs on the fire, and when they lighted the room enough, he studied the old-timer. He didn't see a man to be wary of, but kept his rifle trained for a quick shot. Finally he put the rifle aside, but in easy reach. "You don't cotton to water much, do you?"

"Ain't been around no water fer a mighty long time. Jest 'nuff fer me an' my hoss to drink; couldn't waste it on warshin' my face."

"There's a stream 'bout a hundred yards downslope from here. Figure you couldn't see it when you made camp; it would've been hidden by that land swell."

He went to the corner of the room, picked up two gunny sacks stuffed with hay, tossed one to the old-timer, and put his on the floor close to the fire. "Sit. I'll pour us some coffee." While filling two tin cups, he glanced over his shoulder. "What you doin' in this country ridin' 'round alone?"

The old man chuckled. "Always alone." He squinted one eye and looked at Trey. "I left them mountains over in the New Mexico Territory soon's I seen a powderin' o' snow settin' on trees one mornin'. Gettin' too old to let that cold eat at my bones fer a whole winter. Figgered to come down here to the Big Bend where I kin stay warm."

Bonner slanted the man a questioning look. "You ever wintered in this country before?" He took a sip of his coffee, and before the old-timer could answer, asked, " 'Fore we go any further, I go by the name o' Trey Bonner. What handle you usin' these days?"

"My own. Them what know me call me Jess, Jess Maynard."

"All right, Jess, now I'm gonna answer the question I asked

you. You haven't ever spent a winter in this country, or you'd know it gets cold enough to freeze hell a mile. You ain't done yourself a favor by comin' here." He frowned. "Figure you'd have to go all the way to Brownsville 'fore you found winter weather like you're lookin' for."

Jess stared at the fire a few moments. "Hear tell that town's maybe 'nother three, maybe four hundred miles." He shook his head. "Don't rightly know whether my old bones can stand that long a ride."

His glance swept the room. "See you done put up that wall in the middle so's it'll help hold up the roof. You figger to put any more walls up?"

Trey nodded. "Yep, reckon I will soon's I make up my mind where to put 'em."

Jess again looked around the room, this time giving the space a more careful study. "Tell you what. In my time I done built at least nine cabins, ain't never seen any house with as much space as you got in here. Looks like you figger to stay a while."

Bonner nodded. "Way I'm lookin' at it. Find me a woman, settle down, have some kids, build me a ranch."

The old man's face looked as though it crumpled a bit. "I had that in mind several years back, but somehow I never got around to it. Wished now that I had."

They talked a while longer, then having studied the old man the whole while, Trey made up his mind he could trust him. "You in any hurry to get down to that warm weather?"

Maynard shook his head. "Ain't got nothin' more down there than I got here 'cept better weather. What you got in mind?"

Bonner chuckled. "Was just wonderin' if those old bones o' yours could stand up to helpin' me finish my home? Couldn't pay you much other than feedin' an' keepin' you outta the cold."

"Well, now gosh ding it, why didn't I think o' that, what with me bein' right handy with tools, an' I got them tools right out yonder on my pack saddle." Jess's face shone like he'd only that moment swiped the cheese off the moon.

Maynard stood, poured them each a full cup of coffee, then

sat again. Dawg had followed him around the room with his eyes. The old man studied the vapor rising from his coffee, then looked at Trey. "Ain't needful o' much pay. I panned me out a little dust in them streams along the Rockies. 'Nuff to take care o' my neeecesities o' life like tobacco, whisky, an' a little food now an' then. Jest tell me where to settle down in yore barn an' I'll go git my gear."

"Bring your stuff here to the house. We'll worry 'bout where you can bed down tomorrow." Any mistrust Trey had about the old man he put in the hands of Dawg. He figured his dog wouldn't let anyone get close to him during the night; besides, he couldn't stand the thought of the old man lying out there in the cold.

As the days passed, and the need for a special tool for a special job became apparent, Trey marveled that the old man could go to where he had stashed his gear in the stable and find the exact thing he needed.

Finally, sitting by the fire one night, Trey pinned Jess with a penetrating look. "'Fore you went out in those mountains to get rich, I got it figured that you were a carpenter—a danged good carpenter."

Maynard's face fell into a smug, cat-ate-the-canary look. His lips crinkled at the corners. He shook his head. "Nope, wuzn't a carpenter." His smile widened. "Back yonder in North Caroliny I wuz knowed as one o' the best makers o' some o' the finest furniture a man could buy."

Bonner studied the old man a moment, then nodded. "Shoulda been able to figure that. When you have a tool in your hands you treat it like a piece of fine china, or maybe an expensive musical instrument." He packed and lighted his pipe, then gave Jess a smile. "The way you've planned rooms for the house, gotten my approval, and then gone about putting in walls says you're a mighty good carpenter too."

Jess stood, went to the fire, and picked up the coffeepot. After pouring them each a cupful, he went to Dawg, rubbed his ears, then sat. "Make you a deal, Trey. You got the money to buy the right wood, I'll set in to make you some o' the best furniture you gonna find in this country."

Bonner looked into the dancing flames in the fireplace, then turned his look on Jess. "Old-timer, I got a counteroffer to make."

"Let's hear it."

Dawg stood, stretched, looked from Trey to Jess, then went to Bonner, flopped down, and put his head on Trey's out-stretched leg.

Bonner rubbed Dawg's ears, then pinned Jess with a questioning look. "Way I got it figured, Jess, you won't ever go back to those mountains—too hard on you. So what I have in mind is that you've found a home right here with me."

Maynard opened his mouth as though to say something, but Trey held up his hand to quiet him. "Hear what I got to say, then you say whatever you got in mind." He took a swallow of coffee. "Soon's we get this house finished, let's get busy on puttin' up another house, smaller of course, an' that house'll be yours. That is, if you think you could stand bein' aroun' Dawg an' me from now on."

Jess stared at Bonner a moment, then blinked, tightening his eyelids down, apparently to hide the moisture welling up behind them. "Bonner, I'd like that a shore-'nuff lot if you figger that there girl you gonna bring here someday could put up with an old man bein' underfoot."

"Jess, if she turns out to be so persnickety she won't have you around, I reckon I won't want her here either."

The sun rose in all its glory in the wrinkled old face. "Reckon we got us a deal, young'un. Don't know o' anythin' I could've dreamed that would be better." He nodded. "Yessir, reckon that takes a load o' worry off 'n my shoulders." He shrugged. "Didn't figger to ever go back to prospectin', but didn't know what I'd be doin' if I didn't."

Trey glanced around the big family room. "Well, you've got some o' the furniture made, but reckon we better get started on your place 'fore we get started on more."

Bonner attended two of the dances in town, taking Jess with him to each one. He'd told Maynard about the shots someone had been taking at him, and in fact Jess had witnessed two attempts to shoot Trey. But Bonner had not let the close call slow him down in the work around the house. He wanted to get finished before he set out to find the man, or men, trying to kill him.

Then, weeks later, Trey swept the area with a searching look. Except for the inside work on Jess's cabin, and the task of making more furniture, he thought to take time to try to track the man who'd been using him for target practice. He looked across a sawhorse at Maynard, who diligently sanded the arms for the chair he'd almost finished. "Jess, I'm gonna pack trail gear tonight. Gonna be gone awhile. Figure to leave you here to look out for what's ours."

Maynard slanted Trey a worried look, one eye squinted almost closed. "You goin' after the bushwhacker?"

Trey nodded. "Reckon I'm lettin' it get to me pretty bad. Gotta face 'im, kill 'im, an' get 'im off my back."

"You gonna need me to help ya, young'un."

Bonner shook his head. "No. That no is for two reasons. First, I want you to stay here and watch the place. Ain't had any trouble with Yadro an' his bunch in some time; reckon they're waitin' for Seely to heal 'fore they try me again. Want you to stay here an' shoot anybody who gets in range o' that Sharps fifty you got in your saddle scabbard." Trey shrugged. "Can't think o' anythin' you could do that would help us more'n that."

Jess's worried frown persisted, but he nodded. "All right, but you be danged careful out yonder, young'un."

Bonner's face muscles stiffened. "Been that way all my life, Jess. Gonna get this taken care of, then I'll be back."

He'd never told Maynard about the badge he had pinned to the inside of his belt. Thinking of the badge, RIP Ford had sent him out here to do a job and he hadn't yet decided who was behind Yadro and his men. He'd have to take care of the bushwhacker first or he might not be around to finish his assignment.

Before leaving Austin, he and RIP had talked it over and

decided that if he selected a plot and filed on it it might flush out the man responsible for running the settlers away. He'd never, at first, thought to settle out here permanently.

Everything had changed except the assignment RIP had given him. He intended to keep his word to his best friend.

He packed his bedroll before going to his bed, the work of art Jess had built for him and the bride he had yet to make up his mind to court.

Maggie for the fifth time put the ingredients for supper in her saddlebags. She wanted to cook Trey a good meal, wanted him to eat well.

After getting most of the saddlebags packed, she one by one removed the items and placed them back in their proper place in the kitchen.

She shook her head. She couldn't do this to Linda. Her friend couldn't close her cafe and go to see Trey, and in that the tall cowboy hadn't shown either she or Linda that he intended to court one of them, or maybe neither of them, she would not take unfair advantage.

She'd not been to Trey's place in several weeks. Now, this was the fifth time she'd unpacked her saddlebags. She was determined she'd not take unfair advantage.

After getting everything put away, she poured herself a cup of coffee and sat at the kitchen table. Her mother and father were in the family room.

Sitting, drinking her coffee, she wondered why putting Trey's supper away always left her feeling empty, feeling as though she had abandoned something she wanted very much.

Did she want to see Trey again—very much? She thought about the question she'd posed for herself. Finally she nodded. Yes. Seeing the tall cowboy meant a great deal to her. Were her feelings for him simply those of friendship or something a great deal stronger? Angrily shaking her head, not caring whether anyone could see her frustration, she took a swallow of the hot coffee, choked, and sat it back on the table. It wasn't fair. Why should she have to make a decision about a man who had not shown any romantic interest in either her or her friend? Maybe the old man, Jess Maynard, who Trey had brought to the dances with him was all the company the tall, handsome man needed.

She mentally shook her head, she couldn't accept the idea that any healthy man or woman would voluntarily live a life without someone to care for, to love, to do things for. She realized her thinking came very close to accepting the fact that Trey Bonner had moved from being a cherished friend to mighty close to being much more.

She pondered where her mind had taken her, then decided that she'd go in town, find out if Linda dared to close the cafe for a day, and if so, they'd both go out to Trey's place and fix him supper. She fought that decision, wanting to have Trey to herself, but decided she'd not take unfair advantage.

The next morning she packed her saddlebags with everything she thought might make a good meal, then having eaten slices of Linda's apple pies, she thought to put the pie baking on the widowed cafe owner's shoulders. Linda's pies were delicious.

While riding to town, Maggie wondered how close Trey was to completing his home. She had missed keeping up with what he was doing, and at the dances they'd not had time to just sit and talk. She missed that.

Maggie reined in to the hitching rail in front of the cafe, tied her horse, and frowned. The horse tied next to hers looked like the one Yadro rode. She wondered about the man. He'd not made a move against Bonner since Jim Seely had taken a bullet on their last raid against him. Her thoughts went to her father. Why did he allow the trash to stay at the ranch? Maybe Yadro knew her father in the past. Maybe during the war.

As soon as she opened the door, the aroma of South Texas spicy food and the crowd sitting at the long tables reminded her she'd gotten here at the peak of the noonday crowd. She saw an empty place at the table where Yadro sat with Manse Allard. There was no other empty seat at any of the three tables. Maggie walked past them and on into the kitchen. She looked at Linda and grinned. "Looks like you need help. Want me to wait tables or help back here?"

"Help back here. I know what those out there have ordered. I'll tell you those I haven't gotten to yet and you can fix their plates."

"Tell 'em while you're out there that you're gonna be closed for supper, an' maybe tomorrow. You need to get away from here for a day or two."

Linda scooped a couple of golden biscuits onto a plate and looked questioningly at Maggie. "Okay. Now tell me what I'm gonna be doin' the rest of today and tomorrow."

"I thought you and I could ride out to visit Trey; fix 'im and that old man he's taken under his wing a nice meal, then you could stay at the ranch with me tonight an' come back in time for tomorrow's noonin'."

Linda carefully placed the plate she had been holding back onto the serving table. She looked at Maggie, a soft smile barely breaking the corners of her mouth. "You been out there since we last talked?"

Maggie shook her head. "Not even once."

Linda leaned against the serving table and stared at Maggie. "You've decided how you feel about Trey." Her words were a statement, fact, no arguing.

Maggie's cheeks warmed. She knew they must be as red as one of those roses out by the veranda at home. She'd nursed those bushes through three dry summers. She nodded. "I think so. I wanted many times to go fix him a meal, wanted to go because I wanted, perhaps needed, to see him, but I wouldn't go because I thought it'd be unfair to you." She picked up a biscuit, absentmindedly buttered it, and took a bite. She chewed, swallowed, then said, "Reckon it'd be nothin' short o' fair to the three of us if we gave him an' you an' me a chance to just sit by the fire, eat, drink coffee, an' talk. We never had a chance to do that an' I think we should."

Linda stared at her a moment. "Maggie, if I was in your place, I honestly don't know if I could be that fair." She picked up the plate she'd put on the serving table, filled it, stepped toward the door, and said over her shoulder, "I'll tell these folks 'bout bein' closed, then pack whatever we need to feed those two men out yonder."

* * *

Bonner packed trail gear after supper, under the worried eyes of Jess and the dog. "You sure you ain't gonna need me out yonder, Trey?"

Bonner shook his head. "No. Knowin' you're here watchin' over the place will be better'n havin' you with me. Remember, I got folks here who want to burn me out, kill me, whatever they can do to get rid o' me." He nodded. "Danged tootin' I'll feel a lot better knowin' you're here watchin' after things. Figure to leave Dawg with you. He'll let you know if anybody comes near."

Trey rubbed the big-headed dog's ears. "Now I'm gonna tell you, Dawg. You stay here an' make sure Jess knows 'bout anybody comin' up on the place."

Dawg whined, lifted his big body, and went to Jess. There he flopped and placed his head on Maynard's leg.

The next morning, with the sun high enough to cast reflections from a rifle, or metal of any kind, Trey stood alongside the rock walls of his home and studied the rimrock for sign of anyone up there above him. He studied every inch of the arid, treeless rim. It took him about thirty minutes to satisfy himself that there was no one up there before he stepped toward the path that would take him to the rim. He felt the worried eyes of Jess and Dawg watching him begin his climb to the top; afoot. To take a horse would make it easier to be seen.

Bonner yelled over his shoulder, "I ain't back in three days, send Dawg to find me."

As soon as he reached the top of the rim, Trey slowed, slanted his tracks close to the edge of the rimrock, then slowed more. He'd tried, and failed, to estimate when another attempt to kill him would come. The man trying for his life had not set a pattern. The years Bonner had looked for men he'd always been able to establish a pattern to the way they operated—but not this man. Everything he did seemed erratic. Bonner planned to be just as unpredictable as the man who was intent on killing him.

He worked his way along the edge, fading back into the brush a few yards, studying out ahead of him, then coming back to the sharp dropoff, where sometimes on hands and knees he looked at seemingly scraped turf or broken limbs on the scrub or scarred bits of rock. He found nothing that led him to believe he'd found anything of consequence. He continued his search on into the afternoon. The chill breeze out of the north aided the sweat soaking his shirt to make him close to being comfortable. Mentally, he settled in for a long, tedious chore.

5

BONNER CONTINUED TO stop every forty or fifty yards, fade back from the rim, and drop behind clumps of brush to study the area ahead. He looked for movement, a reflection of light from a weapon, or a bright-colored piece of cloth.

Half of the sun's golden orb sank behind the horizon. Bonner squinted toward it, then decided to make camp. During the day, he'd found two places from which his attacker had fired into the valley, but searching, bent to the ground, circling the places he knew had been the ambusher's selected spot to study and shoot from, he failed to find tracks, or sign of a route the killer had taken from the site.

He sighed. This was like so many times he'd searched for men in the past. It never got easier, and now he'd make a dry camp, no fire, no coffee, and only jerky for supper. He wanted to go back home—but he had to end this now or forever spend time studying the rimrock for sign of someone trying to kill him.

Bent almost double so as to not show any part of himself above the brush he found a small cleared area and spread his blanket.

After putting his rifle, handgun, and canteen within reach, he sat chewing on a strip of jerky, pondering the many ways he'd learned to find a man. The only hard fact he knew of his attacker was that he had always used the rimrock from which to fire, except during the time Bonner had been traveling from Austin to his assigned job. Even then the man had chosen high ground from which to fire. Trey chuckled to himself; if his killer had much experience with firearms, he should have known that a shot from above makes for a damned good chance at missing.

He took a goodly swig from his canteen to wash the jerky down, pulled a folded sheet of paper from his shirt pocket, and tried to read the letter RIP Ford had given him, the letter that had asked for help, the letter that had brought him to this country to try to find those who had killed homesteaders and burned out their cabins. The letter, unsigned, looked as though it had been written by a woman, a woman with some education. Bonner was certain that fact had had a lot to do with Ford responding to her plea. He squinted at the paper a moment and frowned—it was too dark to read, and maybe too sweat smeared to be legible. He put it under his canteen to let it dry during the night, and the weight of the canteen would keep it from blowing away. He shivered. This desert country turned right chilly after the sun set. He slipped under his blankets and soon slept.

Yadro had watched Maggie come into Linda's Cafe, glance at the empty seat next to him, then walk on to the kitchen. Raw bile surged to his throat. He'd bring that persnickety female to her knees one of these days. At the ranch she never acknowledged he was even on the earth. She never said anything to him. She always, if she looked at him at all, looked as though he'd only that moment crawled from the hole under the seat in the outhouse.

His mind went from Maggie to Linda; now there was a real woman. He thought of her a few moments, then shifted his thoughts to Trey Bonner. His anger deepened. Blood surged to his head, making it hurt. That damned sodbuster seemed to have the attention of both of the only women in town worth looking at. Then the pressure in his head lessened. The blood receded. Bonner would soon not be a problem to him or his boss.

Whitey Yadro's thoughts went from killing Bonner to wondering why the sodbuster had come to this country. Yadro couldn't tell whether the tall man intended to farm or raise cattle on the land he'd claimed.

If Seely would only get over his gunshot wound soon.

Yadro wouldn't admit it to himself, but with three men, Manse, Seely, and himself, he would feel a lot better going back out to Bonner's place, get rid of him, and then maybe take over Bonner's house and the entire claim.

He'd never come onto a sodbuster who could fight like the tall man who'd showed up out of nowhere. It was then that Linda came out of the kitchen.

"Folks, I got somethin' to tell ya. A friend of mine needs a little help. So, I'm gonna be gone a couple o' days. Hope to be back tomorrow night." She grinned. "Reckon you're gonna have to cook your own food the next couple o' days."

Groans from those at every table sounded. A cowboy sitting close to the wall shouted, "Miss Linda, we done fergot how to cook since you got to town."

She looked at the cowboy, smiled, and shook her head. "Tell you how to do it, Slim. Slice whatever 'mount o' bacon you figure to eat, put it in a fryin' pan, put it on the fire, roll up some biscuit dough with hot water, put it in the hot bacon grease, an' when they're both 'bout burned to a crisp, take 'em out an' eat 'em along with the beans you had sittin' by the fire in an airtight to warm." Her grin widened. "Ain't nothin' to it, cowboy."

The hard-working men who filled the room laughed.

She stacked some empty plates, held them on her forearm, and went to the kitchen.

As soon as the last customer left, Maggie went to the shed out back of the cafe and saddled Linda's horse while Linda cleaned up the dishes. They soon rode out of town together.

Riding alongside Maggie, Linda looked across her shoulder.

"You sure you wantta do this, Mag? I tell you again, I don't b'lieve I could do it."

Maggie reined her horse around a yucca and slipped her friend a smile. "Yeah, you could, Linda, an' you would, 'cause I think you an' me're more'n just two women who need someone to talk to. We're friends, gal, an' that says a lot."

In the soft sound of their horse's hooves, Maggie barely caught Linda's response, "Yeah, Mag, reckon we could write a book on what it says. I wouldn't take anything for it—not even a man."

They rode in silence for several miles, then Maggie pulled her horse alongside Linda's. "What you think Trey's gonna think when we both show up at his place?"

Linda grinned. "Tell you, girl, most men's head would swell so big they'd have trouble puttin' on their hat." She shook her head. "But Trey probably won't think anything of it except that two friends decided to visit him." She shrugged. "Don't reckon I ever seen a man who's so blind to how he affects women."

Maggie chuckled. "Glad he's like he is. If he wasn't, I figure we'd both have to stay away from 'im."

Those were the last words between them until they topped a rise and looked down on Trey's home. Linda gasped. "My word! How many people you think he plans to live in that house? That's one of the grandest houses I b'lieve I've ever seen."

Maggie nodded. "It is, isn't it." She laughed. "If one o' us is lucky enough to get 'im, reckon the winner better get ready to have a whole gaggle o' children so's we could fill those four walls to the brim."

When within hailing distance of the house, Maggie yelled, "Hello the house."

Jess stepped out the door, a rifle in the crook of his arm. Dawg stood at his side. "Git down, rest yore saddle, an' come on in, ladies. Seen ya soon's you topped that there hill out yonder."

While Maggie and Linda took their saddlebags into the

house, Jess took the horses to the stable. Maggie stood outside a moment to watch him, then followed Linda in.

She wasn't prepared for what the inside held. The last time she'd been out here, the only wall had been the load-bearing one dividing the house in half—and there had been no furniture.

Now, the huge family room had some of the nicest furnishings she remembered seeing, and she saw through wide double doors that the kitchen had been completed with cabinets, a large cast-iron stove, and hooks for the brightly polished copper pots and pans hanging from them.

Jess came into the room while she still looked from the family room to the kitchen. She looked at him. "Jess Maynard, when did y'all do all this work, an' where did you get this beautiful furniture?"

Jess's face flushed a bright red. He looked at the floor just beyond his boot toe, shuffled a couple of times from one foot to the other, then with a shy smile, looked into Maggie's eyes. "Miss Maggie, reckon I gotta take credit fer buildin' this here furniture. Seemed the least I could do since Trey done give me a home, an' me an' him done finished the house right down to rooms fer chillun an' a missus in case Trey ever finds one what'll have 'im."

Maggie swept the room with a glance. "Where's Trey?"

"Tell you how it is, ma'am. He left here 'bout daylight this mornin'. Said as how he figgered to find the varmint what's been shootin' at 'im. Said to look for 'im 'bout three days."

Linda, who had been moving about the room, walked up. "Why didn't you go with 'im, Jess? He's gonna need somebody out there with 'im."

Before she finished talking, Jess shook his head. "He wouldn't hear of it, ma'am. Said he wanted me an' Dawg to watch over the house, an' not to let nobody git close 'nuff to set fire to it. He sets right smart store by what we done here."

Maggie cut in. "He should be more than proud of what y'all have done. Anyway"—she picked up her saddlebags— "we came to fix you men a good dinner, an' reckon we're gonna fix that dinner anyway." She cocked her head to study him better. "You reckon you could eat what two women fix for a change?"

"Why I hope to smile, Miss Maggie. I'll stoke the fire up a mite."

A couple of hours later, the three of them sat at the table. Jess had made certain it could comfortably seat at least twelve people when he built it. They drank their coffee, and judging by the lack of conversation, each was obviously worried about Trey. When about finished, Jess looked from one to the other of them. "Ladies, if y'all ain't gotta git nowhere tonight, I kin show you them bedrooms me an' Trey fixed up an' furnished."

Maggie shook her head. "Thanks, Jess, but my folks would worry themselves sick if I didn't get home sometime tonight. Linda's stayin' with me." She smiled. "But I'm tellin' you right now. Before we leave, I'm gonna see those bedrooms you an' Trey fixed up."

After looking at the rest of the house, Linda and Maggie headed for the Box T, Maggie's father's ranch. Maggie had told Jess she'd be back about noon of the third day to await Trey's return. Linda said her cafe and its clientele would just have to go hungry until she returned, that she'd be with Maggie, that they'd both be back. They rode deep into the night before they rode into the Box T's ranch yard. The ranch hadn't seemed like home since Yadro and his bunch showed up.

Yadro stared down at Jim Seely lying on a bunk at the end of the long room, the bunkhouse. "Seely, you done used that bullet you took as an excuse to lie there in that bunk long 'nuff. We gonna pay that sodbuster another visit. This time we gonna make damn sure he ain't able to walk away from them stone walls he put up."

"Aw hell, Whitey, I ain't feelin' up to it yet. Feelin' mighty weak. 'Sides that, I might bust the scab off 'n that there hole an' start bleedin' agin."

Yadro's look sharpened. "Don't give a damn if you bleed to death. I cut you in on this deal 'cause I figgered to have a whole bunch o' help gittin' it done."

Still staring at Seely, Yadro pulled his Bull Durham sack from his shirt pocket and fashioned a quirly. He pulled a lucifer across the rough denim of the seat of his jeans and lighted his cigarette. "I ain't had much help outta you, but in the mornin' we gonna ride to that pile o' rocks the sodbuster done put up, smoke 'im out, an' blow 'im to hell. You got that?"

Seely stared back at Yadro. Fear pushed hard at his ribs. He was scared of what Bonner could do to them. The tall man had proven he was not a man to take lightly, but Yadro stood there right above him, looking as though he'd shoot him while he lay in his bunk. *That* fear caused him to choke on the huge knot that formed deep in his throat. He nodded. "Be with you, boss. You know I'm gonna do my part." He grimaced. "Jest wanted you to know I'm still hurtin'."

Yadro stared at him another moment. "In the mornin', we ride." He spun and walked to his own bunk.

The next morning, the sun still not breaking the eastern sky, Maggie stood at the kitchen window and watched Yadro, Manse, and Jim Seely saddle their horses, ram rifles into saddle scabbards, each pour a box of what looked like shells into their saddlebags, mount, and ride out.

She frowned. They weren't going to town. They had prepared for war. She would bet her prize saddle they were headed for Trey's ranch. She wrung the dishrag out, hung it on the rack, and went to look for Linda. She found her in front of the veranda bent over one of the rose bushes, apparently breathing the aroma of one of the last blooms of summer. "You saw Yadro an' his men ride out. I figure they're headed to pay Trey an' Jess a visit. That old man's gonna need help what with Trey bein' gone." She turned to go back inside, then over her shoulder, said, "C'mon in. I'll grab us some rifle shells, tell Ma we're goin' to Trey's an' to look for us in two or three days. Won't tell 'em why we're goin'; it'll only cause 'em to worry.

"We'll follow Yadro, an' when he an' his men close in on the house we'll hit 'em from the backside."

About fifteen minutes later, and trailing those she had labeled as white trash, Maggie looked across her shoulder at Linda. "You ever shoot at anybody before?"

Her face frozen into a grim mask, Linda nodded. "Indians, comancheros, an' bandits. Figger I can hold up my end o' this fight."

Maggie chuckled. "Lookin' at your face, danged if I don't believe you're gonna be worse to face than Trey would be—if he was there."

A couple of hours later, Maggie pulled rein and held up her hand for silence. She cocked her head, turned it a little, trying to hear better. A sharp but distant popping sounded. "They didn't take Jess by surprise. Sounds like he's givin' more than he's gettin'." She grinned to hide her fear. "Let's get closer, close enough to see 'em, then we'll join the fight."

They rode close to the brow of the next hill. Maggie again reined in, pulled her foot from the stirrup, unhooked her leg from the sidesaddle and slid to the ground. While pulling her Winchester from the saddle scabbard, she said, "We better lead our horses from here. I figure we're gonna be able to shoot from that pile o' rocks up yonder at the top."

A few moments later they led the horses into the rocks, dropped the reins, and put a large rock on the rein's trailing ends. Maggie motioned Linda to her side. "Figure they're gonna be hid much as they can 'tween them an' the house, but their backsides're gonna be right bare for us to shoot at." She looked into her friend's eyes. "Linda, don't show nothin' for *them* to shoot at."

Linda nodded while they crept to the edge of one of the boulders. Maggie peered around the rock, nodded, and pointed. "Like I thought."

The three men lay alongside the top of a swale not a hundred yards in front of them. All three faced Trey's home. When one of them would raise up to take a shot, more often than not a bullet would come his way before he could pull trigger.

While jacking a shell into the chamber, Maggie glanced at

Linda. "Looks like we made this ride for nothin'; don't look like Jess needs any help."

"We let that bunch stay 'til dark, he's gonna need a bunch o' help." Linda eased her rifle around the edge of the boulder, squeezed off a shot, and pulled back to the protection of the rock.

Maggie at the same time squeezed off her first shot, levered another cartridge into the chamber, and fired again. Her first shot kicked up dirt by the side of Yadro. Her second caused Seely to jump, in fact he sort of bounced. "B'lieve I got a hit on that second one," she muttered.

"Think you're right, Mag. I've seen 'em bounce like that before. A forty-four slug'll cause a big man to jerk like that."

Now, Yadro and Manse had twisted to stare at the pile of rocks. Manse wriggled down the side of the swale, stood, and bolted for his ground-reined horse about fifteen yards away. Yadro ran right on his heels. Seely stayed where he lay, not moving.

Maggie and Linda fired at the retreating two riders as fast as they could lever cartridges into the chamber. One of the riders, Maggie thought it to be Manse, grabbed the saddle horn, leaned forward, but held on. She glanced at Linda. "Score one for you, Linda. Wonder what it's gonna take to make 'em leave this country?"

Her face frozen into a mask devoid of expression, Linda shook her head. "Danged if I know, Mag. But I'm tellin' you right now, if I was them, I'd get to the Box T, pack my bedroll, an' cut out faster'n it take to tell 'bout it."

Maggie rolled the stone off the ends of their horses' reins. "Reckon we better get down there an' see how Jess made out."

"Better make sure those two are long gone 'fore we put ourselves out in the open." Linda picked up the trailing reins of her horse and swung aboard. "I'll check an' see where they are."

About fifteen minutes later, after letting Jess know who they were, they sat at the table drinking coffee. Maggie stood, filled their cups again, and went to the window. "You s'pose they'll be back, Jess?"

"Don't worry. If they's anythin' within a half mile, Dawg'll let us know." He grinned. "Shore didn't figger to have you two pretty ladies back so soon."

"Maggie saw Yadro ride out this mornin' with his two men. She figgered they'd be comin' here, so we grabbed some rifle bullets an' followed 'em." Linda took a swallow of her coffee. "While I'm thinkin' 'bout it, one of Yadro's men is layin' stretched out beyond that rise. He's gonna need buryin' if one o' his friends don't come pick 'im up." She took another sip of coffee. "Reckon we'll take you up on your offer for us to use one o' those bedrooms you an' Trey built."

"Well, now gosh ding it, I wuz jest gonna say the same thing." Jess stood, then sat again. He chuckled. "Here it is the middle of the day—don't reckon y'all gonna be goin' to bed this early."

Maggie glanced toward the window. She'd done this several times since sitting for coffee. "Miss Maggie, I done told ya, Trey ain't gonna be back 'til maybe tomorrow evenin', less'n o' course he finds what he went out yonder to find afore then."

While his three friends sat drinking coffee, Bonner sat wishing he dared make a fire. Instead he sat on his bedroll chewing on another strip of jerky. Today, and the day before, he'd not found a sign that he could follow. The wind shifted the dust such that tracks would disappear only a couple of hours after being made. He thought hunting under these circumstances to be futile. He pondered that a few seconds, then decided that he'd come out here to look for at least three days and that was what he would do.

A couple of hours later, ducking in and out of the chaparral, he got the feeling he was getting close. He couldn't think what had alerted him, but his body yelled at him to slow down, look sharper, and to keep his rifle at the ready. Then he knew what told him to be wary.

A hard, painful knot had formed between his shoulders. He had attributed it to the stooped position he'd been in while searching. Yeah, bending over was tiring, but the pain between his shoulders was a warning he had often heeded while on the hunt. It was a warning that had saved his life many times.

He faded back into the chaparral, squatted on his heels, fingered his pipe, and wished he dared have a smoke. Tobacco smoke would warn his man he was close as well as standing up and shouting, "Hey! Here I am. Come get me." He shook his head. He'd wait to light his pipe until he took care of business. He could really enjoy a smoke with nothing to worry about.

Bonner frowned. Did his prey know he was searching for him? Trey nodded to himself. As cagey as he'd found the man to be at hiding his trail, Bonner was not dumb enough to underestimate the man; in fact, instead of being the hunter, he might even now be the hunted. His neck tingled, making it feel as though the hair at the base of his neck stood on end. He'd better make sure the place he made camp was well hidden and defendable.

He got off his haunches, then, aware the sun had gone from sight earlier than usual, he glanced to the northwest, noticing a dark-gray mass of clouds hanging above the horizon. He was torn between being glad to see them, because if it rained he might find tracks to follow, but he wasn't so glad when the knowledge hit him that he might be both wet and cold that night. "Gettin' soft, Bonner, jest plain damn gettin' used to havin' things easy."

Now, in addition to searching for his bushwhacker, he looked for a place that might shelter him in some small measure when it set in to rain. Finally, not finding the kind of place he wanted, he spread his groundsheet among stunted desert oak, pulled his spare groundsheet over him, and hoped for a short night.

The rain came, a soft, soaking wetting of all under it. Bonner stirred a couple of times during the night and came awake long enough to be thankful the clouds had not brought a gully washer. He managed to stay drier than he'd at first thought.

Daylight came. Only a soft lightening of the heavy gray clouds hanging overhead showed Bonner it was time to roll out of his blankets. He was careful to keep the ground cloths wrapped solidly on both sides of his blankets so they'd stay dry during the day. He used them to sit on while he chewed another strip of dry, tasteless jerky.

He made a hurried task of eating, wanting to get on the trail, see if there might be footprints left in the now-squishy, muddy soil. He wiped his rifle clear of moisture, pulled his oilskin coat over the handle of his Colt to keep it dry, then again bent close to the ground, the spot he'd last looked at before he'd holed up for the night.

Bonner need not have been concerned about finding tracks. The man who made them found him. A hard hit on his shoulder turned him almost completely around. A tug on his trousers told him a second shot came close to knocking his left leg from under him. He dived for the ground, rolled behind a clump of prickly pear cactus and lay still.

Bonner swallowed and tried to rid himself of the hot, brassy taste of fear under his tongue and at the back of his throat. From under one of the broad, thick cactus leaves he scanned the chaparral in front of him.

While searching for his attacker he pulled his bandana from his neck and stuffed it inside his shirt. The slug that had turned him sideways to the shooter had been a solid hit.

He moved his fingers along his collarbone, checked to make sure it hadn't been broken, figured it was still in one piece, and pushed his neckerchief hard against the hole, which bled in a steady stream. He thanked God that the wound didn't gush, which would have indicated an artery had been hit. An artery, and he'd never make it back to his home. He still searched out in front of him.

His ears located his ambusher before his eyes could find him. The sucking squish of mud on boot soles came to him. The sound moved away from him, then the plop of a butt onto a wet saddle and the retreating sound of a horse's hooves slopping through the muddy soil came to him.

About the time he figured his attacker had left, pain replaced the numbness the bullet had caused. Waves of gut-wrenching, muscle-knotting pain pushed through the entire upper left side of his body.

He swallowed a couple of times to keep from vomiting. He closed his eyes tight and clenched his teeth together. The hunt for the bushwhacker was ended—this time. He couldn't continue. He had to get back to his house before he bled to death. It wouldn't be easy.

After waiting for the sounds of the horse to become distant, then disappear, he pushed to his feet. He fought back swirling blackness that threatened to bring him to his knees. Finally, figuring he could walk without passing out, he took a few tentative steps toward home, then feeling that he would make it, planted his feet more solidly and headed back the way he'd come.

After a while, believing the killer would be long gone, Trey walked to the edge of the rimrock and stared down. His house was easily within three hundred yards—if he could have gone straight down. But the way he'd have to go, it was four, maybe five miles to the down trail. He hoped he could make it. He had to make it, or all his dreams through the long, lonely years would have been fruitless; besides, there were two lovely women he wanted to get to know much better.

He thought to stay close to the edge so if Jess should come outside he could fire a shot and maybe get his attention, maybe get him to bring a horse for him. Then he thought better of the idea. His steps were faltering, erratic, and to stagger at the wrong time might pitch him over the edge.

He stumbled on, only now he stopped to rest every ten or so steps. Finally he stopped, stared at the edge, looked over, and figured he would be heard if he fired his rifle into the air.

The afternoon of the third day, Maggie and Linda walked to the window more frequently. Each would stare toward the cliff, then their gaze would travel upward, each hoping to see their friend; no, the man they looked for was more than a friend.

Jess watched them. The rain had gotten heavier. He thought that Trey would be holed up somewhere out of the weather, if he could find a place. He said as much. "Ladies, if I done learned anythin' 'bout that there man is that he's shore 'nuff got the sense to come in outta the rain. Don't figger he's gonna be home tonight."

Maggie turned from the window. "Jess, I'm tellin' you like it is, if he doesn't came home tonight, I'm gonna set out in the mornin' to find 'im."

Jess nodded. "All right, but he left me here to watch the place an' to keep them cabin burners from undoin' all the work him an' me's done got done." He sliced himself off a fresh chew from his plug of Days Work tobacco, stuck it in his jaw, then chomped down on it a couple of times. "Reckon I better do like he said 'less you ladies wantta stay here an' let me go lookin' fer 'im."

Without waiting for either of the girls to answer, Jess stepped toward the door. "Figger I better set that there number-two warshtub out yonder under the roof drain; see if I can catch some o' that rainwater."

He set the tub under the best place he thought to collect rainwater, twisted to go back inside before he got soaked, and heard a shot from above. He ducked, pulled himself around the corner of the house, and squinted toward the top of the cliff.

A man stood up there in plain sight. Jess squinted to bring the figure into focus. His eyes weren't so good anymore. He pulled his eyelids tight, then opened them wide. He could see clearer now—maybe for a few seconds. "Damned if that don't look like Trey a-standin' up yonder in plain sight," he muttered. He shut his eyes tight again, then opened them wide and stared at the figure.

Whoever it was held a rifle up and fired toward the sky. It *was* Trey. Then after firing the second time, Bonner put the stock of the rifle under his thigh and pulled on the lever.

Jess stepped out in full view and waved his arms to let Bonner know he'd been seen. Then Trey put the rifle down and waved with his good arm to come to him. Maynard waved both arms to tell Bonner he understood. He twisted toward the door, stuck his head in, and shouted, "Trey's up yonder on the rim. B'lieve he's hurt. I'm goin' after 'im."

Maggie was first to the door. "Goin' with you."

Jess shook his head. "You ain't. You an' Miss Linda's gonna stay here. Put some water on the stove to boil in case he's hurt bad. I'll saddle a couple hosses. Now git inside an' pertect this here home o' his."

Maggie stared at Jess a moment, then nodded. "All right, Jess, go get 'im. Linda an' I'll cover you in case Yadro comes back."

"Good. Now get yoreself back inside, young lady."

In less than five minutes Jess headed across the creek. The trail to the rimrock started only a few yards on the other side of the creek's bank. Jess worried that the tilt of the narrow path on the way down might make it hard for Bonner to stay aboard his horse; then he decided that if Trey had a problem with it, he'd tie him on. He hoped the footing along the path would not be slick—*that* would make his task more dangerous.

While riding, he studied the brush ahead, hoping the ambusher didn't know he'd scored a hit on Bonner and had made up his mind to follow the tall man and finish the job.

Finally the pressure of his backside on the cantle lessened. The incline slowly leveled such that he sat straight. Now he kept his eyes peeled for his friend. It had taken over an hour to reach the top. Another fifteen or more minutes, about a hundred yards ahead he spotted a hunched-over figure sitting at the side of the trail. If that person had been anything other than friendly, Jess figured he would have joined Trey in the wounded column.

He rode to the man and watched Trey slowly twist his head to look at him through pain-filled eyes. Jess had not left the saddle as quickly in years. He didn't think his old bones could take the shock, but he did it.

"Boy, you jest set still there 'til I can see where you're hurtin'."

"Ain't gonna argue with you, Jess. Don't reckon I could get up if I tried. Got a chunk o' lead in my shoulder. Been bleedin' right steady. Get me on that horse you brought with you an' get me to the house."

Before trying to pull Bonner erect, Jess bent over him and pulled his slicker aside. Trey's whole left side was red. Jess whipped off his bandana, wadded it into a pad, and along with Trey's bandana pressed it to the area over the wound. "Now you jest set there a minute while I git the hoss alongside you."

He ground reined his horse and pulled the spare up to the side of Bonner. "You gonna have to hep me, son. Ain't got the strength to lift you. Gonna try to pull you to yore feet now."

He went to Trey's back, put his arms in under Trey's, locked his fingers together and tugged upward. Trey apparently bunched his muscles and pushed upward when Jess pulled. He came to his feet.

Breathing hard, Jess lockstepped Bonner to the side of the horse. "Damn, big fella, you weigh more'n I figgered a man had a right to. Now take hold o' that saddle horn an' hold tight 'til I can put yore foot in the stirrup."

They struggled a few more minutes and finally hoisted Trey to stand one-legged in the stirrup. Jess grabbed the other leg and pushed it over the horse's back. He slanted a look up at Trey. "You gonna be able to set up yonder without fallin' off?"

Trey nodded.

"Good. I ain't gonna tie you on 'til maybe I have to. All right?"

Bonner shook his head. "Better tie me on; don't figure we could get me back in the saddle if I fell off."

Jess put enough rope around Bonner that to his eyes he thought the tall man looked like a mummy, then led the horses to where the trail slanted downward. He walked alongside far enough to make sure the trail wasn't too slick to be safe, then climbed aboard and headed for the house.

Linda and Maggie busied themselves tearing a sheet into bandages, checking to make sure the water was boiling, and going to the window to see if Jess came down the trail. They made bandages not knowing whether Trey would need them or not.

Linda, a deep crease between her eyes, looked at Maggie. "You reckon Trey just wanted Jess to bring horses so he wouldn't have to walk the rest of the way home?"

Maggie shook her head. "You're grabbin' at straws, Linda. I figure he's hurt—bad."

The hope in Linda's eyes died. The sparkle faded from the green in her eyes, leaving them a dull olive. She nodded. "Reckon I figgered that all along. Jest hoped you'd say somethin' different."

Maggie put her arm around Linda's shoulders. "B'lieve you *are* in love with 'im."

Linda shook her head. "Don't b'lieve so, Mag. I—I reckon he's just someone special to me. Gonna give it some more thought."

Maggie pinned her friend with a straight-on look. "Reckon he's special to both o' us. He's been willin' to be a friend, let us all get to know each other without tryin' to make somethin' happen that has no basis."

Linda nodded. "Maybe that's it. A lot o' men would have tried to get closer—maybe outta loneliness, or wantin' a woman, or for whatever reason. They just ain't many women out here, an' most men'll settle for whatever's there."

Maggie, despite her worry, chuckled deep in her throat. "Tell you what. I don't think that man would settle for anything less than the *real* thing. Reckon that's what makes 'im so special."

She cocked her head, then went to the window and stared toward the creek. Jess, leading Trey's horse, had only then crossed out of the water to the house side of the creek.

She twisted to look at Linda. "C'mon, Jess's home. Looks like Trey's hurt."

They ran for the door.

Yadro slanted a look across his shoulder at the only man he had left of the three he'd brought with him. Manse clung to the saddle horn as though it was his only link with the world. It was.

Before they reached the Box T, Manse slipped to the side, lost the stirrup, and fell to the ground. Yadro cursed. He thought to leave Manse Allard lying right where he fell, then through some shred of decency in him, he reined in, rode back to where the man lay, dismounted, and walked to the still figure on the ground.

"Manse—Manse, you hear me? You gotta git up. We still got work to do. We gotta git that there sodbuster."

Manse didn't move, didn't groan, didn't respond in any way. Whitey felt his henchman's neck. Cold. He knew that once the heart stopped beating, a corpse cooled down pretty quick. Manse was dead.

Yadro cursed again, stooped, put his hands under Manse's armpits and lifted. He had to get him on his horse, had to get him to the Box T. Then he'd have to dig another grave.

Damned if he would dig it very deep. Let the scavengers have him. Digging graves and burying the men he'd brought with him had not been in the bargain.

He'd collect his pay and head out. All the sodbusters had been easy, but this last one? Hell, he'd run into tough men before, but not as rawhide tough as Bonner had proven to be. Yeah, he'd had enough. The boss would raise hell, but let him. If he wanted Bonner out of here so bad, let *him* run him off.

Despite the chill in the air, by the time Yadro got Manse across the saddle he'd worked up a streaming sweat. He cursed Manse, he cursed his boss, and most of all he cursed Bonner. Maybe he should stay and see if he couldn't take care of the tall man from ambush. He nodded. He'd have to think about that.

When he rode into the ranch yard, lights still burned in the bunkhouse and the ranch house.

He didn't bother to take care of his horse or to take Manse from the horse he'd slung him across. He went into the bunkhouse, a chip rode his shoulder. The regular crew of the Box T only looked at him when he came in. None of them spoke; in fact, they didn't acknowledge that he was there, except for the brief glance they gave him.

He stared at each of them, then centered his look on Slim Ramey, the Box T foreman. "Have somebody go take care o' my horse. Allard's out yonder too—slung across 'is saddle, dead, need plantin' in the mornin'."

Ramey, cleaning his rifle, reached to his belt, slipped a cartridge out of its loop, pushed it into the chamber, slammed the breech closed, and casually pointed the Winchester at Whitey. "You want yore hoss taken care of? You want Allard buried? Git after it. Do it yourself. After you git that done, pack yore gear an' git the hell off a this here range. You got that?"

6

A CHILL DANCED up Yadro's backbone. He'd lost the only thing with which he'd ever controlled people—fear. "What's done got into you, Ramey?" Even to him, his question sounded like a whine.

"Ain't nothin' got into me what shouldn't got into me the day you rode in here. Don't know what you or yore boss got on my boss, but whatever it is an' whoever yore boss is, tell 'im I'm comin' after 'im, gonna find out what he thinks he's holdin' over Matt Tedford. Whatever it is, it ain't nothin' I cain't take care of. You got that?"

Ramey shifted his chew to the other cheek, chomped on it a couple of times, and stared into the eyes of the trash that had usurped the peace of the Box T.

The cold, flat gray of Yadro's eyes had turned a murky milk color. Sweat beaded his forehead. The ranch foreman saw only fear in the eyes of the white trash. He pushed his luck. "You come in here with three other pieces o' trash like yourself, an' what we here at the ranch didn't have the guts to do, that man over yonder against the hills has done all by hisself."

Ramey chomped on his chew a couple of more times, spit, and hit the can sitting by his bunk dead center. "You done come up against a real man, Yadro. He done eeeliminated yore backbone. I wuz you, I'd climb aboard that spavined thing you call a hoss an' ride 'til you find people who never heard o' this part o' Texas."

Yadro sidestepped to his bunk and sat, still staring at Ramey. "Don't know what put a burr under yore saddle, Ramey, but I already figgered to saddle up an' ride—come mornin'."

Ramey shook his head. "Uh-uh. You done figgered all wrong agin. You gonna leave here tonight, right now. We'll burn yore mattress an' the hay it's stuffed with come daylight to git the stink outta the bunkhouse." He sucked in a deep breath and let it out. "Now roll yore gear an' git."

Yadro, obviously trying to make a show of some kind of guts, stood, grabbed his trail gear, slammed it onto his blankets and groundsheets, rolled it so as to tie it behind his saddle, and stomped from the room.

His rifle still in hand, Ramey watched while Yadro tied his bedroll to his still-saddled horse. "Lead that other horse outta here, along with the garbage you got slung across the saddle. Bury 'im come daylight if you got that much decency in you."

Ramey stood outside the bunkhouse in the dark until the white-haired gunman disappeared into the night, then went back into the lighted room. He flashed his men a silly smile. "Ain't felt so good in months. Let's git some sleep."

Yadro rode from the ranch yard. A deep, simmering hatred burned his chest, and at the same time a hollow void sat where his guts should have been. He told himself that he'd done what any man would; hell, a Winchester .44 had been pointed at him the whole while. Yeah, any man would have acted the same way as he had.

After riding toward town only about thirty minutes, he reined in and stared back toward the ranch. He fingered the packet of oilskin-wrapped lucifers in his shirt pocket, thinking to wait, give the family and hands time to settle down and get to sleep, then ride back and set fire to the buildings. That thought lasted only a moment.

He glanced at the stiff body slung across the horse he'd

been leading. A chill ran up his back. Ramey and the crew would track him down and he'd end up just like Manse Allard. He reined his horse toward town.

He thought at first to bed down about halfway to town, then ride in, collect his pay, and head for San Antonio. He thought on that a few moments, then decided he'd ride the extra few miles, go to the saloon, drink 'til he washed the scene at the ranch from his memory, then sleep in the hotel. He nudged his horse to a faster pace. He would bury Manse come morning, if he didn't decide to dump 'im out here in the desert somewhere.

Maggie and Linda ran from the house to where Jess had reined the horses in at the front door. Although Maggie's stomach churned as though to empty itself before she could reach the horse on which Trey clung to the saddle horn, she threw a question at Jess. "Hurt bad?"

"'Nuff we better git 'im in the house, cleaned up, bandaged, an' in bed. He done bleeded a whole bunch."

Each of them rushed to help untie Trey and lift him from the saddle. Finally, the two girls, one under each arm, staggered into the family room. They lowered him to the floor in front of the fire after Jess spread a blanket and sheets.

Jess slanted each of the beautiful women a look. "Fur's I could see, he ain't hurt none 'cept he's got a bullet in 'is shoulder. It's blood, or lack of it's got 'im in this shape. I'll have to dig that chunk o' lead outta him. You figger you cain't stomach watchin' me do it, go put on some broth, stay busy in the kitchen."

Linda turned pale, and her throat bobbed a couple of times as though trying to squelch getting sick to her stomach. She headed for the kitchen.

Maggie came to the old man's side. "Let's get it done, Jess. I'll see if I can get his shirt off. Wash it later."

She carefully slipped Trey's arms from the sleeves, thinking at one time she might have to cut them off. Then she went through the pockets and placed their contents on the mantel. She flipped up the corner of the note RIP had given the ranger before he left Austin, decided what it might say was none of her business, slipped her finger from beneath the fold, and put it on the mantel with the rest of the pockets' contents.

She glanced again at the note and frowned. Something about that note tried to trigger a memory. She shook her head, shrugged off the thought, and with Jess's help, rolled Trey's body enough to work his shirt from under him.

She bunched a flour sack, now used as a dish towel, into a pad, lifted the steaming kettle from over the fire, and put it at Jess's side.

The old man held the blade of his bowie knife in the flames dancing above the logs. After giving the fire time to disinfect the blade, he placed it on an edge of the clean sheet and carefully sponged the dried blood from around the hole. Finally able to see where the bullet had entered, he felt the back of Bonner's shoulder to see if the chunk of lead was close enough to the surface that he might cut it out from the back side. It wasn't. He sighed and looked at Maggie. "This ain't gonna be nothin' a young woman's gonna want to watch, young'un. Go on out to the kitchen with Linda."

She shook her head. "You might need help. Get at it."

Maynard stared at her a moment, nodded, and picked up his knife.

About a half hour later, Trey, pale but now sleeping, lay with a clean bandage over the hole Jess had had to enlarge to get the lead out. Jess looked from Trey's sleeping form to Maggie. "Judgin' by the number o' scars on that there man, I'd say he's done seen a bunch o' trouble 'fore now."

Maggie, nearly as pale as Trey, swallowed a couple of times, nodded, glanced from Bonner's still-bare chest to Maynard. "Reckon he has, Jess, but I'm bettin' everything I'll ever have that he got every one of them honorably."

He nodded. "Think maybe you're right." He reached in his pocket, pulled out his Days Work, and carved himself a chew. After tucking it in his mouth, he stared into her eyes. "You think a whole lot o' that man lyin' yonder, don't you?"

Not breaking the lock Jess had on her eyes, she nodded, slowly. "More, a whole lot more than I let myself acknowledge up until now."

"Figgered as much. Now why don't you go get us a cup o' Arbuckles', an' tell Linda to come on out here. Figger she thinks 'bout as much o' this here man as you do."

From the kitchen door, Linda's voice came. "You're right, Jess, but in a different way. Guess it took somethin' like this to show both of us how much we cared for him—and the track our feelin's were takin'." She nodded. "Yep, I figure we both love that man, but like I said, we love 'im in a different way."

She gasped. "Goodness sake. Here I stand lettin' these coffees get cold. Heard you ask Mag to come get me an' the coffee so I brought both."

Through the night they took turns watching over Trey, checking that he didn't turn feverish, checking that his wound didn't start bleeding again, and wanting someone to be awake if he needed anything.

Two days after Jess brought Trey home, Dawg, who hadn't left Bonner's side, stood, growled deep in his throat, and the hair on his shoulders standing straight up, went to the door. The two girls and Jess picked up Winchesters.

Maggie looked out the window, closed her eyes to slits, then smiled. She'd been expecting this visit. At the "Hello the house," she yelled, "Come on in, Slim, we only got three rifles pointed your way. Bet Papa sent you to see what happened to me."

Now in earshot of the house, Ramey yelled, "Dang tootin', little miss. Yore folks're bout outta their minds worryin' 'bout you. Why the gosh-danged hell you treat 'em this way?"

By now, Ramey, at the edge of the veranda, was stepping from the saddle. "Come on in, Slim. Want to introduce you to my friends. You know Linda, but I want you to meet Jess Maynard an' Trey Bonner. Bonner's the one lyin' yonder on that pallet by the fire. He's tryin' to make like somethin's wrong with him so we'll keep waitin' on 'im."

Ramey pushed his hat to the back of his head. He stared at Trey a moment. "Knowed it had to be somethin' like this. You sick or git yoreself shot up a leetle bit?"

His voice dripping sarcasm, Bonner said, "Sure nice to meet you too, Ramey."

Slim's face turned a bright red. "Aw hell, Bonner, didn't mean nothin' by the way I said what I did. Reckon I'm still lettin' off steam by the way Mag's treated her folks. Howdy, men, glad to meet both o' you."

While they got acquainted Linda cooked supper, then after they had eaten and sat by the fire, Ramey told Maggie that he'd run Yadro off, along with Manse Allard's body. "Figger one o' you put lead into Allard."

"Linda did it. I'm glad he's gone, it's long overdue. Papa should have gotten rid of him a long time ago."

From his blanket by the fire, Trey spoke up. "I got some business with Yadro. Gonna find 'im, get what I need to know outta him, then blow 'im to hell."

Slim took a sip of coffee, then asked, "You got it figgered he's the one who shot you?"

"Nope. I gotta find whoever shot me after I find Yadro." He shook his head. "Only take care o' one thing at a time."

Maggie opened her mouth, clamped it shut, then apparently decided to say what she'd started to. "Know it's not gonna do any good to ask, but why don't you let be whatever's drivin' you?"

Bonner stared into her eyes. "Little miss, it's not in me to let be on anything, especially what I got against those two men. One shot me from ambush and has tried many other times to put me down; the other has tried to shoot me, burn me out, run me off." He shook his head. "Don't reckon I got it in me to forgive an' forget such. They gonna pay."

"Knew it was gonna be that way. Don't reckon I'd feel as highly of you if you let it go." Maggie shifted her eyes to look at Linda and Ramey. "I'm stayin' here to look after Trey 'til he gets on his feet.

"Linda, your business has suffered enough. Think you oughtta get back to it. Trey an' I'll ride in to see you soon's he feels fit to sit a saddle." She looked at their cups and stood. "I'll pour us some more coffee."

She came back with the coffeepot, poured, and sat the kettle by the coals. She looked at Ramey. "Slim, in the mornin' want you to go back home, tell the folks what's happened, have Ma pack a bag with some o' my clothes, and send one of the boys back here with 'em. I'm gonna stay 'til Trey's able to get around."

"What you reckon yore ma an' papa's gonna say 'bout you stayin' here all this time with two men you hardly know?"

Maggie's face felt stiff, hardened, then softened. "Ma's gonna understand." She shrugged. "Reckon Papa's gonna be a mite o' trouble—but I'm stayin'. Tell 'im you tried to get me to come home and I wouldn't."

"Aw hell, Mag, you've done enough. You've sat by my side every night. One night I know you didn't sleep a wink. Go on home with Slim, get some rest; Jess'll take care o' me. 'Sides that, I'm gonna be gettin' up an' around come daylight."

Maggie grunted and pinned Trey with the look he'd learned in the last couple of days meant she wouldn't take an argument. "That's exactly why I'm gonna stay, Trey Bonner. You need watchin' like a little boy, or you gonna do somethin' dumb." She shook her head. "I'm stayin'."

Jess laughed. "Reckon she done told you, boy. If I ever learned anything, it's to not argue with a hardheaded female."

The next morning, Ramey headed back to the ranch, and Linda packed the things she'd brought with her when thinking she would spend the night with Maggie. She headed for town to fix lunch for the hungry men who would crowd into her small cafe.

Knowing what had happened to Trey, Linda rode with her Winchester across the saddle in front of her. While riding, she checked the magazine to make certain it was full, then jacked a shell into the chamber. She'd be ready if need be.

About an hour out from Trey's place, she glanced behind. A rider, close to a half mile behind, held his horse to a gallop. She'd noticed him before when he was at least a mile behind. He closed on her. She urged her horse to a faster pace. He still gained.

Her breath quickened. She told herself she wasn't frightened, but that didn't quell her fear. Most men in the West would not dare harm a woman. That didn't make her feel any better. She thought to kick her horse into a run but was fearful she'd kill him before getting to town. She settled back in her sidesaddle, rode most of the time looking back, and when the rider came close enough she pointed her rifle at the man.

"You seem to be in pretty much of a hurry, so ride right on by."

The man, now that he was close, was a well-set-up man, handsome by most standards. But looks didn't show what was inside a man.

He stared at her a moment. "Ain't very friendly, are you, missy?"

"Keep ridin'."

"Missy, I ain't never hurt no woman, wouldn't do such. Why don't we ride on to town together? Be company for us both."

"Don't need company, don't want any. Know you ain't gonna cause me harm long's I point this Winchester at you. Now ride."

The man twisted in his saddle, apparently to see her better. "You that widder woman what runs the cafe in town, ain'tcha?" He nodded. "Yep, you're her. Well, my name's Skeeter Wells. We gotta get to know each other better."

With his insistence, her fear increased. A brassy taste welled into the back of her throat. Then anger pushed its way past the fear. Blood pumped to her head. "I said for you to ride on—get goin'."

She pointed her rifle to the ground in front of his horse, squeezed off a shot, jacked another shell into the chamber, and pointed it at the man now trying to stay in the saddle of his bucking horse. "You were in a hurry to catch up with me. Now get in a bigger hurry to get to town."

He sat there a moment. His look would have punched a hole in her if it'd been a bullet. "Goin', ma'am, but we gonna meet agin." With those words that sounded like a threat to the pretty cafe owner, Skeeter Wells urged his horse ahead. Linda had made an enemy.

Ramey rode to the tie rack in front of the ranch house, slipped from the saddle, and before he could cross the veranda, Matt and Belle Tedford burst through the front doorway. "Where's Maggie? She hurt? Why didn't you bring 'er home?" Their questions came out in unison, as though they'd rehearsed them.

Slim held his hands out in front of him, palms outward. "Hey! Hold on. She's all right."

Matt, big and blustery as always, stepped ahead of his wife. "She's all right? Well, why the hell didn't you bring 'er home like we told you?"

"She an' an old coot who's stayin' with Bonner are tendin' that man who built his home right across the head of the canyon you claimed. An' she seems right happy to be doin' it. He's been shot an' she's tendin' 'im. Said to tell Belle to pack her some clothes an' to send 'em out by one o' the hands." Slim chomped down on his chew, spat, and added, "Reckon I'm gonna do just that. That little woman's as hardheaded as you, Matt."

Tedford hitched up his trousers, stared at his foreman a moment, then twisted to go back inside. He threw the words over his shoulder, "Goin' an' get 'er myself. You don't carry out orders like you use to."

Belle motioned Ramey to follow her inside, then walked up even with her husband. "You're not goin' to go get her. She's a woman grown. We've reared her properly. She's not going to do anything to make us ashamed of her. Now pour yourself a glass of whisky, sit down, and cool off."

Ramey beat his boss, his best friend, to the liquor cabinet, picked up a glass, and poured it full. He handed it to Matt. "Gonna tell you like it is, Matt. That boy has had some pretty good raisin'. He ain't gonna try nothin' funny with that girl we both love." He paused. " 'Cept to maybe take 'er away from all o' us."

Matt, his face still flushed with anger, stared at Ramey. "What you mean, 'take 'er away from all of us'?"

Belle chuckled. "What he's telling you, husband of mine, is that he thinks Maggie's found her man."

Slim nodded. "Yes'm, that's what I'm tryin' to say, only that man don't know it yet. But I got a idear when the time comes Mag's gonna tell *him*. She ain't gonna wait for him to ask 'er."

"Wh-wh-what the hell makes you say that? You've already told us we reared her properly. She won't do such and you know it."

Ramey shook his head. "You shoulda seen that little girl hoverin' over that hurt man like a mother hen. She wouldn't let Linda or old Jess do anything for him. She wanted to do it all."

Matt tossed down about half his drink, coughed, then apparently not mollified one whit, took his hat from the rack, jammed it on his head, and pinned Slim with a look that had caused most men to quake in their boots. "Have one o' the boys saddle my horse. Gonna go get 'er."

Ramey looked from Matt to Belle, hoping he'd get some support from her. He got it.

"Slim, if he wants his horse saddled, let 'im do it himself."

"Well, gol darned it. There y'all done gone an' done it agin. For twenty-five years you folks been puttin' me in the middle 'tween you. I ain't gonna stand for it no more. I'm goin' to the bunkhouse an' git me some sleep." He stepped toward the door, then turned back. "Belle, I'll send one o' the boys up here to pick up Mag's clothes. He can ride along with that there pigheaded man you married all them years ago."

When he cleared the front door, Ramey sent a chuckle into the night. Belle would ultimately win out over Matt—he'd seen the results of their arguments before. She always won.

Yadro sat alone at a table in the back of the shoddy saloon. It didn't have a name. Being the only one in town, no one, including the owner, ever called it anything but "the saloon." Whitey had been there for two days. He'd not been to see his boss.

After dumping Manse Allard's body in a dry ravine out in the desert, he'd ridden into town to the saloon and he hadn't left. The owner had locked him in at night and checked his bottles the next day to see what the man had emptied. He collected pay for them then.

Even in his drunken state, Whitey denied that he feared his boss or Bonner. Then he'd tilt the bottle again, swallow, choke, cough, and face the truth: his boss could have him put in prison or kill him; yeah, he was that good with a gun, and he had witnessed Yadro commit the unpardonable. He'd seen him rape a woman during their trek to the West after Lee surrendered. A man walked to his table.

"Seen yuh sittin' back here drinkin' alone. Man shouldn't oughtta ever drink alone; he does an' he gits to thinkin' bout all the things, good or bad, that he's done." Skeeter Wells swept his hand toward the empty chair across from Yadro. "Want a drinkin' partner?"

Whitey lifted his lolling head enough to see who stood there, studied him through bleary eyes, and the dark of the room didn't help him see. He nodded. "Sit. Ain't never done much good. You don't like that, go sit somewhere else."

Wells laughed. He held out his hand. "Skeeter Wells, what handle you usin'?"

"Don't make no difference; just sit."

While standing at the rough slab of lumber that some around this shoddy little town would call a bar, Wells had studied Yadro sitting alone, dirty, unshaven, and drunk. He thought on the type of man he looked at and decided he might have use for him. He wasn't certain that he'd accomplished what he came out here to do. Yeah, he might need help, and that drunk standing there might be the one to do it—if he could get him sober. That was when he walked back to Yadro's table. And now, as invited, he pulled out the chair across from Whitey and sat. He had brought his own bottle from the bar.

"Yeah, I seen yuh sittin' back here, but I seen yuh several times before that." He nodded. "Yeah, I seen yuh before. Seen yuh three times, an' each time that man at the head o' the canyon run you off after shootin' you up a leeetle bit." He chuckled. "You an' that mangy bunch you had around you run off like a scalded dawg." He poured about two fingers of whisky into his glass, knocked back his drink, and pinned Yadro with a knowing look. "You an' yore bunch wuz either tryin' to burn that man out, or you wuz tryin' to shoot him, or both. Which one you try to do?"

Whitey lifted his lolling head a trifle. "What you talkin' 'bout? Ain't never done none o' that."

Wells leaned across the table to look directly into Yadro's eyes. Angry blood pushed at his temples. He needed help, but this whisky-soaked rag in front of him might not have the backbone to sober up and be of any help. "Gonna tell you right now"—he nodded—"I know what you done. I sat up there on the rimrock an' watched. I watched 'cause I figgered you might do what I wuz hopin' to do myself." He shook his head and shrugged. "But you and that ragtag bunch o' yours didn't have the gumption to git the job done."

Whitey apparently studied on Wells's words. He abruptly sat a little straighter, and his eyes cleared a bit. "What you mean, a job you were hopin' to do yourself?"

His words, slurred as they were, still told Wells he had Whitey's attention. Maybe he could straighten the drunk up enough to use him. He'd keep it to himself that when he'd crossed Bonner's path before he had worn a Texas Ranger badge.

He pushed the cork into his own and Yadro's bottles, picked them up by the neck, and took Whitey by the elbow. "C'mon. We gonna get you sober, then I'm gonna tell you what I got in mind."

7

JUAN JIMENEZ DREW rein outside the shabby town and raked the weathered clapboard buildings with a look that memorized where every building stood and guessed what kind of business they might be. He rubbed the badge pinned to his shirt, took the clasp loose, and put it in his pocket.

RIP had told him before leaving Austin to find Trey Bonner, give him help if he needed it, determine what delayed his friend, have Bonner send a report back, and then for Jimenez to return to headquarters. He'd carry out orders, but damned if he'd stay in that grungy little town a minute longer than he had to. He urged his horse toward town.

Dust kicked up in small clouds under his horse's hooves. In the middle of town he pulled to a stop, glanced at each building, then urged his horse to the neat, whitewashed one. He hadn't eaten since breakfast and now the sun sat at about four o'clock. His stomach felt like an empty grain sack; besides, he might find where to look for Bonner.

The screen door squeaked. Linda looked up from scrubbing a tabletop. The man who came into her cafe would have drawn any woman's look: tall, dark, slim, and as handsome as any man she knew, yeah, including Trey Bonner. "Supper'll be ready in 'bout half an hour. You want coffee while you wait?"

"Be obliged, ma'am."

His words had only a touch of the south-of-the-border music she loved about this country and the people in it.

She poured a cup of coffee and, when placing it on the table in front of him, asked, "Ridin' through?"

Juan shook his head. "Don't know. Been lookin' for an old saddle pard, hopin' to partner up again. When I find 'im I'll probably stop for a while."

Linda went to the coffeepot and drew herself a cupful, then came back to the table. "Not many strangers come through here except once in a while a trail crew stops on their way home." She frowned. "What name your partner using the last time you saw him?"

"Last name I theenk he might have used was Bonner. He might have used that name 'cause it's the only one I ever knew 'im to use—it's his own."

While the man talked, Linda's expression changed from frown to smile; she couldn't keep it from her lips. "You scared me for a minute. I thought maybe Trey might be one o' those who changed names every new town he came to."

"No, senorita, Bonner ees an honorable man."

His words convinced Linda that he *was* Trey's friend. "It's senora, sir. I'm widowed." She nodded. "And yes, I do know your friend, and I know where you can find him."

A man in range garb pushed through the door, found a place to sit, and flopped tiredly to the bench.

Linda looked from the cowboy to the man with whom she'd been talking. "Why don't you take your time eating, then when the place empties out again we'll talk. I'll tell you how to find Trey."

"All right, senora, but first I'd like you to know, I'm Juan Jimenez." He grinned. "That's the *nombre* I been usin' all *my* life."

Linda chuckled and stood. "We'll talk later. I better get

busy. These men look hungry, an' that's not a guess, I been feedin' 'em for several months now."

Belle Tedford poured Matt another drink and went directly to Maggie's bedroom. She packed a bag with everything her daughter might need for several days, pulled the leather straps tight around the valise, buckled them, and went back to the family room.

Matt cast her a look that accused her of being a traitor to his cause; his cause being to keep Maggie with them for the rest of her life. She walked to his side, rubbed the back of his neck, then stood behind him and massaged his shoulders a few moments until she felt the tight muscles relax and soften.

"Ah, my husband, I know how you feel. We are like most parents; we think of our children as just that; we think of them as still being little ones, but children grow up." She leaned over and kissed his neck. "Matt, they grow up and look for the things you and I were seeking when we found each other."

"Yeah, but you an' I knew each other all our lives. I reckon we started figuring we b'longed together when you were still climbin' trees an' hadn't figured out yet that you were a girl."

Belle's laugh started as a chuckle deep in her throat, then erupted into a full-blown laugh. "Yeah, husband mine, if I remember correctly, you were the one who convinced me I was a girl, convinced me we were different." She shook her head, then smiled. "It was a wonderful discovery, Matt, and we, having been reared properly, didn't take undue liberties with our new findings. Our little girl's gonna do the same."

Matt, obviously not wanting to give in too easily, grumped, "Well, I'm here to tell you right now, he damned well better treat 'er right." He nodded. "Yep, we raised 'er right, but if you remember, it wasn't all that easy to push our feelin's aside an' do what we knew was the proper thing to do."

"I remember, Matt." And now, her breath coming in small gasps, she walked around his chair and crawled up into his lap. "But I'm tellin' you, husband mine, we're married now an' don't have to worry 'bout the proper thing." She leaned to kiss his earlobe. "Now, if you're of a mind to, I reckon I'll let you convince me that anything we do now"—she sucked in a tremulous breath—"is right an' proper." Before she could take another breath, Matt had her in his arms, stood, and headed toward their bedroom.

Maggie glanced at Trey, still on a pallet by the fire. He slept. She stared at him, the stubborn cut of his chin softened, and the sun wrinkles at the corners of his eyes smoothed while he slept. He almost looked like a little boy. She reached toward his brow, wanting to smooth his hair back, but pulled her hand back as though from a hot stove. She shook her head.

Maggie Tedford, you don't have a right to be touching him like he's already yours. A lot has to take place before you can treat 'im the way you're yearning to do, she told herself. She stood and stepped back from the man she now admitted to loving. She nodded. Yep, she'd even admitted how she felt to her best friend, Linda.

Jess broke into her thoughts. "You reckon yore pa's gonna let one o' the hands bring you some clothes?"

She shook her head. "Don't think so, but Ma'll change 'is mind. She's right good at doin' such"—a slight smile broke the corners of her lips—"an' I'm just now beginning to know how she does it." Jess only slanted her a puzzled frown.

Trey stirred, opened his eyes, and looked at Maggie. "You still here? You better get on home, little one. Your pa'll be comin' after me with a Greener twelve-gauge shotgun if you don't."

Maggie shook her head. "Nope. Gonna stay an' make sure you don't do any danged-fool thing like tryin' to get up an' do a day's work before you should."

He shrugged, then smiled. "Gotta tell you, Jess welcomes havin' you here to take the load off his shoulders, you know, doin' the cookin' an' cleanin', and such. But me? Well, I'm sorta gettin' used to bein' told what to do an' when to do it."

He nodded and a furrow formed between his eyebrows. "Yep, reckon I'm gettin' used to havin' you around." His smile widened to a grin. "Yep. Fact is, I'm likin' it."

Maggie's face heated. She knew she blushed furiously but

there was nothing she could do about it. She picked up the glass he'd been drinking from and turned toward the kitchen. "I'll get you another glass of water."

The few feet to the water pitcher gave her a chance to gather her composure. Dang that man anyway. Couldn't he see what just being around him did to her? The slow plodding of a horse broke into her thoughts. She listened a moment, figured it might be someone from the ranch, but put Trey's water beside him and picked up her rifle. Jess already stood at the window.

"Looks like one o' yore pa's men." He nodded. "Reckon it is. See he's got a valise tied to the back o' his saddle." He put his rifle back in the rack. "Yeah, it's Ramey. Reckon he's got them things you sent 'im for."

Maggie let her lips crinkle at the corners. Her mother had once again simmered her father down—or maybe caused him to simmer in a different way.

Jimenez glanced at the hill to his left and reined his horse a little more to the right. Linda had given him pretty detailed instructions as to how to find Trey's home. If he had it figured right, he had only to circle the base of the hill and Trey's place should be in sight. He was right.

He reined his horse in and stared. "Lordy day, Trey, I didn't figure you'd have built anything so grand for just you; damn, that looks like a big-time rancher's house, a place you figure to spend the rest o' your life in." He nodded. "An' I reckon that's just what you're plannin'—if that house is yours." He sat straighter in the saddle and urged his horse toward the ranch house.

About thirty yards from the front door, he reined in and yelled. "Hello the house!"

Expecting Trey's deep baritone to answer, he frowned and shook his head when a husky female voice said, "Ride up closer so's I can take a look at you."

Juan urged his horse a few paces closer. "Ma'am, I reckon I've made a mistake. I'm lookin' for a friend o' mine name of

Trey Bonner. Would you be so kind as to set me on the right path?"

A low chuckle answered his question. "You ain't made a mistake, mister, unless you've come to make trouble for Trey, an' it ain't likely you gonna do that with two Winchester forty-fours lookin' down your gullet. What handle you usin'?"

"Juan Jimenez, ma'am. You expectin' Trey home soon?"

"He's home now. Ride on in, step down, an' rest your saddle."

Juan wondered if Trey was in that house, why he hadn't answered his shout? He shrugged mentally and rode to the hitching post. If Trey was in trouble, he would soon find out. He had no choice with two rifles pointed at him.

When he stepped from the saddle, a right pretty girl opened the door. Fact was she was danged pretty, but to his thinking not as pretty as the widow woman, Linda, the one he'd met in town.

"Come on in. Trey isn't spry enough to come out to meet you. He took a bullet in the shoulder a couple days back, an' even though he's grumpy as the dickens I won't let him move around much yet."

The next few minutes were organized confusion while Juan greeted Trey, met Jess Maynard and Slim Ramey, and properly introduced himself to Maggie. Then he told them how he'd found his way out to Trey's. "'Bout the prettiest lady I reckon I've ever seen told me how to get out here. She seemed to know you right well." He grinned. "But I'm here to tell you right now, she didn't prepare me to meet none o' these others, an' she didn't tell me you'd been shot."

Maggie stood. "Supper's 'bout ready. You an' Jess get on down to the stream an' wash up. Jess'll show you the way. Trey says he's gonna sink a well an' buy a pump from Tom Parsons soon's he gets his shoulder well enough to dig."

As soon as Maggie disappeared into the kitchen, Juan glanced at Jess's back and said no louder than it took for Trey to hear. "She know what you do for a livin'?"

Trey, still lying on the pallet by the fire, shook his head.

"Don't want it known hereabouts. I still don't know who's ramrodin' those men who been givin' the settlers hell. Reckon RIP sent you to help me?"

Juan nodded. "We'll talk soon's we get a chance. Also, you can tell me where Maggie and Jess fit into the picture." He grinned. " 'Til then reckon I better do like Maggie said—gonna go get washed up."

Another couple of days and Maggie let Trey get up, but wouldn't hear of him doing anything around the ranch. Juan and Jess stepped in and did the work Trey cut out for each day. Finally, Maggie, seeing how things were going, knew she should go home.

If she continued to stay things would get pretty awkward. She couldn't justify, in her own mind, dragging her care for Trey out any longer. Finally, despite her longing to stay, she directed Jess and Juan, in detail, the things to do, and to make certain Trey didn't go back to work that might tear his wound open.

Before heading out, she lingered by Trey's chair, wanting to touch him, wanting all the things she couldn't have. When she turned from him she felt as though she had torn off part of her own body.

Juan rode with her when she rode from the house. Trey wouldn't—in fact, none of the three men would—allow her to ride alone.

Yadro, now sober, thought to tell his boss he was quitting, then had second thoughts. Why shouldn't he continue to draw his pay, as well as pay for Skeeter. His boss, Timothy Rogers, didn't know that but one of the three men Whitey had was dead. He didn't need to know, now or ever.

As soon as he'd finished the job, killing or burning Bonner out, he figured to head for San Antonio; he'd had enough of this grungy little town. The task he'd been ordered to do fit exactly what he and Wells planned. He looked across the hotel room he and Wells had taken while Skeeter tried to sober him up.

"We gonna both draw wages while we do what we figgered to do anyway. I'll jest draw pay for one o' the men what come out with me an' give it to you."

"How you figger that?"

"My boss brung me in here to get rid of any squatters. I done it easy, up 'til Bonner come in here. Don't know what my boss's gonna get outta it but think maybe he's got a big payday stuck in 'is head." Yadro had been pacing from wall to wall in the small room. He went to the bed and sat. He cast Wells a sly look. "Been wonderin' how I could get myself a big payday when we get the job done I been gettin' paid to do."

Wells frowned and leaned forward in the room's only chair. "You come up with a idea yet?"

Yadro nodded. "Been tryin' to figger a way to take over Bonner's place—they's places along the same track you could take over *if we can get rid o' Rogers.*"

"Thought you said your boss was right gun handy, an' smart."

Whitey studied his new partner a moment. He nodded. "Yeah, he's both o' them things, but don't reckon he's bullet-proof. I figger a bullet throwed at 'im from the side o' the trail, or from the back o' some rocks'll take care o' him same as it will for Bonner." He grinned. "We work it right, you an' me'll be sittin' right pretty." He sighed and wiped his mouth. "Reckon I'll jest have to put off visitin' San Tone a mite longer."

Wells frowned. "Wished this here setup wuz closer to a decent-sized town." He shrugged. "But hell, a man cain't have everything."

Rogers toyed with a pencil, threw it to his desk, and sat frowning at the pencil on which he'd just broken the point. He wondered why Yadro hadn't reported having gotten rid of Bonner?

Yeah, Whitey had gotten one of his men killed, but that left him with two others. Three men should have been able to take care of one man easily. Shouldn't have taken them but a day or two. Now here it was weeks since the homesteader had insisted on filing for that piece of land stretched across the mouth of the canyon.

He'd never seen that stretch of land he'd tasked the white-haired gunman to keep clear of settlers. He didn't figure to waste time and energy riding out there until he could ride to Austin and show the state land commissioner the forged papers that said he'd bought the land from the settlers and that they had packed up their families and headed for California; then he'd see about taking care of Matt Tedford. He'd get the rancher's land without having to do anything except threaten him with what he knew.

But that should be easy. Tedford had folded mighty easy when he'd threatened to talk to the law.

Maggie had been gone only two days when Bonner pushed to his knees and stood. The room swam before his eyes. He leaned against the mantel until his head cleared. Then squeezed his eyes shut, opened them wide, and grunted, "Reckon I let that slip of a girl browbeat me into stayin' flat o' my back longer'n I should've."

He thought to fold the bedding he'd been lying on, then considered that as weak as he seemed to be he might fall flat on his face. He left the bedding as it was.

"What're you tryin' to do to yourself, amigo? The senorita, she say for you to stay in your blankets until Jess an' me say you're strong enough to get up."

Trey looked at his friend a moment, pulled his mouth to the side in a grimace, and nodded. "That's what she said for damned sure—but she ain't here. Figure I won't ever get strong enough to get up an' do a day's work long's I stay flat o' my back. Where's Jess?"

"Down by the corral throwin' some hay to the livestock. Why?" Jimenez never used his Mexican accent unless he thought to charm a pretty female with it.

Trey worked his way to his chair by holding on to the backs of furniture. When seated he looked at Juan. "Better tell you where this assignment stands while Jess is out o' the house."

The slim Mexican pulled a chair to the side of Trey's and sat. "Let's hear it."

It didn't take Bonner more than ten or fifteen minutes to bring Juan up-to-date on all that had happened. He even told him about the trail crew helping him load his wagon. He packed his pipe and squinted at his friend. "Juan, I ain't figured out for sure who I b'lieve is givin' Yadro orders, but I'm beginnin' to get an idea. Tell you 'bout it soon's I get it all straight in my head. But I'll tell you for sure, the one who shot me is not one o' those we're lookin' for."

Juan stood, went to a cabinet along the wall, and took out a bottle of bourbon. He poured them each a drink, looked at the two filled glasses, and put another glass beside them. "Jess'll want a drink too."

He came back with the two glasses and handed Bonner one. "I think we better let Jess know why we're really here. I theenk that old man would die before he'd tell anybody, if we told 'im to keep it a secret."

Bonner took a sip of his drink, stared into the amber liquid, then nodded. "Been thinkin' o' doin' just that. Plus, if anything happened to you an' me, I'd want him to ride to Austin an' tell RIP. You reckon he could make that kind o' ride?"

"Aw hell, Trey, that old man's made of bone and whang leather." Juan nodded. "Yeah, I theenk we tell 'im 'bout us, an' what we want 'im to do in case we buy the farm."

Jess came in as Juan finished approving Trey's suggestion. Jimenez flicked a thumb toward the liquor cabinet. "Poured you one. It's sitting on the cabinet."

Maynard grinned. "Whooee, glad you did. That wind's gittin' right chilly. Drink'll take the chill outta my old bones." He glanced at Bonner. "Glad to see you done decided to ride a loop around what Miss Maggie done told you. You'll git well a helluva lot faster bein' up an' around."

Trey glanced toward the kitchen. "That pot o' stew from last night's good enough for supper tonight. Figure we warm it an' fix a fresh pot o' coffee, an' maybe some cornbread'll be enough. Soon's I get confident in my strength, I'll do the cookin' 'til I get a little stronger."

Jess knocked back his drink, looked at Trey and Juan, picked up the bottle, and poured them another.

When he brought the drinks, Bonner flipped his belt so he could reach the back of it. He unpinned his badge and put it on the table beside him. Juan had done the same. Trey eyed the old man. "Got somethin' to tell you."

Jess looked from the badges to the two men, nodded, and said, "Reckon from what I'm lookin' at y'all both got things to tell me."

Bonner picked up his badge and again pinned it to the inside of his belt. "Gonna tell ya, but I want your word you won't say a word 'bout what you hear 'til one o' us says so."

"Ain't sayin' nothin' to nobody."

Juan grinned. "That's the way we figured it'd be." He looked at Trey. "This's your ball game; you tell 'im, Bonner."

Trey spent the better part of an hour telling Jess about his and Juan's assignment, and asking him to do the things that needed to be done if they couldn't. Then he gazed into his glass a moment and shifted his look back to Maynard. "Ain't told Juan yet, but I'm figurin' to stay here after I get this job done. In case anything happens to me, I want you to take over what I've started here, otherwise we keep on like we're doin' now."

"Now, why in the gosh-dinged hell're you talkin' like that for? Ain't nothin' gonna happen to you."

Trey grinned at the old man. "Neither one o' us would've said that when you brought me down from the rimrock." He shrugged. "You got the whole story 'bout me an' Juan. We gonna play out our hand, an' by then I figure I'll talk Juan into takin' up one o' these preemption tracts for himself." He chuckled. "Boy, I'll bet old RIP'll swallow his cud he'll be so mad."

Juan shook his head. "Don't think so. Knowin' RIP, he'll be happy for us both, an' he'll be even more happy 'cause he kept us from ridin' the owlhoot."

* * *

Saturday dance night came. Linda closed early, brought the number-two washtub in and filled it with warm water. She sank tiredly into the tub and began to soap her body with the perfumed soap she had had Tom Parsons order from New York. She liked smelling good for those who asked her to dance.

Her mind switched to the handsome young friend of Trey's. Wonder if he'll come to the dance? B'lieve I'd like to know him better, she thought. He was such a gentleman, and from the short time I got to talk with him, he seemed a gentle man, but one who could be right hard if need be. She shook her mind from thoughts like that, but hummed "Buffalo Gals" in anticipation of dancing with him—if he came with Trey.

She dressed with care, telling herself she wanted to look nice for Trey even though she'd admitted to Maggie that she didn't think of him *that* way. Then, always honest with herself, she knew it was Juan she wanted to think she was pretty.

The liveryman always placed bales of hay around for people to sit on, and he'd clean the stable's runway between the stalls down to hard-packed bare earth.

Linda wondered if the town would ever grow enough to have a town hall in which to have their dances. She smiled to herself while walking the short distance to the dance. Heck, she enjoyed every dance, regardless where they held it.

Only a few feet outside the huge double doors she stopped and looked at the horses, buggies, wagons, and other horse-drawn vehicles parked outside.

The Tedford coach stood just outside the doors. She frowned and looked for Trey's horse, and finally she nodded. Yes, Bonner was here, and she thought she recognized Juan's horse at the hitching rail alongside Trey's. She went through the opening into the stable. Trey, Maggie, and Juan rushed over to take her in tow.

Jimenez looked down into her face and smiled. "Senora, the other day when I met you I would have bet my pony you couldn't look any prettier, but you've up an' done it." He twisted to look at Trey. "Amigo, reckon we ought to feel guilty from havin' cornered the two prettiest women in this part o' Texas."

Maggie felt her face turn hot.

"Feel guilty if you want, vaquero, but I'm gonna hog every dance with this one if she'll let me."

Maggie took Trey's hand and tucked her tiny one into his. "She'll let you, cowboy." She swept those already there with a glance. "Where's Jess? Didn't he want to come?"

Trey's look sobered. "Yeah, little girl, he wanted to, but with things bein' like they are we left him an' Dawg there to watch the place. I don't feel like startin' my home all over again."

He glanced toward the end of the building. "See Yadro's picked up another of his ilk to travel around with."

Maggie nodded. "Uh-huh, last time I came to town I saw them together. Don't have a reason to figure him as trash, but I've always thought that birds of a feather flock together. Thinkin' that way, I reckon I ain't wrong."

Maggie and Trey danced a couple of dances, then Bonner seated her and went to get them a lemonade. He'd filled their cups and turned to go back to her when Yadro, his look spearing Bonner, leaned over and said something in Wells's ear. Then they hitched up their gunbelts and moved toward the door.

Trey watched them disappear into the dark outside, then handed Maggie her drink. "Hate to do this, Mag, but Yadro an' that scum he's partnered up with just spent a little time lookin' my way, then they left.

"Don't b'lieve they're up to any good. Better get on back to my place. They may be more than Jess can handle." He took a swallow of his lemonade and glanced toward Linda and Juan. "Ain't gonna spoil Juan's night; you can tell 'im after a while what I've done. Let 'im enjoy his time with Linda. They both seem to be havin' a good time."

"They'll see you leave."

"Juan'll probably figure I've gone out to stop by that keg they brought down from the saloon—let 'im think that until he says something."

She put her hand on his forearm, let it slide down to his

work-hardened one, and squeezed. "Be careful, Trey." Then, obviously trying to joke, her voice caught in her throat. "Don't want to spend another couple weeks nursing you back from any more gunshot wounds."

"I promise." He walked out of the stable, hoping no one noticed.

While tightening the cinches on his saddle he shook his head. That Maggie was some sort o' woman. She simply accepted that he had to leave. She didn't try to talk him into letting Jess handle things out at the canyon, or ask him to let Juan know. He chuckled. He'd bet she'd show up at the ranch the next day to see if he was all right.

He frowned, then wondered why she'd care so much. Well, hell, they were good friends. He toed the stirrup, reined his horse onto the trail, and kicked him to a lope. He held him to that pace for about fifteen minutes, then slowed.

He didn't want to ride upon the heels of Yadro, and he had no doubt that the white-haired gunman was on his way out to his ranch. He chuckled. He thought of his place as his ranch even though he'd not yet driven one cow onto his grass.

Nearing the house, he slowed his horse to a walk; his horse's hooves would make little noise in the thick dust. Also, he wanted to listen for the sound of gunshots. The closer he got without hearing the sharp reports of rifle fire, the more worried he became. Then a volley of sound came from the creek side. He'd not been aware that he held his breath waiting, hoping to hear the sounds of gunshots, but he must have because now he slowly exhaled.

Bonner studied the house and the creek bank from where he clearly saw the flashes. He first thought to spur his horse to the front of the house, yell to Jess that it was him, and get inside to help Maynard fight them off.

He shook his head. If he and the old man chose to fight from inside, the bushwhackers would have them pinned down. He wasn't that dumb. He'd stay out here where he could judge where they were by sound, and when they fired the flashes would show him their position within inches.

Jess wasn't in any immediate danger, so under the cloak of darkness, Trey led his horse to the corral, put him inside, loosened the saddle cinches, slipped the saddle off, and slung it over the rail. Now that his horse had water and food, Bonner slipped his Winchester from the scabbard and circled the house toward the creek.

Finally, in easy range of where the gun flashes came from, Bonner sighted in on where he judged one of the bushwhackers stood. He squeezed the trigger, heard a curse, then one of the men Trey judged to be the man Yadro had teamed up with yelled, "The old man's done come outside."

Then a shot from the house put the lie to his words. "That damned Bonner's done tricked us. He must've follered us when we left town. The old man's still in the house." Trey had no doubt this time that it was Yadro who yelled.

"Let's git outta here. We'll find a better way to git 'im." Yadro's partner yelled. They had ceased firing.

Now all Bonner had to fire at was the deceptive location of their voices. He wouldn't take the chance that they'd locate him the same way he'd judged their position. Then one of them threw a last shot toward the house before he heard the sound of running horses. Not thinking he'd hit anything, Trey squeezed off another shot in the direction of the horse's hoofbeats— and surprised, he heard a curse and the words, "The bastard creased me." Then the sound died in the distance.

"That you out there, young'un?"

"It's me. I'm comin' in."

Jess greeted Bonner with a chuckle. "Figgered it wuz you all along. Dawg didn't growl, he jest whined, wagged 'is tail an' stretched out across the floor in front o' the door."

"How'd you know you had uninvited company?"

Again Maynard chuckled. "Dawg told me in plenty of time so's I could even hear them talk about how they'd take care o' me reeeal easy." He scratched his head. "Come on in. Coffee's on. You can tell me how you figgered they wuz gonna hit the ranch tonight."

Before answering, Trey went to the liquor cabinet, poured

him and Jess a drink, then sat and told Maynard why he figured they were headed for his ranch.

"Where's Juan? Why didn't he come home with you?"

"Didn't tell 'im I was leavin'. He an' Linda seemed to be
havin' a good time, so I told Maggie not to say anything 'bout
where I'd gone 'til he asked." He took a sip of his whisky, then
nodded. "Figured you an' I could take care of those two—if I
got out here in time."

Jess stared at Trey a moment, then shook his head.
"Young'un, you got a lot more faith in us than I got." He
knocked back his drink and stood. "You want another drink,
or you goin' to bed?"

"Goin' to bed, Jess. Figure I'll let Juan sleep in in the
mornin'."

Several dances after Trey left for the ranch, Juan and Linda
walked up to the bale on which Maggie sat. A frown creased
her forehead and she kept looking toward the door. She wasn't
aware that her two friends stood there until Linda asked,
"Where's Trey? Haven't seen you dancin' for a while."

"That's because I haven't danced since the second dance."

Linda put her hand on Maggie's shoulder. "Aw now, honey,
you an' Trey ain't had a fallin' out, have you?"

Maggie's face hardened until it felt like old cardboard.
"Wish it had been somethin' like that." She shook her head.
"But no, he's gone after Yadro."

Then she told them about the white-haired gunman, and
what led Bonner to think it best that he follow them and help
Jess defend the ranch, if need be.

"He didn't want me to help, senorita?"

"Said he could take care of it, to leave you alone and let
you two have a good time." She looked up into his eyes, which
had hardened to slate gray. "Tell you, Juan, I never had to do
anything as hard as to just sit here, not tell you when there was
every chance in the world that he needed help."

"Senorita, not sayin' he won't need help, but knowin' 'im
like I do, I theenk he ees better off handlin' thees thing by

himself. I've seen 'im when I knew he needed help, but he'd tell me to stay outta it." He shook his head. "No, alone he weel not have to worry 'bout anyone else; that way he can keep 'is mind on only one theeng."

"Are you gonna leave now?"

Juan shook his head and smiled. "No, Maggie, I'm gonna stay here an' do exactly like he said, only I've got two pretty ladies to dance with now."

Maggie opened her mouth to argue, then clamped her jaws tight. She sat there a moment, got her worry and anger under control, then nodded. "All right, you've seen 'im in these situations before. I trust you know what you're doin'. 'Sides that, he's as much your friend as he is mine."

She nodded, smiled at Linda, and took Juan's hand. "I claim this dance."

Linda smiled and sat in the place Maggie had only then vacated.

Winded, and feeling that her face showed a beet red from the exertion and heat, Juan seated her and held his hand out for Linda. Before they could swing out on the hard-packed earth, Maggie said something that obviously surprised neither of them: "Reckon come daylight I'm gonna ride out to Trey's place. Gonna see if your faith in 'im is justified."

"First, you better tell your folks, an' next, when the dance breaks up maybe you better ride out there with me. Damn sure nobody's gonna bother you with me around."

About four hours after turning in, Trey groaned, rolled over, and glanced at the window to see if daylight brightened it. Dark still showed from outside. He looked at his watch on the bedside table. It showed five-thirty. He threw his legs over the side of the bed and stood to get dressed. "Gonna be another long day," he muttered while tucking in his shirttail.

When he went in the kitchen, Jess stood close to the big cast-iron stove. The old man shivered. "Gettin' almighty chilly these nights. Got the coffee on. I'll whip up some pancakes."

Trey cocked his head, listened, and picked up the sound of

horses. He glanced at Dawg standing by the door, tail wagging. Bonner glanced at Jess. "Better whip up a bunch; Dawg's standin' there waitin' to greet Juan an' whoever he's brought home with 'im."

Jess chuckled. "Bet it's that girl. She's done come to check an' see if you're all right."

Trey frowned. "Wonder why she'd do that?"

Jess's chuckle turned into a laugh. "You ain't figgered that out yet, I danged sure ain't gonna tell ya, young'un."

Before he could say more Maggie yelled, "Comin' in. Juan's puttin' the horses away."

Jess flipped a pancake and looked up from the skillet. "Got breakfast almost ready. Warsh up an' set up to the table."

Maggie stood just inside the door. She raked Trey from head to toe, then twisted to do the same to Jess. "See y'all didn't take any lead. Yadro visit ya?"

Bonner nodded. "He was here. Left mighty quick though."

Maggie frowned, went to the washstand, slowly washed her hands, then pinned Trey with a hard look. "Knowin' you like I do, I would think you'd go after 'im an' put an end to all this."

Bonner held a towel out to her so she could dry her hands. He shook his head. "Wouldn't do any good. I gotta figure out who he's workin' for first, make sure of it, *then* I'm gonna take care o' Yadro, that trash he's partnered up with, *and* whoever's payin' 'em."

Finished drying her hands, she went to the table and seated herself in the chair Trey held for her. As soon as she pulled up to the table Jess put a plate in front of her with a stack of three pancakes. "Go ahead, eat 'em while they're hot." He glanced at Bonner. "Have you an' Juan some in a minute."

Trey sat, then grumbled. "Sure would be nice if we had some fresh eggs."

"Mama might let you have a settin' hen an' a few fertile eggs. You care if I ask 'er?"

"Heck no. But don't pressure her into givin' 'em to me."

Soon, all seated and eating, they talked mostly about

Bonner's plans for his ranch and when and where he intended to find a small herd to buy. He wanted to stock some
whiteface heifers, a good bull of the same breed, and maybe
some longhorns.

After breakfast, and seeing that Maggie had satisfied herself that they were all right, Trey suggested that she could stay
the day, spend the night, or he'd ride home with her.

"Told Mama an' Papa where I was headed before the dance
ended—an' why. Mama smiled and agreed with me. Papa
grumped, growled, and settled down when Mama told him she
saw it my way."

Bonner raised an eyebrow and shook his head. "All right,
that bein' the case you better stay. Know you're tired after
dancin' all night, then ridin' out here. You know where your
room is. Take a nap while we get a few things done."

Yadro and Wells, soon after riding hell-bent for election away
from Bonner's ranch, circled, came back and climbed to the
rimrock. With Wells leading, they saw the sun rise and travel
across the heavens until it stood overhead. Skeeter waved a
hand toward a small butte ahead. "Other side o' that hill's a
ravine. That's where I been holed up the last few months."

Wells knew Yadro had been wondering why he wanted
Bonner dead, but he'd decided he wouldn't tell the white-
haired gunny anything. He figured if he said anything about
Bonner being a Texas Ranger, Yadro would run like a scared
rabbit. That didn't fit his plans. He'd decided he needed help
when he saw the ranger at the dance.

He'd been certain he'd killed him up on the rimrock. The
way he'd jerked, blood blossomed from his chest, and then
he'd crumpled in a heap into the dust after being knocked
backward by the bullet's force, Wells figured justified in his
assumption. Everything in his memory and experience spelled
a sure kill. Now here he was again. The man must be like a cat
with nine lives. He sighed. This time with Yadro's help he'd
get 'im, get 'im good. And he figured if anybody's neck would
be stuck out, he'd make sure it was Whitey's.

Another half hour and they rode into Skeeter's camp.

During some long-ago time water had probably run in a fast stream down the arroyo. It had undercut the bank such that a shallow cave pushed back into what had then been the sides of the stream. Now, many years later, the stream flowed serenely many, perhaps fifty, feet below.

WELLS SHOWED WHITEY where he kept his horses—a riding horse and a packhorse. "Have to go out an' cut somethin' for 'em to eat 'bout every day. You an' me'll take turns."

"I ain't gonna swing a scythe for no damned horse."

Wells face froze into a granitelike mask. "All right. Tie your pony out away from mine. I'll cut hay for mine. Yours can starve to death. Course the day might come when he could save your drunken life if he wuz fed good."

Taking in the look on Wells's face ran chills up Yadro's spine. He was lookin' at a man who would kill him for very little reason.

He'd not seen this side of the man before, and he realized that he knew nothing of him except that he wanted Bonner dead; he didn't know why Skeeter hated the homesteader. He made up his mind to never cross Wells, and after they'd taken care of Trey Bonner, he'd get rid of him. Then the thought hit him that whatever wages he got out of Rogers he'd keep it all.

"Aw hell, Skeeter, I was only jokin'. Now sure I'll cut my horse some hay."

"Every other day you'll cut hay for all three of 'em."

Yadro nodded.

Without another word, Wells pulled the gear off his horse, put it under the overhang, and tethered his horse next to the packhorse.

Then, before starting a fire for breakfast, he sat and cleaned his rifle and six-shooter. He glanced up at Yadro. "You better do the same. Bonner ever manage to track us back here or anywhere he can get a shot at us, we better be able to trust our weapons."

"He ever able to track you very far?"

Wells shook his head. "Tried a few time, but I've shook 'im off. Got lost from 'im." He ran a patch down the barrel of his rifle, sighted down its bore, and carefully stood it next to his saddle. "Me bein' able to lose 'im ain't sayin' he's not any good at trackin'. All I'm sayin' is I didn't leave 'im anything to follow."

"He that good?"

"He's damned good. Oughtta be, he's done enough o' it." Then Skeeter clamped his jaws closed and said nothing else.

Yadro wondered why Wells shut up so fast and seemed not inclined to say why the homesteader had tracked a lot of people. Whitey decided not to push his luck. He figured Wells had been about to paint Bonner as a bounty hunter. That would account for the man he intended to kill being so gun quick.

The bushwhacker finished cleaning his guns, stood, and glanced at Whitey. "Start a fire." He picked up a bucket and headed down the side of the ravine, dipped the bucket in the stream, then climbed the hill. Very little water sloshed from the bucket.

Back at the cave he filled the coffeepot, put a handful of grounds in the pot, and set it by the fire. Then he fastened his gaze on Yadro, his face again rock hard. "You gonna get somethin' straight right now. Camp chores gonna be split even-like. You ain't settin' round here an' watchin' me cook an' ever'thing else. Got it?"

Whitey set his face in what he hoped was as hard as Wells's. "Never figgered it any other way, Skeeter. Why you actin' so mad toward me all of a sudden?"

"Ain't mad. We understand how things gonna be right off,

then they ain't no reason to get mad." He nodded. "That's the way it's gonna be."

An hour or so later, they sat by the fire eating a jackrabbit Wells had gone out in the brush and shot earlier. The bushwhacker stared at Yadro a few minutes, long enough for Whitey to squirm under his steady gaze. "What you lookin' at me for? I ain't done nothin'."

"Jest wonderin'. Bonner knows you've tried to burn 'im out, bushwhack 'im, kill 'im any way you could; wonder why he ain't called you out when you wuz both in town?" He took a bite of the stringy rabbit, chewed, swallowed, then nodded. "Know he ain't scared o' you. He could hold his draw 'til you got yore gun out, then draw an' kill you easy-like." He shook his head. "Jest flat don't make sense."

Trying to save face under Wells's obvious contempt for his gun prowess, Yadro blustered, "You just ain't never seen me pull iron."

Wells's look froze his guts into knots. He shook his head. "Nope, ain't never seed you draw—but I've seed Bonner, an' ain't no man I ever come across can beat 'im. An' I'm talkin' 'bout you, me, an' anybody else you want to name."

The frozen knots in Yadro's stomach turned into one twisted chunk of ice.

Trey let Maggie sleep until midafternoon, then knocked on her bedroom door. "Wake up, sleepyhead. You sleep any longer an' you won't be able to sleep tonight."

Her voice, cloaked in sleep, came through the door. "What time is it?"

"Three-twenty-five. Jess's 'bout ready to start supper."

"Oh my goodness. I'm so ashamed. I should be in that kitchen cookin'."

"No, you shouldn't. Before you went in your room, I filled the pitcher, put soap on the washstand, and put clean towels on the rack. Now just get the sleep outta your eyes an' come on out. I'll have coffee ready for you."

In about twenty minutes Maggie came out all rosy faced from the scrubbing she'd apparently given it.

"Well, now, if I'd known how pretty you are when wakened from a nap, I'd have knocked on your door earlier."

Maggie blushed to an even deeper glow. "If I'd known you could give such nice compliments, I'd have come out sooner."

"Aw, Maggie, I always think you're the prettiest woman I ever met. Just never had a chance to tell you before."

She glanced around the room. "Where's everybody?"

"Jess's in the kitchen. Juan's down at the corral."

"Ooops, I better get out there with Jess an' help 'im. Maybe I can fix somethin' special."

After supper, they sat up late, again talking about plans for the ranch. Maggie mentioned that her father was thinking about sending her back East to finish her schooling. She didn't sound too enthused with the idea. Trey frowned when she told them her father's idea. He wondered why he felt like he'd been kicked in the stomach.

"I'll ride home with you in the morning, Mag. Don't want you traipsin' 'round the country alone. Plus, maybe your mother'll have those chickens and eggs to spare."

Maggie hoped her father would be civil.

After breakfast the next morning, Bonner saddled their horses—Maggie had borrowed one from the liveryman the day before—and they rode toward the Box T.

While riding, they occasionally passed clusters of cattle, mostly whiteface. Trey frowned. If Maggie's father was inclined to be civil toward him, he might feel free to ask the rancher to sell him some breeding stock.

Then as though reading his mind, Maggie pointed toward several heifers. "That what you got in mind to go lookin' for? They're all crossbred, Hereford an' longhorn."

Bonner nodded and took on a wry grin. "Mag, those cattle are exactly the kind I'm gonna try an' find."

"Maybe Pa would sell you some. It'd save 'im the time it'd take to drive 'em to railhead."

Bonner chuckled. "I thought o' that when we passed the first bunch." He shook his head. "I didn't think on it very long though. I don't figure your pa'll give me the time o' day, let alone sell me breedin' stock."

Maggie's jaw set in a hard line. "If you won't ask 'im, I will."

Bonner stared at her for a long moment. "Mag, gonna tell you somethin' right now. I fork my own broncs. Ain't never asked anyone to clear the trail for me; ain't gonna start now."

Her jaw hardened further. Knots stuck out at their backs. Trey would have bet her teeth hurt from the pressure she apparently put on them.

"You don't think anyone can do anything for you that you can't do better, is that it?"

He shook his head. "No, ma'am, that ain't it at all. The way I see it, your pa doesn't like me even a little bit. I don't ask favors of those who don't like me, an' it *would* be a favor. It'd keep me from havin' to spend a couple o' months on the trail, months that would leave Jess, an' maybe Juan, at the ranch alone to keep someone from burnin' down the place—or maybe killin' both of 'em."

He frowned. "Reckon I'm gonna have to put off ownin' any cows o' my own 'til I've killed those tryin' to get rid o' me."

Maggie rode closer to him. "Almost home. You gonna come in an' visit a while?"

Trey chuckled. "Reckon I will if I want to talk to your ma 'bout that settin' hen. Maybe your pa won't shoot me for tryin' to steal all his daughter's time."

Maggie gave a very unladylike snort. "It's not his daughter's *time* he's worried 'bout. He thinks you're tryin' to steal his daughter."

Bonner tried to think of something clever to say, but thought it better to not say anything. An uncomfortable silence engulfed them until they rode into the yard.

Belle Tedford came out onto the porch before they had their horses tied. "Sure glad you rode home with Maggie. I get mighty worried when she's out alone."

"Aw, Mrs. Tedford, I wouldn't let her do anything that might bring harm to 'er. Man don't let his best friend do anything dumb."

Belle laughed. "Her hard head'll get her into as much trouble as being dumb would. Y'all come on in the house outta this chill wind. Lordy day, seems like the wind never quits blowing."

On entering the family room, Maggie looked around. "Where's Pa?"

Belle shrugged. "Don't know. He rode out with some of the crew soon after daylight." She laughed. "He might be gone all day, but something I'll swear to is that he'll be here in time for supper. He might miss his nooning, but not supper."

Trey raised an eyebrow and twisted his mouth to the side. "I'll be long gone by then." He nodded. "I'll make it a point to be."

"Oh pshaw, Mr. Tedford does a lot of growlin', but I never knew him to bite. Now you chillun sit down an' rest your bones while I fix y'all a glass of lemonade."

They talked while they drank their drinks. Maggie asked her mother about sparing one of her hens from the nests, along with eggs. All the eggs were fertile based on the number of roosters in the yard.

Belle went them one better. She included six laying hens, along with a rooster. "Ma'am, I'll surely be beholden to you, an', yes'm, I'd like all you've offered, but I'll have to bring my wagon over to pick 'em up. I'll knock together a couple o' pens to put 'em in."

He wanted to pay for the chickens, but Belle wouldn't hear of it.

After talking through their nooning, Trey stood. "Reckon I better get on back home." He chuckled. "Get there by suppertime. I don't like to miss a meal either, although I've missed a many a one in my time."

Maggie chimed in. "Know that. That's why I try to make sure you eat well when I come over."

They talked until Trey excused himself, went out, climbed on his horse, and headed for his ranch.

Two days later, sitting in front of a roaring fire, sipping their nightly drink, Juan glanced at Trey. "When you gonna go get those chickens?"

"Don't know. Why?"

"Well, I noticed our whisky's gettin' mighty low. Theenk I better ride in town an' get us another few bottles."

Careful to make his face devoid of expression, Bonner nodded. "Why don't you stop in an' see Linda while you're there?"

Juan frowned. "I never thought o' that. Good idea, *compadre*."

Trey chuckled, then laughed outright. "Juan, you're as transparent as that glass you're holdin'. Hell, we got plenty o' whisky. You just want to see Linda."

Juan stared into his almost-empty glass, chagrin pasted his face. He raised his eyebrows and twisted his mouth to the side. He nodded. "Shouldn't have spent all those months trailin' you 'round Texas. You know me too well." He knocked back the rest of his drink. "Tell you what's a fact, partner, you're right. I surely do like that woman. Don't know as I ever saw one I liked more."

"You figure on courtin' 'er?"

Juan scratched his head and frowned. "Ain't considered that, but reckon I'm gonna give it some thought."

Trey grinned. "Yeah, you do that, amigo. From what I've seen at the last two dances, she's already done her thinkin' 'bout you." He chuckled, stood, and went to the cabinet on which sat the whisky. He looked over his shoulder. "Ain't none o' that land on either side o' me been filed on. Why don't you look into it? RIP might be losin' himself two rangers 'stead o' one."

Bonner poured them each a drink, looked at Jess, who shook his head, and filled the two glasses he'd taken to the bottle. Before he could hand Juan his drink, the handsome Mexican surprised him. "What you figurin' 'bout Maggie?"

"Maggie? What about 'er?"

"Well, you stuck your nose into my business, figured turnabout was fair play." He took his filled glass from Trey. "That girl's already showed you in every way I can think of that she's already done her thinkin' 'bout what she thinks o' you. Time you did somethin' 'bout it. Treat 'er right."

"Aw hell, amigo, we're just good friends."

Juan took a swallow of his drink, stared at Bonner a moment, then chuckled. "That's 'bout the biggest lie I ever heard outta you, but you go on believin' it's that way if you want."

Jimenez packed his pipe and lit it. "One of two things gonna happen if you keep thinkin' like you're doin'; first, if you don't say somethin' to her right soon, she's gonna say it to you, an' second, y'all don't say nothin' to each other an' she keeps on comin' over here, her pa's gonna shoot hell outta you."

Juan's words caused Trey to pull his brow into sharp creases. He nodded. "Yep, reckon I'm gonna have to do a whole bunch o' thinkin' 'bout what you've said." He stood, knocked back his drink, shrugged, and said, "Let's get to bed. Lot to do tomorrow."

Yadro had given Wells's words about Bonner's quick gun a lot of thought, day and night. Finally, while eating a jerky breakfast, he chewed, swallowed, and pinned Skeeter with a worried look. "We gotta do some plannin' 'bout how we gonna take care o' Bonner."

Wells swallowed the coffee he'd only then sipped. "'Fore you waste a lot o' words, we ain't gonna be able to git 'im from the rimrock. I've watched him study it like a man studyin' a book; by now, he knows every rock, lump o' dirt, cactus, everything along the cap." He shook his head. "We gotta figger somethin' else."

Yadro nodded. "Way I got it figgered. Buckin' 'im in town, stand up an' head-on won't work either if he's as good with that handgun as you say he is."

Wells's face hardened. "He's that good—maybe better."

Yadro pulled his bowie knife and sliced off another slice of jerky, clamped his jaws into it, bit off a bite, chewed, and swallowed. "Skeeter, most people, once they've done somethin', tend to do it the same from then on."

"What you gettin' at?"

"I figger he has to go to town ever so often, an' I figger he's gonna take the same trail to get there. We gonna have to move our camp to some o' them piles o' rock along the trail an' wait for 'im."

Wells nodded, then shook his head. "Sounds good, but if either one o' those men who've settled in with him are with 'im, we better wait for a better time. Don't think we can handle more'n Bonner. 'Sides that, that old man ain't no slouch with a long gun."

"Good. Let's move camp."

About a half hour before sunset Matt Tedford rode to the stable, took care of his horse, and went to the pump to wash up for supper.

When he went into the kitchen from the back door, he looked at Belle. "Maggie come home from takin' care of that nester?"

She glanced at him, pulled a sheet from the oven loaded with crisp, golden biscuits, then turned to face him. "She's in her room. Trey rode home with her to make sure she was safe. We had a nice visit. No disagreeable incidents at all. It was nice."

Matt gave her a hard look. "Don't see why she figures she has to take care o' any hurt stray that comes along. Seen 'er do it with animals, but not human bein's."

He went to the sheet of biscuits, took one off, spread butter on it, took a bite, chewed, swallowed, and shook his head. "If she's looking at 'im like a woman does a man, don't know why she couldn't have picked one with more promise than a damned squatter. She couldn't live in a nester's cabin after the nice home we've given 'er."

Belle wiped her hands on her apron, pulled a chair from the table, and sat. "Matt Tedford, you're talking about something you know nothing about. Why don't you take a day off an' ride over there an' look at the shanty you think she might be unhappy living in, then come back here an' you and I'll continue this discussion. 'Til then I won't discuss it with you anymore."

She stood, checked the water she had boiling for the last ears of autumn corn, poked a fork into the beans boiling next to it, and put the corn in the water. "Go tell Maggie supper's ready."

Juan rode into town about the time Trey had said the noon rush would be over, one-thirty. He shivered from the chill wind, thought to go to the saloon for a stomach-warming drink, but tied his horse in front of the cafe.

When he went through the door into the cafe, Linda's smile warmed him more that a drink of anything would have, and her "Hi, vaquero," made him feel at home—not that he'd ever had a home.

"Hi, pretty senora." He grinned. "Had some business to take care of but couldn't pass up the chance to see you first."

"I'll bet Trey told you the best time to get here so we could visit a while."

He nodded. "You're right. He told me if I wanted to be able to visit that this was the best time to time my gettin' here."

She drew them each a cup of coffee, glanced at him, went to the stove, put a steak on to cook, then sat. "Thought maybe you'd be hungry an' wouldn't have stopped for a noonin' on the way in."

He nodded. "You figured right. I wanted to get here, see you, then go to the land office."

"You thinkin' 'bout filin' on some land?"

It seemed to Juan she sort of held her breath when she asked him that. He nodded. "Yeah. Think if there's anything that ain't taken close to Trey's place I might file for some o' that preemption land."

To his thinking, she let her breath out and seemed to glow. Maybe she wanted him to stay. "I figure I can't keep driftin' over this land forever; gotta tie my horse in one place pretty soon, or I'll find myself an old man still lookin' for the other side o' the hill."

Linda stood, checked his steak, turned it, filled their coffee cups, and sat. She smiled, and not bothering to hide her pleasure at his words, said, "I'm so glad, then I'll have four close friends here. I count Jess as a good friend too."

Juan nodded. "An' you couldn't pick a more steady one

than that old man. Yep, I reckon we'd all be better off with more friends."

They spent a pleasant couple of hours visiting and getting to know each other better. The dances hadn't given them much chance to talk. Juan glanced at the wall clock, pendulum swinging back and forth, and saw it was four o'clock. He stood. "Better get over to the land office if I want to see the agent today."

"You don't, an' you'll have to stay in town 'til tomorrow."

Juan frowned. That might be a good idea. "'Stead o' tryin' to see 'im now, I could get a hotel room, have a couple o' drinks, an' if you'll let me, I can help you around the kitchen for the supper hour. Then after you close we could visit some more."

Her blush made her even more beautiful to Juan's way of thinking. Then so softly he barely heard, she said, "That's a wonderful idea, Juan."

The next morning, Juan ate breakfast, went to the land office, found it not open for business, and sat on the bench in front of the general store to wait. Finally about seven-thirty, Rogers opened the front door.

When Juan went in, feeling grumpy about anyone who started their workday this late, and not liking the musty smell of the office, he said, "Don't keep very early hours, do you?"

Rogers shrugged. "Most of the land around here's already taken. Not much need to open earlier."

"I want to see what's still available."

Rogers spread a map on his desk, looked up, then back at the map. He drew a circle around all the land in the foothills. "All this land's already taken. One man by the name of Bonner insisted on settling in there, but he won't be allowed to stay. Matt Tedford's already ranchin' that land along with a couple other big ranchers."

The longer he talked, the more irritated Juan became. "Well now, senor, just happens I've looked that land over and I have it in mind to file on that parcel that stretches across the canyon next to Bonner. It, like Bonner's, has some pretty good springs on it, provide water for a modest herd. I doubt those *big ranchers* you mentioned own even one acre of the land they're runnin' cows on."

"I will not let you file on that land, mister."

Jimenez's face heated. Hot blood pushed into his head. He clamped his teeth, swallowed, and took a deep breath. "Senor, I ain't asked anyone to let me do anytheeng since my mama used to tell me what I could and what I could not do.

"You get out the papers, fill 'em out properly, put the right parcel number on 'em an' get 'em mailed to Austin on the next stage. *Comprende?*"

"And if I don't?"

"I'll write Austin, ask for a ranger to come investigate your operation here, and try to get you replaced."

"Bonner threatened to do the same thing, mister. It won't work. I have friends in Austin."

"Make out those papers, give 'em to me, an' I'll put 'em on the stage myself."

"I have to mail them, an' I promise you I won't do that."

Juan nodded slowly. He had his temper under control. "Yeah, you'll do it. Bank on it, I'll check to make certain you do. Now get to it. I've wasted as much time messin' with you as I intend to."

Twenty minutes later he walked out the door of Rogers's office. Anger still roiled his gut. He'd thought old RIP had taught him to keep a tight rein on his emotions better. But only a few moments ago he'd found RIP had not made much progress in that direction.

He took a deep breath, and even with the dusty, dried on the stem smell of grass, he felt better. He'd been itching for a fight. He knew he'd only now gone round one. From what Trey had told him about Rogers he figured the fight had only started. The thought made him feel good. He'd been wondering who might be paying Yadro to take out the settlers. Now he had a good idea who. He'd have to see what Bonner thought.

Matt Tedford saddled his horse, thinking to help the hands work cattle. Finished with saddling, he toed the stirrup, sat there a moment, then changed his mind.

Belle had suggested that he take a look at the "shanty" Bonner had thrown together to keep rain, snow, and cold away. Now he intended to do that.

He told Ramey he'd not be riding with him, that he had something else he wanted to get done. He reined his horse to the south. He'd not been on that part of his range in quite a spell.

While riding, he looked with approval at the sleek sides of his cattle. He nodded to himself; they had plenty of tallow on their bones to carry them through the winter, and the heifers, many of them, were heavy with calves. They should bring in a good crop before Christmas.

He studied the ground a few moments. Crushed grass and sometimes kicked-up earth showed a faint trail. Neither he nor any of his hands had been riding this way since spring roundup. The only one with business over this way was Maggie. Anger pushed into his throat.

The longer he thought of Maggie being interested in the squatter, the grumpier he got. He looked on Bonner as nothing more than a sodbuster, or maybe a two by twice ragtag rancher who might run a few cows of his own and steal enough Box T cattle to keep him in food and clothes.

He followed the dim trail Maggie seemed to be in the process of establishing until it joined the one that led into town. He'd ridden it only a couple of hundred yards when, from a pile of boulders alongside the hill he rode on, he caught the glint of sunlight reflected from metal. A rifle barrel maybe? He swung his horse downhill to stay out of rifle range.

He frowned. Bonner wouldn't be sitting up there. Matt could think of no reason why the man would be there when his shanty was only a few miles farther.

According to Maggie, whoever had shot the sodbuster had ranged up above Bonner's place, along the rimrock, to take his shots. Matt pondered that a while. He couldn't think of anyone who would benefit from the man's death, except he himself. Then he thought of Yadro. He knew that Whitey had been attacking the settlers, and it was whispered he was also the one who'd burned several of them out—or caused them to disappear—but he'd heard the slim gunman had left the country. Had he?

Tedford urged his horse on to the top of the next hill. He looked down on the mouth of the canyon he understood Bonner had filed on. Close to the stream, a large, comfortable stone house stood. A house larger than his own, and from what he could determine from where he sat his saddle, its construction was solid, well done. He couldn't help thinking, almost admiringly, the boy had come to stay. That place, if it was Bonner's, was meant to house a family. Again anger pushed into his throat. Bonner and Maggie's family? He didn't want to think about the answer to that.

Dawg stood, ears peaked, and growled deep in his throat. His shoulder hair stood straight up. Trey frowned, glanced from the dog, looked in the direction Dawg's head pointed, then pulled his Winchester from the rack by the door. He walked outside, looked up the hill, squinted to shut out some of the glare, and looked at a man alongside the hill. He studied him a moment. Looked like Matt Tedford. He cradled his rifle in the crook of his left arm and waved to the man to come on down.

For a moment, it looked like Tedford reined his horse to go back up the hill and leave. Then he pulled his reins to the left and came toward Trey.

When within earshot, Bonner yelled, "Come on in, step down, rest your saddle. 'Bout to fix my noonin'."

He waited until Tedford got closer, then said, "You don't like me. I don't particularly give a damn 'bout you either, but no need to leave here hungry. Come on in."

Tedford stepped from the saddle and went through the door Trey held open for him. Once inside he stopped as though hit in the gut. He swung his massive head to look at Bonner. "Don't reckon you're what I been figurin'."

"Yeah? An' what you been figurin'?"

Matt grunted, then pinned Trey with a piercing look. "If I told you that, you'd give even less of a damn 'bout me." He glanced around the room. "Never knew you could buy furniture of this quality anywhere closer than New Orleans. It's mighty pretty." He stood there a moment. "Where's the kitchen? Help you fix our noonin'."

They went to the kitchen where Tedford showed as much appreciation for it and its trappings as he had the family room. "Well, while you're in a mood to look, I'll show you the rest of the house. Don't reckon we have to be friends for you to see how I live. Know you must've ridden over here to see what kind o' shack I might've built."

Tedford smiled. "You got me there, boy. I did in fact want to see what kind o' place you might've put up." He shook his head. "Gotta say, I'm surprised." Again, he admired the furnishings as much as the house. "How the hell you get it hauled in here without wreckin' it?"

"Didn't haul it. Jess—he'll be here shortly to eat—Jess made every stick of it. He's right handy."

"I should smile. Don't reckon I've ever seen any finer, anywhere."

They talked through their nooning, and although not a visit of camaraderie, their conversation was one of guarded enmity, one in which each was careful to stay away from subjects that would cause rancor. Matt and Jess seemed to take a liking to each other right off.

When Tedford toed the stirrup to leave, Bonner gave him a cold smile. "Next time you ride this way, you'll see more indication I came to stay. Gonna build Jess his own house here next to mine, an' I figure to have stone stables too." Then he made a pointed statement to see Tedford's reaction. "Need to go to San Tone, buy a few head o' cattle, but not gonna leave here 'til I kill whoever it is tryin' to kill me. Then I'll go."

Tedford frowned. "Somebody gunnin' for you, boy? Somebody other than the one who shot you a few weeks ago? Maggie told me all about that shootin'." This was the first time Maggie's name had been mentioned.

Trey nodded. "Two, don't know who either of them are—but I'll find out, and then they better fish or cut bait 'cause I'm comin' after 'em." He thought to thank Tedford for all the help Maggie had been, but decided to drop the subject.

Then just as Matt reined to head home, Bonner hit him

with the barb that had been stuck in his throat. "Don't know who shot me, but I figure it was that rider o' yours, Whitey Yadro. I get better proof, he's a dead man."

From his saddle, Tedford looked down at Bonner. "Be good riddance." He shook his head. "But you're wrong; Yadro doesn't ride for me, hasn't for several weeks now. Fact is he never rode *for* me an' I won't discuss how he came to be on my place." He kneed his horse to ride home.

Trey stood there and watched the rancher until he disappeared over the brow of the hill. Tedford's words backed up the opinion Linda had voiced when he first came into this country. If Yadro didn't, and hadn't, ever drawn pay from Tedford, where did he fit into the picture? He pondered that a few minutes, then went in the house to dry the dishes left from their nooning.

Through the kitchen window, Belle watched the crew ride in. She searched them for a sight of Matt. He wasn't among them. Her breath quickened. Where was he? He usually worked right along with them. She went out and cornered Ramey. "Slim, didn't Matt ride with you today?"

Ramey shook his head. "Said he had somethin' else he had to do. He rode toward the hills. He should oughtta be home soon though. Reckon he wanted to take a look at them cows we got grazin' to the south o' here. I seen 'em the other day. They're fat an' sleek as any man could want."

She nodded and went back inside. Slim might think her husband had gone to check on the shape of his cattle, but Belle had an idea he had done exactly as he had done. He'd gone to see what kind of place Trey Bonner had. She smiled to herself. If the man had put up a soddy, and Maggie loved him, it wouldn't deter her one ounce. She remembered when she and Matt had decided to come West—she would have come with him regardless what he intended. She went ahead with preparing supper. It would be ready when he got home.

Maggie came into the kitchen and without being told what needed doing set about helping her mother. "Didn't see Papa when the crew rode in; he gone to town?"

Belle smiled and shook her head. "Nope. Think he rode over to see what kind of place Trey's building. Hope they don't have a squabble if they meet up over there."

Maggie looked her mother in the eye. "Trey's a gentleman. He won't argue with Papa. Especially if Papa is invited into his home." She cocked her head. "Reckon that's Papa now. Sounds like a single horse." She smiled. "Papa's gonna be mighty surprised to see the shanty Trey's built for himself. Be nice to see 'im eat crow."

When Matt came in, as always, he went straight to Belle, gave her a hug and a kiss, and as always, she told him to wash up before hugging her—but she didn't try to break free of his arms.

"Slim said you'd gone out alone to take a look at the cattle down south of here."

Matt cast her a sheepish look. His face reddened. "Aw hell, Belle, you know why I rode out that way."

"Well, what do think?"

He cleared his throat, grimaced, and shook his head. "Hell. I reckon that boy's come to stay." His face brightened. "An' honey, you should see the furniture in his home, an' I do mean a home. He has nothing to apologize for."

Maggie snorted. "I can't see Trey apologizing even if he'd thrown up a soddy, but I believe, Papa, the home he's built far outshines any ranch house in this country."

"You want me to grovel, Mag, reckon you have good grounds for it. Tellin' your ma only a minute ago, that boy's come to stay." Then as though reluctant to say it he pushed it between his lips, which looked stiff as leather. "Reckon any girl would be proud to call it home."

Maggie knew his words came hard, but she also knew he had partially accepted the fact that he might lose his daughter to Bonner. Now if only Trey would think the same way.

9

TREY AGAIN LOOKED out the window for signs of Jimenez. Still nothing. He frowned. Hell, his ranger partner wouldn't stay in town this long unless he'd run into trouble. He shrugged; Juan could take care of himself. Then he shook his head, strapped on his gunbelt, pulled his rifle from the rack, went in the kitchen, and told Jess he worried about Juan and was going to town to make sure he was all right. "You feel all right about holdin' down the fort alone?"

"Aw, Trey, with Dawg here to tell me somebody's comin' an' from what direction, I ain't got a worry in the world. Go find that boy an' bring 'im home. Me, Dawg, an' my old Sharps'll keep everthin' all right here."

Trey smiled to himself. "That boy," as Jess called him, could outfight, outshoot, and raise more hell than a whole company of rangers. He went outside to saddle up. Then when he rode out of the yard, he shouted to Jess, "Might stay in town tonight. Depends on what Juan's up to." Jess only waved.

As soon as he left his ranch yard, Bonner tuned every sense to his surroundings. Getting shot was one thing, but taking a slug due to carelessness was a thing for which he would not take blame.

A few miles out, he again swept every crease in the land, then he homed in on the pile of boulders alongside the trail. He frowned. He'd passed that pile of rocks every time he went to town; why did he now feel edgy about riding close to them? Heck, since getting shot he jumped at shadows.

He urged his horse ahead, squinted at the boulders, shook his head, and reined to ride around them outside of rifle range. His horse had heeded the pressure on his neck only a step or two when a spray of dust kicked up in front of him, and then he heard the sharp crack of a rifle shot.

Bonner dug heels into the sides of his pony, laid low along the neck of the horse, and pulled rein about twenty yards out of range. He left the saddle on the run, drew his Winchester from the saddle scabbard when he left his pony, and threw himself flat behind the lip of the swale he found himself in. He gulped air. His guts twisted and turned. Soon his breathing slowed and he put his mind to wondering from whom the shot might have come. He would have bet Yadro was on the other end of that bullet. He might have to kill the white-haired gunman before he found out who had him on his payroll. Since his visit with Maggie's father, he was less sure that Matt Tedford was the kind of man who would pay someone else to do his shooting.

Then he thought of the bushwhacker who'd been shooting at him from the rimrock. He mulled the two men over in his mind, Yadro and the bushwhacker, then settled on Yadro. The rimrock shooter had stayed up above him thus far with an easy escape route and wasn't likely to change.

He lay there ten or fifteen minutes waiting for another shot. None came. He wriggled his way toward the rocks, hoping to get in range without taking a bullet. He held to the circle of the swale's lip until he figured he could pour lead into the boulders. Maybe rock chips would spray the gunman. He figured there to be but one man against him.

He blew through his nose to rid himself of the dusty smell raised from the dried grass. Maybe there would be a telltale odor; maybe the shooter had coffee boiling. He quit trying to guess what might tell him more about his attacker and inched closer. Finally, as close as he felt comfortable, along with staying out of sight, he studied the pile of rocks.

After a few minutes he spotted what he wanted. A space between boulders, low to the ground, and another about shoulder level to a tall man. He took careful aim at the upper opening, squeezed off a shot, jacked a shell into his rifle and put another through the same opening, then shifted his aim at the lower one. Two more shots left his rifle.

Cursing and shots came at him. Good, he'd stirred up his assailant. He squeezed off another two shots into the upper opening. More cursing, then the sound of running horses—at least it sounded like more than one horse. It could be a trick.

He lay still, expecting more lead to be thrown his way. He stayed where he was another fifteen minutes, then slithered back to where he'd ground reined his horse. He thought to try to catch the drygulcher, then realized that his chance of catching him was slimmer than slim.

Now almost certain whoever had been in the rocks was long gone, he rode to them, his gut muscles tight as a bowstring, braced against the possibility of a point-blank shot. None came.

He rode into the opening and, staying in the saddle, checked the kind of camp the man had set up. The smell of coffee wafted from the steaming ground where the gunman had dumped the pot of Arbuckles' before grabbing up his belongings and heading out.

Bonner took several minutes to examine the camp. He determined that two men had occupied the space and that they had been there more than a couple of days. Had Yadro taken on a partner?

He left the pile of boulders and, riding carefully, studied the ground, then nodded. Two men rode fast, side by side. After another few minutes he convinced himself the two headed for town.

He pulled rein and sat there a few moments, then nodded. If they headed for town they could stop anywhere along the

way to take another shot at him. He pulled his horse off the
trail, then after getting far enough to the side of it so as to be
out of rifle range, he again headed for town.

He rode slowly. He wondered if Yadro, if it was him, would
stay in town or ride out again. He shook his head. It made no
difference. He didn't intend to call him out anyway, not until
he found who he worked for.

Then, Bonner wondered, if he could get the rifleman alone,
could he sweat the information out of him?

Skeeter Wells and Yadro rode from the rocks like the devil had
scooted up behind their saddles. Whitey wiped blood from his
face. Blood had flowed freely when rock fragments peppered
his face; now only a thin trickle oozed from each small hole.
"Damned lucky none o' them slivers caught my eyes. Woulda
blinded me for sure."

"Way those bullets ricocheted around inside them rocks we
both lucky one o' 'em didn't catch us dead center."

Yadro glanced at Wells across his shoulder. "I'm gonna
shoot 'im somehow, an' when I get 'im on the ground, gonna
make 'im pay for this. Gonna git 'im good."

Wells grunted. "You better hope when you walk up to 'im
he ain't breathin' no more. Like I told you, he's one damn
salty gent." He nodded in the direction of town. "We gonna
get to town right sudden. You gonna stay in there where you
can be seen with your face bleedin' like it is?"

Whitey nodded. "Don't see why not, ain't nobody in there
knows how I got hurt."

Wells shot him a cold, disgusted look. His mouth pulled
down at one corner. "It ever enter that stupid head o' yours
that Bonner was headed for town, that he's gonna be there
soon after us, that when he sees you he's gonna know exactly
how you got that peppered-up face, and then he might take it
onto himself to see if you can shoot a man while facin' him?
He did exactly what he tried to do when he put that shot
'tween them rocks."

"What you figger I oughtta do then?"

Wells's brow creased, he squinted toward the horizon a

moment, then turned his gaze back to Yandro. "Wuz I you, I'd git us a room at the hotel. You stay in it an' I'll git us a bottle at the saloon, an' we'll stay in that room 'til I'm sure Bonner's gone back to his place."

Whitey frowned. "How you figger to jest roam 'round town? He's gonna see you easy as he could see me."

Wells smiled a cold smile, none of it reaching his eyes. "Bonner don't know me; he knows you. Helluva big difference."

Yadro shook his head. "Don't know now how we gonna get 'im under our guns. He's right cagey."

The bushwhacker stared at the gray, unpainted buildings ahead. "I don't know either, but gotta think on it awhile. I'll think of a way."

Bonner kept the town on his right shoulder until he'd circled it far enough to come into it from the north, then he rode to the back of Linda's Cafe, knocked on the door, and without waiting for her to answer, opened the door and went in.

The supper crowd jammed the place. Noise buffeted the walls. Linda couldn't have heard him if he'd tried to break the door down.

The first person his eyes locked on was his ranger partner. Jimenez scooted over to make room on the bench next to him. "Didn't know you figured on comin' to town."

Bonner gave him a sour look. "Didn't 'til you decided to spend the rest o' your life in here." His look changed to one of chagrin, eyebrows raised, the corners of his lips tight. He shrugged. "Hell, partner, I got worried 'bout what you might've got into here in town. Thought I'd ride in an' check on you."

"Anything happen out our way since I been gone?"

Bonner chuckled. "Not 'til I took it in mind to ride in here. Couple gents decided to bushwhack me." He shook his head. "Don't know why but I decided to skirt that pile o' boulders closest to the house. Soon's I turned off the trail they took a shot at me. I caused 'em to dust outta there. They headed toward town. You see Yadro an' another of his kind ride in together?"

Jimenez shook his head. "Ain't noticed, ain't been lookin'. After supper I'll wander over to the saloon. Might be I'll see Yadro there with somebody else."

Bonner grinned. "Good. I'll keep Linda company while you're gone."

"I ain't worried. I seen Maggie an' her ma an' pa ride in a few minutes ago. Figure Mag can keep *you* occupied."

"Aw hell, Juan, you know Mag an' me are just good friends."

Jimenez chuckled. "Whooee, ain't you gonna be surprised when you wake up some mornin' an' realize how strong that friendship is, along with the man-woman feelin's you got goin'—even if you don't know it yet."

"Aw hell."

Maggie followed her parents into the hotel lobby, but just before stepping through the door, she saw Juan come from the cafe. Her heart swelled such as to shorten her breath. She wondered if Trey had come in with him.

In the room her father had rented for her, she dumped her bag on the bed, stuck her head in the door to her parent's room, and told them she was going to the cafe and wanted to see Linda.

She felt no guilt about the little white lie; she did want to see her friend, but that could have waited until she and her parents crossed the trail for supper.

She couldn't wait to see if Trey was there. She hadn't seen him since her father rode back from his snooping trip out to Bonner's place. And to her thinking, his attitude about the cowboy had changed. She wanted to see them in the same room, see if there was any semblance of softening between them. Trey was just as hardheaded as her father.

As soon as she stepped through the door, she saw Linda leaning over a table to take an order. Then her gaze swept the room. It seemed that each time she came to town, it and the surrounding area gained more people.

Then she spotted Trey. He sat, his back to the wall, his eyes studying each person in the room. He lifted his eyes to look straight into hers. "Howdy, Mag. Juan said he saw you an' your folks go in the hotel. What brought you to town?"

"Needed flour, bacon, an' a bunch of stuff to keep us eatin' good. What you doin' in town?"

Trey chuckled. "Came in to check on Jimenez. He came in a couple days ago, supposed to have been back at my place before now. Figured I'd better see if he'd gotten into any trouble here in town." He frowned. "Never thought to ask, but ain't this town got any sort o' name?"

Maggie grinned. "You mean you don't know?" Then without giving him a chance to answer, she poured them each a cup of coffee, came back, and sat next to him. "Tell you, in answer to your question, the first people here when asked that question answered, 'no name.'" She chuckled. "People started callin' it No Name, then when more people came in they, an' the post office, shortened it to one word, Noname, only they pronounce it Non-a-me." She took a swallow of coffee. "Reckon that came about when they read it."

Trey slowly shook his head, then frowned. "Towns sure get their names in strange ways; towns like Gun Barrel City, Mule Shoe, an' other places here in Texas. Figure other states got places like that too."

She took a deep breath of the spicy aroma coming from the kitchen. It reminded her how hungry she was after the short ride from the ranch. She changed the subject, wanting to see how Trey responded. "Hear you had a visitor the other day."

He nodded. "Yep. Your pa came to see me. Ain't made up my mind why, but I think he wanted to see whether I'd put up a shack on land I figure he still thinks of as his."

"Back off, Trey; if he makes a friendly move, why don't you take it at face value?"

He grimaced. "I've made that mistake before a few times. Now I figure to wait a while an' see if they really mean it."

She snorted. "Men! Every danged one of you are like a mule. Takes someone to hit you in the head with a heavy board to get your attention."

He laughed, took a swallow of coffee, and nodded. "Reckon you're right." He glanced at the door. "Your folks just came in. Want 'em to sit with us?"

Maggie frowned. "Thought I'd get a chance to visit with you, but yeah, let's slide over; make room for 'em."

Trey seated Belle. Matt seemed a little reluctant to sit, then apparently thought it would be rude if he took a seat someplace else.

While eating, they visited. After the crowd thinned, Linda sat with them. To Maggie's way of thinking, a stiffness dampened the words between her father and Trey. She shrugged mentally. Heck, give 'em a chance to get to know each other. She thought when the ice melted they might grow to be friends, but right now she'd take what she could get.

When her folks left, Maggie told them she'd stay and help Linda clean up before she closed. Linda and Belle gave her a smug look, almost as to say, "Yeah, we know you're staying to spend time with Trey." They didn't put their thoughts into words; they didn't have to, since their looks were enough to cause her face to turn hot with the blood that rushed to it bringing a rosy blush.

Bonner didn't know what brought the blush to her face but she sure was pretty when she looked that way.

He visited until Juan came to the door, caught his eye, and leaned his head toward the hotel. Trey stood, asked the girls if he and Juan could come visit after Linda closed for the day. Getting their approval, he went to see what Jimenez had found out.

They met in the middle of the street. "You got a room at the hotel?"

Juan nodded. Trey frowned and said, "Think I'll stay in the livery tonight. Ain't sharin' a room an' bed with you, an' danged sure ain't payin' fifty cents for a room to sleep one night in. Let's go down there an' talk. You act like you've found out who Yadro works for."

They talked while they walked toward the stable. Juan shook his head. "Don't know for sure, but I theenk I'm 'bout to decide who it is. An' I tell you right now, it ain't Mag's pa."

"I decided the same thing. I figure if Matt had somebody

who was steppin' on 'is toes, he'd take the fight to 'em without bringin' in a gunny."

Juan grinned. "Nope. Matt's figurin' you're tryin' to take more than his land from 'im. He ain't accepted that idea yet."

Trey thought about what Juan said, then frowned. Hell, seemed like everybody he knew in this town was trying to push Maggie and him together. His frown deepened. He thought of the time he'd put a barrier up between the two of them, wanting to make sure he didn't cause either of them to mistake physical longing for much more.

They walked into the livery, out of the chill wind. Bonner glanced at Jimenez. "You got somebody else in mind who might be runnin' settlers out o' here?"

Juan nodded and shrugged. "Yeah, I got a thought on it, but I ain't sure yet. Let me tell you what I done, an' what kind o' reaction I got."

When they had climbed to the hayloft, they pulled over a couple bales of hay to sit on and settled on them comfortably. Bonner pulled his empty pipe from his pocket, sucked on it a couple of times, then put it back in his pocket.

Juan grunted, "Was wonderin' if you'd lost your mind gettin' ready to smoke here where everything is burnable."

"Nope. Just wishin' we'd picked a different place for you to bring me up-to-date."

Jimenez nodded, then told him about his filing on land next to Trey's and the reaction he got from Rogers.

Bonner smiled. "Don't know what you got in mind, but you couldn't have told me anything that makes me any happier." He sat back and shook his head. "So I'm gonna have to put up with you for the rest o' my life?"

"Looks like it. RIP's gonna have a conniption fit when we tell 'im."

Trey grinned and shook his head. "Think you're wrong. He'll be happy for us. Hell, it'll be like two of his own children settling down. But sounds like you're figurin' Rogers has somethin' to do with runnin' the settlers outta here?"

Juan nodded. "Yeah, but we gotta get a lot more evidence before we go about tryin' to pin killin's an' burnin's on 'im."

He looked into his friend's eyes. "You ever took the time to go to those cabin sites and rake through the ashes?"

Bonner shook his head. "Nope. But I'm tellin' you right now, you laid out what I'm gonna be busy doin' the next few days. It'd be good to have you with me, but after what happened to me today—or almost happened, I b'lieve one o' us oughtta stay right close to Jess. Hate like hell for 'im to get hurt on our account."

Juan nodded. "We'll play the hand that way, then when you get back, I'll go do the same thing, then we'll put our thoughts together an' see what we come up with."

"Sounds good."

A couple hundred yards down the street, in their hotel room, Wells poured two drinks and handed one to Yadro. "You think o' any way we gonna take care of Bonner while I was gone?"

"Got an idear. Think maybe we need some help; think I should oughtta send for a couple o' my friends."

"You got enough money to pay 'em when they git here? They ain't gonna come less'n they's somethin' in it for them."

Whitey grimaced, took a swallow of the raw whisky, coughed, and shook his head. "Geez, I never thought o' that." He took another swallow of his drink. "Reckon I might get some o' my kinfolks to come—we sortta come runnin' when one o' us is in trouble. I got a couple o' cousins I figger will come if I tell 'em they's free land out here. They'd probably come anyway if they knew trouble wuz camped on my doorstep."

Wells stared at the man he had picked to help him kill the ranger, the man he'd pulled out of a bottle thinking he might help. "Know what, Whitey? You're so damned dumb it amazes me that you ever got anybody to follow you in any kind o' game; fact is it makes me wonder how the hell you lived this long. Looks like somebody would've killed you jest fer bein' so stupid."

"Why you always puttin' me down in the dirt, Skeeter?

Know I ain't real smart, but I got enough sense to figure what we can get outta this."

That got Wells's attention. If there was more in it for him, other than the satisfaction of killing the ranger, he'd take whatever he could get. "Yeah, what you got figured?"

"Land, lots of land."

"Where's all this land you gonna get?"

"Right here, right down by them hills where Bonner's done built hisself a place."

The wind went out of Wells. He shook his head. "Gonna tell you somethin', Whitey, I won't stay in this godforsaken country any longer'n it take me to saddle up after we kill Bonner. I'm gonna go back to where they's people, women, good whisky. I got a farm what'd fit exactly where I'm goin'. Nope. Soon's I see the ran . . . , er, see Bonner in the ground I'm cuttin' out." He took another swallow of the rotgut, shivered, and pinned Yadro with a look that he intended to drive right through him. "Know what, Whitey? You git them kinfolk o' yores out here, show 'em the land you're talkin' 'bout, an' *they'll* blow your damned head off."

Yadro stood, poured each of them another drink, then sat on the edge of the bed. When Wells returned from the saloon with the whisky, he'd told Whitey to move to the bed. He took the only chair in the room.

"Why you hate Bonner so much, Skeeter?"

Wells stared at Whitey a long moment, then shook his head. "Ain't none o' yore damned business. You jest better figger how lucky you are that I'm sidin' you in this."

Yadro's eyes took on a hot, red look. Anger. Skeeter took some degree of satisfaction in antagonizing the cheap gunman. When he'd sobered him up, he'd hoped for more help in getting Bonner, but with every moment he spent with the dumb bastard, he took on more doubt as to whether Whitey would ever be any help. He sighed. Hell, he would use him as long as he could do anything that might be of use, then he'd get rid of him.

He stood. "Gonna leave you the bottle. I'm goin' back to

the saloon. If Bonner's there, he might say somethin' that'll tell me where he's gonna be the next few days." He knocked back the rest of his drink, coughed, and continued, "He lets it out where he's gonna be, it'll save us a lot o' time huntin' 'im."

"Wish I could go with you."

"Sure. Come on, but don't act like you know me. That way, if Bonner's there, when he kills you I won't have to take a hand in the gunfight he's gonna push on you."

Yadro settled back on the bed. "Reckon I'll stay here."

Wells headed for the saloon.

Trey and Juan spent another half hour in the stable trying to figure whether their suspicions were reasonable and finally decided they would have to do more searching for hard evidence.

Trey stood, swept his hand across the seat of his jeans to rid himself of any clinging hay, glanced at the door through which bales were swung into the loft, and saw that darkness had settled on the land. "You goin' back to Linda's?"

Juan nodded. "Maggie gonna be there?"

"Yeah. Figure she an' Linda gonna spend as much time together as they can. They don't get to see much of each other."

Jimenez chuckled. "So you figure they'll be glad for us to use up some o' their visitin' time?"

"Why, hell, we're their friends too." He nodded. "Yeah. They'll be glad for us to be there."

When the two rangers got to the cafe, the girls had finished cleaning up from the day's business. Linda opened the door at their knock. "Thought it might be you. What kept you so long?"

Trey looked at Juan and grinned. "See there, told you they wouldn't figure we were hornin' in on their visit time."

Linda frowned and cast a questioning look at Jimenez. "What's he talkin' about?"

"Aw, we were just wonderin' if we oughtta come over an' crowd in on your visitin'."

"Well, you dang sure have better come over." Maggie's face flamed. "Oh heck. What I mean is, we're all friends; the two o' you are always welcome."

Bonner nodded. "Just what I told Juan." The two girls looked at each other, and their expressions were of pure joy.

They talked long into the night, then when Maggie stood, saying she better get back to the hotel, Trey stood, took her arm, and looked at Juan. "See you here for breakfast 'bout six. All right?"

Jimenez nodded.

Bonner walked Maggie to the door to her room. She turned to face him when he told her good night. She was much too close for his comfort. Her breasts brushed his arm when she turned. Her face raised to look into his eyes. Her lips slightly parted. She ran her tongue over them. Her eyes wide, her breath came in short little gasps. An expectant, hopeful look pulled him toward her, then without thinking, only feeling, he pulled her into his arms. His world centered in the sweet nectar of her lips.

After what seemed only moments he relaxed his arms and stepped away. "Shouldn't have done that, Mag."

"You sayin' you're sorry?"

He shook his head. "No, ma'am, can't say I am. What I am sayin' is, I'm mighty glad your folks are right next door."

"Trey, if they'd been standin' right here with us an' you hadn't pulled me into your arms"—she chuckled—"I b'lieve I'd have pulled you into mine. I been wantin' that kiss a mighty long time."

"Mag, I gotta tell ya, I been wantin' the same thing, but I ain't let it happen."

"Why?"

He frowned. "Well, I been studyin' on that. Ain't figured out whether it's 'cause we want each other—you know, like a man an' woman—or whether there's more to our feelin's. Wantta make danged sure o' that, then we gotta talk a whole lot more."

She grinned, then a laugh came from deep in her chest. "You kiss me like that and we won't need to talk." She placed the palms of her hands flat against his chest. "Now you go away. See you an' Juan in the mornin' for breakfast." She twisted to open her door then turned back to him. "Oh yes, an' you do a lot more thinkin' 'bout why we wanted that kiss." She chuckled, opened the door, and disappeared inside.

She'd not started getting ready for bed when a light tapping on her door broke into her thoughts about what had happened only a few moments ago. She opened the door. Her mother ducked into the room while Maggie closed and locked the door.

"Couldn't you sleep, Mama?"

"Was asleep. Something woke me. I lay there a while, couldn't get back to sleep, then I heard you and Trey walk to your door." She smiled. "Guessing how you feel about him, I was terrified you'd invite him in, then goodness knows what might've happened."

Maggie walked to the edge of the bed and sat. "Mama, if Trey was as good at guessing how I feel as you are, there's no doubt it would've happened." She shook her head in wonder. "He kissed me, an' I was mush in his hands." She shrugged. "Even now, I sit here wishing he wasn't so danged honorable; said we both needed to do some thinkin' 'bout how much we really *felt* 'bout each other, not just the hurtin' an' wantin' a kiss brought on." She nodded. "Reckon he's right, but I already know the answer 'bout me. I knew it soon after I met 'im."

Belle, still standing inside the door, went to her daughter and squeezed her shoulder. "Yeah, an' I think that's why your father takes such a hard edge toward the boy." She nodded. "Let things happen in their own time."

"All right, Mama, but seems like Trey's time an' my time're set on different clocks."

Belle stepped toward the door. "Now you go on to bed, daylight'll be here before you know it."

Lying on a pile of hay only a couple hundred yards down the street, sleep came slowly to Trey. He thought about Maggie, wondered why they had such strong feelings for each other, and knew the answer while he pondered the problem.

The fact was, he had known how he felt about her since soon after their first meeting, but he had a job to complete and a gun could put an end to his dreams. He pushed a little more hay under his blanket and went to sleep.

* * *

Dawg pushed himself to his feet from the comfortable place in front of the fire, the place he'd chosen to be his. He stretched, his stomach almost touching the floor. He straightened and went to the door, tail wagging.

When the dog stood, Jess reached for his .50-caliber Sharps, then put it back in the rack when Dawg's tail wagged. He glanced out the window toward the trail and in the distance saw one rider approaching. He soon recognized Juan and wondered why Trey wasn't with him. He asked that question as soon as the slim Mexican got in hearing distance.

"Tell you what he's doin' soon's I take care o' my horse."

Jess went back to the kitchen where he'd been preparing their nooning.

When Jimenez came through the door he told Maynard that Bonner might be gone a couple of days, that he'd check out the cabin sites of each of the settlers before coming home.

"Considerin' how much he's been shot at, don't you reckon you shoulda gone with 'im?"

Juan chuckled. "Know what, old-timer? We spend more time worryin' 'bout each other than a heifer worries 'bout her newborn calf." He shrugged. "If I'd have figured Trey needed me along, figured he couldn't take care of himself, you know I'd be right there with 'im."

Jess frowned, then obviously accepting what Juan had said, he nodded. "Reckon you're right."

"You know danged well I'm right; 'sides that, he worried 'bout you an' insisted that I come see if you were all right."

Jess laughed. "Danged if we ain't mighty good friends. C'mon, set up to the table, I done got our noonin' 'bout ready."

Trey rode about a mile out the trail with Juan when they left town that morning, then he branched off toward the cabin site of the homestead nearest his home, the one Jimenez had filed on only a couple of days before.

He had no idea what he expected to find, other than a pile of cold ashes, but he wanted to put his mind to rest that Yadro hadn't left some clue as to what had happened to the man who'd built his home there.

After about an hour, his back muscles tightened enough to cause an uncomfortable feeling bordering on pain. He knew the feeling well. He slipped his Winchester from the saddle scabbard and rested it across the pommel. The easy, relaxed ride had ended.

With every step of his horse, Bonner's eyes shifted from one big yucca to another, from it to the brow of a land swell, from there to the edges of dry washes.

Abruptly, he reined his horse to the east. In the past, such a maneuver had caused whoever shadowed him to change his position enough for him to discern movement. It didn't work.

Then he checked his back trail. He still saw nothing he could identify as approaching danger—but now his senses honed to extra sharpness. They took in all in front of and behind him.

Another couple of hours and the blackened skeleton of the cabin stood before him. He stepped from the saddle, still clutching his rifle.

Only a couple of steps toward the charred ruin and dust jumped in a fine spray in front of him. The bullet whined off into the distance.

Bonner, his guts churning, dived for what was left of the door frame, hit the ground, and rolled into the ashes of the front room of what had been a two-room shack. He searched in the direction from which the shot had come. He didn't see anyone. He hadn't expected to.

He lay there a few minutes, the smoky stench of burned wood and ashes assailing his nostrils. The burned-out fire had been rained on and left nothing but the unpleasant odors. He picked up a short length of wood, maybe three feet long, and tossed it through the door opening. Two bullets hit it before it hit the ground, the sharp, cracking report of the shots closely followed the erratic movement of the board when the bullets changed its course.

Bonner pursed his lips and blew a silent whistle. Whoever

had fired those shots was one damned good rifleman—fast, accurate, and had obviously moved closer for a better shot. Trey, judging by those last shots, thanked God the shooter hadn't bothered to get closer before he fired the first shot.

Without moving anything but his eyes, he searched all that he could see, looking for better cover. Then he glanced at the short shadows. Only a short time past high noon. Damn! If that gunman had it in mind to keep him pinned down, he could only look forward to a long, cold stay here in these burned-out boards and ashes.

He tried to estimate from where the shots had come. No luck. There were a hundred places out there that could hide a gunman, all within rifle range.

Who would be hunting him? He thought of Yadro, then discarded the thought. *The shooter from the rimrock!* He had to be the one—but why, and who was he?

While pondering that question, and despite the chill in the air, he sweated. It soaked his shirt, cooled and chilled him to the bone, then more sweat flowed to do it all over again.

His eyes swept across his horse, standing with head drooping, looking to be asleep. The thought ran a shiver up Bonner's spine. Asleep. If it entered the rifleman's head, and being a bushwhacker, Trey had no doubt the man would kill his horse.

No one would deliberately shoot a horse, but a man so devoid of common decency as to shoot from ambush would take any advantage he could think of. Bonner sweated harder, then blood pushed up behind his eyes. Anger pushed at his brain so hard he thought to climb to his feet and charge where he thought the rifleman to be.

He sucked in a deep breath, then another, and pushed anger to the back of his mind. You lose your head, Bonner, an' your horse won't be the only thing to die. Settle down, he thought.

Hoping to draw fire from the shooter, he jacked a shell into the magazine and fired, then did it again. The ambusher bit on his ploy. Shots slammed into the charred wood above his head.

He rolled to lie behind the part of the wall that appeared to be less damaged than the rest. Bullets kicked a spray of ashes into his face, but he made it without feeling the slam of a shot into his body. Two of the boards close to the ground had burned so as to leave a crack between them. He glued his eyes to the crack, studied everything close to from where the shots had come.

Hour after hour, he lay there. The sun sank toward the horizon. The chill deepened. He shivered.

10

EVERY FEW MINUTES Trey tensed the muscles in his legs, back, chest, and arms, hoping to take some of the stiffness from them, and if lucky, some of the cold. His horse still stood ground reined. The lower the sun sank, the higher Bonner's hopes rose that his attacker would not shoot the proud animal.

He had not fired a shot in a couple of hours, hoping the bushwhacker would think he'd hit or killed him. Hoping the man would get careless and walk in on him. That didn't happen.

He again cast an eye toward the sun. Only half of the blood red orb stood above the hill to his west. His hopes raised. Soon it would be dark. Then maybe he could make a break for it.

His only escape route lay in back of the cabin, and in that direction he'd have to go into the canyon behind the walls. Right now, he'd welcome any route that offered protection. His horse still stood there, hipshot, standing on three legs.

Bonner figured he could escape on foot, but that didn't make him feel any better. There might not be water in the canyon, he wouldn't have supplies—they were tied to his saddle—and he'd be afoot miles from his place. Even though no one could see him he shook his head. He decided that when he left here it would be sitting atop his horse.

Another half hour and the soft pastel shades of the evening sky faded to a velvety blackness. He eased to his feet, careful to make no noise. The bushwhacker knew where he went to ground. Any sound would draw shots. He thought about where his horse stood and decided to walk to the side about twenty yards and come in on the buckskin from an angle he hoped his assailant would not suspect.

He put each foot solidly on the ground after his boots had searched for dry rubble from creosote bushes or yucca leaves. When he sensed brush under his feet he carefully eased it aside with his boot toe, then he'd take another step.

When he thought he'd come close to his horse, the soft nose of the buckskin nuzzled his arm. The touch startled him and caused his stomach muscles to tighten—he might have walked up to his attacker with the same lack of sensing a presence.

He gathered the reins into his left hand and toed the stirrup. He sat there a moment, thinking that as black dark as that which surrounded him, he might cut out for his house.

Then he thought to try to ride out slowly, hoping to make little or no noise. He cast both of those ideas aside; the best way to get gone would be to dig heels into his horse and ride hell-for-leather into the canyon, hoping the horse didn't step into a hole. He turned the thought into action.

With the first leap of his animal, shots sprayed in his direction, but missed. The rifleman would have to be the luckiest man alive to score a hit by shooting at the sound of his horse.

In the confines of the canyon it got darker, wrapping around Bonner like a blanket. He slowed the horse and rode carefully, letting the big animal pick his way along the rock-strewn ground. After a few minutes, he stopped, twisted in the saddle, and cocked his head to listen. No sound of pursuit.

He thought to stop where he was, maybe a quarter of a mile from where he'd started and wait for daylight. Mentally he shook his head. He'd get farther into the rock-walled scar in the earth, then wait until he could see a place to fort up, maybe a pile of boulders. Then he'd be able to see anyone approaching, although he didn't think anyone in their right mind would follow him into the close confines of the walled-in slash in the earth.

Bonner climbed from the saddle and led the horse, still not willing to chance crippling him. After about half an hour, the buckskin quickened his pace, pushing Trey to a pace just short of a jog. He wondered what caused the faster pace, then grinned into the night. Water.

His horse had stood outside the burned-out cabin most of the day, and the smell of water would cause him to move faster. Bonner followed willingly; water meant he'd have coffee and a hot breakfast come daylight. He took care of his horse, spread his blankets, and lay staring at the distant stars. He'd not sleep, but intended to keep his ears tuned for sound through the night.

Skeeter Wells cursed, and as fast as he could jack shells into the chamber of his Henry, fired at the sound of the running horse, then realized if he scored a hit it would be a miracle. "Damn him. I had 'im an' let 'im get away—again."

He thought to follow Bonner into the canyon and had toed the stirrup when he stopped, frowned, and shook his head. If he followed the ranger, he'd be riding into a sure ambush. Bonner had the upper hand now, and at this point Wells was certain the ranger had no idea who it was that hunted him. He wanted to keep it that way.

Plus, he'd seen the lawdog in stand-up gunfights, and also seen what he could do with a rifle. Fear did not govern him, but caution entered his every decision.

He thought to sit out here until daylight, or daylight of the next two or three days, and shoot Bonner when he came out. He sat there a long moment, his brow puckered, then shook his head. Figuring Bonner didn't know him, or why he was being hunted, Wells decided to keep it that way; there would come a better opportunity.

He reined his horse toward Noname. He'd eat breakfast as soon as the cafe opened, then get some sleep. He'd kick Yadro out of the narrow bed so he'd have ample room to relax.

Whitey had wanted to come with him, saying he might get

a shot at Bonner, saying two guns were better than one; he'd offered a dozen reasons, but the one reason he kept to himself? If Rogers paid good hard cash for Bonner's scalp, Yadro intended to keep it all. Wells could read him like a book. He knew what the white-haired gunman thought before he thought it.

Back in Noname, still too early for the cafe to open, Skeeter went to the saloon and nursed a couple of whiskys until Linda opened for business.

He was the first person to enter the door, and the pretty lady who ran the place was alone. He took a seat next to the kitchen door, and when she came in to take his order he slid over on the bench. "Come sit down, pretty lady. We can talk 'til people come in; get to know each other better."

While he talked, his eyes drank in her body, full breasts, slim waist, and flared hips that brought his breath out in ragged gasps.

She stared at him a long, tense moment. "Mr. Wells, we know each other as well as we ever will. I don't want to know you any better. Fact is I don't want to know you at all. You want breakfast, order it or get up and leave."

Before he could respond, the front door squeaked and Juan Jimenez came in and sat at the end and across the table from Wells. From long habit he freed his holster of the encumbrance of resting on the bench.

He sensed a strained atmosphere as soon as he sat. He looked at Linda. "Anything wrong, ma'am?"

She still stared at Wells, and without turning her head, said, "Nothing I haven't already made perfectly clear to this *gentleman*." Then still staring at Wells, she asked, "You gonna eat, drink coffee, or leave?"

Wells again raked her body with a look that to Juan seemed to undress her as his eyes slowly traveled down her body and back up again. "Reckon I'll eat. Steak, eggs, and coffee."

While Wells's eyes traveled the length of Linda's body, Jimenez's blood heated. By the time the bushwhacker's eyes had again reached Linda's face, Juan's anger had boiled, then cooled to an icy calm.

He shifted only a fraction of an inch on the bench, enough for his fingers to brush the walnut grips of his Colt. He stared into Wells's eyes. "I only this moment changed the man's mind, Miss Linda. Don't reckon if he eats anywhere today, tomorrow, or anytime, it ain't gonna be here in your cafe."

Without moving his gaze from Wells, he nodded. "Stand, don't let your hands swing anywhere close to your side gun, an' get the hell outta here."

Wells placed his hands flat on the table and pushed to his feet. "What the hell put a burr under your saddle, cowboy? I ain't never done nothin' to you. Fact is I don't even know you."

"You don't know me, but if you ever look at this lady with dirt drippin' from your eyes like it just was, you ain't ever gonna know anybody again." Jimenez motioned toward the door with his head. "Now move. Get outta here."

Wells stared at the ranger a long moment, then nodded. "Gonna remember you, cowboy. They'll came a time when we might see if you can use that handgun you wear."

His face stiff as old saddle leather, Juan kept his eyes on the bushwhacker until the door slammed behind him.

"Wh-what in the world brought that on, Juan?"

Trying to push his anger to the back of his mind, his words came out stiff and cold. "He looked at you like he was tryin' to take your clothes off. Didn't like that. Nobody better ever look at you like that when I'm around."

To his surprise, Linda's face glowed, a beautiful flush pushed to her cheeks. "Does it make a difference, that much difference to you, Juan?" Her voice came out velvet soft.

His brow puckered. Why *did* it make such a difference to him? Then as though awakening in a new world he answered his own question. His answer brought on hope that she would let him court her. That decision formed his answer. "Ma'am, I don't reckon I ever want any man lookin' at you like he did. Fact is, much as I think of you, I want to be the only man who ever looks at you with hunger in his eyes." He spread his hands, palms facing her. "Ain't got no right to say such to you right now, but maybe you'll give me the right someday."

A soft smile crinkled the corners of her lips. "Juan

Jimenez, let's say I'm givin' you the right, gave you that right soon after I met you. I—I . . ." A customer pulled the door open, came in, and sat.

"Howdy, Miss Linda, how 'bout a double order o' flapjacks."

Juan resented the man coming in, then guilt flushed him. Hell, he had no business feeling toward the man as he did. Linda ran a cafe; the man came in hungry and deserved to be fed—but he *did* wonder what would have happened if they'd been alone.

Bonner sensed rather than saw the coming of day. The black dark softened, then lightened such that he could see the outline of his horse, then without being aware of it, daylight pushed the darkness into rocky crevices.

The water his horse found in total darkness proved to be a pool about a quarter of an acre fed by two springs trickling from cracks in the rocky wall of the canyon. Trey stepped away from the water's edge and cast his gaze toward the mouth of the earth's scar. He studied every rock, bend in the trail, brushy growth for sign that he wasn't the only one deep in this gully. The only sign of life was a six-point buck standing a couple of hundred yards out. He tested the air, looked toward the pool where Trey stood, hesitated, then bolted into the rocks on the slope behind him.

Although knowing no one could hear him, Trey said, "Bet I horned in on your watering hole; bet you been comin' here since you first looked on the world." He shook his head. He'd fix breakfast, scout his back trail, then leave the deer to his range.

He fixed and ate his meal, saddled his horse, toed the stirrup, and holding the big animal to a walk, headed for the mouth of the canyon.

He figured whoever his assailant had been had either left or taken up a place to shoot toward the opening from which Trey must emerge, unless there was an escape route at the other end of the canyon.

If he wanted to continue the attack, Bonner thought his ambusher would be within rifle range of where he soon would be riding. He stepped from the saddle, ground reined his horse, and darting from cactus growth to large boulder to drywash, he gained the entrance through which he'd come the night before. He squatted behind a boulder only large enough to cover his body and inch by inch studied the terrain in front and to the sides of where he was.

He spent an hour looking. He looked until he thought he could point out every blade of the coarse desert grass. Finally, he went back to his horse, mounted, and rode toward the burned-out abandoned cabin.

He rode past the cabin to where he thought the shooter had taken up station for his bushwhacking. He searched every inch of ground for some clue as to his attacker. He found only spent brass from .44-caliber cartridges and tracks from a single horse leading toward Noname. Tracks in the fine dust left no identifying marks.

"He headed for town; it ain't likely I could figure who he was if I followed him there." Like most men who spend a great deal of time alone, Trey voiced his thoughts aloud. He pulled his pipe from his vest, packed it, and lighted it. He sat there enjoying the taste of it, then nodded. "I came out here to see if the folks who lived here left any clue as to what happened to 'em. Reckon I'm gonna do what I came to do."

He rode to the back of the burned-out skeleton, ground reined his horse, and went inside. The scorched remains of a cast-iron stove sat in the middle of the back room along with cookware—pots, pans, ladles, and cooking forks with the wood burned away from the handles. In the front room, the heat-twisted heads and feet of three iron beds stood against the wall. A metal chest sat at the foot of a bed. It had been pried open and whatever contents it had held, mostly clothing, lay scattered in the ashes beside it. He stood in the middle of the waste, shook his head and frowned. If the people who lived here had left, they'd have taken their belongings with them. But he saw no bones to indicate they'd died in the fire. Where were they?

He thought on that a few moments, then, his face stiff, feeling frozen, he started circling the cabin, knowing what he'd ultimately find: shallow graves and scattered bones.

Only a few feet from where he assumed the back door had been, he found what he'd guessed he would—four sunken spots in the earth. The dimensions of the spots were obviously those of graves that would accommodate two adults and two children.

A lump in his throat threatened to choke him. He'd seen many such indications of the brutality of man, but they never ceased to tear his emotions apart. Holding his teeth tight together, his face frozen, he toed the stirrup and headed for the next cabin along the hills.

During the day, and the next one, he searched through the remains of burned-out cabins where families had dreams of making a new start, dreams of raising their families in peace—and found evidence of their having met the same fate as the family he found in the first site. He headed back toward the home in which he hoped to spend the rest of his life.

Wells rode into town, tight jawed and gut churning. The damned ranger had thwarted his efforts once again to get his revenge.

He'd spent a long, cold night waiting for Bonner to make a mistake, and now he wanted a hot breakfast and a drink of that rotgut whisky, but the hot breakfast would have to wait.

He cast a longing look at the neat, whitewashed little building. Jimenez might be there and Wells didn't want to have trouble with him; that trouble would have to wait until after he settled with Bonner.

He cast another look at the cafe and wondered which he wanted most, the hot breakfast or that good-looking woman who ran the place. He reined his horse to the hitching rack in front of the saloon.

When he walked into the dark interior, he waited inside the bat-wings and the wooden door inside it, which kept out the now-chill winds. When his eyes adjusted to the darkened room, the first person he saw was Yadro sitting at a table close to the bar. He walked to the table. "What you doin' outta the room? Somebody see you who knows what happened out on the trail an' we'd both be in trouble."

Yadro shook his head. "Naw, I seen Bonner an' that there gent he's done took up with ride out just after daylight yesterday, an' Tedford an' his woman, along with his daughter, left soon after. Ain't nobody else got any idea what happened out yonder on the trail." He frowned. "You find out what Bonner wuz gonna do?"

Wells went to the bar, got a drink, and came back. He nodded. "Yeah, I took a few shots at 'im an' he ran like a scalded dog." He shook his head. "Damned if I reckon I'll ever git 'im cornered where I got a clean shot at 'im." His stomach growled. "You et breakfast yet?"

Yadro shook his head. Wells knocked back his drink, shivered, and tossed two bits on the table. "When you go eat bring me a couple o' biscuits with a fried egg in 'tween."

"Why don't you come with me?"

"'Cause I'm cold, tired, an' hungry. Do like I say. Eat an' bring it to the room."

An hour later, Wells sat on the chair and Yadro on the edge of the bed. Whitey frowned and cast Wells a questioning look. "You never said where you tangled with Bonner."

"Aw hell, I wouldn't say I tangled with 'im, but I seen 'im nosin' round that old burned-out cabin at the head o' that ravine next to the one he built his place on. That's when I took a few shots at 'im."

"He have time to do any lookin' around?"

"Didn't give 'im time to do nothin' 'fore I opened up on 'im. Why?"

Yadro's look shifted nervously from Wells to stare at the floor, then back to his partner. "Tell you, Wells, I don't want nobody stickin' their nose into what's around that cabin."

"Somethin' 'round there you don't want nobody to see?"

Sweat popped out on Whitey's forehead, and he fidgeted. "Naw, ain't nothin' there. It's just that that's the place I figger to settle on. Don't want nobody gittin' interested in it 'sides me."

Wells watched Yadro squirm a moment, then nodded, and forced a cold smile to his lips, but his eyes remained flat, not letting any humor show at their corners. "You killed them people who built that cabin, didn't you, Whitey?"

From somewhere Yadro got enough nerve to talk back to Wells. "That ain't none o' your business, Skeeter. I got my job to do. Ain't asked you to help 'cept for the two of us to git rid o' Bonner. When I see that man dead, you an' me're through. I won't owe you nothin' an' you won't owe me nothin'. Right?"

Wells had found out what he wanted to know. If he ever needed it, he had something to hold over the sleazy gunman. In fact, in the next few days he thought to revisit that cabin and do his own searching. He thought he knew what he'd find.

When Bonner stepped from the saddle at the edge of the porch, Juan said he thought he'd be home before then. "What kept you so long? You run into any trouble?"

Trey chuckled and shook his head. "Uh-uh, no trouble, 'less gettin' pinned down all that first day, then shiverin' an' shakin' all night in the cold, an' hopin' I wouldn't have to dodge bullets all of this day." He grinned. "If Jess ain't 'bout got supper ready, I might chomp down on Dawg. I'm starved."

Dawg apparently recognized his name. He came to Trey, rubbed his side along Trey's leg, and whined. His master rubbed his head and scratched behind his ears. "No, I ain't gonna bite down on you, Dawg. Done got to thinkin' too much o' you."

After dinner, the three friends sat by the fire, sipping coffee spiked with whisky. Trey, thinking about Jess and wanting to get him situated in his own home before the nasty winter weather set in, suggested they begin to lay it out and start building on the morrow. They said that was a good idea. Then Juan added, "After his, you reckon we could start on mine?" They agreed to that also.

Bonner took another swallow of his coffee. "Know what? I gotta go to San Tone, or maybe El Paso, an' see if I can find any good cattle for sale. Don't know how I'm gonna manage that unless you two'll stay here an' keep those jaspers from burnin' me out."

Juan nodded. "We'll do that, but I figure if you want somethin' other than longhorns, which ain't nothin' but rawhide an' bones, you'd be better off goin' to San Tone." He stood and threw another log on the fire, then frowned. "Why don't you swallow your pride an' ask Tedford to sell you some. He's gonna have to make a drive pretty soon or his range is gonna get overgrazed."

"Ain't askin' him for nothin; I'll get my herd somewhere else."

Jimenez raised his eyebrows and grinned. "Know what, Trey? I theenk maybe you're one o' the hardest-headed rannies I ever run into." He nodded. "Course I've known that for a good many years now." He shrugged. "Do it your way; me an' Jess'll back your play."

They talked a while longer, finished their coffee, and went to bed.

The next morning, Juan and Trey encouraged Jess to lay out his home the way he wanted—for comfort and convenience, not to save on the labor it would take to build it.

With the three of them working, cutting and shaping slabs of rock, hauling it, and getting it seated in the hard earth, they had the foundation laid. Bonner slanted a look at the old man. "You sure this's gonna be big enough for your needs?"

Jess nodded. "Don't want a big place to take care of. Figure you an' Jimenez gonna need me around to do some cookin' an' stuff like that." He grinned. "Yep, figure I'm gonna be right busy hepin' y'all with your needs." He grinned. "I added a leeetle bit o' room for my furniture-makin' tools."

Then he let out a laugh that came all the way from deep in his chest. "And, from what I been seein' when y'all are around them two pretty girls, you both gonna be gittin' hitched, then they's gonna be some little ones runnin' 'round here. Reckon I kin take care o' young'uns good as anybody."

Bonner looked at Juan and shook his head. "Meddlesome old goat, ain't he?" He pulled his mouth to one side and raised one eyebrow. "Gotta say that 'cause I ain't give it a thought 'bout hitchin' up with Maggie."

Juan grinned, then burst out laughing. "The hell you haven't. But if you haven't you're a bigger fool than I ever figured you to be."

By now, Trey's face burned like it was on fire. His only comment? "Aw hell."

Matt's chair sat close enough to Belle's such that they could talk without having to raise their voices to be heard across the large room. He looked at her, trying to keep the misery and fear from his look and voice. "Belle, tell me true, what's your opinion o' that cowboy who's built his home on our land?"

Belle pinned him with a look he'd learned many years before that said he would get exactly what he'd asked for.

She nodded. "All right, Matt Tedford, you seem bent on stickin' your nose into Maggie's business." She glanced around the room, obviously to make certain Maggie wasn't there, then she turned her attention back to her husband. "I'm gonna answer you the best I know how. First, Trey built his house on government land; it's not ours, never has been. Second, that young man's as honorable as any you have ever known. Third, we, you and I, are gonna keep our noses out of Maggie's business.

"She's a grown woman, a grown woman we reared to be a lady. I trust her, and I trust Trey Bonner." Her look softened and she chuckled. "You and I didn't have anyone interfere when we began to get ideas about each other."

"Yeah, but we grew up together, our folks knew each other before we were born."

Maggie nodded. "True enough. You know what that tells me? Well, it says about as clear as it can that Maggie an' Trey have a lot of time to make up for, time they've missed not knowin' each other."

Matt frowned. "You're pretty well sold on that young'un, aren't you?"

Belle nodded. "And I'm gonna tell you right now, Maggie is too, so let them settle their lives the way that best suits them."

He stared into the drink Belle had poured him only moments before, then looked into her eyes. "Tell you what, wife of mine, it won't be easy but I'm gonna play the hand the way you say."

Belle chuckled. "Matt, it won't be easy because you'd keep Maggie here with us until we were all too old for it to matter." She cast him a tender smile. "You wouldn't want to deprive our daughter of the kind of happiness we've known, would you?"

He shook his head. "No—but I still say it won't be easy."

He stretched, then yawned. "Better get to bed. Start roundup in the mornin', an' brandin' won't be easy either; we got a pretty good calf crop this fall."

Belle smiled; this was the opening she'd been waiting for. She thought to do some more meddling.

Wells kept a sharp lookout on the town. He wanted to make certain that any time the ranger and that partner of his were in town, he kept Yadro out of sight. He now thought the stranger who'd hooked up with Bonner was also one of RIP Ford's boys. However, only a day or two more and Yadro's face should be healed enough for him to roam about town. His estimate as to Whitey's face healing proved accurate.

Wells visited the burned-out cabins and came to the same conclusion that Bonner had. None of those people had ever left; they'd been buried on the land they thought to live on the rest of their lives, and they had lived on it *the rest of their lives,* albeit very short ones.

11

TIMOTHY ROGERS ATE breakfast at the cafe, then went back to his office. He sat and pulled the topographic map to the edge of the desk in front of him. He studied it. He'd marked in yellow crayon the two claims Bonner and Jimenez had told him they would file on.

The longer he looked at the map, the more angry he grew. His face heated. Pressure built behind his eyes. His head throbbed. Why had those two busybodies come in here? He'd had it all planned where he could get legal claim to thousands of acres.

He'd get Tedford's entire ranch, home, outbuildings, everything. All he had to do to run Tedford off was to tell him that he was the one who knew what he'd done right after General Lee surrendered the Confederacy. He had no doubt that the rancher would pack up his family and leave; then he'd have it all.

He might even keep Tedford's daughter. He didn't give a damn about her as a woman, he just figured being a married man would give him status in the town, and he planned to make the town grow—with businesses, his businesses, he planned to build *his* town.

Yadro had gotten rid of the others who threatened to upset his plans, but with Bonner he'd failed miserably; not only had he failed to take care of the squatter, but he'd gotten all of his men killed. Now one of Bonner's friends had shown up and from what Rogers could determine, the friend was as salty as Bonner himself.

He pushed the anger aside, telling himself that a cool head would solve his problem much easier than a decision made in anger and haste.

He pondered what must be done, and the longer he thought on it the more convinced he became that he'd have to do the job himself. He didn't want to go back to being direcly involved in his get-rich-quick schemes as he had before getting the goods on Matt Tedford. He much preferred to sit behind the scenes and pull the right strings—let someone else do the dirty work and he'd keep his own hands clean. But Yadro had shown he wasn't capable of getting it done.

He thought to kill the white-haired gunman; no one would miss him. They'd think he had decided to drift. He frowned and shook his head. Why kill the dumb bastard? Maybe he could still be of use; maybe when he decided what to do about Bonner and his friend he could set it up to make it look like Yadro had committed whatever it was he decided to do. He smiled. It sure was nice that most people were stupid.

He put his mind to how to get rid of Bonner and his friend Juan Jimenez. He had to get that done before he broke the news to Tedford for him to pack up and get out.

Rogers had never been to the government land freed up for settlement by the Preemption Act. He had not seen the cabins built by the settlers, and he'd not seen the place Bonner built, but from what Yadro told him, Bonner's place was no shack. He'd come to stay. But burning him out wasn't an option; stone didn't burn—he'd have to try something else.

Jimenez glanced at Bonner. "You decided yet who you think is behind Yadro burnin' those settlers outta their homes?"

Trey nodded. "'Bout as good an idea as I can come up with." He shook his head. "Thought from the very first that maybe

Matt Tedford was the one, then I backed off that idea, then convinced myself I backed off 'cause he was Maggie's pa."

He let the corners of his mouth crinkle in a wry smile. "Then, *compadre,* I met the man." He picked up his coffee cup, took a swallow, grimaced, dumped the now-cold coffee in the bucket they kept for that purpose, and poured the three of them another cup. "Tell you how it is, if Matt Tedford wanted somethin' like that done, he's the kind o' man who'd look his targets in the eye an' tell 'em what they were gonna do." He shook his head. "Tedford's no murderer."

He cast Juan a questioning look. "You got any ideas 'bout who's behind the whole scheme?"

Jimenez nodded. "Been thinkin' on it pretty hard. Ain't got any real solid evidence to go on, but I'm beginnin' to think pretty hard about that land agent, Rogers." He frowned. "You think maybe I'm takin' the wrong fork in the trail?"

Jess put his say into the conversation. "Been listenin' to the both o' you fer some time now. From all you've said, reckon I'd agree with Juan." He chuckled. "Now all you two Texas Rangers, tough lawmen, gotta do is come up with the proof."

Bonner cast the old man a sour look. "Don't know why I didn't send you on down the trail soon's you showed up at my door."

Jess chuckled. "Know why you didn't, you seen that Dawg liked me right off. You trust that dog's opinion more'n you do yore own."

Trey drank the last of his coffee, stretched, and stood. "Reckon I'm gonna turn in. We oughtta finish the walls of Jess's cabin tomorrow, then we gotta see 'bout gettin' some two-by-fours to hold up his roof "—he nodded—"an' yeah, we gotta see if Parsons's got any more o' those sheets o' tin roofin' material. If he ain't, we gotta get 'im to order some. We don't an' we gonna be stuck with that old man sittin' in here with us all winter; drinkin' our whisky an' stickin' his nose into our business. Fact is, I bet another month an' he'd be tryin' to get both of us married off."

Jess slapped his knee and laughed. "Either o' you had any

brains at all an' you'd done been married. You ain't gonna find no women, nowhere, what's any better'n them two."

Trey again growled that he was going to turn in, and he did—but he thought long into the night about Jess's last words.

The next day while hauling rocks, shaping them, placing them, and watching Maynard's house take on its own personality, Bonner continued to think of Maggie.

The old man was right. Maggie and Linda were exceptional women—strong, smart, compassionate, and as he'd found, Maggie was passionate, a trait he constantly had to fight himself to keep from taking advantage of.

He thought Linda would be just as much so as Maggie with the right man. He frowned. Maybe Jess had been able to look inside both him and Jimenez and seen what they hadn't admitted to themselves. Well, maybe they hadn't acknowledged it because they each had a job and an obligation to complete for the Texas Rangers, then they could get down to serious thoughts of the two girls.

About midafternoon, the three men stood shoulder to shoulder, and even in the chill air all were soaked with sweat. They stared at the completed walls of Maynard's house. Jimenez put words to his thoughts, "Damn, she's gonna be a beauty soon's we get a roof on 'er."

Jess nodded, very slowly. "Yep, she's a beauty." Then he looked each of them in the eye and, his voice somewhat subdued, asked, "Y'all gonna make me stay in 'er—or you gonna let me come up to see you, a lot?"

Bonner came close to giving him a joking answer, then clamped his jaws shut. His answer would be important to the old man, one that could hurt his feelings.

He threw his arm around the bony old shoulders. "Oldtimer, I reckon if you don't spend a considerable time in the big house, my feelin's would be hurt. Fact is we gotta build Juan a place next an' he's gonna want you to spend some time with *him*."

Jimenez nodded. "Damn tootin'."

Jess gazed at them a moment, his Adam's apple bobbed twice, then a smile brighter than a sunrise covered his wrinkled old face. "Well now, gosh ding it, I'm shore glad to hear you say that. Figgered on cookin' you an' Maggie a whole bunch o' meals; give y'all time for sparkin'."

Trey stared at Maynard a moment and didn't refute his inclusion of Maggie in his statement. Juan only allowed his lips to crinkle at the corners.

Skeeter Wells now allowed Yadro to come to the saloon in that his face no longer showed the raw, pink look of fresh scars. He knocked back his drink, poured himself another, and looked at the white-haired gunman sitting across the table from him. "Go back to the bar; don't want no company right now. Got some thinkin' to do."

Whitey stood and headed for the bar like a whipped dog, tail tucked between his legs.

Wells studied the slim retreating back, then stared into the drink he'd poured. Was he as rotten as Yadro? He mentally shook his head.

He knew the man he tried to kill. Yeah, he shot from ambush, but only because he knew from having seen the ranger in fights that there was no way he could match Bonner in a stand-up gunfight, and if he got himself killed before evening the score, there would be no one else to take up the fight. The ranger had killed his kin. He had to pay for that.

But Yadro? He was trash. He took money to kill people he had no reason to, people he didn't know, people he'd never seen before. He killed them only to have more coins to clink in his pocket.

Those shallow graves he'd found behind each burned cabin held people who'd had dreams, who'd gotten married, had children, and worked to make their dreams come true. He shook his head. He couldn't kill innocent people. No, he couldn't make claim to being a *good* man, but he did have reason to do what he tried to do.

His thoughts centered on Bonner. The ranger had taken Wells's two brothers to Austin, gotten them tried and hanged.

The lawdog had then run down his cousin in Laredo who wouldn't submit to arrest and tried to outdraw Bonner. He came in a poor last. They'd buried him there in the border town.

What else had Bonner done? All Wells came up with was that the man did his job. He brought men back for the law to determine whether they were guilty or innocent, and if guilty, what would be their punishment. It was usually hanging.

If they put up a fight, they paid the price. If his own family had not been ones who paid the price, Wells thought he might have admired the tall ranger for being one helluva fighting man, but not for being a lawdog.

He slipped into wondering how to get the ranger under his rifle sights. He wanted to get back to the rimrock above Bonner's house and wondered if the only way was up the trail alongside the stone house. He shook his head. He'd climb to the mesa somewhere else and try to find the right canyon at the mouth of which the lawdog had built his house; then he'd be able to pick the time to ambush him, and if he missed, as he'd done several times, he would have a well-known trail to evade capture.

Maggie looked across the breakfast table at her father. "Papa, you an' me need to talk. You gonna get balky as an old mule, but this is somethin' you gotta hear now so you can digest it, get mad, get over it, an' learn to accept it."

Matt looked her in the eye. He knew that what he was about to hear was a thing he feared, didn't want to accept, maybe never would. "Get it said, Maggie. We've never been ones to beat around the bush."

Knots bulged at the back of his daughter's jaws. Matt figured at that moment she had taken the bit in her teeth and would not take any kind of argument.

"Gonna tell you, Papa, I've found the man I want to marry. Ain't gonna ever be another.

"I know every time you an' he get within ten feet of one another you get your hackles up. You might as well keep a tight rein on your feelin's 'cause if I can make it happen, he's gonna be around for the rest o' my life."

He studied the set of Maggie's features: lips held in a straight line, eyelids drooped to form slits over her eyes, jaws clamped. His stomach, already queasy, churned. His breakfast, a meal he always enjoyed, turned sour. If she'd kicked him in the stomach, he could not have felt worse. "You're talkin' 'bout that squatter Bonner, I reckon. Has he already asked you to marry him?"

She shook her head. "He hasn't said anything; fact is I'm gonna have to do somethin' to make him realize I'm the woman he's been thinkin' of for a long time. He's tryin' to decide whether his feelin's are only man-woman feelin's, or whether they're feelin's that'll hold us together through all sorts of problems."

Heat again pushed into Matt's head. He tried to squelch it, but it didn't work. "What you mean, 'he's tryin' ' to decide whether his feelin's are 'man-woman feelin's'? He been gettin' familiar with you?"

He stood, his chair toppled to lay on its side. He pushed his Colt down into its holster and made sure the thong was over the hammer to hold it in. "Gonna go see that man. We're gonna have an understanding right now. He's gonna stay away from you."

Maggie stood and glared across the table at her father. "You're not gonna go see him. He's never done anything to me that I didn't almost beg 'im to do—even then all we did was kiss, and he told me he shouldn't have; although he did say he wasn't sorry. Glad he said that 'cause I sure wasn't sorry; fact is, Papa, I wanted 'im to kiss me again. Now you sit down an' let's finish this talk." She picked up the coffeepot and poured them another cup.

He looked at Belle. She sat where she'd always sat. Not an emotion showing. Just looking at her, he guessed she had already known all of what had been said. He had never known betrayal by his own wife.

The starch went out of his backbone. He felt alone in the world, felt as though he'd lost his best, maybe his only friend. "Belle, you been knowin' 'bout this all along?"

"Most of it, Matt. Fact is, I suspected it from the very first time Maggie came home after meeting the boy. She had a glow about 'er that a young woman seems to get when she's in love; maybe she didn't even know it herself. That was the way it was with her." She shrugged. "She didn't know it back then, but I did."

"Why didn't you do somethin' to stop it?"

"Because I didn't want to. Our daughter deserves her chance at happiness, at life, the same as you and I had." She shook her head. "Oh no, Matt, I didn't do anything to stop it." She clamped her hands to her hips and stared at him. "An' I'm tellin' you right now, you're not gonna do anything either. Now sit down an' drink your coffee."

She topped off their coffee, looked at Maggie, and sat next to her. Matt stared at them a moment then sat. He'd lost the battle—maybe the war. He didn't have to like it. Belle's next words cut into his thoughts. "I expect you to be civil to Trey Bonner when we meet again. You don't even have anything to judge him by. He hasn't tried to take Maggie from us yet."

"I have a strong belief Trey will come to you both and ask permission to court me before he takes us any further." Maggie laughed. "If he doesn't come askin', I'm gonna come tellin'. Gonna tell y'all that I'm gonna go courtin' *him*."

Matt tried to keep his anger, but in the face of his women-folk felt it drain from him. He didn't stand a chance. He nodded. "I'll leave things be—for now."

Maggie shook her head. "No, Papa, you're gonna leave things be for good." Her voice softened. "Papa, think about what you're doin'. You don't want to create a world in which you an' I are constantly at odds, constantly at war with each other."

She sipped her coffee, looked into the coffee still in her cup, then fastened her eyes on her father. "Papa, I've made up my mind. I'm gonna marry Trey, if he'll have me. I'm the one reaching for happiness, reaching for my man. He hasn't and wouldn't do anything before asking your permission." Her shoulders relaxed, her face begged. "Papa, if you have to get angry an' take your love away, then I reckon I'm the one you need to target. Hope you won't, Papa, 'cause I love you more than anything—'cept Mama an' Trey. Reckon I love each one o' you as much as the other, 'cept in different ways."

Matt stared at his daughter. The wind went out of his sails. The pressure in his head lessened, the tightness in his chest eased, his shoulders slumped. He shook his head. "Mag, I reckon I love you so much it terrifies me to think o' losin' you, to think some man has taken my place."

"Papa, not he nor anyone else can take your place." Her voice softened such that he barely heard her. "You see, Papa, he'll be takin' his own place, the place he's meant to have, the place I been savin' for him all my life."

Matt stood, walked around the table, and took his only child into his arms. They stood there like that for several long moments while Belle's smile bathed them both in sunshine.

Bonner chopped and split stove wood, while Juan and Jess cooked supper. When they called him in to eat, and they were at the table, Trey took a bite of venison, chewed a few moments, swallowed, and frowned.

"What brought on the frown, Trey?" Juan sliced himself another bite.

"Just thinkin', partner, why don't we put up the sides of your place before we go in to see Parsons 'bout orderin' those roofin' sheets. That way we gonna know pretty well exactly what it's gonna take." He cut another slice of venison and put it on his plate. "Plus, I figure you gonna want a place 'bout the same size o' my house." He grinned. "You gonna need a pretty good-sized house for all those children you an' Linda gonna have."

Jimenez surprised him. He smiled, then nodded. "Reckon you're right, Trey. I been thinkin' since that old goat at the end o' the table started puttin' his nose into our business. He's right, 'bout you an' me both. Soon's we finish our ranger job, make sure RIP's satisfied, I'm gonna go in town an' do some serious courtin'."

Bonner nodded. "Been thinkin' 'long those lines myself." He stood, went to the stove, picked up the coffeepot, and poured them each a full cup. "Wish I could think o' some way to make Rogers come outta the woods, take a shot at us . . . somethin'."

Jimenez squinted at the center of the table, then lifted his look to Trey. "Know what I been thinkin? The answer we been lookin' for might not be here. I'm figurin' we might find what we need to know in Austin. There has to be some record of any action on those claims of the folks who got burned out." He nodded. "The more I slant my thinkin' that direction, the more I'm convinced one o' us needs to go back to the capital an' check it out."

Jess stood and started clearing the table. Trey pushed back to help the old man. "First, we gotta get your house started, an' make sure Parsons has the roofin' sheets."

Two weeks later, a couple of layers of rock set in the earth for Juan's house, Trey thought they could estimate close enough what they'd need from Parsons. "No need for both of us to ride in there 'less Jess don't mind holdin' down the fort."

Jess grinned. "Course I don't mind. I figger Juan's gonna want to go sparkin' Miss Linda, an' you're gonna pay a visit to that there Rogers, an' see can you learn any more 'bout what he's up to."

Bonner nodded. "You're right, old-timer, but the more I think on it, the more I b'lieve the answer's right here, but we're likely to uncover what we need to know in Austin." He shrugged. "At any rate I figure we'll go into Noname an' see what's changed since we were in last."

The next morning when the eastern sky showed first light, Bonner and Jimenez were almost to the outskirts of town. They'd left Jess and Dawg to keep each other company—and keep the place safe.

Juan looked across his shoulder at Trey. "Know what I figure?" He nodded. "Well, I'm gonna tell ya. We're so early we can go to Linda's place, eat breakfast, then visit awhile 'fore Parsons opens his store for business. And, I ain't said nothin' to you 'bout what I want to talk to 'im 'bout after we get through orderin' the stuff we gonna need to finish both Jess's place an' mine."

"What we gonna talk to 'im about?"

Jimenez shook his head. "Ain't thought it out yet. Hoped maybe you an' Parsons might help me get my thoughts straight on it. We'll wait 'til we can get all three together an' discuss it."

About the time he ended his sentence they reined in in front of the cafe. When they stepped from their horses, Trey reached in his shirt pocket, pulled a sheet of paper from it, unfolded it, and glanced at the figures he'd taken so much time measuring and writing to come up with. He again folded and put it in his pocket. He glanced at Juan. "When I made this list, I kept yours and Jess's stuff separate. I'm gonna pay for his, an' if you're short on cash I figure I can let you have a few bucks."

Jimenez chuckled. "Trey, you an' me have lived much the same kind o' lives." He shrugged. "Hell, man, like you, I still got most o' what I've made since I went out on my own." He nodded. "'Preciate your offer, but I can handle my end o' it."

They stepped to the boardwalk, pulled the screen door open, and stepped into the smells of brewed coffee, frying bacon, potatoes, and steak.

Bonner sucked in a deep breath. "Dang! Didn't know how hungry I was 'til I drew in some o' these smells." He shook his head. "Danged if I don't b'lieve I could eat the south end o' a northbound skunk."

Jimenez frowned, shook his head, and bunched his shoulders up around his neck, then let them drop. "Tell you how it is, I don't figure Linda's got any skunks in 'er kitchen. If she ain't, I'll head out an' see if I can find one for you."

Bonner pulled his mouth to the side in disgust. "Think you're smart, don't ya?"

There were only two people in the room other than Linda. She motioned them to take a seat at the table closest to the kitchen. "We can talk in between me takin' orders an' cookin'."

Juan frowned. "Jest wonderin', 'fore you get too busy, you got a south end o' a northbound skunk back there?"

"Have I got *what?*"

Bonner grimaced. "Aw hell, Linda, he's tryin' to be smart, but he ain't got enough 'tween his ears to get the job done."

Jimenez laughed, slapped his knee, then laughed again. "Ah, *mi* amigo, I was jest tryin' to be helpful."

Linda put a cup of coffee in front of each of them. "I'll bring your breakfast in a moment."

Juan frowned. "We ain't ordered yet. How you know what we want?"

She stared at him a moment, then grinned. "Every time y'all come in here, you take some of everything I have in the kitchen." She shook her head. "Didn't see as how this time would be any different."

Bonner smiled. "Bring it on. If he don't eat it, I reckon I'll take care o' what he don't want."

Two hours later, having eaten and visited, Bonner and Jimenez stepped into Tom Parsons's store. He came to the front to greet them. "What y'all need that I might have?" He looked at Trey. "Know you don't need anything much, but maybe Juan does. Hear tell he's buildin' himself a house 'bout the same size as yours, Bonner."

"Don't know where you heard that, but it's true." Trey dug in his shirt pocket and pulled out the list. "Fact is, we built two houses. You remember Jess Maynard?" At Parsons's nod, Bonner told him that the three of them had built Jess a house too.

Then after the storekeeper saying how nice he thought it was that they'd take care of the old man in that way, Trey shook his head. "Now, Tom. That old man earns everything we do for 'im. He won't have it any other way."

Bonner unfolded the sheet of paper and placed it on the counter. "Notice I have two lists here. The long one's for Jimenez, the shorter one is for me. Keep the prices separate."

Parsons studied the list a few moments, then shook his head. "I'm gonna have to send to San Tone for most o' this stuff; ain't got near enough on hand to fill this order."

"We figured as much. That's why we didn't bring a wagon with us." Jimenez frowned. "Sure hope you can get it here 'fore really bad weather sets in."

Parsons nodded. "Think it'll be here."

"Now that that's taken care of, I need to try a suggestion on you an' Trey." Jimenez placed his hands on the counter behind him and jumped up to sit on it. "Soon's y'all are ready to listen, I'll lay it out for you."

Parsons grunted. "Looks like you're ready, so I reckon Bonner an' me'll stand here an' listen. Lay it out."

Juan pinned him with a look. "Tom, you're sort o' the town leader, so the way I got it figured it ought to be up to you to do this." He rolled a quirly, put a lucifer to it, and seeing both Trey and Tom were listening, he nodded and continued. "The town's gonna grow, so while it's still thinkin' 'bout it we should oughtta have everythin' in place an' ready to operate when it does."

Parsons looked squint eyed at him. "What're you talkin' about?"

Juan took a drag off his quirly, blew smoke out toward the ceiling, and again looked at the storekeeper, then to Bonner. "First, we need a mayor, an' soon's he gets his town council set up, they need to hire a lawman."

Parsons shook his head. "We don't have any money to pay a town marshal, or a mayor for that matter."

Jimenez grinned. "Didn't figure you'd be askin' for a salary."

Parsons frowned. "Me? What the hell you thinkin', young man? Tell you right now, if we have a town meetin' you ain't gonna railroad me into bein' mayor."

Juan opened his eyes wide and tried to give Parsons an innocent look. "You sayin' you won't accept or perform your civil duties?"

"Wh-wh-why, dammit, I'll accept my responsibilities as much as any man." Tom looked at Trey. "Tell 'im, Bonner. You know damned good and well I ain't no shirker."

Trey shrugged, raised his eyebrows, then shook his head. "Can't tell 'im that, Tom. Sounds to me like you don't want to accept your responsibilities, even though you're the leadin' citizen o' this town."

"W-w-well, dammit, I'll do my duty anytime, anywhere."

His brow creased, and his eyelids drooped over his eyes in a half-angry squint. "You gotta help me get the business people together for the meeting you're talkin' about."

Bonner nodded. "We'll do that. You gonna have to chair the meetin'. Jimenez an' me gonna have to sit there an' keep quiet bein's we ain't citizens of the town. Course we'd be happy to chime in if we're asked."

Parsons studied each of them a few moments, then grimaced. "Why do I believe you two young devils have sucked me into something?"

Juan grinned. "Maybe it's 'cause we have done exactly like you figure, but it does need doin an' you're the one to do it."

Parsons stood there a few moments, stared at the floor, then nodded. "You boys're right. I've had some o' the same thoughts for quite a while now. Yep, it's a thing we gotta do, an' I do want y'all to help me do it."

Parsons glanced at the two of them. They stood there grinning like a couple of kids caught with their hands in the cookie jar.

Bonner nodded. "Looks like we gonna have us a real town. Let us know when you wantta have this town meetin'." He looked at the slip of paper he'd handed Parsons. "Go ahead an' order everything on that list. Soon's you get it we can finish our building job." He stepped toward the door and said over his shoulder, "C'mon, partner. We gonna get back to my place 'fore dark, we better ride."

Timothy Rogers wrote the last words on the three sheets of paper, read and reread them, then nodded. They sounded legal to him. They read as though a lawyer had written them. Now he needed someone to sign them and another person to sign as a witness.

He pushed back from his desk, stared at his handiwork, frowned, and wondered if Yadro could read or write. If he couldn't, it fit his plans better, but maybe, at the very least, he could write his name.

The white-haired gunman would do as told, but where could he find a witness? He thought about that for several minutes, then decided he'd forge the signature of a witness. Hell, he could claim that a man traveling west had been handy, so he'd talked him into signing the three deeds to the property of those Yadro had gotten rid of. The deeds included the property Bonner and Jimenez would claim they had filed on. But he'd already taken care of that.

Finally, after sitting there studying on his course of action for several minutes, he pushed back from his desk, wondered where he might find his puppet, then decided he'd probably be in the saloon, where he spent most of his time instead of staying out in the brush where he might have the opportunity to get a shot at the two squatters who threatened to upset his plans. Plus, maybe that trash Yadro had hooked up with might be there.

Should he pull the white-haired gunman's friend into being a witness? He frowned. No. He wanted no more individuals to know what he did than absolutely necessary. He'd forge the witness signatures. He headed to the saloon.

As soon as he stepped into the dark room, stinking of unwashed bodies, stale alcohol, and tobacco smoke, the same revulsion hit him that always assailed him when having to go in the make-do structure.

To his thinking, the only men who patronized the saloon were the scum of creation. It never entered his mind that those men who came in the place for a drink were hardworking men trying to find a break in the drudgery and danger of their everyday lives. It served a useful purpose.

He scanned the room for the man he needed, then saw him sitting at a table with the man he rode with. Rogers walked to the table, looked down at the two, and with a flick of his thumb motioned Yadro to step away from where he might be overheard.

Whitey glanced at Skeeter Wells and shrugged. "Be back in a minute."

Before getting to Rogers, he said, "What you want, Boss?"

Rogers glanced around the room to see who might have heard the gunman call him "boss." He caught Yadro's shirt in his left hand and pulled the gunny toward him. "Damn you, don't ever say anything like that where people can hear you. You know damned well ain't nobody s'posed to know we know each other." He released the handful of shirt, and under his breath said, "Come down to the office after dark. Need you to do something."

He stepped toward the door, thought to ask if Yadro could read and write, then decided he'd find that out where the air he breathed was more to his liking.

Outside, he glanced at the sky, saw that the sun had passed high noon, and decided to go to the cafe for his nooning.

Trey and Juan, after leaving the general store, went back to the cafe not wanting to make the ride back to the ranch on an empty stomach. They had finished eating and sat smoking and drinking coffee before getting on the trail for home.

Bonner drained his cup and held it aloft to signal Linda he'd like another cup, when Rogers came in. He halfway stood, then sat again. He'd make sure the land agent had sent the papers to the capital before he left. He looked at Jimenez. "Gonna put a burr under Rogers hide 'fore we leave." Juan nodded.

They drank their coffee, smoked, and deliberately waited until the land agent had his dinner in front of him, then stood and walked to where he sat.

Bonner stood there a moment, waited for Rogers to look up. "Just figured I'd check an' see if you sent those papers to Austin yet—the papers sayin' Jimenez an' I've filed on those two parcels o' land we told you to get the papers ready to send in."

A hooded look came over Rogers eyes. "Haven't had time yet. Gotta tell ya though, there's other people interested in those two plots."

Hot blood pushed to Bonner's face, and a knot pushed into his throat. He swallowed, pushed his anger to the back of his mind. "You tellin' us there's others interested? Well, I'm tellin' you, those papers better be in Austin when one o' us gets there—in the next few days. They ain't, I'm goin' to the rangers an' report you for dereliction of duty. Then, they don't take care o' it, I'm comin' back here an' blow your damned stinkin', crooked brains out. You got that?"

Rogers's face flushed, then went white as one of the puffy clouds that sprung up during summer but never gave rain. He made as though to stand. Bonner put his hand on his shoulder and held him in his seat. "Uh-uh, now, you don't want to stand. You try it an' I'll knock your sorry butt back so hard you'll bounce. Got that? Now stay there, eat your cold dinner, an' count yourself lucky I don't beat hell outta you."

Trey looked at Juan. "C'mon, let's head for home 'fore this garbage stinks up Linda's Cafe so's we can't stand it." They headed for the door.

Outside, Jimenez stared at Trey a moment. "Never knew you to push a man so hard."

Bonner's face, feeling like dried mud, pinned him with a look. "That's my home. Gonna take my wife to it, raise my kids there, ain't nobody gonna crook me outta it."

12

Rogers watched the two tall men walk from the cafe. He swallowed, tried again to choke back the brassy taste of fear in the back of his throat. He'd lost all desire to finish his meal, but continued to place bite after bite of the cold, now-tasteless food into his mouth. His thoughts rested on those phony land titles he'd drawn up for Yadro to sign.

His first inclination pushed him toward going back to his office and destroying the papers he'd labored over, then greed and hate pushed his fear aside.

If he didn't make a move to get that land soon, his carefully laid plans would account for years wasted—trailing Matt Tedford here after the war, finding the source of some of the precious water, getting Yadro and his bunch to take care of the settlers once they'd filed on the land, and fixing it so the land transfer to him could not be traced.

As for Tedford's ranch, he figured getting it would be a cinch, or he'd destroy any claim Tedford ever had to an honorable reputation. He'd already threatened the rancher and knew his threat had been taken seriously, or Tedford would not have buckled to letting Yadro stay on his ranch when he'd made the demand that the white-haired gunny do so.

He pushed the cold food from in front of him, thought to order a hot cup of coffee, then decided he'd better get back to his office; he had things to do to make sure the loose ends were tied together.

Back at his office, Rogers walked to his desk, opened the top right-hand drawer, looked at the .44 Colt resting there, then shook his head. He'd not wear a belt rig; he didn't want anyone to know he'd taken to going armed.

He nodded, pulled a shoulder rig from the drawer and shrugged into it; then he took a snub-nosed .38-caliber Smith & Wesson revolver from beside the .44 and dropped it into the hand-tooled, well-oiled holster. He felt better.

Bonner and Jimenez rode side by side, each keeping a careful watch for drygulchers. Bonner had suggested they do so in that he'd not seen Yadro before leaving town.

About halfway to Bonner's place, he frowned, then looked at his fellow ranger. "Juan, if you an' Jess can take care to see we don't get burned out, think I'm gonna go see RIP."

Juan smiled. "Wondered when you were gonna come up with that idea. If you hadn't, I was gonna say I should go."

Trey shook his head. "Naw, reckon I'm the one what oughtta go. I need to make a report to the boss, check on what Rogers might have done—or not done." He flicked his gaze around the terrain, then again looked at Jimenez. "Reckon I better see if there's anybody got maybe four, five hundred head o' mixed breed cattle, an' a good whiteface or Durham bull they'll sell me."

"You find them cows, you gonna have to hire a couple o' drovers to help get 'em back here."

Bonner nodded. "Thought o' that. Also, I been thinkin' it's early to say anythin' to RIP 'bout quittin' the service. We find what we think we gonna find about Rogers, we gonna need these badges we got in our pockets."

He made another sweep of the ridges, swales, and dry washes with a studying gaze, then looked across his shoulder at his partner. "Aw hell, Juan, don't mean to sound like I'm figurin' to hide behind my star."

Jimenez smiled, a cold smile devoid of humor. "Know you wouldn't do that no more'n I would, but when it comes to a showdown, it sure will be nice to have the thing in our pockets that'll eliminate a bunch o' stupid questions, an' maybe trouble with the law."

Trey nodded. "Way I got it figured."

Matt could have stood there holding his daughter in his arms forever, if he knew she'd still be sitting at his fireside, but somewhere during that time his heart let go and cut the ties that soon would belong to a man he'd treated unfairly.

He stepped back from Maggie. "Mag, I know I've treated you badly; an' that boy you've chosen, don't reckon I've treated him any better—fact is, back home in Virginia I wouldn't have treated a Yankee as badly as I've treated 'im." He pulled his pipe from his pocket, packed it, and lit it, hoping to hide the tears behind the cloud of smoke. "Why don't you get Ramey to ride over to the Bonner place with you in the mornin'? Invite that young feller to dinner. I promise you I'll be nice to 'im, maybe even eat a little crow."

Tears welled into Maggie's eyes. She smiled through them. "Oh, Papa, he wouldn't want you to do that." She gasped. "Oh, my goodness. Don't you dare let on we've had this talk. He ain't said a word to me yet." She nodded. "Course we know we're mighty attracted to each other, but he hasn't made up his mind yet as to what the attraction." She smiled, then nodded. "Course I could tell 'im, but I b'lieve it'll be sweeter when, all by himself, he comes to the conclusion I've already reached. Yes, I'll go see if Slim'll go with me in the mornin'." She didn't waste any time in heading for the bunkhouse.

Rogers sat behind his desk, and for the dozenth time glanced at the window to make certain dark had set in. Damn that white-trash gunny he'd hired. Why didn't he come on? He'd specifically told him to come after dark. It had been dark for over an hour. It was then footsteps sounded on the boardwalk in front of his office.

He stared at the door and as soon as Yadro came through

it said, "Where the hell you been? I said after dark, not mornin'."

Whitey slouched to the chair in front of the desk and sat. "Didn't think you'd want me comin' soon's it got dusk dark, so I waited 'til now."

Rogers stared at his hireling, fingered the sheaf of papers in front of him, then shrugged. He might as well find out. "You read an' write, Yadro?"

Whitey shrugged. "Some. Ain't very good at it. Back East I went to school 'til the fifth grade, quit 'fore I could get started good."

"Can you sign your name?"

Yadro nodded. "Yeah, so's most could read it. Why?"

"Can you read enough to sign somebody else's name?"

"Yeah, if you got it spelled out so's I can tell what to put on paper." He frowned. "What you want me to sign?"

Rogers wondered what and how much to tell the gunny, then decided to tell him nothing. "None o' your damned business. You're gettin' paid to do what I tell you." He reached in the bottom drawer and pulled out a bottle and two glasses. "We'll have a drink, an' I'll tell you what I figure you need to know. I'll tell you this though. It's not anything that'll get you in trouble with the law."

Whitey grinned. "Hell, boss, it's a little late for me to start worryin' 'bout that. You ready for me to sign? It might take me a while to figger out what letters to write down."

It was then that the land agent decided to have Yadro sign as the witness rather than the buyer. He figured he could do a better job of phonying up the signatures of nonexistent people. He poured them each a half glass of whisky and slid the one for Whitey across the desk. "No, I'll just have you sign your real name as the witness. Let's drink, then we'll get down to business."

Tom Parsons, after he'd locked up for the night, spent several nights visiting business owners and residents of Noname. This night he sat across the table from Ian Murphy, the saloon owner. "All right, Ian, I've told you what those two settlers have brought up, an' I agree with 'em. If this town's ever gonna amount to anything, we gotta have a plan for how we gonna get there."

He took a swallow of the drink Murphy poured as soon as he came in, and pulled out a chair to sit, a signal Parsons always wanted to talk. "Now I'm gonna tell ya, those two boys don't want to interfere with the way we run our town. They know they aren't citizens of the town, but they also know they wantta be able to come into a town that's law-abiding."

Murphy stood, freshened their drinks, then frowned. "Hell, Tom, I agree we need exactly what you say, but where we gonna git the money to pay for all that law an' order stuff?"

Parsons grinned. "Been thinkin' 'bout that. It won't cost us a dime."

"Aw, c'mon, know damned well a person don't never git somethin' for nothin'."

Parsons shook his head. "Didn't say we'd be gettin' it for nothin'. I said it wouldn't cost us any money, but it *will* cost us some o' our personal time. We gotta be willin' to spend time in meetin's, time watchin' out for lawbreakers—you know the kind o' stuff I'm talkin' 'bout."

Murphy nodded. "Yeah, I been in towns what was tryin' to grow before. Glad to see them boys're thinkin' ahead." He took a swallow of his drink, pulled papers and tobacco from his pocket and rolled a quirly, lit it, and stared at Parsons. "Tell you what's a fact though, Tom; I really don't want to see the town grow very much, don't want it to get all clustered with a bunch o' people. You know the kind I'm talkin' 'bout."

Parsons frowned, stared into his drink a moment, then with an effort, kept his face solemn. "You ever figure out the business that's responsible for bringin' in the whores, gamblers, gunmen, and trash in general?"

Murphy's face turned several shades of red to settle on one about on a level with igniting a stroke. "Now dammit, Parsons, you know I got that kind o' business; but you know me good 'nuff to know I ain't gonna let none o' that trash ever come into my saloon to raise hell with my friends."

Any surge of levity Parsons had felt evaporated. "Ian, I was only tryin' to put a burr under your saddle." He nodded. "You bet I know you'll run the kind of watering hole we all want in this town."

He took another swallow of his drink, shivering as the strong, raw drink went down his throat. "You see, I've watched some o' that kind o' trash come into our town, visit you in your business, then saddle up an' leave town. Yep, all by yourself you been keepin' our town as clean as one man could ever do it." He shook his head. "Hell, Murph, I know you could have had a business twice the size o' the one you got if you was willin' to squelch your beliefs in order to make a dollar."

He stood. "Reckon I'll go see Linda, let 'er know what we're plannin'; don't know as how bein' a female we'd want to put 'er in a dangerous situation, but she needs to know, an' she needs to see if there's any way she figures to help."

Dawg dragged himself away from his favorite place in front of the fire, growled, stared toward the trail, then his tail wagged furiously.

Trey pulled his hand back from reaching toward the gun rack. He glanced at Jess. "We got friends comin'. Reckon Dawg figures they're his friends too."

Jess chuckled. "Figger you got that nailed down right tight." He chomped on his cud of tobacco cuddled in his right cheek. "Bet you my next payday Maggie's out there on the trail. That old dawg loves that woman o' yores much as you do."

Bonner cast the old man a hard, tight-jawed look. "First place, that ain't much of a bet, 'cause you ain't gettin' a payday; second, she ain't *my* woman"—he nodded—"an' yeah, I 'bout decided the feelin's we got for one another ain't all from man-woman wantin' an' need." He shook his head. "Ain't sayin' that ain't part o' it, a good part, but I 'bout figured we got a lot more feelin's than that."

"When you gonna tell 'er bout them other feelin's you got?"

Trey pulled his mouth to one side in a grimace. "Old man, that ain't none o' your damned business."

Jess bent, slapped his knee, and laughed until tears rolled

down his cheeks. Bonner opened the door in time to invite Maggie and Slim Ramey to step down and rest their saddles.

"Y'all c'mon in, maybe you can stop this old reprobate from stickin' his nose into my business."

Ramey swung his leg over his horse's rump while Trey held his arms up to help Maggie slide off her sidesaddle. He held her a moment longer that was necessary. She stared into his eyes. "Want me to climb back aboard an' let's try that again?"

Trey grinned. "Yeah, b'lieve I didn't handle you gently enough."

She shook her head. "Uh, knew I shouldn't have asked a smart alec that." She headed for the door. "Jess got dinner ready yet?"

"Why, you hungry?"

"Naw, I usually talk to hear myself talk. Heck yes, reckon Slim an' me're both starved. Haven't had a bite since breakfast."

Trey choked back a laugh. "Uuuh-uh, gracious goodness, that's been all o' four hours ago. Poor little girl, ain't had a bite to eat in almost half a day."

Maggie stopped at the door. "If, as any *gentleman* would, you'd invite me in, I'll tell you what caused me to make such a long, food-depriving ride."

"All right, cart yourself inside an' let me in on the big secret."

Inside only a few feet, she turned to face Bonner. "Want you to come over for supper; you can stay in the guest bedroom."

Before she finished, Trey shook his head. "Aw now, little one, you know your pa don't like me. Last time I spent any time over there when he was home, he treated me like a renegade Comanche."

Her look never left his eyes. "Trey, this is Papa's idea. Think he wants to show you he can be decent."

Bonner stared at her a moment. "You say anything to 'im 'bout me maybe buyin's some of his breed stock?"

Maggie shook her head. "Haven't said a word. Knew you'd get madder'n ole billy hell if I did."

He thought on her words a moment, then nodded. "When?"

"Think we can make it back by sundown?"

Trey smiled. "Don't think so. Besides I noticed you an' Ramey packed for overnight. Shame to waste all that time gettin' acquainted while we're alone."

"Gettin' acquainted? Why, dang you, Trey Bonner, I nursed you back from near death, looked on a lot o' your naked body"—she turned a bright red—"well, looked on your naked chest, listened to you grump when I wouldn't let you saddle up an' go to work, w-w-well, dang it, I figure we're right well acquainted right now."

Trey let a sly smile crinkle the corners of his mouth. "Not near as much as I figure on happening someday." Blood rushed to her face again.

The next day, Slim, Maggie, and Bonner left his new home early enough to get to the Box T in time to talk a little before supper. They left Jess and Dawg to watch the place; Juan had spent a couple of days piddling around the walls they'd put up for his future home. Besides, he'd said he didn't want to take a chance on anyone wrecking the work they'd gotten accomplished.

Rogers never took his eyes off of Yadro's labored effort to put his name to the fake land transfers he'd drawn up. When Whitey finally sat back against the back of his chair, sweating like a plow horse in the middle of a day's work, Rogers said, "Get a good night's sleep. Want you to head for Austin in the morning and get these filed at the state land office."

Yadro shook his head. "I ain't very smart, Boss, but I'm tellin' you, it won't be a good thing for me to file these papers. Figure bein' they have somethin' to do with your business they'd take more to you doin' whatever it is you gotta do."

Blood rushed to Rogers head; his hireling bucking him, even making a suggestion didn't set right. He pushed back his anger, held his whisky under his nose, and inhaled its aroma. Pressure decreased at the back of his neck. Yadro might be right. Besides if he took the papers himself, he could make certain everything fell into place the right way, the way he planned it.

He stared at his white-haired gunny. "Gonna leave in the mornin'; don't want you doin' anything. Leave those buildin's those two settlers put on their place alone, I might have use for 'em."

He took a swallow of his drink, stared into the now-empty glass a moment, then nodded. "Think if you get a chance to put a bullet into either one o' those sodbusters you can do it without gettin' yourself killed, or makin' it obvious that maybe you had orders to do it?"

Yadro stood. "Reckon if the chance comes, I'll be mighty careful to know ain't nobody around to tie me to you." He left the room tight jawed.

Skeeter Wells shifted his position on the rock slab against which he'd been sitting for several hours, hoping to get a shot at Bonner. The only person he'd seen around the new building was the friend of the man he wanted to kill.

He'd thought to take a shot at him just for the hell of it, but pulled his rifle sights off of Jimenez. He wouldn't kill a man only because he'd befriended the man he wanted to wreak revenge upon.

While Wells sat there through the long, chilly midday, Jimenez had dug several holes in the back of where the original burned-out cabins had stood. He'd carefully picked up bones, human bones, and placed them on a canvas sheet.

He'd then dug other holes alongside each other on the side of the hill adjacent to the house he and Trey were building. He sorted the bones as to the size of the person they belonged to and placed them in a grave befitting the size of the person. He covered the graves and put a rough wooden cross at the head of each.

Some shred of decency in him made Wells feel good, feel a swelling in his chest toward the man he'd never met. The smell of dried grass and dust gave him a sudden urge to sneeze. He squelched it, giving himself a headache with the blood forced to his head. If he'd allowed the sneeze, his closeness to the man covering the graves might have gotten him shot.

He sat there another hour or so, hoping that Bonner would

show, then finally he figured he might as well get on back to town. He wasn't going to kill the man below him, and his stomach told him he'd not eaten since breakfast. He'd get back and let that pretty lady who ran the cafe fix him a good steak as long as Jimenez wasn't in town. He wriggled from his perch, slid back to his horse, mounted, and rode toward Noname.

Maggie led Slim and Bonner to the front of her father's ranch house. They slipped from their horses and handed Ramey the reins so he could lead the horses to the stable, unsaddle them, and feed them. Maggie led Trey to the veranda.

Before she could pull the door toward her, it opened and her father came out to greet them. He held out his hand to Bonner. Trey hesitated, then grasped Matt's hand. Tedford's grip was firm, sincere.

"C'mon in, boy, wantta apologize for the way I've treated you."

A surge of admiration pushed into Trey's throat. It took a big man to offer an apology. He waited for Maggie to go ahead of him, then went in ahead of Tedford, who went to a cabinet in the corner of the room and poured them each a drink. He looked at his daughter. She shook her head.

Matt handed Bonner his drink, and still standing, said, "Mr. Bonner, reckon for many years I've considered all the land I could ride across in a day or two as mine. Didn't have a legal claim to it, never filed on it, or paid anybody for it, but I came here first and thought on it as by my bein' here, havin' cows on it, made it mine." He took a swallow of his drink, coughed, and looked Trey in the eye. "You of a mind to, I'd like to be friends."

Bonner never broke his gaze from Tedford's. After a moment he nodded. "Reckon I knew how you felt, sir, figure I woulda felt the same." He shook his head. "Don't see as how I intend to take any graze away from you; that valley back o' my house'll graze more cattle than you an' me together will ever put on it." He nodded. "Don't see any reason why we shouldn't be friends."

Tedford grinned. "Good. Now that that's settled, knock back that drink, have a seat, an' I'll get you another." His smile widened. "Gonna pour one for Belle an' Maggie too."

Although the chill of the meeting had gone, a degree of stiffness remained. Only after an hour did Trey relax; Tedford seemed genuinely wanting to be friends, and Maggie and Belle, although not contributing much to the conversation, sat there glowing.

After supper, sitting at the table drinking coffee, Tedford brought up the subject Bonner wanted to avoid. He'd still not settled on how much he trusted Maggie's father, but Matt dumped it right into the middle of the conversation. "Course I know you been shot 'cause Maggie stayed at your place takin' care o' you, but she tells me that wasn't the only time you been shot at. You got any idea who might want you dead?"

Trying to give himself time to figure out Tedford's reason for bringing that into their visit, he took a swallow of coffee. Was the man trying to find out who he suspected? Was he trying to see whether Bonner figured he might have had a hand in it? Trey decided to lay his cards on the table.

"Mr. Tedford, I know who's been shootin' at me; have known almost since his first attempt."

"Why haven't you called 'im out?"

Bonner shook his head. "Wouldn't solve anything. Figure he's workin' for somebody. When I find who that is, I'll take care of 'em both. 'Til then, I'm hopin' the shooter'll lead me to 'im. If I kill the man shootin' at me, the one who's payin' 'im will just go find someone else to do his work."

Matt frowned; he obviously gave Trey's words more than a little thought, then he locked gazes with the ranger. "Mr. Bonner, you have every reason to think I might be the one payin' the man you know is shooting at you. Think by now you have made up your mind what kind o' man I am. Think you've decided whether I'd hire someone to shoot a man I wanted dead."

He took time to pack his pipe and light it, then pierced Trey with a straight-on, penetrating look. "Gonna tell you, son, if I had a reason for wanting you out of the way, I'd look you in the eye an' say what I had on my mind. You can take those words to the bank."

Despite the seriousness of the words between them, Bonner smiled, grinned, then laughed outright. "Damn, Mr. Tedford, as ferocious as you looked just now, all you'd have to do is growl at me an' I'd probably run like a scalded cat."

Matt sat there, obviously stunned at Bonner's reaction. Belle and Maggie choked, then laughed along with Trey. Tedford swung his eyes from one to the other, then a belly laugh rumbled up from his stomach.

After each of them dried their eyes from the tears the laughs had forced, Bonner shook his head in wonder. "Sir, we've 'bout put everything on the table, might's well get it all aired out, then we can sure 'nuff be friends."

Maggie stood, went to the oven, pulled out an apple pie, the aroma of which had been about to drive Trey out of his mind for the past thirty or so minutes, and she cut them each a quarter of it. Trey took a bite, a swallow of coffee, and again looked into Matt's eyes.

"Gonna tell you straight out, sir, I thought at first you mighta been the one, then I met you an' had different thoughts, but I'll tell you now, I got a good idea who the man is—but I ain't got any proof, nothin' that would stand up in court, if we had a court, and nothin' that, if I had to shoot 'im, would convince me I'd done the right thing."

Matt chewed on the last of his pie, loosened his belt, and sat back in his chair. He seemed to want to say something, seemed undecided, then apparently made up his mind. "Son, I got somethin' rollin' 'round in the back o' my head; haven't decided yet whether I have it right, but when I make up my mind I'm thinkin' right, I'll tell you what an' who I think it is." He nodded. "If I tell you that much I'm gonna have to tell you the rest of the story. I'm not ready to do that yet."

His face fell, went solemn, as though just thinking about what he might do tore him apart inside. "Fact is, son, I might not ever have the guts to spill it all to you. It's not somethin' I'm at all proud of." He glanced at Belle. "My wife doesn't even know what I may tell you someday, but if I tell you, I'll tell Belle and Maggie at the same time."

During the course of the evening, Bonner told them he'd be out of pocket for a few days, told them he had business to take care of, told them that getting his business done in Austin might give him the pieces he needed to solve the puzzle of who had tried to kill him.

They kept the things they talked about to more mundane things. Trey, even if he'd had a burr under his saddle about something, wouldn't have brought the subject up. He wanted to keep things friendly since Tedford seemed inclined to be satisfied to keep things more friendly than he would have thought possible only a few hours ago. The subject of stocking his ranch with breeder stock never came up. Bonner decided to wait.

Most of the supper crowd had eaten and left by the time Wells pushed the door open to Linda's Cafe. He took a seat on the bench close to the kitchen and waited for her to come wait on him.

She put a cup in front of him, poured coffee into it, and stood back waiting for him to order.

He gave her a direct look, nodded, and said, "Ma'am, I know I might a scared you out there outside o' town the other day, but I want you to b'lieve I really did want company. I meant you no harm." He shrugged. "Fact is, I've done a lot o' things I ain't proud of, but harmin' a woman ain't none of 'em. I wouldn't ever hurt no woman, never have, never will." He shook his head. "Jest want you to know I'm sorry."

Linda studied him a moment. "Mr. Wells, you did scare me. A woman has reason to fear any who she doesn't know, especially when she's out alone like that." She nodded. "I accept your apology." She smiled, told him what she was serving for supper, took his order, and disappeared into the kitchen to fill his plate.

Wells watched her go into the room that sent the wonderful aromas out to where he sat. For some reason he felt good about apologizing for his actions on the way into town the other day, and at the same time shame flooded him that he'd scared her.

She placed his food in front of him and went back into the kitchen. Skeeter ate slowly, chewed every bite to a frazzle. His mind turned his reason for being here every way he could turn it. He might as well have eaten a plate filled with cotton.

Finally, he shook his head. There was no way out of it. He had to kill Bonner. The ranger had been responsible for the deaths of at least three of his family, and back in Henderson, in East Texas, if a man caused your family hurt, you had to reciprocate or ride in shame the rest of your life. Fact was, he'd heard somewhere that the Bible demanded an eye for an eye, and a tooth for a tooth; well, how about a life for a life?

After a while, he stared at his plate and was surprised to see it empty. He knew it had been good food because he'd never eaten a meal here that he didn't enjoy. He stood, thinking to go to the saloon for a drink, then changed his mind. After eating, a drink didn't sound good. He left a quarter by his plate to pay for his meal and headed for his room.

There, he shucked his gunbelt, hung it on an arm of the chair, and stretched out on the bed. He lay there staring at the ceiling.

He'd never gotten involved in the lawless activities of his kinfolk; he'd been happy farming his quarter section of land, courting the girl he'd gone through the fifth grade with, going to church on Sundays, and having dinner on the grounds. It had been a good life. Why was he taking up a fight with a man he knew only by sight, knew only good enough to train his rifle sights on?

Lying there, he mentally shrugged. His family still lived by the code they'd brought with them from Kentucky, a code that demanded you get even, a code you lived by or left the family hearth in disgrace.

His eyes got heavier, then closed. He thought of the girl in the cafe. She was a decent woman. He'd not bother her. The last thing he thought before letting sleep take him? He had to settle with Bonner before heading home. Family honor demanded it.

On the way back to his ranch the next morning, after Belle and Maggie made sure he had enough food in him to help him survive long enough to get home—pancakes, eggs, venison sausage, and coffee strong enough to float an anvil—Bonner sighed, loosened his belt to gain a little comfort, and thought of the night before.

He wondered what caused Matt to want to bury the hatchet. He pondered that for several minutes, all the while studying the landscape for sign of danger. Finally, he shook his head. He couldn't figure it out, but he felt good that he and Maggie's father could sit in a room with each other without being on edge, feeling that he had to be on his guard the entire time.

He pushed any doubts he'd had about Matt to the back of his mind. In fact, he decided the rancher had nothing to do with burning the settlers out. He wasn't that kind. Then if not Tedford—who? He thought on that for another quarter of a mile. He would bet his saddle that he knew, and that Jimenez had it pegged also, but he needed proof.

He'd said he would go to Austin. Maybe he should stay here long enough to see if he could uncover something he could take to the capital and investigate. When he rode into his ranch yard he still muddled around in indecision.

When he went into his front room, Jess sat at the desk, a sheet of paper in front of him. He looked up at Trey. "Dawg seen you comin' while you wuz still a mile out."

Bonner glanced at the sheet upon which Maynard had been writing; a list stretched down half the page. "What you makin' a list of, old timer?"

Jess tongued his tobacco cud to the other cheek. "Need some special wood to make me some furniture." He gave Bonner a sly sidewise look, a smile creasing the corners of his mouth. "Need a really special sort o' wood to make Maggie a weddin' present, somethin' I got in my mind, somethin' I done give a whole bunch o' thought."

Trey stared at him a long moment. "Why, dang you, you old goat, you're bound an' determined to get me married, ain't ya?"

The gate to the stove's firebox stood open. Jess cut loose with a stream of tobacco juice into the open door. He always left it open for that purpose. He cocked his head to the side, squinted one eye toward Trey, and nodded. "Yep, gonna do what you ain't got 'nuff sense to do yoreself. You don't ask that girl pretty soon, reckon I'm gonna have to do it for ya."

"W-w-why, damn you, Jess, I'll just bet you're that much of a busybody." Bonner stepped back and studied the old man he'd grown to love. "Tell you like it is, Jess, I've got some things I gotta do. You know that." He pulled over a chair, straddled it, and looked Maynard in the eye. "I've 'bout made up my mind how I feel 'bout Mag. Soon's I get done with this assignment RIP sent me on, I figure I'll have everything settled in my mind such that maybe I'll ask 'er." He threw Maynard a sheepish look. "Guess I might as well admit it, ain't no maybe about it, I'll ask 'er. Reckon I made up my mind some time ago. Think you seen it 'fore I did."

"*Maybe* you'll ask 'er?" Jess chewed furiously a moment, spit, and pinned Trey with a look. "Maybe hell. Like I done told you, I ain't givin' you much more time. You got all kinds o' sense 'bout a lot o' things, but you ain't got a gut in yore head when it comes to women. Figger somebody's gotta take charge." He nodded. "Yeah, an' you admittin' jest now that you'll ask 'er ain't gonna git me off 'n yore backside 'til you do it." He shot another stream of tobacco into the hot maw of the stove.

"Yeah, you don't b'lieve me so you're gonna go ahead an' do what you've already made up your mind to do." Trey nodded. "You've elected yourself as the one, an' there ain't nothin' I can do 'bout it." He shook his head. "Damn! For an old goat who ain't ever spent thirty minutes with a woman, you sure have become a right knowing man. Gonna have to ask you more what I oughtta do 'bout most things."

Jess grinned. "Go right ahead, young man. I might surprise you with what I know." He chuckled. "Reckon after takin' care o' some o' yore business, an' buildin' Maggie a weddin' present, gonna have to steer that other young ranger in the right direction. He ain't got no more sense than you 'bout womenfolk."

Tedford, unusually quiet after telling Trey good-bye, pulled his hat down low on his forehead and walked down to the corral. He hung his arms over the top rail and stared at the fenced-in horses. He turned his problem over in his mind.

Within days after the War between the States, he'd committed what many times since then he'd justify to himself as being his right; then the next moment he'd wonder if what he'd done might qualify as the crime of the century.

His conscience stayed awash with guilt, reluctant to admit he'd done something of which he should be ashamed, or something any man would have done without a twinge of conscience.

Many times in the last few years if there had been any law close by, he'd have gone to them and admitted his act—but there was no law within two hundred miles, so he'd let it stay inside him, eating his guts out. Only two men other than himself knew what he'd done, and one of them held it over Tedford's head. Many times Matt had thought to go into town, call that man out, and kill him. Every time, he'd shake his head and unconsciously push his Colt .44 down hard into its holster. He'd not add a killing to his guilt.

Then his thoughts centered on the young man Maggie had, in no uncertain terms, told him she intended to spend the rest of her life with. What about the man of Maggie's choice, and what about Maggie?

Matt, being honest with himself, knew he'd been unfair; Trey Bonner was as decent a man as he'd ever met. He couldn't let Maggie pursue something that might wreck her and Bonner's future that, if they knew what he'd done, might change their decisions. His problem instead of being one he alone had to live with now involved his entire family.

He stood straighter, squared his shoulders, and headed back to the house. Before he let things go too far, he'd call a family meeting . . . and include Bonner. He'd tell them the whole story. They'd have to judge him as their own moral and legal standards dictated.

He stopped a few yards short of the house. Should he tell Maggie first so she might stop her pursuit of Bonner?

13

TREY, LEADING A packhorse, lifted his hand to Jimenez and Maynard. "See you in a week or two."

Hours later, well on the trail to Austin, he breathed deeply, pulled in the smells of dried grass, dust, and the hint of mountain cedar. The shackles of town fell from his shoulders. He'd long been hemmed in by the few miles it took to ride from his ranch to town and back. For many years, the horizon or the other side of the next hill had been his only constraints. He felt good looking down a trail with no end that he could see. Then he thought about his feelings.

An endless trail had many lonely hours. Did he really like that sense of freedom? Would a life with Maggie fence him in? She seemed like the kind of woman who, if her man said he wanted to hit the trail, would pack and go with him. He pondered that a few moments, then the feel of freedom returned. Freedom was knowing he had it whether he ever used it or not. He smiled to himself. Maggie would never fence him in.

Then he thought about the trail. Was it getting to the destination at the end, or was it what one could encounter along the way? He decided that the unknown encounters along the way were the things that made the trail tantalizing. He pulled his thoughts in to make certain he looked at the things about him. It wasn't like him to ride along daydreaming; he rode in dangerous country—hostile Indians, outlaws, and forces of nature still abounded. He sighed. Someday this country would be tamed, civilized. He wondered if he wanted that to happen.

He squinted into the distance. Now about high noon, the sun shone brightly, although not warmly. He wore his sheepskin and felt good in it.

He nodded. As thought earlier, a rider rode ahead of him. The distance prevented him from identifying the man; it had to be a man, for no woman would be out here alone. He thought to urge his horse to a faster pace, catch up with whoever rode ahead of him, and have company along the trail. He shook his head. Maybe the man who rode there wasn't one he cared to share the trail with. He decided to wait until after dark, scout out the man's camp, and see who he might be.

Several hours later, after the sun had long disappeared, Bonner sighted flickering firelight only a quarter of a mile ahead, maybe a little less. He slipped from his horse, ground reined him, pulled a pair of moccasins from his saddlebags, looped the reins of his packhorse over the saddlehorn of the saddle he'd sat in all day, and set out toward the eerily dancing light of the fire. He walked knowing that even a slight noise in this quiet desert air would carry far. When he got close enough that sounds might carry to the camper, he searched out the ground with the soles of his moccasins, taking care that nothing he stepped on would make a noise.

Still about a hundred yards from the camp, Trey frowned. The man hunkered by the fire looked vaguely familiar. He squatted, rolled to his knees, then went flat of his stomach. He crawled and slithered to within perhaps thirty or forty yards. Then lying still, he raised his head such that he could see all in the camp plainly. The man he saw caused anger to well into the back of his throat, anger caused by crude treatment from business dealings with the man and suspicion raised from those dealings. Rogers.

Bonner relaxed against the ground to think. His first impulse was to slither back out of hearing range, stand, and walk back far enough out to build a fire the other side of some land swell and make camp.

He frowned into the darkness. Maybe if he caught up with the land agent, rode with him, he could get a clue as to what he was up to. He thought on that a few moments, shook his head, and decided he'd stay behind Rogers to his destination and see what he did once there. He hunched his back, got to his hands and knees, and crawled far enough that he felt safe enough to stand and walk away.

Bonner wanted to ride a wide circle around Rogers and get to Austin ahead of him, but between where they rode and the state capital the trail branched off toward many places; San Antonio, Fort Worth, and many others. Trey decided he'd better stay behind the land agent.

Four days later, in time for his nooning, Bonner closed in on Rogers when he rode down the main street of Austin only fifty or so yards behind the land agent. Getting this close in the cluttered traffic posed no threat. Wagons, mounted riders, dogs, and foot traffic all jammed the street ahead of him. He kept his eyes glued to the top of Rogers's hat. He didn't want to lose sight of him now. Any place the land agent stopped might point to why he'd come to the capital.

Rogers showed no hesitation. He walked his horse to the front of the state land office, hitched him, then went in the building.

Bonner wanted to follow the man in, but on second thought looked at the store next door. The bench in front of it had seated on it all it could hold. Trey walked to the store's wall, backed up to it, and slid down to sit on the boardwalk. He kept his eyes on the door of the land office. After about an hour, Rogers emerged, untied his horse, and walked across the street to a hotel. Bonner stood and headed for the land office.

At the desk, he described Rogers and asked what business he'd had with the office. Of course he might have been filing reports from the area for which he was responsible, but a nagging suspicion tugged at Bonner; in fact anything the agent might do engendered suspicion on Bonner's part. Also, he didn't rely on those in the state office knowing Rogers; there were many men in that position around the state.

The man who waited on him cast Bonner a slit-eyed look, then asked, "What business is it o' yours what anyone else wants here?"

Trey reached to his shirt pocket, fingered his ranger's badge, pulled it out and placed it on the counter in front of the man. "You can tell me now, or I'll have RIP Ford sign an order for it. Show me an' it'll save us both a lot o' time."

The clerk shrugged, reached in the drawer under the counter ledge, and pulled two sheets of paper from it.

The first thing Bonner saw was that the papers were a deed to land in the Noname area, *and the next thing was identification of the plots he and Jimenez had previously filed on.*

The deeds stated that on payment of twenty-five cents an acre ownership was transferred from three people he'd never heard of to a Charles Bascom, also someone he'd never heard of; but he *had* heard of the witness—Yadro. And he would bet everything he'd ever own that the three people who'd supposedly sold the property were those whose bones Jimenez had buried alongside the slope overlooking land now claimed by him and Bonner, *and* he'd also bet that Bascom was Rogers. He'd get proof of that.

"Gonna ask ya to keep these papers separate from any other business you do until I contact you again. Even if this Bascom comes back in, *do not let him have them.* Tell 'im you had to send them to another office. All right?"

The clerk nodded. Bonner told him he'd be back, maybe in a day or two, but he'd be back. He headed for RIP's office.

When he pulled the door shut behind him, Ford glanced up, stood, and came around his desk, hand extended. "Well, now, I'll be double danged. Trey, how you doin'?" He looked over Bonner's shoulder. "Jimenez with you?"

Trey, still gripping RIP's hand, shook his head.

Ford let go of Bonner's hand. "He should a caught up with you. I didn't hear from you almost the whole summer so I sent 'im to find you. Dang! Hope nothin's happened to the boy."

Bonner chuckled. "Settle down, RIP, ain't nothin' happened to 'im. Left 'im out yonder at Noname to keep 'is eye on things."

Ford, holding Trey's upper arm, steered him to a chair, almost pushed him into it, went around his desk, and poured them each a cup of coffee. He sat and looked at Bonner. "Why the hell haven't I heard anything outta you?"

Bonner shrugged. "Didn't have anything I could back up, didn't have anything up 'til less'n a hour ago. B'lieve I got somethin' now, but I'm gonna ask ya to let me an' Juan handle it to make sure."

"Won't let you do anything 'til I hear what it is. Tell me what you have."

Trey grinned. "Gonna take a little while, sir."

"I have time, get on with it."

Bonner set in to tell his boss everything that had happened. He skimped over his and Jimenez each filing on a parcel of land, and their initial suspicions of Tedford, then he got down to the details of filing on the land, Rogers's attitude when they did, and his only now finding that the land agent had not submitted their claims, but had less than an hour ago turned in a deed for the claim under somebody else's name.

He looked RIP in the eye. "Gotta ask ya, sir, don't do anythin' right now. Juan an' me, well, I want us to find out who this gent is who supposedly bought the parcel from them who settled there." He took a sip of his coffee, swallowed, then nodded. "Reckon Juan an' me know who the man is but want to nail it down tight, then we'll bring 'im in for you to get tried before a court of law."

Ford pinned Bonner with a look that would pierce steel. "Can I count on the two of you to bring him in, count on the two o' you to not be judge, jury, an' executioner?"

Trey shook his head. "Can't promise you that, sir." He shook his head. "All I can promise you is that we'll try."

He pulled his shoulders up around his neck in an exaggerated shrug. "You been in more gunfights than I reckon Jimenez an' me put together. If he tries to pull a gun on either one o' us, we'll send you a corpse." He shook his head. "But I promise you we'll *try* to bring 'im in alive. He's right here in this town, right now, but I want to let 'im get on back to Noname. See what he does then."

Ford studied Bonner a long moment, then nodded. "You never lied to me yet, son. Know you an' Jimenez'll handle it within the law. You got my approval."

Bonner stood, told RIP he'd hear from him when he'd solved the case. He left.

Guilt plagued Trey when he walked out on the street. He'd not said it, but he'd let RIP think he and Juan had filed on those land parcels in order to determine who might be the guilty party in the land steal.

And he'd said nothing about Linda and Maggie. And he'd not said anything about resigning from the rangers. He had a weakness as far as emotional things were concerned. He avoided confronting those things, then when he couldn't sidestep them any longer, he'd bull into them head-on, making himself seem hard, seem to be a person who didn't give a damn.

He shrugged mentally. That was the way he was, and he didn't know how to change. Now he wondered what to do next. He thought to check into the availability of some good breed stock, but first he wanted a drink. He walked to the nearest saloon.

When Bonner toed the stirrup and rode from Tedford's ranch house, Maggie took her father's arm, hugged it to her breasts, and looked up at him. "Papa, don't know how I can thank you. I think you made Trey think you liked 'im."

Matt put his hand over Maggie's small, work-hardened one she held his arm with. "This'll surprise you, little one; I do like 'im. He's a likable man, an' I believe an honorable one. That's the kind of man I want for you—if I have to give you to anyone, he's got to be a man I respect." He nodded. "I think maybe Bonner's that kind of man."

He stepped away from his daughter, turned toward the corral, and said, over his shoulder, his voice strangely gruff, "Gonna ride over west o' here, thought I saw a bunch of unbranded stock. Wantta get it all done 'fore winter sets in. The calf crop is better'n I expected this fall. Gonna have to sell some of the yearlin's soon, or the range is gonna be overgrazed."

Maggie wanted to tell him that Trey wanted to buy a good bull and a few heifers, in fact she opened her mouth to say so, then clamped her jaws shut. If she said anything about what Bonner wanted, she'd be stepping into his shoes, at least she thought that was the way he'd take it. Mentally, she shook her head. Nope, that was a man's business. She'd wait for him to say something to her father.

Through the afternoon and evening, Maggie did the things she and her mother did every day: washed dishes, washed a load of clothes, cooked supper, ate and cleaned up from the supper mess, then the time came she'd waited for—bedtime. The time she could lie in her bed and think private thoughts about Trey. Thoughts she wouldn't share with anyone, thoughts so private she could feel her face warm and knew she blushed in the darkness.

Shame never occurred to her. He was her man whether he yet faced up to it, admitted it. She didn't shrink from admitting she wanted him, wanted him lying beside her, his hands, lips, and body searching her body, getting to know all of her. Warmth flooded her, centered heat in parts of her she had seldom given a thought. She perspired. She hurt from wanting. She forced herself to take her mind somewhere else, but then she realized she'd be right back to wanting Trey beside her. She stared at the ceiling for a long time that night. Dawn cast a rosy, pink cast upon the land before she slept . . . with a smile.

Whitey Yadro moped around the saloon after Rogers left. He wanted, when his boss got back from his trip, to be able to tell him that he'd killed both Bonner and Jimenez. He wanted that, but didn't have the guts to seek them out and get it done.

Wells wouldn't be any help; besides, all he wanted was the tall Texan dead. He had something eating on him where that man was concerned. He showed no interest in killing the Texican.

Fear ate at Whitey's guts when he thought of trying to take either of the two men on alone. Everything he'd done in the way of killing, he'd always had several men with him, men of his own stripe, and there were none of that kind left in the Noname area that he could think of..

He would not admit to fear. He thought about being able to tell Rogers he'd taken them out until he decided to ride out toward Bonner's place, stake it out, and maybe he'd get lucky, maybe he could get one of them.

He drank himself into a stupor the day Rogers left for the capital, then the next morning he saddled his horse and rode toward the hills.

He got within a half mile of Bonner's house before he pulled off the trail and looked for a vantage point where he could look at all that went on around the ranch yard.

He scanned the area. The Texican shoveled hay to the riding stock, then turned toward the house. Yadro hurried to his horse, pulled his rifle from its scabbard and went back to the rock behind which he'd been hiding when he saw Jimenez. The Texican had disappeared.

Whitey cursed himself for not taking his rifle with him when he stepped from the saddle and vowed to never again get separated from it. He thought he could have gotten at least one of those Rogers wanted killed.

Jimenez shoved the pitchfork into the haystack and turned his steps toward the house.

As soon as he stepped through the doorway, Jess put his rifle back in the rack. "Jest comin' to get you. Dawg bristled an' growled a few seconds ago. They's somebody out yonder, Juan, somebody Dawg don't like."

Jimenez frowned. He wanted to sneak out the back and see if he could spot whoever or whatever it was that raised Dawg's hackles. His frown deepened. He shook his head. There was no way he could get out there and get a good look without exposing himself to a shot. He glanced at the dog, who still stood looking out toward the hill in front of the house.

"Jess, reckon Dawg's got 'im located pretty close, but there's no way we can get out there to take a look. Gonna swing the door open, stand behind it an' see what I can see."

"Now, young'un, don't you show any part o' yoreself. Even if whoever's out yonder ain't a good shot, he's in close enough he cain't miss."

Jimenez nodded. "You take hold of Dawg. Be just like 'im to go runnin' out there after whoever it is."

He stood there, partially hidden by the door. He scanned the ridge, swept his eyes down its sides, then focused on a cluster of rocks at the right side of the ridge. He stared at the rocks, and for several minutes, never took his eyes from them—then a reflection of sunlight bounced from the edge. His gut muscles pulled tight. He nodded, slowly raised his Winchester, and sighted in on where he thought he might dust the man. He squeezed the trigger.

Simultaneous with the sound of his rifle and the spray of rock dust from the boulder, a puff of powder smoke jumped from behind the rock. Jimenez spun into the room, dropped his rifle, grabbed his shoulder, and cursed.

Jess, still holding Dawg by the scruff of his neck, hurried to the door, closed it, and turned to Juan. "Where you hit?"

"Shoulder. Got me pretty good. Don't be a damned fool an go out there tryin' to get a shot at 'im. If he stayed put, he'd kill ya; if he left, it'd be a waste o' time. I think I heard a horse leavin' them rocks mighty fast soon's his shot sounded."

Jess hung his rifle back on the gun rack and went to Jimenez. He pulled his shirt back from where the most blood showed. He nodded. "You wuz right, he got ya pretty good. Now sit still. I gotta see if that slug hit any bones or clipped yore lung."

While he checked the shoulder, his fingers probed the area around where the bullet entered, then he stripped Juan's shirt down his shoulder and looked at his back. "Went all the way through, didn't hit a bone."

He stepped back, looked at Jimenez squint eyed, then held his hand under Juan's mouth. "Cough, cough, dammit, an' spit in my hand." He pinned Juan with a look. "Go ahead, spit in my hand. I can wash it with lye soap. Gotta see did that bastard nick yore lung."

Jimenez looked into Maynard's eyes. His own eyes now had to be pain filled. "Gonna cough now." He drew in a breath, pushed it from his lungs in a hacking cough, then spit into the palm of Jess's hand.

Jess studied the spittle a moment, then went to a window where better light shone. He spent several minutes looking for flecks of blood in every bubble of the phlegm Jimenez had coughed up.

He'd been frowning; now his brow smoothed. He smiled. "Reckon they ain't nothin' wrong with you I cain't doctor. Bones're all right, lungs're all right."

Jimenez held a cloth Maynard handed him to his shoulder, grimaced, and shook his head. "Damn! Trey gets shot an' Maggie comes over to take care of 'im." He shook his head. "Was hopin' Linda might be needed."

Jess chuckled. "Reckon I could ride in an' git 'er, but you don't need to cause 'er to lose that much business. Figger she can use what money she makes in that cafe o' hers."

Juan nodded. "Just my luck." He frowned, looked to be thinking, then nodded. "Jess, I seen some aloe vera plant out yonder. It'd be right good, if when we're sure that bushwhacker is gone, if you'd try to gather a few leaves an' milk 'em. That stuff's mighty good for any kind o' open wound."

Jess cocked his head, one eye closed to squint at him. "Jest gonna ask ya if they wuz any o' them plants close by." He folded two rags into pads and placed them over the holes in Jimenez's back and shoulder, then tied a strip of cloth around his chest and shoulders to hold the pads in place.

He glanced at Dawg, who had again curled up by the stove. "Reckon that danged shooter's done gone. Point me toward where you seen them plants an' I'll go git us some."

Jimenez tried to talk Jess into waiting a while to make certain the bushwhacker was indeed gone, but Jess shook his head, saying that the sooner he got the sticky sap from the aloe vera on, and in, the ranger's wounds the better. He'd already poured whisky into each hole "to kill the germs," as he put it. He took a healthy swallow of the rotgut whisky in between soaking the bandages and pouring the whisky in the raw holes. He even offered Jimenez a swallow while he doctored him.

Wells, in the middle of his noonday meal, looked up when Yadro came through the door. His meal, which he'd been enjoying, abruptly became tasteless. Whitey swung his legs over the bench and sat next to him. Wells slanted him a look across his shoulder. "Where you been?"

Yadro swung his head to look about the cafe. "Ain't gonna talk 'bout it in here, but think I got one of 'em. Tell ya 'bout it when we git back to the room."

Wells nodded, then turned his attention back to his meal. He hoped the one Whitey thought he'd gotten was not Bonner. Bonner was the one he had left home to take care of. In fact, he caught himself hoping Yadro had not "gotten" either of the men.

He wondered at his thoughts. Why should he care which man, if any, the cheap gunny had shot? He ignored Whitey while he finished his meal.

His thoughts had gone back to that quarter section of land he wanted more and more to be cultivating, planting, and harvesting, and that girl he'd known since the fifth grade.

He thought of the ranger he'd almost killed up on the rimrock. He smiled to himself. He'd never told Yadro the two men who'd filed on that land Rogers wanted were Texas rangers. He thought if he told the gunny who they were that he'd saddle up and put West Texas behind him. In fact, if either he or Yadro shot either of the rangers, there would be nowhere in Texas they'd be safe from the law. That was something he'd have to give more thought. He'd never be able to go back to his farm.

He glanced at the gunny's plate and saw that he had only finished half his meal. Wells stood, and without a word, left. He had never cottoned to the cheap killer, and now he wanted as little time around him as he could make possible.

Back in his room, he remembered seeing Rogers leave

town leading a packhorse. He wondered where the land agent headed. Wondered if he'd told Yadro he was leaving, then figured he didn't give a damn whether he'd told him or not. His thoughts shifted to the tall pines, green grass, sandy soil, and the rains of East Texas. He wondered that his thinking took that turn more and more.

Bonner sat at a back table staring into his drink. He took a swallow and let it rest on his tongue a moment, wishing Ian Murphy had whisky of this quality in his watering hole. Then his thoughts turned to Rogers. How could he and Juan make certain they kept the land they'd not only filed on but built on as well?

There must be other crooked land agents in the state, but Rogers was the one he and Jimenez had the misfortune to have dealings with. Thinking of Rogers, blood slowly pushed up behind Bonner's eyes, pushed pressure and heat to his brain. His fingers caressed the walnut grips of his Colt. His anger grew. He'd kill the sorry bastard. Kill him slowly. All the work he'd put into building his place; all the dreams he had of marrying, having children, raising cattle, a vegetable garden. Even though he hadn't put a face to the girl he'd marry until only recently, he now saw Maggie tending the things around a house that turned it into a home. Yeah, Maggie filled out, completed his dream. Rogers threatened to destroy everything. His blood reached the boiling point. He nodded unconsciously, even though no one would know he nodded. Then he shook his head. Hell! He carried a lawman's badge. He'd sworn to uphold the law. His best friend, RIP, had reared him to respect law and justice.

Justice. That word alone kept him thinking. Law had nothing to do with justice. It would be beyond the law for him to simply call Rogers out and kill him, but justice, by any definition, would be served.

But he'd accepted the Texas Ranger badge he carried in his pocket to serve the law. He thought a long moment, grimaced, and mentally nodded. He'd stay within the law as long as he could—as long as it didn't encroach on his dream.

* * *

In the same saloon, Rogers sat at a table back in the shadows at the back of the room, only a couple of tables from where Bonner sat, *and he looked at the ranger and recognized him as the squatter who'd filed on land he had only a few hours ago taken steps to make his own.*

His smug contentment of having accomplished part of what he'd spent over a year trying to set up evaporated. All he had left to do was take over Tedford's ranch. Then he'd be in control of all of that for which he'd plotted. *If* Bonner didn't mess the whole thing up. He couldn't let him do that.

What the hell was the nester doing in the state capital? Would he go to the land office and check on whether his claim had been lawfully filed? He pondered that question awhile, drank his drink, and ordered another. He moved from the chair against the wall to one that faced away from Bonner in case the nester looked his way.

After turning all the probabilities over and around in his mind he shook his head. If Bonner did go to the land office, he'd surely find out his claim hadn't been filed. Rogers shook his head. He couldn't take that chance. He knocked back his drink and stood. He'd go to a saloon where the element hung out who would rustle, rape, or kill *for a price*.

The price! He didn't have that much money left; wouldn't have until he took over Tedford's ranch and sold off some of his cattle. If Tedford stayed and decided to fight, Yadro could take care of him, but Bonner was a different story.

A chill ran up Rogers's back. The preemption act, an act of government he hadn't counted on, would turn his plans upside down. Trey Bonner would fight tooth and nail for his legal rights and Yadro hadn't been able to kill him or scare him off. Now here he was, right here in Austin. Unconsciously, Rogers patted his billfold. He'd find somebody to kill Bonner at *his* price, one that he could afford.

He pulled his coat tighter around him to ward off the night chill and walked briskly toward the seedy part of town, an area where the saloons catered to drunks, cowboys, people who worked and sweated for a living, and those who wouldn't work, but would do anything for a dollar. He considered himself too good to patronize a place of that nature, but this was different; he needed someone who would do what he wanted done.

He passed two saloons as being a step above the kind he looked for. He came to the front of one, hesitated, then pushed through the bat-wing doors; it was not yet cold enough to close the heavy wooden one against the weather.

He walked to the bar, stood at the end, and ordered a drink. When the bartender put his drink in front of him, he asked, "Know anybody lookin' for work?"

The man looked at him, frowned, then shook his head. "Most o' these men in here have already settled in for the winter." He shrugged. "They, most of 'em, have been with their ranches or employers quite a spell now. They ain't about to leave." He picked up the drink he'd only a moment ago put in front of Rogers, swabbed a ring of moisture from under it, and put it back.

He stepped toward the middle of the bar, then turned back. "There's a couple in here, out o' work, probably wouldn't take a job if offered one—but they always have money. Don't know what they do to earn it. You wouldn't want that kind workin' for you." He again stepped toward the middle of the bar.

"Wait a minute. I can watch 'em pretty close. Won't need 'em for long. How 'bout pointin' 'em out to me. I'll check 'em out an' see if I can handle 'em."

The bartender shrugged, then pointed to a table close to the back wall. "The clean-shaved one an' the bearded one sittin' with 'im always got money, an' spend a lot o' time in here."

The land agent nodded, put a dime on the counter for his drink, knocked it back, shuddered, then headed toward the table with the two men.

When he approached the table they looked up at him. "The man tendin' bar told me you two men might be huntin' work."

"Don't know where he got that there notion," the clean-shaved one said. He turned to his partner. "You tell 'im anything like that?"

The bearded one shook his head and laughed. "You know damned well I ain't said nothin' 'bout wantin' work." He cocked his head and stared at Rogers. "What kind a job you hirin' for?"

The land agent looked at them a moment. His back muscles tightened. The leaders up his neck pulled against his head. How did he figure to handle this when he came in here? He couldn't just say to these men, or any men for that matter, that he wanted a man killed and that he wanted them to do it.

He shook his head. "Reckon I made a mistake, men. Don't b'lieve y'all would do the kind o' work I need done." He nodded. "Thanks anyway." He spun and headed for the door.

He sweated, his breathing came hard. He seldom did anything without thinking it through, planning every move, and here almost in a panic he'd approached two men to do something that would require his in-depth knowledge of who they were, knowledge of their past, and knowledge that they would and could do what he required.

Almost back to his hotel, his nerves settled down, he coldly calculated his next move, and that move included getting Bonner dead, if he had to do it himself.

Bonner figured if there was any chance Rogers had seen him, he'd figure on his land steal being discovered, and there was a chance the land agent had seen him crossing the street, going in a saloon. He might have seen him go into the courthouse when he went to see RIP. That being the case, he'd better keep his guard up.

The first thing he checked was the hotel register. He nodded. Rogers had a room in the hotel only three doors down from the one in which he stayed. He'd have to be careful to not be seen when he entered or left his room. He frowned. Also, he'd better take care while in his room asleep. That would be an opportune time to try to murder him.

He went back to see RIP. After pouring himself a cup of the chief ranger's coffee, he sat and stared across the desk at his boss. "Colonel, I need you to do somethin' for me. Want you to get those two deeds from the land office an' keep 'em 'til I can go back to Noname an' arrest the man Rogers hired to do his killin' for him."

RIP nodded. "All right. But why don't we take Rogers into custody now, before you go back?"

"Tell you how it is, Colonel. I'm sure, but ain't got enough to prove Rogers is the one tied in with those fake names on the deeds, or that he's the one who hired Yadro, an' Yadro is the one who witnessed the transfer. I need him to testify. Then we need to charge him with the murder of those settlers."

He took a swallow of coffee, then followed it with a deep breath. "Aw hell, sir, reckon I need to get back there an' write down everything I know, an' then write down all the things I have yet to prove." He pulled his mouth down in a grimace. "Reckon what I'm sayin' is that I want an airtight case on that slime." He grinned. "Plus, there's some personal things I gotta take care of. One of 'em I figure I might have to interpret the law on my own. There's a man down yonder who might need a little help."

RIP cleared his throat and leaned to rest his arms on his desk. He pinned Bonner with a steely stare. "Don't want to know what you're going to do *on your own*. Don't tell me a damned thing about it. All right?"

Bonner smiled, stood, and held his hand out. "See you again soon's I get this sorted out so's I know exactly what Rogers has done an' can prove it. Gonna head back to Noname 'fore daylight. I won't be seein' you for a while."

RIP stood, leaned across his desk, and clasped Trey's hand. "Be careful, son."

Bonner smiled, showing little or no humor. "That's one thing you can always bet your last dollar on, sir." He left and headed back to the hotel. He figured to get a good night's sleep before hitting the trail the next morning.

In his room, he thought to sleep in the chair and rig the bed to look like someone slept in it, then shook his head.

Damned if he'd let a two-bit crook like Rogers rob him of a good night's sleep when he had to spend the next day in the saddle, sunup to sundown. He placed the back of the chair under the door handle, removed his hat and boots, then placed his .44 next to his hand, shut his eyes, and went to sleep.

Sometime during the night he came instantly awake. He

lay still, all his senses trained to define what awakened him. The door scraped and opened a crack, enough to show a sliver of light from the hall. He eased his legs over the side of the bed to stand. The bedsprings squeaked as soon as his weight shifted, then made more noise when he placed his hands down beside him to stop his movement.

The door closed and footsteps sounded on the wooden floor, but didn't go far. They stopped. The soft sound of a door being unlocked, pushed open, then a slight *snick* when it shut caused Bonner to nod into the dark. Rogers.

He strapped on his Colt, reached for the door, then had second thoughts. He didn't want the land agent yet. Besides, if he went after him now, he figured Rogers would fire through the door and he might catch a chunk of lead. He shook his head. He didn't want that to happen either. He pushed the chair under the doorknob more securely and went back to bed.

14

SKEETER WELLS HAD not seen Bonner or anyone from the foothills ranches in town lately. He wondered at that. There had been a dance only a few days ago, and Bonner and Jimenez never missed a dance.

Not knowing where any of the foothills bunch were preyed on his mind until he decided to find out. Yadro hadn't come back from the cafe yet, but Wells didn't figure to tell him what he had in mind anyway. He rolled his bedroll, cleaned and oiled his Winchester, loaded it, and went to Parsons's store. He would be gone a few days and needed provisions.

While riding toward the hills, he wondered how he could again get to the rimrock without riding by Bonner's place. He pondered that a few moments, then decided he'd have to skirt the canyon that ran in back of the ranger's claim and find another trail to get him to the mesa and ultimately the rimrock.

He studied the cactus, sage, alkali soil, and terrain devoid of trees of any kind, except those that grew along the banks of streams, and water of any source was as scarce as trees. He frowned and shook his head. Many people found this land to their liking, but his land, land where he grew to manhood, was as different as night and day from the landscape he looked upon.

Without thinking, he neck-reined his horse toward the east, then wondered at his action, pulled the reins to stop, and sat pondering what unconscious motive had caused him to do that. Abruptly, he grinned. "Come on, old hoss, we're going home. I ain't got nothin' personal against that ranger. Ain't gonna try to kill 'im, jest gonna go find that lil ole girl from school, marry 'er, grow kids an' cotton, an' live the kind o' life a man's got a right to."

He straightened in the saddle, urged his horse ahead, and headed east. For the first time in months he let a tune come to his lips, then he sang "Buffalo Gals." His voice bounced back to him from the hills. He smiled.

Two days later, a horse and rider came into view. Wells thumbed the thong from the hammer of his Colt. He had no reason to expect trouble, but in this day and time a man never knew what he'd encounter.

The sun, now low in the west, shone directly into the face of the man approaching. Wells studied him, thinking the closer he got that he'd seen the man around Noname. Then it became clear. The ranger. The man he'd come out here to kill. Here was his chance. He could go home without anyone, family members or people in his hometown, questioning his honor.

He thought on that a moment. Bonner had no reason to expect trouble from him; in fact they'd never met formally, although they'd seen each other on the street, or in the cafe, or saloon in Noname, so why not stop and see what kind of man he'd set out to shoot from ambush?

Their horses brought them to within speaking distance. Bonner tipped his hat. "Howdy, neighbor, what you doin' so far from home?"

"Ain't leavin' home now. I'm goin' home, an' every step this ole hoss takes he's gettin' me closer to my own fireside." Wells kept his face toward the ranger.

He'd not try for a head-on gunfight. If he tried at all, he

knew he couldn't beat Bonner; he'd seen him handle a gun, and there was no way anybody he knew could outdraw or out-shoot the tall Texan.

Wells had the advantage of having the sun behind him. He could study the ranger without it being obvious. He took in the man's tall, well-built frame, and he judged Bonner would be considered handsome by most women. The ranger looked at him with an open, honest stare, a look men would trust. All in all, he measured up as being likable, and Wells found him-self far from *disliking* the man he looked upon.

Then the ranger surprised him. "Neighbor, it's right close to sundown, time to make camp; why don't we share a fire?"

Wells frowned, swallowed, then nodded. "Why not? We both have to eat an' sleep." He glanced back toward his packhorse. "I got enough coffee an' stuff without us both unpackin'."

Bonner had recognized Wells as being the stranger who had taken up with Yadro. He'd considered riding on after his greeting, but then thought he'd like having the man where he could watch him.

Also, in that, as he'd suggested, sunset closed in on them and they'd each be making camp soon, their camps wouldn't be far apart, not far enough apart that the stranger couldn't sneak back to his camp and shoot into it. He admitted to him-self that he had no reason to suspect the man, but as he'd al-ways heard, "birds of a feather flock together." He nodded to himself. Yeah, he wanted to study the man up close, and hav-ing him in camp with him he could know if the man did any-thing to suggest that he intended to harm him.

They introduced themselves, then set about making camp. While Wells took provisions from his packsaddle, Bonner went about gathering sticks and small pieces of wood and building a fire.

Later, sitting across the fire from each other drinking their after-supper coffee, Bonner swept Wells with a studying look. The man was less than six feet tall, blocky built, and by his dress and behavior, gave the impression that he didn't belong in the west.

He looked more like a sodbuster than a cattleman or cowboy.

His clothes were those of a farmer: bib overalls, brogans instead of boots—about the only thing Western on him was his straggly straw hat.

"Seen you around town, Wells. You an' that white-haired man, the one who seemed to consider himself a gunfighter, were right friendly. Y'all been friends long?"

Wells looked into his cup a long while, apparently wondering how to answer. When he raised his eyes from his cup, he looked directly into Bonner's. "Never were friends, Bonner. Reckon we both needed a friend, an' after talkin' awhile found we had somethin' in common."

Bonner grunted. His hand rested close to his Colt. "Somethin' in common? You mean, in common like tryin' to kill me?"

Wells choked on the swallow of coffee he'd only then put in his mouth. He spewed it out in front of him, then making it clear he'd not go for his .44, he held his cup with both hands out in front of him.

"Bonner, I wantta level with you, but I got it figgered you'd kill me 'fore I got through."

His face feeling stiff as dried, weathered leather, Bonner pinned the ambusher with a look that didn't give an inch. "Try me."

Obviously careful to make any move he made a friendly one, Wells reached for the coffeepot with his right hand, poured himself a full cup, took a sip of the boiling hot liquid, then returned Bonner's look. "It's a long story, Ranger Bonner. Take a while to tell it."

Trey let a thin smile break the corners of his lips. "So you know I'm a ranger. Yadro know it too?"

Wells shook his head. "I never told 'im. Figger if he knew, he'd have packed his bedroll an' left this part o' the country. Didn't want 'im to do that. Thought I might get on the same payroll as him, 'til I found out what he wuz doin'."

Bonner nodded. "All right, tell me your story; I got all night."

Wells nodded. "Gotta start back a couple o' years."

Bonner nodded. "Go ahead."

Wells started with the code his family brought with them

from the mountains of Kentucky, that of upholding family honor when a thing was done to them by an outsider.

Then he told Bonner about his three kinfolk being brought in, tried, and hanged, and that he'd been the one picked to even the score for their deaths.

Then he told him about his, only in the last few days, wondering why he should give up everything he wanted in life to get revenge on a man for doing his job, an honorable job of bringing to justice men who had committed crimes against honest law-abiding citizens. Revenge on a man he didn't know.

He held his hands out, palms up. "That's the honest truth, Ranger Bonner. An' far as I know, ain't nobody in that town knows you're a lawman 'cept me."

Bonner stared into Wells's eyes. "You haven't told me the whole story. Now finish it." His voice had no give in it; the words could have been chipped from granite.

"You gonna take me in, git me hung from an old unpainted gallows like my cousins an' uncle?"

Bonner found himself admiring the honesty of the man across the fire. "Finish your story."

Wells sat very still, his shoulders pulled in close to his body as though trying to protect himself from the words being dragged from him. He visibly relaxed. "All right, Bonner, here's the rest of it." He threw the remains of his coffee off to the side. It had gotten cold. He poured himself another cup and faced Bonner across the fire. "Reckon I might's well lay it all out. Figger you got it sorted out anyway." He took a deep breath. "Them shots throwed at you from the rimrock? Well, they wuz my doin', an I got to thinkin' lately, thinkin' for the first time, that I ain't killed nobody yet, didn't want to kill nobody, an' I better quit an' go home where I knowed folks, where I wouldn't be throwin' lead at a man I didn't even know."

"You didn't only throw lead at me, you damned near killed me. You can an' should hang for that—or maybe I should shoot you now an' leave your carcass to be picked bare by the coyotes."

Wells's Adam's apple bobbed twice, and he swallowed

again. "Reckon whatever you decide ain't gonna be more'n I deserve, Bonner." Then to Trey's surprise, Wells face smoothed, then he smiled. "Tell you one thing though. For the first time in months I feel like a man, feel like a whole load's been lifted off 'n my shoulders." He took a swallow of his coffee. "You gonna tie me up for the night so's I won't run? Know you gotta take me in, know I gotta pay for shootin' you. It's the law, an' that's what you obey."

Long and hard Bonner studied the man across the fire. He understood what he'd been told. He'd known several people from the mountains, even some out here in Texas who had the same code as the man he looked at.

He believed Wells, but his training, his way of life, the people he'd known wouldn't let him trust the man without reservation, but he came close to it.

"Tell you what I'm gonna do, Wells." He hunched his shoulders and shook his head. "Don't know why I'm gonna do it, but I'm sure as hell gonna do it 'cause I b'lieve what you've told me, an' I b'lieve you ain't again gonna make a try to kill me." He never took his eyes from the man from East Texas. He nodded. "Yep, I b'lieve what you've told me, but you still ain't told it all. What about those settlers Yadro killed and buried in shallow graves behind their burned-out cabins?"

Before Bonner finished talking, Wells's head turned from side to side. "Ranger Bonner, he must've done all that before I met up with 'im. He never said nothin' to me 'bout what he wuz hired to do, or who hired 'im. I didn't know what he'd done 'til I went out yonder one day an' found the graves." He shrugged. "B'lieve that's when I began to think 'bout cuttin' out for home. Never done nothin' that low-down, ain't gonna neither."

Bonner had been so intent on absorbing every word Wells said that he'd let his own coffee get cold. He threw its remains aside, poured himself another cup, then took a swallow. He had kept hoping while Wells talked that he'd say he'd witnessed Yadro murdering the nesters, or tell him the name of who hired him to get rid of those decent, hard-working people.

When Wells finished talking, disappointment washed over

Trey. The one he wanted was the one who brought all the trouble to people who'd never harmed him. He studied the stocky man sitting across the fire, studied him a long time, a time in which the sodbuster began to squirm.

Finally, he mentally nodded. Yeah, he'd been shot by the man across the fire, but from everything he'd said, he'd been following some misguided code that his parents, and those before them, had drilled into their children from birth.

He searched his soul for an answer as to whether he thought Wells would ever again follow what he'd been taught. What would be gained by taking the man in and getting him hanged? He studied that question a few moments and decided that if he took him in for trial, he'd hang a man who would never again break the law.

He nodded to himself, then said, "Wells, know it's almost black dark, but I'm tellin' you to pack your gear, saddle your horse, an' get the hell outta here 'fore I change my mind."

He took another swallow of coffee, stood, and pointed east. "Git goin'. Take care o' that farm you got. Marry that girl from school an' don't ever let me see you in this part of Texas. You do, an' my mind might've changed by then. Now git."

Wells's jaw, if it had been long enough, would have fallen to his chest. Bonner's last two words spurred him to frenzied action. Trey had never seen a man get ready and get on the trail any faster.

After Wells got lost in the darkness, Bonner broke camp and moved to another site. He thought he'd done the right thing, but just in case he figured to play it safe.

He smiled to himself. He'd only a few moments ago done exactly what RIP had warned him not to do; he'd set himself up as judge, and jury, and nearly become the executioner. But he'd set the guilty man free.

He felt a wave of pride flow over him despite his hand unconsciously massaging where Wells's bullet had hit him. Maybe he should listen more often to the man inside him who wanted to get married and live a life as devoid of danger as times would allow.

In a couple of days he'd be home. Only a few miles from

"home" Maggie lived. He figured to go see her first thing. He gave that some thought and changed his mind. He'd better see what Yadro was up to first.

He'd not decided how he'd make Yadro tell him who the person was whose name was on the deeds he'd witnessed, although he'd settled in his own mind that that person was Rogers. He thought the land agent would not have made the trip to Austin for anyone other than himself. And he knew the land agent was the one who'd hired Yadro to get rid of the settlers. He *and* Jimenez knew it, but how to prove it?

The questions? One would, if answered by the white-haired gunny, incriminate Rogers, and the other would incriminate both of them. But how to get Yadro to confess such that it would stand up in court? A hard knot formed in his chest. Maybe he'd again have to disobey his best friend, RIP. He didn't want to, but sometimes justice was best served by one man becoming judge, jury, and executioner. A chill ran up his back at the thought. It meant he'd deliberately have to set out to kill a man—maybe two.

While in Austin, he'd not heard of any cattle of the quality with which he wanted to start his herd. From that he wondered if there were any of that quality close to Noname that might be for sale.

Yeah, Maggie had thought her father might sell some of his, but Trey didn't want to push his luck with Matt Tedford. They'd only recently gotten on terms that might be called "guardedly friendly."

He made a cold camp a couple of miles from where he'd turned Wells loose, slept, and before daylight saddled and, still more than a day from his ranch, headed for Noname.

Each day Jimenez's wound pained him more, then as the healing began, it itched, and he became harder to live with. He griped about everything until finally, Jess, standing by the stove tending a sheet of biscuits, turned to him. "Tell you how it is, Juan, I'm 'bout ready to turn you out that front door, give the man who shot ya another chance, or let you see if you can take care o' yourself good as I been doin'."

Jimenez stared at the old man and felt shame wash over him. Jess had done everything a mother would do to make him comfortable. He'd cooked, changed bandages, taken care to put aloe vera sap on his wound, and even sliced fat bacon and bandaged it to his wound when it looked red and angry as though about to start festering.

"Aw hell, Jess, I'm sorry. Know you been takin' care o' me good as Linda would. Reckon I'm just gettin' well enough that I need to get to doin' somethin'. It's made me feel like a danged parasite lettin' you do everything."

A slight smile crinkled the corners of Maynard's eyes. "Juan, it ain't that there bullet hole what's been eatin' at yore gizzard so much as bein' tied down an' not bein' able to ride in there an' see that girl."

He slipped the biscuits from the tin onto a plate and put them on the table. He sniffed. "Danged supper smells right good even if I do say so myself. C'mon, let's eat."

When they were seated at the table, Jess ladled up a bowl of stew and passed the kettle to Jimenez. He cocked an eye at the ranger. "Tell you what, that bullet hole's done healed enough such that if you ride reeeal easy-like, you could ride in an' see Linda. Think maybe she'd like that much as you."

Juan made as though to stand. "Whoa up, young'un. I didn't mean right this minute." He grinned. "Come daylight I'll help you saddle yore hoss. You can ride in then."

An hour before the sun lightened the sky, Jimenez and Jess stood alongside Juan's horse, while Jess pulled the saddle cinches tight. "All right, climb aboard. 'Spect to see you back here tomorrow bright eyed an' bushy tailed. Now git on outta here." As soon as Jimenez toed the stirrup, Jess slapped his horse on the rump.

Juan gave his wound every consideration on his ride to town. He held his horse to a walk, being careful to not break open his wound and start it bleeding. When he tied his horse in front of the cafe, even though having been careful, sweat ran between his shoulders and down his face. He realized then that as tense as he'd held himself against jarring, he had been using his muscles as though doing a hard day's work.

His was the only horse at the rack. Between meals. He thought he might be the only one in there with Linda. He smiled to himself; he'd planned it that way.

He pulled the door open, and before he could pull it closed, Linda stood only a foot or more outside the kitchen. "Where have you been? Haven't seen you or Trey in so long I thought you might've left town."

Gingerly, careful not to pull on his wound, Juan went to the back table, sat, looked at her, and nodded. "Bonner's been gone a few days; went to Austin. I took a chunk o' lead an' ain't been gettin' around too spryly. Soon's I could, I come in to see ya."

A couple of steps and Linda stood by him, her hand on his arm. "Oh, Juan, I'm sorry. Are you doin' all right now? Noticed you weren't movin' very spry."

"Yeah, I'm doin' okay." He winced, then frowned. "Anythin' been happenin' since I was last in town?"

She shook her head. "Not much." She seemed to give his question a moment's more thought, then shrugged. "Fact is, that white-haired gunman is the only one of that bunch still in town. Course the ranch hands're still comin' in, but Wells an' that land agent ain't been in since you an' Trey were here last."

Jimenez pondered her answer a few moments. If Wells had been gone, he figured Yadro had been the one who put lead into him.

He thought about Rogers. He figured the land agent would kill a man, shoot him from ambush if he could get him that way, but until desperate he'd not get involved in a shooting; he'd not want anyone to tie him to a violent act, so he'd keep his reputation as clean as possible.

Having put the blame for his shooting where he thought it belonged, angry bile bubbled to the back of his throat. He'd kill the bastard, put all six shots into him. He looked at Linda. "Yadro been in today? Figure he's the one who shot me. Soon's I see 'im figure to ask 'im 'bout it."

"Juan, please, don't look at me like that. Your eyes, they're black, cold, hard." She placed her hand on his shoulder. He winced. She pulled her hand back as though having touched a hot stove. "Oh, Juan, I'm sorry. I hurt you."

He shook his head. "Naw, now, it's just a little tender."

Then, not letting her thought go, she said, "Please don't go get yourself shot again."

He stared at her a moment. Tears flooded her eyes. Then they spilled over and ran down her cheeks. The anger drained from him. His thoughts left the white-haired gunman. His only concern was that he'd caused her to cry. She cared, really cared whether he put himself in danger. He covered her hand with his right one. "I'm sorry I made you cry, little one. Reckon I let my troubles show too much. Reckon I brought them in here an' dumped 'em on you. Didn't know it would mean that much to you."

He stood, took off his bandana with the intent to wipe her eyes, but in the same instant she was in his arms, sobbing. "D-d-didn't think it would mean much to me? Y-you Texican gigolo, why do you think I take every minute I can spare from my business to be around you, touch you, dance with you, and only you? I-I'm not even polite enough to dance with Trey when you're around."

He took her by the shoulders and pushed her a few inches from him, then pulled her into his arms again, put his finger under her chin, and tilted her head. Then his lips claimed hers, soft, sweet as honey, and pressing to his as though she'd been hungry for this for a very long time.

He didn't want to let her go, but a customer might come in. He made as though to push her away. She clung to him like a cocklebur. "Don't push me away, Juan, don't ever push me away."

"Little one, I'd keep you here like this forever"—he smiled—"but I'm afraid we'd cause people to talk."

She stepped back, her face a frozen mask. She looked scared. Gently, he dabbed at her tears. Her eyes locked with his. "Now you know. Reckon you think I'm a hussy. You got every right to think that way. You never said anything 'bout you an' me, but I just flat threw myself at you."

He threw his head back and laughed, then pinned her with a look that let his heart show in his eyes, soft and caring. "Know what, honey? I rode in here today to ask if you thought you might love me, even a little bit. If you said you thought so, I was gonna ask you to marry me. So reckon I'll do that right now." He tilted her head to look up at him again. "Linda McKinsey, you reckon you could learn to answer to Linda Jimenez?"

A tremulous smile creased her cheeks. "Reckon I could. I been makin' believe like I was answerin' to that name for some time now. Are you sayin' you want us to get married?"

He chuckled. "There ain't a doubt in this world but what that's exactly what I'm sayin'. Will ya, Linda, *mi amore,* will ya marry me?"

A customer walked in, but Juan didn't want to see or hear him. He pulled Linda closer.

Yadro, looking at his unfinished meal, wanted to leave with Wells, but decided he'd catch him later. He thought about what he'd done after shooting through the door of Bonner's place and wondered if he'd been seen.

After firing through the door, blinking bullet-generated dust from his eyes, he'd climbed aboard his horse and spurred him into an all-out run. When he finally pulled him down to an easy gallop, he sweated more than the horse. His hand trembled holding the reins. He looked behind, and then looked again. He'd been doing this even when he had his horse on the run. He pulled a shell from his gunbelt and pushed it into his rifle's magazine. He'd be ready if they got on his tail.

From the top of the hill outside of town, he looked down on Noname and breathed easier. He'd put his horse in the stable, rubbed him down, gotten to the cafe and eaten. He'd let on that he'd been in town all day for any who looked at him. By the time he walked in the door of the cafe his nerves had settled such that he'd quit sweating and his breathing slowed.

As soon as he walked through the door he saw Wells and sat at the table with him. When he got his meal, he wondered that he'd not seen Rogers since early the day before.

He wanted to tell him that he'd gotten one of the men he was supposed to kill. Then he wondered if he had in fact hit anyone through the door. Maybe he wouldn't say anything to

Rogers about what he'd done until he was sure that he'd gotten one of the squatters.

He hardly noticed when Wells stood and told him he'd see him back at the hotel. His meal only half finished, he continued eating, continued thinking of what he'd gotten out in the foothills.

Finally finished eating, he stood, paid for his meal, and left. At the hotel, he expected to see Wells. They could go to the saloon, and he'd tell him what he'd done over a drink, but the room stood empty. He frowned, then glanced to the spot where Wells usually dumped his saddlebags. They were gone—and his bedroll was gone also. His frown deepened. Where the hell had the man gone? He felt safer when the stocky man was close by.

Maggie wakened before daylight a week after she'd had the friendly dinner with her family and Bonner. And, since then, she had spent every night lying in her bed thinking about Trey. Thinking those thoughts that turned her body into hot jelly.

She *had* to tell someone, talk to someone, and the only one she could talk to and be completely truthful was her best and only friend, Linda, except for her mother. Besides, Linda had been married; she's experienced all of the things that Maggie only dreamed about in her make-believe world. She nodded to herself. Linda would tell her if her feelings were realistic—or immoral.

When she went down to breakfast, she told her mother she would ride into town; she wanted to see her friend and talk to her.

Belle smiled. "You want her to tell you how married life is." She nodded. "I think you need to do that. I'm not sure I could tell you the things you want answers for." Her smile turned into a grin. "Fact is, daughter of mine, I think I might let modesty stand in the way of giving you the kind of answers you're gonna be askin'." She laughed. "For that matter, I don't believe you'd ask the questions of me that you'll ask Linda."

Maggie took a sip of her coffee. "Mama, you know I've

already told you; Trey hasn't said a word to me 'bout marryin', but reckon we might as well be married judgin' by the thoughts I'm havin' 'bout 'im."

Belle stared at her daughter a moment. "You've grown to be a full-grown woman. Those thoughts are ones that I believe most grown women think, although most would deny to their death that they ever thought of anything below their shoulders."

She chuckled. "Honey, your father an' me were raised by *very* proper Southern families. Through the years we've admitted to each other that *our* thinkin' was of the things we've grown to cherish during our marriage." She nodded. "You gonna stay overnight?"

Maggie laughed. "You think I'm stuffin' all these clothes into my valise only to bring them back this afternoon?"

Three hours later Maggie sat in Linda's kitchen. She'd tried to help with the noon meal until Linda had placed her hands on hips and told her in no uncertain terms to sit down and stay out of the way, that there was room for only one cook in her kitchen. Linda cut a slice of apple pie, poured a cup of coffee, and placed them on the work table beside her friend. "There now, get busy on that."

Maggie studied her, she seemed smug, seemed to be prettier than usual. "Somethin' has happened. You're flushed and I don't think the heat in here has anything to do with it. You seen Juan lately, like maybe last night?"

Linda cast her a smile that glowed. She nodded. "He came to town yesterday. Got something to tell 'bout that visit, but I'll wait'll we close for the night."

"Did Trey come with him?"

Linda shook her head. "Trey's in Austin. Juan didn't know when he'd be back." She frowned. "You ever notice that neither o' those two ever said anything 'bout why they came to Noname in the first place, and how they both seem to have money to buy whatever they need over yonder at Parsons's store, an' what business either of them could have in the capital?"

Maggie frowned. She had wondered at some of those things, then accepted that wanting land and a place to build a home were sufficient reasons. She told Linda her reasons for accepting why they were there.

Linda grinned. "Tell you, honey, I don't care why they're here, I'm just glad they are."

While riding, Bonner mulled over all he knew to be a fact, separated the things he could prove from those he thought were still on the hazy side of provable, and in the middle of his problems he thought of the note RIP had gotten that triggered him into sending a ranger to Noname.

He stopped, opened his money belt, took the sweat-stained note from it, read it, read it again, then studied the handwriting. It looked like a woman's neat lettering, not at all the careless scrawl of a man.

The request stated that settlers were mysteriously disappearing and asked that the rangers investigate. He thought about the handwriting a few moments, wondered if he'd seen it before, then cast that question aside. Hell, he'd not seen anyone's writing except Rogers's, and this was not his. Whoever had sent it had good reason to do so. He wished he knew who did it; they might have information he could take to RIP.

He rode into his own stable in midafternoon, took care of his horse, and went to the house. Dawg greeted him like a warm blanket; he jumped, rubbed his side against Bonner's leg, licked his hand and face, and wouldn't leave him until he literally pushed the dog away, and made him lie in his favorite place by the fire.

Trey turned his attention to Jess. "Damn, you'd almost think Dawg missed me. Maybe I should have taken 'im with me."

"Glad you didn't, Bonner. That dog saved our bacon. Even with his warnin' us, Juan took a bullet in his shoulder." With those words Bonner wanted to hear the details.

It took three cups of coffee and two pipes of tobacco for Trey to get the full story, but while getting it, Jimenez sat there grinning like a mule eating briars.

"What the hell you grinnin' at?"

Juan, still grinning, said he'd tell his friend after he got the story of what Bonner accomplished in Austin.

Trey started at the beginning and told him all that had happened, then gave him a head-on look. "'Less we can get some proof 'bout us filin' on our claims, you an' me have built somebody some mighty nice homes."

"Hell, Trey, we know the answers to the whole story. Don't see how anybody'd doubt a thing we'd say."

Bonner raised an eyebrow and stared at his ranger partner "You think what we have would stand up 'fore a jury?"

Juan frowned, obviously thinking about Bonner's question, then he shook his head. "Don't reckon so." He shrugged. "You come up with anything we can do?"

Bonner stood. "Gonna get some more coffee." He sniffed, caught a whiff of the whisky both Juan and Jess had had a drink of only a short while before he got home. He nodded. "Yep, gonna get some coffee, an' splash some o' that whisky in it, then tell you what I figure."

He again sat, took a swallow of the doctored coffee, then pinned Jimenez with a look that seemed to cause him pain to answer. He shook his head. "Juan, Jess, the only answer I can come up with is for me to kill Yadro, then call Rogers out an' kill *him*."

Jimenez rolled a quirly, lighted it, then, staring at the end of it, shook his head. "You know that ain't the answer, partner. We've lived by the law too long to do that. You turnin' Wells loose probably broke some law, but that ain't like deliberately killin' a couple o' men." He shrugged. "We gotta find another answer."

Trey nodded "Yeah, like proof." He looked at Jess. "Smells like you've already put supper on to cook. How long 'fore it's ready? I'm hungry enough to chew on the leather in my holster."

Jess chuckled. "Save yore holster, young'un. We can eat anytime you're ready." He glanced at Juan. "'Fore we set down to the table, I figger you wantta hear what Jimenez has done got 'imself into." He chuckled, then laughed and slapped his knee. "That young'un's done got hisself into a whole lifetime o' misery."

Trey pulled his mouth down at one corner, lifted an eyebrow, and shook his head. "You beat me to it, didn't you?"

Juan, looking like the cat that ate the canary, hunched his shoulders. "Beat you to what, partner? Hell, I ain't done nothing'." Then he grinned. "Ain't done nothin' 'cept gettin' Linda to say she'd marry me."

Trey nodded. "That's exactly what I was talkin' 'bout." He stood, went to Jimenez, and grabbed him by the shoulder, the one that hadn't taken the bullet. Grinning, he said, "Congratulations, old friend. Now I reckon I better not waste any more time. No point in causin' the preacher to have to make two trips to Noname."

Juan frowned. "I was you, first I'd try to find out why Matt Tedford let Yadro an' his bunch horn in on the Box T's operation." He squinted at Bonner. "Figure I'd want the answer to that 'fore I did anything."

Trey shook his head. "Ain't nothin' could change my mind 'bout Maggie."

"Maybe not, but we were sent out here to find some answers as to why and how those settlers disappeared. Appears to me we'd want to know if Tedford was involved."

Abruptly all the joy left Bonner. An empty hole filled his chest, his stomach turned over, and he thought he might throw up. He stared into his empty cup, then nodded. "Reckon I better talk to Matt 'bout that 'fore I ask Maggie. She'd wantta know if I came out here to take her pa to Austin." He hunched his shoulders. "Ain't gonna make no difference how I feel 'bout 'er, but it might make one helluva difference how she feels 'bout me."

Trey moped around the ranch the next couple of days, torn between wanting to see Maggie and the thing he knew he had to clear up between her father and him. He decided to go see her despite what per pa might have done. He had time to confront Tedford with his part in Yadro and Rogers's scheme to get control of all the grasslands within forty miles. He'd just be careful not to put himself in a situation where he and Maggie were alone. Also, he had time to further investigate what Matt Tedford might have done. With *that* thinking, he shrugged. He only put off the inevitable.

* * *

Rogers, after failing in his attempt to sneak into Bonner's room and shoot him while he slept, was careful to stay out of sight until he checked the livery and found that the sodbuster had paid his bill and left Austin. He thought to see if he could catch up with him, circle to get ahead, and shoot him from ambush.

He studied on it a while. He was sure that he could still run Tedford off his range with no more than the threat of exposing him as an outlaw. The only thing that stood in his way of controlling all of the range and water around Noname were the two sodbusters. He thought he had taken care of getting their land, but he'd feel a lot more sure of it if they were dead.

With no one to challenge his claim he'd be safe. But he couldn't take care of them unless he got himself back to Noname. Then he thought of Yadro.

He could tell him he no longer needed his services; the fact was, the white-haired gunman had done nothing to earn the money he'd been paid. Well, yeah, he *had* gotten rid of the nesters. That might come home to haunt him. Maybe he'd better get rid of Yadro too.

Thinking he'd carefully thought of everything that might ruin his chances of attaining his goal, Rogers packed his saddlebags, rolled his bedroll, and pointed his horse's nose west.

Yadro checked the livery to see if Wells still boarded his horse there and found that he'd paid his bill and left. The white-haired gunny felt as though he'd been hit in the stomach. He'd always had those around him to back up any trouble he might get into. Now he had no one.

Then he wondered to what he'd signed his name on those papers for Rogers. He thought about that until he convinced himself that those papers might tie him in with the disappearance of the settlers. He'd light a shuck once the land agent got back. But he needed to cover his trail; besides, Rogers owed him a month's pay. And he might get a shot at Bonner before he left.

Anger bubbled into his throat. *That* sodbuster single-handedly killed off Seely, Allard, and the others who had done his bidding. They'd been good men, Seely and Allard especially.

Then a hollow settled in his chest and his mouth dried. He knew the feeling only too well—fear. The tall sodbuster was hell on wheels with a gun. Yadro thought again about trying to kill Bonner, then decided he still might get him from a ravine, escarpment, or even a swale if he dared get close enough for a safe shot.

Bonner got out of bed earlier than his usual five o'clock rising time, bathed, dressed in his best clothes, except for the one suit he kept for special occasions, saddled, and headed for the Box T. He'd play the cards the way they fell, but he'd try to stay away from any subject that would lead to the settlers' killing, or to any declaration of love for Maggie.

15

WHEN TREY RODE into the Box T ranch yard, Maggie met him at the hitch rack. She practically pulled him from the saddle, then she hugged him, stopping just short of pulling his head down and pressing her lips to his. "Oh, it's so good to see you're back. Linda said you'd gone to Austin."

He nodded. "Had somethin' needed takin' care of over that way." He frowned. "Might have to make one more trip, then figure I'll be through, figure I can stay here an' not leave again."

She wanted to ask what was so important in the state capital, but swallowed her words. His business was his own, but like she and Linda had talked about, neither of them knew what brought Trey or Juan to Noname. Whatever it was, she was glad they'd come.

"Come on in, we can have a cup of coffee while our nooning finishes cookin'.

"Papa left here early with Slim. Said somethin' 'bout drivin' those whiteface cattle to a separate part o' the range. He figures to sell off a bunch of them. He should be back in time for supper."

When she mentioned her father thought to sell some of his crossbreed stock, Bonner's head snapped around. "He's been mixin' Herefords an' longhorn, hasn't he? Wonder if he'd sell me a couple hundred head. I didn't find any that suited me while I was gone, an' that was one o' the things I hoped to get done."

He nodded. "Well, in addition to not bein' just what I wanted, most of them had already been put on the trail to Abilene."

Maggie smiled. "You don't know how close I've come to askin' 'im if he'd sell you a small herd, but then I figured that'd be man business." She shook her head. "Not ever gonna butt in where I ain't been asked. But seems to me it'd make good sense for y'all to get together on that; it'd save Papa from a long trail drive, an' save you from havin' to hire drovers an' push a herd across some mighty dry miles."

Bonner only nodded.

About half of the bloodred sun had already sunk behind the hills to the west when Matt came in, dusty, sweat crusted, and looking tired. He shook Trey's hand and said, "Saw your horse in the stable. Glad to see you, boy. Linda told Maggie you'd gone to Austin on business. Didn't know you were back."

Trey figured this was a good time to edge into talking about cattle, and that he needed to buy some breeding stock, but he'd wait until Tedford cleaned up.

After Matt had washed the dirt off of him, changed clothes, and poured them each a drink, Bonner held his drink up in a silent toast, then looked at him straight on. "Matt, one o' the things I went to Austin for was cows. I need to start me a herd. Figure to start with a couple hundred head o' mixed breed, then think I'll see can I round up some o' those mavericks in the Big Bend." He shrugged. "Figure I can grow my herd a little faster that way."

He frowned and took a swallow of his drink. "Gonna need a couple o' good bulls too. You reckon you have any you'd like to sell?"

A deep crease pulled Tedford's brows together. He nodded.

"Kinda thought to bring that subject up. The boys have already rounded up an' trail branded the ones I figured to sell." He took a swallow of his drink. "I was out yonder today takin' a good look at a herd I'd kept on separate pasture, some yearlin's an' some three-year-old heifers I wanted to keep another year. Most o' those three-year-olds will drop calves in the spring."

He stood, went to his desk and shuffled some papers around, found his tally book, and came back and sat. He shook his head.

"I hadn't thought to sell that bunch"—he smiled—"but tell you, boy, if we're gonna be neighbors, I'll think right hard 'bout it. I have a few whiteface bulls, mostly half Hereford and half longhorn. Be glad to sell you a couple but I wouldn't recommend breedin' 'em. If one o' the other ranchers 'round here have some good registered stock, that's what I'd get a hold of. You'd have a lot heavier beef to sell."

He shot Bonner a wry grin. "You ask me, I figure you gonna have to make another trip to Austin or maybe Fort Worth to find a couple you'd feel good 'bout puttin' in with those cows you figure to up breed with."

"I cain't talk for Jimenez, Matt, but I think he might be needin' 'bout the same thing I need for starts."

Matt nodded, then said, "Send 'im over when he's ready. We'll talk 'bout it." He stood and poured them another drink. "Why don't you stay over tonight, then I'll get Slim to ride with us an' we'll look at that bunch I been tellin' you 'bout."

Trey smiled, then it turned into a grin. "Damn, Matt, you slick-tongued devil, reckon I'll do that bein' I brought clothes along with that in mind." Their laughs merged.

Later, sitting with a cup of coffee and talking about the things that Trey might have missed while he was gone, Maggie opened her mouth to ask him if Juan had said anything about having proposed to Linda.

She snapped her mouth shut. That would sound like she might be asking if he'd made up his mind what the two of them would be to each other. She would not push the issue. If he didn't know by now, maybe he didn't care enough to spend the rest of his life with her. That thought wasn't acceptable, but for now she'd steer clear of that subject.

After supper Trey suggested they take a walk. Belle looked at Matt with a slight smile crinkling the corners of her lips and eyes, then looked at Maggie. "Get a wrap, it's chilly outside; your pa an' I'll probably be in bed by the time you get back."

Maggie stood and while letting Trey help her with her coat told her mother they'd be quiet when they came in.

They walked out beyond the outbuildings. The scent of sage, dust, and dried grass wafted on the light, chilly breeze. Maggie hugged Bonner's arm to her, and neither of them broke the silence for a long time. Then Trey, still taking short steps to match Maggie's, said, "Mag, I didn't just come over here to talk 'bout cows with your pa. Wanted to do this right, want to talk to 'im 'bout parting with more than his cows, then if he says it's all right, I want to talk to you."

"Oh, Trey, you mean . . ."

"I could mean a lot, most anything, but you an' me ain't gonna talk 'bout it 'til I talk to Matt an' Belle. All right?"

She held his arm tighter. "Yeah, Trey, reckon I gotta accept it for now, but if you'll let me act like one o' those saloon hussies an' ask you to kiss me, reckon it'd make it more all right."

He stopped and swung her around in front of him. He chuckled. "Little one, I'm sure glad you asked. Don't think I'd have ever thought of it." He pulled her close to him, and yes, it was *all right*.

The next morning Bonner, Tedford, and Ramey sat their horses at the edge of a bowl-like pasture. By Trey's estimate, the bowl held about seven hundred head of cattle, all upgraded to whiteface. He would like to have any of them. They were all fat and would winter well. "Matt, you give sellin' me some o' those cows any thought last night?"

He nodded. "Didn't take much thinkin'. Yeah, cut out the ones you want; we'll go to the house an' dicker on the price, I'll have Maggie make out a bill of sale, an' then I reckon you can say you're in business."

Bonner took another look at the scattered herd. "Tell you

what. I don't see any there I would call a cull. If you'd let Ramey an' a couple o' your boys gather two hundred head an' drift 'em on down to that canyon back o' my place, then turn 'em loose, we can go back to your place an' I'll pay you for 'em."

Tedford twisted to look at his foreman across his shoulder. "You heard the man, Slim. See you in 'bout four days."

Ramey rode back far enough to meet up with three of the Box T hands, told them what Tedford wanted, and said he'd ride with them until the cattle were on Bonner's range.

Matt and Bonner haggled over the price while they rode. When they agreed on an amount, Trey was more than satisfied, and Tedford looked to be happy with the deal also.

At the Box T ranch house Maggie made out a bill of sale for the cattle, had her father and Trey sign it, then handed Bonner a copy. She'd made two copies while working on the first one.

Trey went in another room, loosened his trousers, pulled his money belt from his waist, and went back into the room where Matt and Maggie awaited him. He counted out the agreed-upon amount and handed it to Tedford, who stared at him, frowning. "You carry all your money around with you like that all the time, or did you just bring it over here with you in case we agreed on a sale?"

Bonner grimaced. "Hell, Matt, I ain't got any place to keep it 'cept with me. Been keepin' it in a money belt every since I earned my first copper.

"Noname ain't got a bank an' I couldn't ride a hundred miles every time I needed a few dollars. Reckon I could make me a hidin' place somewhere in my house." He nodded. "Gotta think 'bout that."

He looked at the bill of sale, folded it, and put it in his vest pocket. He picked up his money belt, frowned, and pinned Matt with a challenging look. "Just thought o' somethin'— why don't you start a bank in Noname? Bet it'd be a good business to get into, an' we need one right bad."

Tedford stared at him a moment, then shook his head. "Boy, you've lost your mind. I don't know anything about bankin', an' I sure don't want the responsibility of holdin' other people's money. I lose a nickel of it, an' I'd spend the rest of my life tryin' to pay it back."

Bonner shrugged. "Just a thought, Matt." He nodded. "Yeah, reckon a man would have to know somethin' 'bout all the paperwork an' all. Well, maybe we'll get us a bank one o' these days. Gotta grow a little more."

Trey wanted to hang around long enough to get Tedford alone so he could talk with him, but it didn't happen. He wanted to see if maybe he could get any information out of him as to why he'd let Whitey Yadro come on his ranch with the trash he'd brought with him. There might be a good, honest reason, but as long as he'd been a ranger he'd never heard of one. Plus, alone with Maggie's father he might have a chance to see what his reaction would be to the idea of Maggie marrying him.

The four of them sat at the breakfast table and drank coffee until Trey knew he'd better get on the trail or he'd be after dark getting back to his place.

He'd ridden about ten miles when he pulled his horse to a stop, pulled out the bill of sale, and studied it with a swelling of pride putting a lump in his throat. Hell, here he was, a cowboy old RIP had dragged away from the edge of stepping outside the law to being a respectable rancher.

He took one fold in the paper, prepared to put it back in his pocket, then frowned. He opened the paper and studied it again. Where had he seen that handwriting? He stared at it a few moments, shook his head, folded it, and put it back in his pocket. Where had he seen it before? He shrugged. It would come to him if he didn't try to force it.

Yadro, on this morning, followed the same procedure he'd been following since Rogers left town. He left the hotel, went by Rogers's office, rattled the door, then headed for the cafe. This morning the door opened.

He went in among the musty smells of old paper and a long-undisturbed dusty interior. Rogers sat at his desk.

"You get either one o' those sodbusters while I was gone?"

Whitey shrugged. "Don't know. I shot at one of 'em through the door of Bonner's place, don't know which one, an' don't know whether I hit 'im or not." He grimaced. "All I know is he ain't been around town since I fired at 'im."

Rogers stared at his desk a moment, then looked at the gunman straight on. "Tell you right now, you didn't shoot Bonner; he was in Austin same time I was."

"What wuz he doin' in there?"

Rogers pulled his shoulders up around his neck. "Damned if I know, an' I know you're gonna find this hard to believe, but I didn't go ask 'im."

Rogers's sarcasm got lost in the fuzzy, whisky-soaked confines of Whitey's mind. He shook his head. "Don't figger a sodbuster knows nobody in the capital, an' slick as he is with 'is handgun, they might be a wanted notice out on 'im, so it figgers he'd stay away from the law much as possible." He again shook his head. "Don't know—jest don't know."

Rogers pinned him with a look, one he couldn't look away from. "When I hired you, you said you were right handy with that iron you got strapped to your leg; what's the matter with you takin' 'im on in a face-on gunfight?"

Now Yadro had no trouble looking into Rogers's eyes. "Tell you how it is, Rogers; Wells told me he's seen that man pull a gun in at least two fights. He says ain't no man he ever seen could get a gun out as fast, told me straight out after seein' me practice draw that I'd be dead 'fore I come close to clearin' leather." He shrugged. "That's why Wells didn't face 'im, even as bad as he wanted 'im dead."

"What'd Skeeter Wells have against 'im?"

Yadro picked up a pencil lying on the desk, twirled it around in his fingers a moment, tossed it back to the desk, then shook his head. "Don't know. He never said, an' when I tried to get 'im to tell me he never even said where he knew the sodbuster before."

Rogers picked up the cup of coffee he'd been drinking when Whitey came in, took a swallow, set it down, and said, "Find Wells, an' both o' you go after those two, those *two,* you hear me?" His voice had risen with each word.

Yadro stared at him a moment and knew the voice he heard came from abject fear. He felt better knowing he wasn't the only one who might be afraid of the tall man. Then with a feeling of smug satisfaction, he grinned. "Rogers, Wells has done disappeared, gone, ain't seen 'im in several days. Figger he's done pulled his freight."

"Somethin' happen to make 'im do that?"

Whitey stood, walked to the side wall, turned, and came back. "Don't know. I seen 'im at the cafe, thought to see 'im when I got back to our room, but he wuz gone, bedroll, saddlebags, an' all."

Rogers slid a double eagle across the desk. "Get provisions, then get out there in the chaparral an' stay there 'til you can come tell me you killed both of 'em."

Yadro picked up the coin, fingered it a moment, then asked for his pay he had coming. "Gonna do what you said, but I need to have some walkin' 'round money; ain't had none for a spell now."

Rogers stared at him a moment, pulled out his wallet, and peeled off several bills. "You cut out on me, Yadro, an' I'll track you down an' shoot you so full o' holes you couldn't hold a pint of that rotgut whisky anywhere in your body. You'd leak it out faster'n you could pour it in. Now get out. Come back when you can tell me they're both dead."

Still a couple of miles from home, Bonner couldn't clear his mind of the problem RIP sent him out here to solve. The more time Bonner spent with and around Tedford, the more he convinced himself the rancher couldn't be involved with the likes of the white-haired gunman and the killing of the settlers.

But why had he allowed Yadro and his bunch to literally settle in on his ranch and take over his bunkhouse? In his experience, the only times he'd seen decent people kowtow to the likes of Yadro was when at some time in their past they'd done something of which they were ashamed and fearful it would be discovered—then someone like the white-haired gunman had shown up with a threat to expose them.

Although he couldn't imagine Tedford being involved in

any kind of shady dealings, it might be possible. He'd have to think about that, and if need be he'd put the question directly to him even though it might wreck their fragile friendship.

The only thing he could think of to get information out of Yadro was to take him down without killing him, then if he had to, he'd get the information from the gunman in a fashion that RIP would never approve.

How could he get him to talk without killing him?

How could he take him down without killing him? He thought of picking a head-on gunfight, then hitting him in the shoulder with his first shot. He shook his head. He was good with a handgun, but there were few, maybe none, who could face a man known to be fast and deliberately try to hit him in some noncritical area.

Those dime novels they wrote in New York put out junk like that, but out here, in real life, he couldn't imagine going against a man with the intent to only wound him; he'd be trying to commit suicide—or be a total damn fool.

He topped a ridge. His house stood at the entrance to the canyon below. Now he had a small herd to put on the lush canyon grass. He had a sense of pride that filled his chest. Now he could claim to be a rancher. He had a home and cows, but he'd not done the one thing that would spell happiness for him. He'd not asked Maggie to marry him.

He hadn't closed the door before Jimenez and Jess Maynard hit him with the questions. "You ask 'er? She say yes? When y'all gonna tie the knot, get in double harness?"

Bonner dropped his saddlebags, then, pulling his face into a hard mask, stared at them. "What the hell y'all talkin' 'bout? I did just what I went over there for; I bought me a small herd o' those whiteface cows, paid for 'em, an' Ramey an' a couple o' the Box T riders are gonna drive 'em onto my range tomorrow."

He walked directly to the cabinet Jess had made, opened the door, pulled out a bottle, and poured himself a half glassful of rye. He tossed down a good slug of it, then faced his two friends. "Aw hell, tell you the truth, I only had one chance to ask Mag to marry me, but I got to thinkin', wonderin' if maybe I shouldn't wait 'til after I talk to Matt about why he let Yadro come in an' take over like he done." He knocked back the rest of his drink. "Figure 'fore I mess up her life, Tedford an' I gotta have a talk."

Juan shook his head. "Trey, I just flat don't b'lieve Matt Tedford's got anything to hide. Hell, I'd marry that girl an' let the chips fall where they would."

Bonner shook his head. "Just wouldn't be fair. Wouldn't do such to a girl like Mag. Wouldn't do such to any woman."

Juan pulled his badge out and stared at it a moment, then looked at Trey. "You know, we been wearin' these badges a few years now, ain't ever done anything to tarnish 'em. Neither you nor me are gonna start now.

"We know Rogers is tryin' to steal our claim from us, but we gotta get proof, an' we know Yadro killed those settlers, but we still can't prove who hired 'im." He nodded. "Yeah, we know the answer to that too, but we ain't got proof of that either."

He went to the cabinet and poured them each a drink. He went back to where the three of them had stopped in the middle of the room and handed them their drinks. His mouth drew down in a grimace. "Hell, we got work to do, but first let's sit an' enjoy our drinks."

Before Maynard dished up supper they talked about keeping their herds in the canyons behind each of the houses they had built, and that as soon as Parsons got the material for Jimenez's house they'd finish it and he and Linda could get married and move in.

Then they studied on what brands each of them should register. When they'd decided, if no one else already had them, they'd turn them in.

Tedford and Ramey rode from the ranch together the next morning. Neither spoke a word for over a half hour, then Matt reined in. "Slim, we gotta talk."

Ramey nodded. "All right, Boss; been wonderin' when you'd get tired of your problem eatin' your guts out. Let's talk."

"Quit callin' me 'boss.' Never have been. We've always been partners, even though you never claimed it."

He stared at his foreman, and partner, a few moments. "Slim, I can't let that boy ask for Maggie's hand in marriage without lettin' him and my family know of that thing I did back there in that copse of maple trees in Virginia." He shook his head. "Just wouldn't be right.

"Then I think I'll go to the law an' tell 'em what I did, an' let 'em do with me what they figure is just."

"Matt, you an' I know you didn't pull that thing off all by yourself. I was a party to it just as much as you." He nodded. "An' yeah, I figger it's time we got it off our chests. I knew as soon as I seen Maggie gettin' all full of love for that boy that we was gonna have to do somethin'. Don't know where the closest law is, but first we gonna have to sit the whole family down an' talk 'bout it—includin' Trey Bonner."

"It won't be easy, old friend. I hate to drag you into it."

"Matt, I dragged myself into it back yonder in Virginia. Don't worry 'bout me. I love Maggie almost like she were my own."

"There best come a time, an' real soon, when we can get 'em all together. Come hell or high water, I'm gonna feel a lot better when it's done."

Whitey Yadro folded the money Rogers paid him, slipped the double eagle into his jeans pocket and left.

He went to Parsons's store, bought enough provisions to last a week, went to his room, got his bedroll and rifle, then went to the livery.

Midafternoon, the gunman looked for a place to set up camp, a place he could get back to and then back to town without being seen once he had fired on at least one of the sodbusters. His mouth dried such that he couldn't muster enough spit to wet his lips. A brassy taste settled at the back of his tongue. And the fear that now permeated his body forced a hollow into his lungs.

He tried to get rid of the fear. He thought of being able to shoot both of them before they could get on the chase. He thought of getting one, and later getting the other without once getting himself in a shoot-out. He tried every way he knew to take his mind off his problem and get rid of the fear. None of them worked.

He stopped, pulled the roll of bills from his pocket, fingered them a moment, and all the while wondering if Rogers would really track him down if he just kept riding. The fear returned. Although he'd never seen the land agent handle a handgun, he had the feeling the man was no slouch. As confident as Rogers was, Whitey thought he might be a lot better than most. He didn't figure to test him.

A distant rumble caused him to take his thoughts from his troubles and look across the terrain toward the hills. Black, roiling clouds hung above the crests. Lightning cast spears at the land below, and moments later a crashing sound pushed at his ears. Damn! Unless he could find some rock piles to shed some of the rain, he'd spend a wet, miserable night. Not only a night of misery, but one that would make it impossible to not leave tracks a child could follow. He turned his attention to finding a comfortable campsite.

A few scattered raindrops kicked up dust in front of his horse, pelted his shoulders, then stopped. He rode toward a large jumble of boulders, then a gust of wind announced the coming of the storm.

Water fell in sheets. He had no time to get his slicker out before every stitch of clothing and his saddle were soaked. A few seconds later he found what would pass for a cave. A large boulder rested on others as large. He'd found what he looked for only seconds after everything he owned became drenched. He cursed his luck, then scanned the area for wood. He could sit out the storm by a fire. No wood lay under the shelter, and only a few small sticks of dry mountain mahogany came under his searching look out where water soon soaked it. He again cursed, then stripped the tack from his horse and hobbled him out on a patch of grass. He was already wet so Yadro thought getting wetter wouldn't matter.

He came back to his saddlebags, pulled from them one of

the two bottles he'd bought before leaving town, pulled the cork from it, and turned it up. He pulled the level of whisky down about two inches before he stopped swallowing, then slammed the cork back with the butt of his hand and stared out at the rain. He judged Bonner's ranch lay only about a mile from these rocks he'd stopped in.

He wondered at his chances of both sodbusters being out where he could shoot one, then the other, getting his horse, and making a run for town. Once there his horse's tracks would blend with those of other horses and he'd be safe.

His thoughts went to the times he'd seen the two men outside together. He nodded. There had been many times, but they had been busy building the house back then. He shrugged, pulled the cork from the bottle again, took a swig, and figured he'd have to wait and see. He didn't want to get one, then have to come back to try for the other.

He glanced at his bedroll. At least his blankets were dry; his groundsheets had held the rain away. He again wished for dry wood, then spread his blankets and crawled between them.

The next morning he set his mind to watch Bonner's house until he got the shot he wanted. He planned to walk to a spot from which he could watch, then changed his mind. He'd better take his horse and his belongings, because as soon as he got in his shots he'd be running all out.

He led his horse, staying below the lips of swales, making certain neither of them showed above the crests. When he considered he was close enough for accurate shooting, he ground reined his horse and, going to his belly, inched his way to the top. He left his hat hanging on the saddle horn. A little thing like a hat showing had gotten many a man dead.

He studied the ranch yard below him. No activity. He lay there, sweat running down his face and between his shoulders. The rain had brought in cooler weather, but Yadro sweated, his nerves pulled tight as a bowstring. He tried to relax, but it did no good—always the thought of missing and not having enough time to toe the stirrup and making a run for it kept his nerves pulled tight.

Movement. He pulled his rifle to his shoulder and sighted on the man walking toward the corral. Then he loosened his hold on his Winchester.

The old man went to the corral, hung his arms over the top rail, stood there a few moments, then went to the stream, dipped up a bucket of water, and returned to the house. Damn, come on out, sodbusters. To shoot the old man would only alert the two men he wanted.

Rogers waited until he saw Yadro ride from town, then he opened his desk drawer and pulled out a stack of currency. He counted it—less than five hundred dollars, the only money he had left of the sixty-five hundred he'd brought into this stinking little town.

He thought on that a few moments, then decided he'd make it last, and after Whitey took care of business he might be able to get some of it back. He had to kill the gunman anyway, so maybe he could get rid of him where no one would witness it.

He pushed the stack of money back into his desk drawer, then pulled his snub-nosed Smith & Wesson from the holster beneath his coat, unloaded it, cleaned and oiled it, then reloaded it with fresh cartridges.

He slipped it back in its holster. Then, his fingers toying with his coat's lapels, he pulled the pistol and reholstered it several times. He nodded with satisfaction. He could still get it out as fast as ever, especially if the person didn't know he packed a weapon, and he had no reason to believe either of the men he'd rooked out of their land would have the slightest idea a town man packed gun.

He thought of Yadro. He'd give the white-haired gunman one week to get rid of the sodbusters, then he would get rid of all three; that would end his problems, except for scaring or running Tedford off his range. He smiled, not feeling any humor.

Skeeter Wells rode hard the next day, wanting to put as many miles between him and Bonner as his horse could stand.

When he made camp that first night he sat by the fire studying his good luck.

Then he thought of the man he'd tried to kill and almost had done so—a decent, law-abiding man, a man who forgave him for what he'd come close to accomplishing.

Then Yadro flashed across his memory. A man he'd not let come in his house back in the piney woods of East Texas. Shame slowly built in him. He felt like insects crawled on him. He swallowed the knot forming in his throat. He'd always considered himself a decent man. But a decent man would not have associated with the likes of Whitey Yadro. The white-haired gunman was what those in his family always thought of as white trash. The picture Wells had of the kind of man he had always tried to be didn't fit with his actions of late.

He went to sleep that night thinking of the people he'd grown up with and the two with whom he'd been associated back in Noname, Yadro and Rogers, although not so close with the land agent.

The next day he passed through Austin in midafternoon. By sundown he made up his mind. Bonner had told him to never again let the sun set on him in West Texas. Now he was going back. Going back to offer his help to the man he'd tried to kill.

If he could atone in any way for the thing he'd almost done, he could truly go home feeling good about himself. If the people of his hometown looked down on him for not completing his ride for vengeance, he considered their opinion of him not nearly as important as his feelings about himself.

He slept that night under the canopy of a large oak tree close to a clear-running spring. The next morning, he turned his horse's head back the way from which he'd come. If the ranger didn't shoot him on sight, he might be able to help in some way. That little girl from the fifth grade would have to wait a while longer.

The fact was, he couldn't remember whether he'd told Bonner what he knew of Rogers's involvement in the settlers' deaths, even though he hadn't taken an active part in their murders. He knew the land agent gave Yadro money on occasion, but he did not know what his orders to the gunman were. Maybe he could find out.

Yadro spent three days alongside the swale, watching every time anyone came from Bonner's house. Not once during the three days did more than one of its occupants come from the house at a time.

The evening of the third day, Whitey slithered from his station at the bottom of the swale, stood, and went directly to his saddlebags. He reached in, moved his hand about, and knew he had figured right. He was out of whisky. He toed the stirrup and headed for town. He'd loaded all his gear on his horse that morning.

He came into town along the back side of the buildings, not wanting Rogers to see him. He went in the back door of the saloon, stood there in the dark, and checked each person in the room. He'd seen most of them around town, but the man he looked for was not there. He went to the bar and bought two bottles of rotgut, then, about to leave, he saw Wells come through the bat-wings.

Whitey waited until Skeeter bought a drink and went to a table at the back of the room. He walked over and pulled back a chair. "Where the hell you been the last few days?"

Wells cocked his head to the side, stared into Yadro's eyes, and shook his head. "Don't see as how that's any o' yore business. Ain't nobody around here been payin' me. 'Til they do, I come an' go as I please." He took a swallow of his drink, shivered, and put the drink back on the table. "Fact is, I'm leavin' agin in the mornin', an' don't want no company. What I'm gonna do is my own business."

"If you gonna go out yonder to shoot that sodbuster, the two o' us might as well get paid for it."

Wells gave him a smile that would have frozen hell a mile. "The two of us?" He shook his head. "Anything I do, I get all the pay fer it." He nodded. "'Til I ask fer yore help, stay the hell away from me. I'll come to you when that time comes."

"Aw hell, Skeeter, why for you mad at me?"

"Ain't mad at nobody. Jest don't need no help doin' what I gotta do. Stay away from me so I don't get blamed for some damned fool thing you mess up tryin' to do. Okay?"

Whitey nodded. "That's the way you want it, Skeeter, that's the way it'll be. You know where I'm stayin', only Rogers told me to stay out yonder in the chaparral 'til I get done what he's payin' me to do." He shrugged. "Reckon come daylight I'll be gettin' back out there."

Daylight? Wells changed his plans. He had meant to wait'll after sunup to try to get to the Bonner ranch. Now he thought it would be a good idea to see if he couldn't get there tonight—if the ranger would let him get close enough to talk without shooting him. He shrugged mentally. He had to give it a try. To his way of thinking, he owed the lawman for what he'd done for him.

Wells knocked back his drink and stood. He looked at Yadro. "I need you, I'll come for you. 'Til then, stay away from me."

Not wanting any questions from the white-haired gunman, he turned on his heel and left.

As soon as he got outside, he went to the livery and got his horse and packhorse. He'd not bothered to pull the saddle off when he got to town, thinking even then to try to get to Bonner's place before midnight. It'd be quiet that time of night, except for the coyotes yowling, and maybe he'd be able to rouse those in the house before he got close enough to get shot.

16

WELLS RODE THROUGH the chilly night, and even with the discomfort, he had a feeling of peace crowded a bit with anxiety, anxiety of getting safely inside Bonner's house. He shrugged mentally. He'd have to take the chance if he wanted to ride back to East Texas in total peace.

He approached as close as he thought he might without catching a chunk of lead, and close enough that he felt certain he could be heard, then he opened his mouth, and as loudly as his vocal cords could stand, yelled, "Hey, Bonner, Wells here, want to talk peaceful. Gonna ride in now, hands in the air." He did this until a light showed through the front window.

Inside the house, Dawg got up, growled deep in his chest, went to the front door, and stood, his hackles standing straight up.

Bonner rolled to his side, threw his legs over the side of the bed and stood. Jess and Juan were already pulling rifles from the gun cabinet. Trey swept the room with a glance, then said, "Light a lamp, then get back in the dark corners."

He cocked his head, thinking he heard a yell. He didn't catch what the person said at first, then the words came clear through the still night air. He opened the front door a crack, and yelled, "Come on in, Wells. Keep your hands clear of weapons. Thought I got rid o' you." He wondered what could bring the man back here; he should have been home by now courting that little ole girl from the fifth grade.

In only moments, the East Texan rode to the hitch rack in front of the veranda. "You gonna let me come in, Bonner? Know you ain't got any reason to listen to me, but I got to thinkin' maybe I had somethin' you needed to know. I come back to tell you." He still sat on his horse. "Let me put my horse outta sight. Don't want anybody to know I'm here."

"Go take care of your horse. Put 'im in the stable, leave your rifle in the saddle scabbard, an' come on in." Wells's hands were clear of his side gun, so Bonner opened the door, stepped outside, and held his rifle on the man. "I'll be standin' here, my rifle pointed straight at you, so don't try anything I might take wrong."

Wells shook his head. "Only come to see if I can help, Ranger. Be right back." He headed for the stable.

Trey said over his shoulder, "Jess, put some coffee on to boil; don't know how long this is gonna take, but I figure we might get somethin' useful outta this man." He looked at Jimenez. "He ain't bad, he was just livin' by a wrong set o' rules."

In a few minutes the East Texas farmer came from the barn. Bonner stepped aside to let him in enter the house. "You come visitin' at mighty strange hours, Wells; come on in. Cof-fee'll be ready soon."

Wells looked at Dawg, held by the scruff of his neck by Jimenez. "That dog bite?"

"Come on over an' rub 'im 'tween the ears. Long's you don't make a motion toward one o' us you'll be all right."

Wells studied Dawg a moment, grinned, and walked to him. In a few moments Dawg's tail wagged. The would-be bushwhacker slanted a look at Bonner. "This's how y'all al-ways knowed when they wuz somebody out yonder in the brush." A faint smile creased his lips. "I had a dog once. Gonna get me another when I git home."

Juan growled, "*If* you get home. Depends on why you came back here."

Wells's grimace showed he'd taken that into consideration. He shook his head. "Tell you how it is, Rangers, I got to thinkin'; after what you done fer me, we oughtta set down an' talk, see wuz they anythin' I know what you need to know."

Bonner studied the farmer a few moments. He was a likable cuss, had a sense of honor, but it had been misguided until now. He decided he'd trust the man.

They pulled up to the table and talked until Jess stood, poured them each a cup of coffee, and again sat.

Bonner pinned Wells with his hardest look. "What you think you know we need to know?"

Skeeter shook his head. "Don't know, Bonner, jest got to wonderin', if they wuzn't somethin' else I might do. Got to thinkin' them two men in yonder at Noname don't know I ain't gonna try to shoot you no more. Thought if they wuz things you need to know maybe I could get an answer fer 'em. I could maybe make like I wuz gonna work with Yadro."

Bonner frowned. He wondered how he could trust a man who'd turn on those he'd worked with, then as though reading his mind, Wells said, "I got to wonderin' if turnin' on Whitey an' his boss wuz right down dirty, dirty as a dog." He took a swallow of his coffee, looked at Jess, and grinned. "Good Arbuckles'."

He turned his attention back to Bonner and shook his head. "Tell you, Ranger, I wuzn't never friends with 'em, never drew a copper from neither of 'em, never—aw hell, I jest flat didn't like Yadro, never wuz friendly with 'im; fact is, wuz downright uncivil to 'im." He took another swallow. "We wuz never friends, so I decided I wouldn't be a low-down skunk for tryin' to repay you fer what you done fer me."

Trey smiled. "Well, farm boy, reckon you just answered the question I had floatin' round in my head. All right, start when you met Yadro. Tell us everything you can remember; what you did, what you talked 'bout, did you ever meet Rogers face to face? If you did, did he offer you a job?" He leaned back in his chair. "Don't miss a thing."

A pale gray cast to the sky touched light to the windows before Wells sat back and said, "Don't reckon they's a thing I left out. You want me to go back to town an' see does Yadro figger he needs help? He done said he did, but I'll give 'im another chance to admit it. Maybe I can meet Rogers and see does he know anything I ain't already told you."

Trey nodded. "Yeah, think whatever you can find will help." He looked at Juan. "What you figure, partner?"

Jimenez shrugged. "Damned sure can't hurt. Figure we know the answers right now, but I'd hate to take what we got to RIP."

Skeeter glanced at the windows. "Daylight already. You got a corner I can curl up in an' git some sleep 'til it gits dark agin? Yadro's out yonder in the chaparral waitin' fer a shot at either one or both o' you. He sees me come outta here, what we decided fer me to do won't work." He grinned. "Fact is, he'd most likely put some lead in me, an' it wouldn't be that he'd mistake me fer one o' you."

Bonner chuckled, looked at Wells from head to toe, decided he was clean enough, and offered him his bunk to sleep in. He looked at Jess and Juan. "Reckon this's another day we won't be gettin' outside work done." He stood, stretched, and shook his head. "Don't know as I ever sat so long in my life 'less it was in a saddle."

"Think I'll take a long look at the outside, see can I spot where Whitey's holed up for the day." With those words, Jimenez took his rifle from the cabinet and walked to a window.

"The last time you stood close to a window or door he put lead in you. Be danged careful, young'un." Jess stood and poured himself another cup of coffee.

Whitey stretched out on the wet sod from the rains of the night before. He'd managed to get enough of a fire burning with the damp, mostly wet wood to cook breakfast. It smoked something fierce, but he'd spent a hungry night and damned if he would do without something to eat when he had to start a long day.

Before he'd left to start his day of surveillance, he'd carelessly tossed the dregs of his coffee on the smoldering fire, packed his gear, and gone to the top of the hill.

Now, he looked back toward the place he'd camped. Smoke, in a thin stream, rose from the boulders. He cursed, thought to go back and make sure he put it out, then figured to hell with it.

He turned his eyes back toward Bonner's house, then studied the mouth of the canyon and on back into it as far as he could see. Cattle, quite a herd. He wondered when they'd been brought in. They hadn't been there when he went in town.

Maybe Rogers would be interested in them. If he could take out Bonner and that other man who'd also filed on land that Rogers wanted, along with telling him there was a nice little herd along with the deaths of the two men, maybe there would be a healthy bonus in it for him.

He put his gaze back on the house. He studied the door, tightly closed from what he could see, then he searched the edges of each window. One of them looked as though the curtain pulled back from the edge. He put his sights about where he thought someone might be standing, then shook his head. Hell, if there wasn't someone there, he'd alert them that he was out here. He'd not only draw shots from them but might get hit, and for sure he'd have to abandon his place of surveillance. It wasn't worth the chance.

He lay there all that day and on into the second day when he noticed another layer of clouds to the southwest. Going to rain again. This time of year brought frequent storms. The hell with it; he'd stay until night, then go back to Noname, drink some whisky, and sleep dry. Rogers would never know.

In the rain, Maggie rode into town to see Linda. They'd agreed long before that she'd come to town rather than cause Linda to have to close her cafe and lose business. Plus, she'd not seen either of the men who'd settled at the edge of the hills.

She had expected Jimenez to come see her father about selling some stock. At least if he had come, she would have had news of Trey. Also, they had both uncharacteristically missed the dance. They wouldn't do that if everything was all right.

She wondered if they'd had more trouble. Maybe one or both of them had been shot. Ramey said he'd not seen either of them when he'd driven the herd into the canyon, and he'd not stopped to speak because he wanted to get the hands back on home range. There was work to be done there. Yes, she needed to see Linda.

When she went into the cafe, Linda had only then finished cleaning up from the supper crowd. She came to give Maggie a hug, but a frown accompanied the greeting. "You seen Juan or Trey?"

Maggie shook her head. "In addition to wanting to talk, that's the main reason I came in. You reckon something's wrong?"

"Don't know." She went to the front of the cafe, locked the door, came back, and led the way into her room. She brought them tea, and they sat. "I know one thing for sure, neither of us know what those two do, why they ride the hills so often when they don't have cattle to look after, and mostly, knowing them like we do, why haven't they gone after the ones who shot them." She grimaced. "It's not like either of them to let something like that ride. Seems like they're waitin' to find out somethin' 'fore they do anything."

"I've wondered the same thing, honey, an' wish whatever it is they are lookin' for that they'd find it. I know danged well Trey wouldn't have ridden all the way to Austin to see if there were cattle there that he could buy.

"If at the time he didn't feel like askin' Pa to sell 'im some, he'd have ridden to one o' the closer ranches in the area." She shook her head. "I know we sound like two old hags. We haven't any right to question what they are up to." She pulled her mouth down at the corners. "Well, reckon *you* have a right, *you're* gonna marry Juan, but I ain't got any right to meddle in Trey's business."

Linda studied her a few moments. "He hasn't asked you yet." It was a statement, not a question.

Maggie shook her head. "Almost, but then pulled off. Said he had somethin' needed takin' care of first, an' too, he said he wanted to do it right, wanted to ask Ma an' Pa for permission."

Tears welled into her eyes. She never cursed, but she gave in to the anger tearing at her heartstrings. "Oh, dammit, Linda, he's gonna ask Ma's an' Pa's permission when I've already given him permission to do whatever he wants with me."

The dam broke. Tears streamed down her cheeks, and the next thing she knew she was in Linda's arms sobbing her heart out. "Oh, I love 'im so much, want 'im so much, want to feel 'im pressed close to me, an'-an' all he thinks about is somethin' else he has to do first."

Linda stroked her hair and caressed her back until the tight, painful knot between her shoulders eased.

"Mag, my man's said the same thing to me. He won't set a date for us marryin' 'til after he an' Trey finish somethin' they think they have to do."

Maggie stepped back from her friend and wiped her eyes. "Linda, I've always made it a practice to keep my mouth outta men's business—tryin' mighty hard to do it now, but it's gettin' awful hard."

Linda placed hands on hips and gave her a straight-on look. "Tell you what, you might make it a practice, but I ain't got any such notions in my head. Next time we get 'em together, I'm gonna just flat lay it out, say it like it is. I think we've got a right to know what's goin' on."

Maggie nodded. "Reckon gettin' 'em mad at us ain't gonna be any worse than keepin' our mouths shut an' hurtin in every part of our body. Yep, let's do it your way." Her tears now gone, she smiled.

Matt held his favorite horse's leg between his own while he dressed a hoof to the shoe he'd only a minute ago nailed into place. Slim came in and stood there watching.

Tedford cocked his head to look at him. "What's on your mind?"

"Well, I been thinkin' 'bout what you an' me were talkin' 'bout the other day, you know that thing we did back in Virginia."

Matt nodded. "So have I, old friend. What about it?"

Slim pulled his shoulder up around his neck. "I got to thinkin', I ain't never seen you spend a cent o' that money. What'd you do with it?"

Tedford chuckled. "You're standin' on it, every penny of it."

Ramey frowned, then shook his head. "You tellin' me you buried it here in the stable?"

"That's what I did. I kept thinkin' I'd give it back"—he shook his head—"but tell you the truth, I couldn't figure out who to give it to."

Slim took the rasp from Matt's hands. "Here, let me finish with your horse." Matt stepped to the side while Ramey straddled the horse's leg. Then he looked sidewise at his boss. "Matt, I been givin' that a lot o' thought too. Ain't come up with any kind o' answer that didn't leave me thinkin' whoever we offered it to didn't have no more claim to it than you an' me."

Matt shrugged and stepped toward the door. "That's my thinkin'." Then while heading for the door, he said over his shoulder, "Go ahead an' finish with my horse, then come on up to the house; we'll have a cup o' coffee"—he chuckled—"an' a tad o' that good rye whisky Murphy's been able to buy outta New Orleans lately."

About thirty minutes later, Ramey came in, Tedford poured their drinks, and they took chairs close to each other. Matt heard the rattle of pans in the kitchen so he knew Belle was busy back there. Maggie had gone to town. They could continue their talk. "Been thinkin' 'bout callin' a family meetin', an' gettin' Bonner here also, then tellin' them what we done." He shook his head. "Can't let Mag and that boy get married without knowin' what I did. Course he ain't said nothin' 'bout marryin' Maggie yet. I might be jumpin' the gun." Holding his face stiff and hoping void of all emotion, he said, "I might have to go to prison, probably will. Won't be fair to Mag or Bonner."

"Aw hell, Matt, if it comes down to that, I'll take the whole thing on my shoulders." Ramey shrugged. "I ain't got nobody who'd care, no family who'd really give a damn."

Before Ramey could finish his sentence, Matt shook his head. "No family? Nobody who'd give a damn? Nobody who'd care? Hell, Slim, me an' my family are all those things to you. No way it's gonna be like you said." He stared at his friend, knew they were at a stalemate, knocked back his drink, stood, and took both their glasses to the whisky cabinet and refilled them. The afternoon waned.

Bonner squirmed and looked at the windows to check the wan light that had never gotten better all day, and now the day came close to ending. He'd wake Wells when it got good dark; the threatening rain had never come like he hoped it would. Hoped Yadro out there in the chaparral would spend miserable, rain-drenched time. Then the anger that had been riding under the surface boiled up to put the taste of brass in his throat and pressure against his skull. "Come dark, after Wells leaves, I'm gonna go out there an' see if I can flush that white-haired bastard out."

"You gonna get yoreself shot full o' holes agin." Jess sliced another potato into the frying pan, then looked over his shoulder at Trey. "Why don't you give Wells time to see what he can find out?"

Jimenez cut in. "I'll go check 'im out. I'm a pretty good Indian."

Trey pushed his anger aside, then chuckled. "That gunshot to your shoulder isn't healed good enough for you to be crawlin' around out there in the brush." He grinned. "'Sides that, I'm 'bout to go crazy as a rabid skunk settin' in here doin' nothin'. Figure it's like we're all in prison. Gonna end that."

They woke Wells, ate supper, and he and Bonner slipped out the back door together. "If I know Yadro well as I think I do, I'd bet my farm in East Texas he's gone back to town for whisky, an' if he feels reeeal lucky, he might even sleep in the hotel tonight."

Bonner nodded. "Hope you're right, but I want to find

where he's been camped, where he's picked to lie up yonder waitin' for a shot. I find that, we'll be able to shoot with a good likelihood of hittin' somethin'. At least we'll scare hell outta 'im."

They stayed together, thinking to split when they found Whitey's camp, and every time the farmer made a noise, Bonner's gut tightened. Damn, didn't those East Texas boys learn anything about how to get around in the woods?

They traveled on their stomachs, rifles cradled in the crooks of their elbows as they dragged themselves along the muddy ground.

Bonner thought the pile of boulders from which Yadro had fired at the door would be the best place to check first. Yeah, it would be dumb of the gunman to use the same place, but Bonner figured him for being stupid enough to do just that.

While crawling, the tall Texan tested the air every few minutes for smoke. Still only about a hundred yards from the pile of rocks he'd not picked up any scent. Maybe there hadn't been enough dry wood for the ambusher. Finally, he dragged himself in among the huge boulders. He waited until Wells came even with him, then put his mouth close to the farmer's ear. "Don't stand. Don't talk. Don't make any noise at all." Wells nodded.

Trey stood, moved about in the camp, and soon decided it was an old one, hadn't been used for maybe a couple of weeks. Where the fire had been, the ashes had caked and the charred coals were slick from rain and wind. He put one close to his nose and sniffed. It had not seen flame in some time.

He swung his gaze in a half circle. Another pile of boulders stood out about fifty yards behind where he and Wells now were. He bent, dropped back to his knees, then his stomach. "Stay here," he whispered, then inched toward the only other place he thought Yadro might be camped.

After what seemed hours, but was only about a half hour, he drew up to the nearest of the rocks, found a crack between two of them, and peered into the opening. Nothing. Then he listened, hoping if there was anyone there he could hear him breathing. Still nothing.

Not yet convinced he'd been wrong, he slithered around the edge of the pile of rocks, found an opening, and crawled into a small level space, partially sheltered. A space that might have kept rain off anyone choosing to camp here, and a still-smoldering, smoking pile of coals said someone had been here not too long ago. Bonner nodded into the dark. Yadro had been here, but had left, probably soon after dark. He checked the area for Whitey's horse, found where he'd been staked, but it too was gone. He stood. "Come on up, Wells. There's no one here. Or better yet, if you're goin' to town tonight, get your horse an' cut out. I'll find some way to contact you; see if you found anything Juan and I might use."

"I find anything you might use, ranger man, I'll come straight to you. Won't worry 'bout anybody findin' I been workin' with you. By then won't do 'em any good to know what I been doin' anyway."

"You ever think they might blow your damned head off once they know what you're doin'? Uh-uh. You let me come to you when I know you'll be safe." He chuckled. "Want you an' that lil ole girl you knew in the fifth grade to get married an' have a whole passel o' kids."

Wells chuckled. "Kinda had that in mind, Bonner. But, right now, reckon I'll head fer town, soon's I get my horses."

They walked back to the house together. Wells went straight to the stable. Bonner went in the house, looked at Juan, and nodded. "Gone." He went to the cabinet, poured the three of them a drink, knocked *his* back, then grinned. "That drink ain't gonna get the mud off'n me, but it sure will get the chill outta my bones."

Jess took a small swallow of his drink. "You young'uns been cooped up in here quite a spell. Why don't the both o' ya saddle up an' go in town?"

"Ain't nothin' in there for me. Jimenez is the only one got a reason to go in there. 'Sides that, Jess, you ain't been to town in a long while. Know it's too late to go now, but in the mornin' saddle up an' go see some people 'sides me an' Juan."

Jess shook his head. "Hell, Bonner, I got everything I want or need right here on this here ranch. You done give me a

home, young'un, that's all I ever needed. I like it right here."
He took another sip of his drink, then frowned. "Jest thought
o' somethin'. If one o' you goes into town, stop by Parsons's
an' see if that wood I ordered has come in yet. Gotta git busy
on Juan an' Linda's furniture."

"You think Parsons is gonna know if the grain an' everythin' is all right to make into furniture? I won't know, an' I
doubt if Juan will."

Jess shook his head. "Naw, now, Parsons knowed what I
needed. He ain't gonna slide nothin' off on you. Not that I
think he would anyway. He's a honest gent."

Juan went to the gun rack, got his rifle, swung his gunbelt
around his hips, buckled it, and headed for the door. "I'm
goin' in tonight, right now. You comin', Trey?"

"Naw, I'll wait'll mornin'. Ain't nothin' in there for me
tonight."

Jimenez left like a kid headed for the candy store. On the
ride in he wished Bonner had come with him, but when he
knocked on the back door to the cafe, even though it was well
after midnight, he smiled, glad he had Linda all to himself.

A shuffling of feet inside the door told him Linda had
heard his knock. "Yes, who is it?"

"Me, Linda, Juan. Know it's late, but I couldn't wait any
longer. Had to see you."

The door swung open. "Oh, am I glad to see you. Maggie
an' I were just sayin' tonight we hoped y'all hadn't got into
more trouble."

"Maggie here?" Disappointment flooded him; he felt
empty inside. Disappointment because he'd not have Linda to
himself, and that under the circumstances Trey hadn't come
with him. He shrugged mentally. Bonner would be coming in
soon after sunup. He'd probably come here first, and if Maggie wasn't here, he'd ride the short ride on out to the Box T.

When he went in, both girls had their hands to their head,
fluffing their hair, obviously trying to look presentable in their
night robes. "Juan Jimenez, you ever come in here like this
again, I'm gonna make you stand out there in the dark 'til I get
dressed an' brush my hair."

"Aw, Linda, I think both you women're 'bout as beautiful as any I ever seen."

"Quit the blarney. You an' Maggie can talk while I put the coffee on. I asked Mr. Parsons to get a bottle so I'd have it for you men when you came to town. I'll spike yours. Now sit while I take care o' the coffee."

Aware that Maggie hadn't taken her eyes off him, he looked at her and nodded. "Yeah, Trey's all right. Wait'll Linda comes back in an' I'll tell y'all why we ain't been in town lately."

After a bit, when the three of them sat drinking their coffee, he told them that he, Trey, an' Jess had been pinned down without a chance to go outside to even chop stove wood. "Bonner finally got mad enough to bite nails, slipped out, checked out the places he thought a bushwhacker might be, found 'im gone, but he'd been there, an' he come back an' told me. That's when I decided to come to town even if it was awful late."

Linda smiled. "Glad you did. Now we can get a good night's sleep."

They talked until the sky turned a bleak gray, showing little light. Linda sighed. "So much for getting a good night's sleep. I have to get ready for the breakfast crowd."

Juan stood. "We'll help."

While they were busy setting up for the meal, Linda cornered Maggie. "When Trey gets here, you reckon we oughtta ask them what danged business they got that's important enough to keep 'em from comin' to see us?"

"I'm tempted, Linda, but they have enough trouble restin' on their shoulders without you and me givin' them a rough time right now. Soon's they get to a point where they seem to be out from under whatever troubles they got, we'll unload on 'em. Okay?"

Linda nodded. "Well, all right—for now."

Jimenez hadn't cleared the ranch yard before Bonner was shucking his clothes. "Let's get some sleep, Jess. Don't figure we need to keep watch tonight. Dawg'll tell us if anybody's snoopin' 'round."

"Jest gonna say that. I'm 'bout ready to go to sleep a-standin' here."

Despite the little sleep they'd had lately, both were up before daylight. Trey decided they better cut stove wood in case they got trapped inside again. He took the wet sticks from the rick, put them aside until he got down to dry wood, then proceeded to split what they needed.

Abruptly, in mid-swing, he frowned, put his ax aside, and dug in his pocket. He studied the note RIP had given him, the one in which someone asked for ranger help to see what had been happening to the settlers.

He looked at it a long time, then nodded, and after the fashion of those who spent a lot of time alone, said, "Bet my saddle I got it figured." He picked up an armload of split wood and headed for the house.

Inside, he went to the desk Jess had built for him and took the bill of sale for the cattle from the top drawer. Maggie had written the papers for him and her father to sign. He put the two papers side by side, looked from one to the other, and nodded. "Yep, ain't no doubt but what she wrote both o' these." He put the bill of sale back into the drawer, thought to put the note with it, then shook his head.

Should he let Maggie know he was the ranger who'd answered her plea? "Don't think the time is right. Better get some more facts, but this sure doesn't hurt my thinkin' that Matt hasn't got a danged thing to do with what happened to the nesters."

"What the hell you mutterin' 'bout, young'un?"

"Just figured somethin' out that's been botherin' me for a while, Jess." He stood. "You gonna be all right if I go to Noname?"

Jess said not a word until he'd gone to the gun rack and picked up his Sharps. "Ain't nothin' me an' Dawg cain't take care of, young'un." He smiled. "Why don't you go see that little gal you been pinin' over while you at it?"

Trey grinned. "Kinda figured on doin that." He slung his gunbelt around his hips, buckled it, took his rifle, and went out the door. "See you in a couple o' days."

His ride to town, uneventful and boring, gave Bonner time to think about what he and Juan could do to wrap this case up, resign from the rangers, and get on with their lives.

When he stepped from the saddle, he had come no closer to coming up with a peaceful arrest than he'd been all along.

Shrugging out of his slicker—a fine mist had fallen all the way in—the first one he saw when he pulled the door shut behind him was Maggie.

She and Jimenez waited tables while Linda cooked. He went straight to her, and despite the cowboys giving them each a hoorahing, he gave Maggie a good hug. "Reckon Juan told y'all why we hadn't been in the last few days." He frowned and accepted the cup of coffee Jimenez handed him. "If somethin' don't break soon, I'm gonna force it, even if I gotta have a gunfight to do it."

"Oh, Trey, I don't know what it is that's so important to you and Juan, but please don't do anything to get you hurt."

He smiled. "Little one, I'm 'bout as careful of gettin' my tender pink skin punctured as any man you ever seen." He took a swallow of his coffee, then held his hand to just below his rib cage and blew a gust of air into the room. "Damn, that coffee's hot enough to boil my insides."

He sat, put his cup in front of him, and wondered if now was the time for him to approach Tedford about the case he and Juan were on. He mentally shook his head. No, he wanted to get the Rogers and Yadro relationship wrapped up first. He convinced himself that getting some answers from Maggie's father could wait. He'd use this time to enjoy being with Maggie.

Wells pushed open the door to the room he and Yadro had shared. The white-haired gunman had been there; his gear, still damp from the mist, was piled in a corner of the room, but Yadro had already gone. Skeeter nodded. It fit. The gunny had come back to town for whisky. He thought to get some sleep before he had to share the bed with the dirty bastard.

He removed his boots and hat and had unbuttoned his shirt when Yadro showed up. Wells cast a hard look at him. "Figured you'd still be out yonder watchin' Bonner's place. What'd you do, run outta whisky?"

Whitey had a full bottle in each hand. He nodded. "Run outta whisky an' dry clothes. Thought long's Rogers don't know I'm in town, it shore won't hurt to spend a little time in here."

"He's gonna raise hell if he catches you." Then Wells, acting as though it had only then occurred to him, said, "You reckon he'd let you an' me take every other day out yonder?"

Yadro frowned, then shook his head. "Don't know. Don't b'lieve he's gonna want any more people knowin' what he's tryin' to git done. Tried to git 'im to hire you once before, but he made me promise that I'd act like I wuz the one what hired you." He shook his head. "Jest don't know."

Wells took out his Colt, removed the shells, and proceeded to clean it. Then he slanted a look at Whitey. "Know you killed them families, every one of 'em out yonder at the base of them hills. You ever figure he's got enough on you to git you hung?"

Yadro nodded. "Give that a lot o' thought, but got to thinkin', I got as much on him as he has on me."

"He any good with a handgun?"

Whitey shrugged. "Don't know. Ain't never seen 'im handle one, but I got an idear he's probably right slick with that short-barreled thirty-eight he carries under his arm."

Wells nodded. He felt certain Bonner would want to know about that. "He ever tell you why he wants them people dead, everybody dead, includin' them two salty men still out yonder?"

Whitey shook his head. "Naw, he ain't told me nothin' 'cept when I asked he'd always tell me it wuzn't none o' my damned business."

He cast Skeeter a sly grin. "He wouldn't tell me nothin', but when he got me to sign them two papers, I got to figgerin' the whole thing's 'bout land, all this land out here."

He picked up one of the bottles he'd brought to the room

and dug at the cork. "Don't know whether he figgers to keep the land and ranch it, or maybe parcel it out an' sell it. He ain't gonna tell me neither." He continued to worry the cork until he pulled it from the neck of the bottle. He tilted it and swallowed, his Adam's apple bobbing several times before he pulled it from his mouth. He held the one-third-empty bottle toward Skeeter.

"Naw, I et a little while ago, don't feel like no drink right now." Yadro looked relieved at not having to share.

Already half undressed, Wells finished getting ready for bed. "You goin' back out yonder tomorrow?"

Yadro shook his head. "Nope, gonna stay right here in this room. Gonna drink my whisky, then in a couple days gonna go see Rogers and see can I get some more money outta him."

Skeeter raised his eyebrows. "You pull that kinda stuff on 'im an' he catches you, you might find out can he use that thirty-eight."

"He ever tries it an' I'll kill 'im." Whitey grinned. "I ain't never told you I'm right handy too." He nodded. "I shore ain't had no reason to prove it lately, but I'll take care o' him, sortta figgered on it anyway, soon's I b'lieve he's 'bout run outta money."

Wells acted as though he gave Whitey's words a lot of thought, then he looked at the gunny. "Be a lot safer to git 'im from behind."

Yadro nodded. "Been thinkin' 'bout that, but I don't never know where he's gonna be. Have to keep watch on 'im."

17

YADRO AND WELLS talked on into the night. Wells continued to try to get even a tidbit of information that Bonner could use.

With his teeth, Whitey pulled the cork on the bottle he'd opened, took another drink, then slanted Wells a lopsided, sly, drunken grin. "Know what I figger to do? Well, it jest come to me. Think I'll stick 'round here 'til I see Rogers, then I figger to tell 'im I want a thousand dollars a head fer them sodbusters. Tell 'em they're a lot more dangerous than them nesters he sent me after. He only paid me a hunert dollars each fer *them*—man, woman, an' child."

When he said "woman and child," Wells's chest felt like it emptied of air, his guts wrenched, and his mouth dried. He wanted to pull his Colt and kill the sorry bastard sitting on the edge of the bed. Instead, he picked up the full bottle sitting on the floor at Yadro's feet, pulled the cork, and took a long swig; anything to get the stink of Whitey's unfeeling words from his memory.

Then he thought if Yadro did that, and if Rogers really was any good with that underarm gun he carried, he might pull it. He didn't think the rangers wanted Yadro dead. He was the only witness they had. But he couldn't think of any way to dissuade the drunken slob. He figured to hell with it, he'd get some sleep.

At breakfast the next morning, Wells saw Bonner and Jimenez sitting at the back table. Yadro still slept off his drunken stupor back in the hotel room, so he walked back and sat next to Trey.

He ordered. Then while eating, he whispered out of the side of his mouth, "Whitey ain't goin' out yonder to yore place. Gonna stay in town an' see Rogers, gonna hit 'im up for a thousand apiece fer yores an' Jimenez's scalps. Figger Rogers ain't gonna stand for that. They gonna have gun trouble."

Then, almost finished with his meal, he whispered, "Rogers carries a thirty-eight hideout under 'is right arm." He took the last bite of food, stood, and left.

Bonner thought about what the farmer had told him. He frowned, then nodded. He and Jimenez could feel free to move about without thinking they would get a slug between their shoulder blades, and the knowledge that Rogers packed a hideout could very well save his life.

Then he wondered when he and Juan should pin on their badges. When they did, and he made any attempt to arrest Yadro, he'd have a gunfight on his hands, that is if Whitey survived a shoot-out with Rogers.

With the murders Whitey had committed, he would not submit to arrest. One murder charge and he'd hang, and he needed Yadro alive to testify against Rogers. He shook his head.

Jimenez, sitting on the other side of Bonner from where Wells had sat, stared at his partner. "What the hell you doin'? I been sittin' here watchin' you an you been noddin', shakin' your head, frownin', hell, you been doin' everything but talkin' out loud."

Bonner grinned. "Been spendin' too much time with myself." He stood, and picked up his dishes. "Gonna get us another cup o' Arbuckles' after I clean up these dishes, then I'll tell you what Wells told me. We need to talk 'bout what we gonna do next."

Juan pulled his mouth down at the corner and shrugged.

When Trey came back, he motioned Juan to come with him. "Told our gals we were gonna go see Parsons. We'd be back soon."

As soon as they came through the doorway, Parsons told them he'd gotten the wood that Jess wanted and that the rest of Jimenez's stuff to finish his house came in the same wagons.

He went back, picked up a piece of the wood Jess had wanted, then, looking at them, he'd rubbed his hand along its length in what Bonner would have called a caress, and told them that he'd never seen a prettier grain and most of it came free of knots.

Any doubts disappeared that Trey had had about Parsons ensuring that Jess got the quality of wood he desired. The man must have done some woodworking of his own sometime in the past. "Next time we come in we'll bring a couple wagons an' pick this stuff up. Might be a while though, Jimenez an' me got a couple things to take care of first."

Tom grinned. "Long's y'all pay me for it, I'll keep it 'til the cows come home."

Trey smiled. "'Til the cows come home"—they had the same saying back home.

When the two men left Parsons's store, they walked along the muddy street to the edge of town, only a hundred or so yards, then started back. While they walked, Bonner told Jimenez what Wells had said.

"What we gonna do now? We know who did what, an' if we can keep one of 'em alive to take back to RIP, we can get on with makin' a life for ourselves."

Bonner chuckled. "Hell, Juan, you an' me have already had a mighty good life, thanks to old RIP." He frowned, stepped over a pile of horse apples, then looked at the gob of mud he'd collected on his boots. He'd better clean them before going back in the cafe. "To answer your question, I been thinkin' 'bout the same thing." He nodded. "Come up with a answer too."

He pulled his pipe from his vest pocket, packed the bowl with rough-cut tobacco, lit it, and squinted at his partner. "I figure we still ain't got all the answers. Figure Matt Tedford's gonna tell us a few things 'bout how all this come about. Next time I'm out to his place, gonna sit down an' flat-out ask 'im."

Juan, his face as sober as Trey had ever seen it, looked him in the eye. "Hate to see you do that, Trey. You realize it might mess up everything 'tween you an' Maggie?"

Bonner nodded. "Thought 'bout that too. Whatever I find ain't gonna make no difference in the way I feel 'bout 'er, but it damned sure might make a big difference to her. I ain't gonna let 'em know you an' me are rangers 'til after Matt gets his say."

"You figger that's fair?"

"Fair ain't got nothin' to do with it. RIP sent us out here to do a job. Gonna do it come hell or high water."

Juan snorted. "Never had a doubt but that's what you were gonna say." He rolled a corn-shuck quirly, lit it, and slanted Bonner a look that went right through him. "That badge we're totin' means 'bout as much as life to you, don't it?"

Bonner stopped in the middle of the street and gave back as direct a gaze as he'd received. "Tell you how it is, partner, when I got swore into this outfit, I took it as meanin' to give my life on any day long's I was servin' Texas. Ain't never changed my mind." He nodded. "An' yeah if I lose Maggie, reckon it'd be like losin' my life." He shrugged. "A man's gotta do what he thinks is right."

Juan slowly moved his head from side to side. "Don't know if I could do that."

Bonner forced a chuckle. "Hell, partner, you'd do the same thing I'm gonna do. The star we carry means as much to you as it does me. 'Sides that, when we took that oath, we gave our word." He stepped up on the boardwalk in front of the cafe. "Ain't never known one o' us to break our word."

They scraped the mud from their boots and went into the warmth and spicy aroma of Linda's cooking. As soon as they could have lunch, Bonner thought to ride to the Box T with Maggie. He'd have that talk with Tedford.

* * *

Yadro sat alone at his usual table against the back wall in the saloon. Wells hadn't come with him, said he didn't want a drink. He'd bought a bottle and had emptied almost half of it. He stared into the now-empty glass.

The longer he thought of telling Rogers how much he wanted to kill the two sodbusters, the better he liked the idea. With two thousand dollars he might even go to New Orleans; he'd heard they liked people like him down there—a man who needed money and would do whatever it took to get it.

Despite the volume of whisky he'd put down, he still thought clearly. Every man who came through the heavy wooden door came under Whitey's gaze. Until he sneaked back into town, hoping to avoid running into Rogers, he'd intended to wait until the weather got better, then he'd go back out. But *now* he thought to wait until he could see the land agent and tell him the price had gone up. Then his wish came true. Rogers came in, closed the door behind him, and obviously swept the room with a glance, then came toward the table where Yadro sat. To give himself an edge in case Rogers decided to use his gun, Yadro slipped his from its holster and held it under the table out of sight.

After lunch, Maggie and Trey headed out of town toward the Box T. Bonner looked across his shoulder at the woman he might lose before the afternoon ended. "Mag, gonna have a talk with your pa. Gonna ask 'im some questions that might come down hard on you, hard enough you might never want to see me again. Hope it don't come out that way, but it might. Just want you to know, whatever happens I'll love you, want you the rest o' my life."

Maggie stared at him, then shook her head. "Goodness gracious, don't know what it could be, but don't b'lieve nothin's gonna change my mind."

"We'll wait an' see."

When they rode into the yard, Matt had only then stepped from the barn. He came over, shook Bonner's hand, and before Trey could step from the saddle, said he was only then thinking about sending a rider to Trey's place to ask him to come over for a powwow.

"Matt, that's why I come over. Need to sit down with you and you an' me have a head-to-head talk."

"Bonner, what I got to say needs to be said to you, Maggie, an' Belle. It's gonna affect every one o' you. C'mon, let's go in the house, I'll round up Belle, an' we can get started."

Inside, they were seated at the kitchen table; all had a glass of rye in front of them—Matt had insisted the women have one also, said they'd need it before he got through. Then Slim Ramey came in. "Figured this here talk y'all 'bout to have included me, so I invited myself to the party." He poured himself a drink and pulled up a chair.

Tedford eyed Bonner. "What was it you wanted to bring into the talk?"

Trey didn't feel so brave about asking the question he must. The chance of losing Maggie loomed larger with his every breath. "Gonna ask what connection you have with Rogers, Whitey Yadro, an' the murders of those nesters." There! He'd said what he had to. Maggie gasped.

Tedford took a swallow of his drink, coughed, took another swallow, and put his glass back on the table. "Tell you what brought us to this point"—he nodded—"an' yeah, I have an involvement. Didn't figure it was any o' your business 'til you an' Mag seemed to be gettin' to like each other every day, then I thought to be fair to both o' you, y'all both better know what I did."

Ramey cut in. "What we both done—years ago."

Bonner reached to his shirt pocket, pinning Tedford and his foreman with a look that showed both determination and pain. "Ain't gonna ride under a false flag. Gonna tell you why I'm more than interested in all this, an' why I got a right to know. Don't want either o' you to say anythin' you might regret later."

He pulled his badge from his pocket and placed it on the table, then pulled the note he'd decided Maggie had written and placed it beside his badge.

He looked at Maggie. "You wrote this note, didn't you?" She nodded. "Well, my boss, RIP Ford, sent me out here to find out what was goin' on. He gave me orders to put a stop to it an' bring those to court who were guilty of a crime."

Without exception, each of them stared at the Texas Ranger badge. Each of the faces Bonner looked at reflected a different emotion: Maggie and Belle, puzzlement; Tedford and Ramey, resignation.

He shifted his look to Matt. "Gonna tell ya straight out. I'm gonna do what I took an oath to do, regardless who it hurts. All of it put together might cause Maggie to shy way clear of me, but I'm gonna do it. That'd break my heart."

He picked up his badge and pinned it over his pocket. "I figured to play it square with you, let you know I'm the law, so don't say anything that might hurt you in a court of law."

Matt shook his head. "No, Bonner. Slim an' I've been talkin' 'bout this off an' on for the last fifteen years. We decided we had to get it off our chests regardless of the outcome."

He stood and freshened their drinks, then again sat. "Gonna lay it out exactly like it happened." He took a drink, swallowed, then proceeded. "I'm gonna make this as short as I can without leavin' anything out.

"During the war, I was a major, and Slim here was my top sergeant. Only a few days before the war ended, I got orders to meet a wagon that had a load of gold ingots, gold that would help the South in its war efforts. The orders said for me to bring that wagon to headquarters."

He mopped sweat from his brow, shrugged, and continued, "I took Slim with me. He could shoot a rifle an' hit what he shot at from a thousand yards. I thought his protection would be enough. Didn't want to make it obvious we were haulin' something of value.

"Anyway, where we were to meet the wagon was a two-day ride. By the time we got there, we heard in a town we passed through that the war had ended, that General Lee had surrendered. We verified the story in the next town. Ramey and I talked about it; what could we do with the wagon when we took charge of it? There would be no headquarters to turn it in to. There was no one in command. *I* was the one last in control. Whoever we gave the wagon to would keep it. We couldn't see giving it to the Union; we'd fought them too long for us to help improve the state of their depleted coffers.

"Well, the two men who'd been driving the wagon turned it over to me. I signed for it, then Ramey an' I sat there in that copse of maple trees and stared at each other. I reckon I got the idea first. Hell, I didn't know who to turn the shipment over to, so I suggested Ramey an' I keep it. Nobody could ever claim it, in fact the ones who knew about it were probably headed for home.

"Slim only nodded. Now I want you to know he didn't have a thing to do with it. Despite the officer-enlisted crap, we were best friends, and he only went along with my suggestion.

"Anyway, we kept the ingots, went home, gathered up Belle an' our baby daughter, burned what was left of our plantation buildings, and came west." He spread his hands, palms up, then shrugged. "I've still got those gold bars. Never spent a penny of 'em. They're buried out yonder in the stable. Wondered where I could find any law to tell my story to." He grinned, although one lacking in humor, then raised his eyebrows and shrugged. "Reckon the law found me."

Bonner stared at him, knowing the look he gave the rancher would freeze hell a mile. "You got any idea how much that gold's worth?"

Tedford nodded. "Last time I checked on what gold sold for an ounce, I figure there's over a quarter million dollars buried out there."

Bonner stood. "You mind me bein' rude an' askin' for another drink?"

Tedford jummped to his feet. "Hell, it's right selfish of me not to have offered." He grabbed the bottle from the shelf and poured them all another. "Haven't finished my story yet. Gotta tell you how all that ties in with this problem we have out here."

Bonner nodded. "Go ahead."

"Well, the paymaster knew about the shipment and the orders I had. He followed me out here, watched me build my ranch, then saw settlers moving in, and I reckon thought he could get rich without havin' to hit a lick.

"He feenagled himself a position out here as land agent and put his plan to work. He wanted all that land up against the hills as well as all the land I ran my cattle on. The settlers who had filed on those parcels were a problem; he wanted it all, but how to get rid of them? He hired Whitey Yadro an' his bunch, threatened to expose me as a holdup man from the war, moved Yadro onto the Box T, an' they proceeded to do their dirty work until you came in here. Despite my protests, I didn't do anything to stop him. The land agent? Of course it was Rogers."

Bonner sat there a moment, held his drink up to the lantern, peered through the amber liguid, frowned, and wondered what to do next. He glanced at Maggie, then Belle. They both sat there staring at Matt, who held himself erect, his head held high, a proud man ready to take what punishment the law would throw at him.

Bonner lowered his glass from the lantern. "How long ago did all this take place, Matt?"

Tedford looked at Ramey, then back to Trey. "I'd say close to fifteen years ago. Why?"

"Did you know what Yadro was doin' while livin' in your bunkhouse?"

Tedford grimaced. "Reckon I should have, but I didn't. Think maybe I didn't want to know so strong I stayed away from the hills." He shook his head. "No, I didn't know." He took a huge swallow of his drink, then looked at Bonner straight on. "Know you gotta do your duty, Trey, so when you gonna take me to Austin?"

Trey frowned and stared at the table a moment. What was it that RIP had pounded in him not to do? Not to be judge, jury, and executioner? Well, damn it, one more time, Bonner, then you better resign, he thought. He looked at Tedford. "You ever hear of the statute of limitations, Matt?"

Tedford shook his head.

"Well, the statute of limitations is the time allowed for chargin' a person for committing a crime. There's not one for murder, but there's one for takin' somethin' that don't b'long to you. Here in Texas it's seven years, so 'cordin' to the law you ain't liable for takin' that gold."

He grinned. "'Sides that, who could you give it back to? There ain't nobody with a claim to it—the Confederacy don't exist no more an' you don't know who sent it to them. An' I cain't see that you did anything wrong where the settlers were concerned except keepin' your eyes closed, not wanting to know what went on over there against the hills."

His grinned widened. "Reckon you're a mighty rich man. You might even find somebody to run a bank for you. I ain't got nothin' to charge you with."

Although happy with the way things turned out, he avoided looking into Maggie's eyes. Yeah, she'd asked that a ranger be sent, but he had done his job without his badge, even deceived her when he suspected her father of being deeply involved in the attempt to rook people out of legally filed-on land. No one knew he and Juan were rangers except Jess and Wells.

Then in his own mind he justified keeping his job secret from her. Hell, he hadn't known who sent the note to RIP. If she wanted to get mad at him for doing his job the way he figured was best, wanted to say no when he asked her to marry him, he'd figure it for the best—but deep inside he knew he could never think it best if he lost her.

Belle stood. "Time to start supper." She looked at Trey. "You'll stay. Eat with us?"

"Ma'am, didn't figure I'd be welcome after the secret way I had to operate an' tryin' to get Matt to talk 'bout his part in this whole thing."

"What would you have done if Matt had been involved in this entire scheme?"

"Reckon I'd have done my duty, ma'am. I took an oath, an' I took the State of Texas's pay." He shrugged. "Don't see as how I had a choice."

She smiled. "Trey Bonner, I don't see that anyone could fault a person for doing his sworn duty." She nodded. "Yes, I for one say you're welcome." She looked at Slim. "You're gonna stay too, then after supper you an' Matt gotta decide what you're gonna do with all that money."

After they'd eaten, they talked, and it seemed to Bonner that any chill there might have been between them thawed— somewhat.

Maggie looked expectantly at him. "What now, Trey?"

He pulled his mouth down at the corner. "Don't want to, but I gotta finish this assignment. Gotta go in an' take care o' Yadro and Rogers. After that, I'm gonna resign an' get on with things."

"What things?"

He looked at her straight on. "We gonna talk 'bout that after I finish." He didn't push it further. Hell, Whitey might kill him. He had to take the gunman alive and that wouldn't be easy.

She walked to his horse with him. He put his toe in the stirrup and was about to swing to his saddle when she touched his arm. "You gonna leave without givin' me a kiss?"

He dropped his foot to the ground. "Didn't know how you felt toward me, didn't think you'd want me to kiss you."

"Trey Bonner, if I ever refuse to let you kiss me, it'll all be over between us." She shook her head. "I don't think it's over; fact is, I think it's just beginning."

He took her in his arms, and the badge pinned to his shirt didn't push them farther apart.

On the short ride back to town, he put his hand on his badge thinking to take it off. He dropped his hand back to his side. Anything he did now would be done as a lawman.

When he pulled rein in front of the saloon, most windows in town showed dark. Only the golden glow of lantern light in the windows of the watering hole indicated that some were still not in bed. He thought a drink would feel good before he went to the hotel.

When he pushed through the door into the room, many voices made a cacophony of sound. Yadro stood against the back wall, his right hand hanging limp at his side. That hand held his smoking six-shooter. A man lay on the floor at the side of the table.

Bonner walked to the body, flipped it over with the toe of his boot, then bent to closer examine it. Blank, dead eyes stared back at him. Rogers's dead eyes.

He straightened. "Who done it?" He asked the question, but his look never left Yadro, whose look glued to the badge pinned to Bonner's pocket.

The road to hell was paved with good intentions. Bonner's earlier thinking to try to shoot Yadro in the shoulder—just wound him so he could use him as a witness—all of those thoughts went into that road to hell. With the white-haired gunman already standing with his gun in hand, it would be impossible to draw and deliberately fire at his shoulder.

Bonner shoved aside any thought of doing anything other than killing the gunman—and knew that even at his best he'd take lead, maybe die right along with the nester killer.

He took a deep breath. "Yadro, you're under arrest."

The gunman's face twisted into a snarl, his eyes shot venom, his hand raised level to point at Bonner. All action slowed. In Bonner's mind, racing faster than a freight train, he had time to kill the trash standing there before he went down.

He threw himself to the side, and his hand swept for his Colt. Yadro's gun blossomed flame. He fanned the hammer again. A fanned gun seldom hit what the shooter intended.

It flicked through Trey's mind that maybe he had a chance. His right leg went from under him. Another sledgehammer blow hit his side. But holes that hadn't been there before showed in Yadro's shirt. Two of them close together in the middle of his chest. Whitey still held his hand to sweep the hammer back again—then it moved back. Bonner saw another hole appear in Yadro's chest before Yadro's last shot hit him. The world went black. His last thought was that he'd gotten the white-haired bastard.

Later, much later, Bonner thought he pulled himself from a deep, dark hole. An inch at a time, he thought he clawed at the sides of the hole to pull himself into light. He'd opened his eyes only a slit, but he could see a hazy light ahead of him. He forced his eyes wide and saw leaning over him the prettiest picture he'd ever beheld.

"Maggie, where'd you come from?" His voice was only a whisper.

She smiled, leaned farther over him, and touched his lips with her own. "I've been here all along. Long enough for you, in your delirium, to say how much you loved me. Long enough for you to ask me to marry you." She took a tremulous breath. "Long enough for you to come back from death."

"Aw now, I never figured to die." His words still coming in a whisper, he said, "Had to give you a chance to make me miserable for the rest o' my life."

Maggie put her cheek to his. "If that's a proposal, it's all right. *I* asked Mama's an' Papa's permission for you to court me. *I* told them I was gonna say yes, an' now I don't wantta hear 'bout any more business you gotta attend to; *we're gettin' married.*"

"Gotta go to Austin, report, resign, an' have a honeymoon. Be fun. Jimenez an' Linda'll be havin' theirs too." Then RIP's words came to him: judge, jury, and executioner. He grimaced.

No one knows the American West
better than

JACK BALLAS

Hanging Valley
0-425-18410-2
Lingo Barnes is on his way to Durango,
Colorado, when he stumbles upon the
kidnapping of Emily Lou Colter.
Now he must save the girl and keep
himself out of the line of fire.

Land Grab
0-425-19113-3
Cord Fain is going to teach his ruthless
former trail boss that when it comes to
stealing land from its rightful owners,
possession is nine-tenths of the law—the
rest is blood.

B303